I0681515

Textbook written according to revised syllabus of S.Y.B.Com.
prescribed by University of Pune from 2014-2015.
Also useful for other universities in Maharashtra.

COST & WORKS ACCOUNTING

(PAPER - I)

Prin. Dr. Kishor N. Jagtap

Dr. Sunil D. Zagade

Dr. Sunil S. Shete

Dr. Hanumant M. Jare

Diamond Publications

COST & WORKS ACCOUNTING

Prin. Dr. Kishor N. Jagtap, Dr. Sunil D. Zagade
Dr. Sunil S. Shete, Dr. Hanumant M. Jare

First Edition : June 2014

ISBN : 978-81-8483-579-3

© Diamond Publications

Type Setting :
Diamond Publications

Cover Page :
Sham Bhalekar

Published by :
Diamond Publications
264/3 Shaniwar Peth, 302 Anugrah Apartment
Near Omkareshwar Temple, Pune - 411 030
☎ 020-24452387, 24466642
info@diamondbookspune.com
www.diamondbookspune.com

Sale Distributor :
Diamond Book Depot
661 Narayan Peth
Appa Balwant Chowk
Pune 411 030
Tel. - 24480677, 66020282

PREFACE

It is a matter of great pleasure for us to present this book to our esteemed readers. This book has been designed as standard text on Cost and Works Accounting - I for S.Y.B.Com as per June 2014 Pattern.

This book comprehensively covers the entire syllabus of Second Year B.Com. Course of University of Pune effective from June 2014-2015 onwards. It has been written to meet the requirements of students of S.Y.B.Com. Some of the special features of the book are as follows:

- Full coverage of the revised syllabus of S.Y.B.Com.
- Chapter outline at the beginning of each chapter to give a bird's eye view of the topics covered in the chapter.
- Pointwise explanation of each topic in the chapter.
- Topics are logically arranged in numbered paragraphs exactly according to the modified syllabus.
- Proposed questions at the end of each chapter.
- Extensive use of diagrams, tables and various forms to give visual view of key concepts and techniques.
- Conversational, lucid and simple language.

Every effort has been made to provide the readers with most up-to-date and authentic material on the subject.

We are very grateful to our publisher Mr. Dattatray Pashte who have rendered all possible assistance in bringing out this book. We wish to acknowledge our deep gratitude to staff who have assisted and helped us in preparing this book. We will consider our efforts amply rewarded in case the book proves useful to the students and teachers of the subject.

Suggestions of readers are welcome and shall be acknowledged with gratitude.

With best wishes.

Prin. Dr. Kishor N. Jagtap
Dr. Sunil D. Zagade
Dr. Sunil S. Shete
Dr. Hanumant M. Jare

CONTENTS

CHAPTER 1

BASICS OF COST ACCOUNTING

INTRODUCTION

In old days, the scope of accounting was limited. The business and its accounts were managed by the businessman himself. But today, the nature and scope of accounting has changed tremendously. The application of science and technology to industrial units has made the nature of business more complicated. The business units keep various accounts which cover mostly the financial aspect of business. Financial accounts show the profit or loss or financial positions of a business on a particular day. These accounts provide useful information to owners, creditors, government, tax authorities, investors, employees because they are closely associated and interested in functioning of business. But the information provided by financial accounting is not sufficient from the view point of management. Management is interested to know much more financial information. Management of business has to take various decisions regarding the production, sales, cost control, etc. Management is more interested in knowing the cost of product or services. The information regarding the cost of product or services is not provided by financial accounting. So, in order to fulfil the requirement of management, cost accounting has been developed. It is the branch of financial accounting but it provides basic and important information to management regarding cost of producing and selling an article. Cost accounting helps in reducing the cost of production and thereby profit of industrial unit can be increased.

Thus, cost accounting has primarily developed to meet the needs of management. Today, the scope of cost accounting has been considerably increased and it is mainly used in controlling the operations of business. Cost accounting is now used in profit and non-profit organisations engaged in manufacturing and non-manufacturing activities.

1.1 CONCEPTS OF COST, COSTING, COST ACCOUNTING AND COST ACCOUNTANCY.

In Cost Accounting concepts such as cost, costing, cost accounting and cost accountancy etc. are commonly used. But they are not synonymous. Each term is having specific meaning. These terms are defined as under.

i) Cost :

The most common meaning of cost is the amount of expenditure incurred on a particular product or thing. Further, word cost means "money cost" of a production. Another meaning of cost means opportunity cost which means the sacrifice made for not utilising the other alternatives. In short, the word cost is defined from various angles. The term cost is defined by different authors as under.

ICMA London defines the term cost :

1) "as the amount of expenditure, actual or notional, incurred on or attributable to a given product or service."

2) According to **Anthony and Welson** "Cost is a measurement in monetary terms, of the amount of resources used for some purposes." Business transactions involve both revenue and cost. The difference between revenue or cost is either profit or loss. If the revenue is more than the the cost, it is a profit. If the cost is higher than revenue it is a loss.

3) According to **Oxford Dictionary** "Cost is the price for something."

4) **Shillinglaw** defined cost as "Cost represents the resources that must be sacrificed to attain a particular objective."

5) According to **Crowningsheild** cost represents "an expendi-ture made to secure an economic benefit, generally resources that promise to produce revenue, The resources may have tangible substance (material or machinery) or they may take the form of services, wages, rent, power."

6) **W.M.Harper** defined 'cost' as, "the value of economic resources used as a result of producing or doing the thing costed."

7) **The A.I.C.P.A. Committee** defines costs as "the amount measured in money of cash expended or other property transferred, capital stock issued, services performed or a liability incurred in consideration of goods or services received or to be received."

Expenses are defined by the committee as "including all expired cost which are deductible from the revenues."

From the above definitions, it is clear that cost has variety of meanings. The meaning of cost depends upon the purpose for which it is used, the situation under which it is empolyed and the intention of people who use it. The cost may be direct cost, indirect cost, prime cost, opportunity cost, conversion cost, controllable cost, marginal cost, standard cost etc. In short "cost is the total of all expenses incurred, whether paid or outstanding, in the manufacture and sale of product or those incurred in giving a service."

ii) "Costing."

The concept "costing" is defined by various authors as under.

1) **ICMA London** defines costing as "the techniques and process of ascertaining cost." This technique consists of all principles, rules and regulation, which are required, for the ascertainment of cost of product and services. The technique of costing is dynamic and everchanging. The technique of costing involves four steps, namely (a) collection of expenditure (b) classification of expenditure according to elements of cost (c) Allocation of expenditure to cost centers or cost units and (d) Apportionment of expenditure to cost centers or cost units. Thus, costing is the process of ascertainment of cost of product or services.

2) **Harold James** defines, "Costing is the proper allocation of expenditure, whereby reliable cost may be asecrtained and suitably presented to afford guidance to producer in control of their business."

3) **According to Wheldon** "costing is the classifying, recording and appropriate allocation of expenditure for the determination of costs of products or services and for the presentation of suitably arranged data for the purpose of control and guidance of management. It includes the ascertainment of every order, job, contract, process, service units as may be appropriate. It deals with the cost of production, selling and distribution."

In short, costing is the technique of ascertaining the cost of product or services. This technique is dynamic and changes with the change in time. The cost is ascertained by using the techniques of arithmetic memorandum and various cost statements. The cost further may be ascertained either from historical records or by using the techniques of standard costing or marginal costing. Costing is useful in various sectors and it helps industries and businesses as under.

a) Costing helps the management to take various decisions.

b) It helps the industrial organisation by controlling the cost and thus brings stability in industrial organisation.

c) Costing helps to face competition, particularly during the period of recession by curtailing the cost from various angles or by elimination of wasteful expenditure.

d) Costing is useful for quoting correct prices for tenders and quotations.

iii) Cost Accounting

The terms "costing' and "cost accounting' are interchangeably used and therefore there is a technical difference between the two. Costing is simply cost finding technique and cost Accounting denotes the formal accounting mechanism by means of which costs are ascertained by recording them in the books of accounts. In simple words, costing means finding out the cost of product and service and cost accounting means costing using double entry system.

The concept cost accounting is defined by some authors as under.

1) **According to Walter Scott** "Cost Accounting is the branch of general accounting and covers the application of accounting principles relating to recording, classifying and analysing of cost within the organisation."

2) **Kolher** defines Cost Accounting as, "that branch of accounting dealing with the classification, recording, allocation, summarisation and reporting of current and prospective costs."

3) **Shillingglaw defines** "Cost Accounting as a body of concept, methods and procedure used to measure, analyse or estimate the cost, profitability and performance of individual product, departments and other sequences of company's operation, for either internal or external use or both and to report on these questions to the interested parties."

4) **Van Sickle defines,** "Cost Accounting is the science of recording and presenting business transactions pertaining to the production of goods and services, whereby these records become a method of measurement and means of control."

5) **ICMA London** has given the most appropriate and an authoritative definition of cost accounting and it is as under. "Cost accounting is the process of accounting for cost from the point at which expenditure is incurred or committed to the establishment of its ultimate relationship with cost centres and cost units. In its widest usage, it embraces the presentation of statistical data, application of cost control, methods and ascertainment of profitability of activities carried out or planned."

From the above definition we can summarise the main features of cost accounting as follows.

1) It is a process of accounting for costs.
2) It is concerned with cost ascertainment and cost control.
3) It records income and expenditure relating to production of goods and services.
4) It involves the presentation of right information to the right person at right time so that it may be helpful to management for planning, control and decision making.
5) It provides statistical data on the basis of which future estimates are prepared and tenders and quotations are submitted.
6) It establishes budgets and standards so that actual cost may be compared to find out deviations or variances. It provides cost control techniques to management.

7) Cost presentation is also one of the important parts of cost accounting. For cost presentation different forms and statements are prepared for efficient reporting.

iv) Cost Accountancy :

Cost Accountancy is a very wide term. It includes the various aspects such as costing, cost accounting, cost control, cost audit and budgetory control. It means and includes the principles, conventions, techniques and systems which are employed in a business to plan and control the utilisation of its sources. It is the application of costing and cost accounting principles, methods and techniques. It is the science, art and practice of cost control and the ascertainment of profitability. Thus, it is a comprehensive term.

The Institute of Cost and Management Accountants London defines cost Accountancy as "the application of costing and cost accounting principles, methods and techniques to the science, art and practice of cost control and the ascertainment of profitability. It includes the presentation of information derived therefrom for the purpose of managerial decision."

Thus, cost accountancy is the science, art and practice of cost accountant. It is **science** because it is a body of systematic knowledge having certain definite rules, principles and aim which a cost accountant should possess for proper discharge of his duties and responsibilities. It is an **art** because it requires certain ability, skill and personal talent. These are used by cost accountant to solve the complicated problems in management. The method of solving the problems may differ from person to person and one situation to another. Thus, cost accountancy is an art. **Practice** includes the continuous efforts of cost accountant in the field of cost accountancy. Such efforts also include the presentation of information for the purpose of managerial decision making and keeping statistical records. The theoretical knowledge alone would not make a cost accountant able to deal with intricacies. He should thus have sufficient practical training.

In short, Cost Accountancy is an art, science and practice of cost accountant.

1.2 LIMITATIONS OF FINANCIAL ACCOUNTING

The industrial units or manufacturing concerns prepare Profit and Loss Account and Balance Sheet at the end of every year. They exhibit the profit or loss and financial position of industry or business. They cannot provide a sound base for the measurement of performance of business. Many a times, Profit and Loss Account shows superfluous profit. It is not a real profit. Similarly, balance sheet is also managed and therefore cannot disclose the true and fair position of a business. Cost accounts provide the useful information for judging the performance of industry. Thus, management gets required information only because of cost accounting. In short, cost accounting has been developed as a separate branch of accounting out of the limitations of financial accounting. The limitations of financial accounting are summarised as follows.

1) It provides only historical information : Financial accounting is mainly historical. It gives information about the cost already incurred. It does not provide day-to-day cost information to management for making effective plans for future. It provides only post-mortem analysis of past activities of industry.

2) No classification of expenses : In financial accounting department or process or productwise expenses are not shown and thereby the loss of one department may be made up from the profit of other department. Further, expenses are not classified as to direct and indirect, fixed and variable and controllable and uncontrollable and thus financial accounts fails to control the cost at each stage of production.

3) It shows only overall performance : Financial accounting does not give a clear picture of operating efficiency, when the prices are increasing or decreasing on account of inflation or depression. It provides information about profit, loss, cost etc. of collective activities of the business as a whole. It does not give data regarding costs by departments, product, process, operation and sales territories etc.

4) Not helpful in price fixation : In financial accounting, costs are not available as an aid in determining prices of the product, services, production order and line of products. So proper price fixation is not possible from the available information of financial accounting.

5) No performance appraisal : In financial accounting there is no well developed system of standards or norms to appraise the efficiency of organisation in the use of material, labour and overhead costs by comparing the work of labourers, clerks, salesmen and executives which should have been accomplished in producing and selling a given number of product in the allotted period of time.

6) No material control system : In financial accounting there is no proper system of controlling materials and supplies. It results in losses in the form of obsolescence, deterioration, excessive scrap and misappropriation.

7) No labour cost control : Generally, there is no system of recording loss of labour time i.e., idle labour. Labour cost is not recorded by departments or jobs or processes and thereby no proper incentive method is applied to efficient workers.

8) It is static in nature : Financial accounts do not provide only the historical data but they are also static in nature. They are not dynamic. They cannot incorporate the changes of modern times which may take place in business.

9) No data for comparison and decision-making : Financial accounts do not supply useful data to management for comparison with previous period and for taking various decisions like introduction by new product, replacement of labour by machine, make or buy decision, product to be continued or discontinued, investment to be made in new products or not. etc.

10) No analysis of losses : Financial accounting does not provide complete analysis of losses due to defective material, idle time, idle plant and equipment, inefficient labour, sub-standard material etc. The causes of avoidable and unavoidable wastage cannot be disclosed by financial accounting.

11) Inadequate information for reports : Financial accounts do not provide adequate information for reports to outside agencies such as banks, government, insurance companies, and trade associations. Thus, outside agencies cannot use the financial accounts for the preparation of reports.

12) No cost comparison : Comparison is the foundation of modern management control. But financial accounting does not provide data for comparison of costs of different periods, different job or departments.

13) Danger of manipulation of Financial Accounts : Financial accounts are manipulated, if the management wants to disclose better or prosperous position of business. When the company wants to raise additional capital, very often, assets are overvalued or essential provisions like depreciation or reserves are curtailed or neglected. In short, financial accounts may not disclose true and fair position of business.

14) Not helpful to management : Financial accounting does not help in forecasting, planning, organising, co-ordinating and communicating various activities of business. Thus, it fails to control the activities of business.

15) It fails to ascertain break-even-point : Break-even-point is a point where revenues and costs of product are equal. This position helps the businessman in taking various decisions. But financial accounts do not help in ascertaining the break-even point.

1.3 ORIGIN OF COST ACCOUNTING

Origin of Cost Accounting :

Cost accounting is the branch of financial accounting. It is developed due to industrial development and out of the limitations of financial accounting. The origin of cost accounting can be traced back to 5000 B.C., when Sumerians started accounting. But the scope of accounting was very limited. It is always said that "Necessity is the mother of invention". Cost accounting is the outcome of such necessity for industries or businessmen.

In ancient days, production was made according to the family needs and hence there was no need to maintain accounts. Thereafter, barter system was developed and commodities were exchanged according to the needs of two parties. Barter system resulted in the development of trade and commerce. But even at this stage, accounts were maintained on a small scale by limited businessmen. Further, Industrial Revolution of 18th century is considered to be the turning point in the field of industry. Due to industrial revolution, production was made by factories on large scale and in anticipation of demand. Due to large scale production, there was a severe competition among the producers for selling their products. This resulted in the development of marketing and each producer was trying to produce his product with maximum efficiency and at lesser cost. All these factors can be economically handled, if proper cost accounts are kept and thus cost accounting was started.

The most rapid development in cost accounting took place after 1914 with the growth of heavy industries and mass production methods when costs other than material and labour constituted a significant portion of total cost of production. The scientific management movement led by Dr. F. W. Taylor gave impetus to the development of cost accounting because it contributed to the use of standard cost in planning manufacturing operations and in evaluating performance.

In the beginning, cost accounting was ascertaining the cost of product or services. But in modern times the need of cost accounting is enhanced as it is providing valuable information to management. The requirements of management may be summarised as follows.

1) Forecasting : Various budgets are prepared on the basis of forecast of cost and revenue. Similarly, various cost estimates are also based on forecast of material labour and overheads. Such information is provided by cost accounts which helps the management.

2) Planning : Planning is thinking in advance i.e. looking ahead and deciding in advance what to do, how to do, when to do, who is to do it. In planning, management is concerned with laying down objectives and determining the courses of action to be followed out of several alternatives available to achieve objective. Thus, planning is concerned with future activity and it formulates budget to meet the objectives of the organisation.

3) Decision Making : Since management has to make a choice of course of action out of several alternative courses of action available, it involves decision making. All rational decisions are based on accounting information. Like fixation of price, increase or decrease in price, make or buy decision, continuation or discontinuation of product, etc.

4) Control of Material, Labour or Overhead Cost : Cost accounts keep efficient check on stores and materials, labour and overheads. Various techniques of material control are applied in order to avoid the excessive locking up of capital in stock of material and stores. Idle time is kept as low as possible and by proper classification of overheads into controllable and uncontrollable or fixed and variable manner. It helps to control the material, labour and overhead costs.

5) Cost audit : The operation of a system of cost audit in the organisation will assist in the prevention of errors and frauds. It will help to improve cost accounting methods and techniques to facilitate prompt and reliable information to management.

6) Controlling : Controlling is that part of management activity whereby managers compare actual performance against the planned performance, find out the deviations and take remedial steps to remove the deviations. Thus, cost accounting helps management to control all activities of industrial unit.

7) Measurement of performance and efficiency : Cost accounts provide the use of standards to assist management in making estimates and plans for future and provide the basis of management efficiency. Actuals are compared with predetermined standards to determine the operating efficiency. Cost accounting helps in controlling wastages of materials, idle time and overheads. Thus, it helps to measure the performance and efficiency of organisation.

Thus, cost accounting helps management in various activities and in various circumstances.

The development of cost accounting in India is of recent origin. Costing is playing vital role after independence, when the Indian Government started laying emphasis on the industrial development of the country. In India, The Institute of Cost and Works Accountants (ICWA) has been set up in 1944. Further, provision of cost audit under section 233 B of the companies Act 1956 has given impetus to the development of cost accounting in India. Now Government is empowered to appoint cost auditor under section 233 B of the Companies Act 1956, where it is necessary. Thus, cost accounting is developed particularly during 19th and 20th century.

1.4 OBJECTIVES OF COST ACCOUNTING

The objectives of cost accounting are ascertainment of cost, fixation of selling price, proper recording and presentation of cost data to management for measuring efficiency and cost control. The aim of costing is to reduce the cost and thereby increase the profit of industry. But the objectives are changing day-by-day due to the development of business and industries. The main objectives of cost Accounting are as follows.

1) Ascertainment of cost : The main purpose or aim of cost accounting is to ascertain the cost of product or service and thereby control the cost. For the ascertainment of cost, different techniques and systems of costing are used under different circumstances. The ascertainment of cost of production of every unit, job, operation, process department or service includes (a) Cost finding, (b) Cost recording, (c) Cost analysing and (d) Cost reporting.

2) Determine per unit and total cost : The aim of cost accounting is to determine total cost and per unit cost of production. Further cost is also ascertained at different stages of production and thereby cost of each stage of production can be calculated.

3) Control of cost : Control aims at improving efficiency by controlling and reducing cost. This objective is becoming increasingly important because of growing competition. Cost accounting keeps effective control on stock of raw material, work-in-progress, consumable stores, finished goods, labour and overheads and thereby reduction of cost is possible. Cost reduction is always possible by means of cost control techniques as well as operational research and value analysis techniques.

4) Determination of selling price : Cost accounts provide requisite data for fixation of selling price of product or services. In the period of depression, cost accounting guides in deciding the extent to which the selling price may be reduced to meet the situation. For fixing the selling price total cost of production, expected profit, market condition, volume of sales etc. are considered. Among all these factors, cost of production plays an important role in price fixation.

5) Elimination of wastages : Cost accounting shows wasteful expenditure at different levels of production to the management. For example, wastage in material, idle time in labour and increase in cost of overheads are detected by cost accounting and measures are taken to control such wastages at proper time.

6) Preparation of cost estimates : Many times the manufacturing concern accepts the orders of customers. Each job may be different and may require different treatment. Before the introduction of job, cost estimate is to be made in order to fix the selling price. Under cost accounting system, preparation of cost estimate is possible. Thus, preparation of cost estimate is also one of the important objectives of cost accounting.

7) Fixation of standards for measuring efficiency : Another objective of cost accounting is to fix the standard for measuring efficiency of various business activities. In costing, the technique of standard costing is generally used for evaluation of performance. Standard costing determines the standards and these are compared with actuals. If there is any negative variance, it is removed.

8) To provide basis for operating policy : Cost accounting provides cost data to management, which is useful for taking the decision. Some of the decisions which are based on cost data are :

i) Whether the production should be increased or decreased.
ii) Whether to close the business or continue.
iii) Whether to produce the product or to buy from outside.
iv) Whether to continue with existing plant and machinery or to replace it.
v) Introduction of new product.
vi) Selling below cost decision etc.

9) Preparation of accounts and reports : Cost accounts collect the cost data and statistical information which is used for the preparation of cost sheet or cost estimate. The value of closing stock is also determined by cost accounts. By using the value of closing stock final accounts of concern are prepared and thus the operating efficiency of concern is determined. It also organises an effective system of reporting which provides the required cost data to management in time.

10) Conduct internal cost audit : Cost account organises the internal audit system to ensure effective working of various departments. It also provides a specialised services of cost audit in order to prevent the errors and frauds and to facilitate prompt and reliable information to management.

1.5 ADVANTAGES AND LIMITATIONS OF COST ACCOUNTING.

The limitations of financial accounting may be restated as the advantages of cost accounting. The advantages of cost accounting generally depend upon the installation of cost system. A sound system of costing is to be installed depending upon the type of product, manufacturing methods, size and type of organisation and the selling and destribution methods.

Then it provides the following advantages.

A) Advantages to the Management :

A company having proper cost accounting system will help the management in the following ways.

1) Reveals profitable and unprofitable activities : A sound system of costing reveals the profitable and unprofitable activities of various departments or processes. If some departments or processes reveal unprofitable activities, steps can be taken to eliminate the losses or inefficiencies occuring in any form such as idle time, under utilisation of plant, wastage of material etc.

2) Helps in cost control : Cost accounting helps in controlling the costs with costing techniques like standard costing, marginal costing and budgetory control.

3) Helps in decision making : Cost accounting supplies suitable cost data and other related information for managerial decision making. It is a best decision making tool. Decisions regarding introduction of new product, replacement of old machinery, make or buy decision, increase or decrease in production etc. are generally based on the information given by cost accounting to management.

4) Guides in fixing selling prices : Cost accounts assists management in fixing selling prices of product, particularly during depression period when the prices may have to be fixed below cost. In normal course, cost is considered the most important factor for fixing the selling price. Management adds reasonable profit to cost and thus selling price is determined.

5) Helps in inventory control : Cost accounting provides a sound base for inventory control. For checking the stock of manufacturing concern, periodic and perpetual inventory control systems are used and thereby discrepancies in stock are detected. Further, perpetual inventory control system helps in the preparation of interim profit and loss account and balance sheet can be prepared without actual stock taking as closing stock of raw materials, work in progress and finished product can easily be ascertained.

6) Helps in cost control : Cost comparison helps in cost control. Comparison may be made from period to period of the figures in respect of the same unit or factory. In cost accounting, techniques like standard costing and budgetory control are used to compare predetermined and actual activities and thereby discrepancies can be corrected at proper time.

7) Helps in increasing profits : Costing helps in increasing profit by disclosing the sources of loss and wastage and by suggesting such controls so that wastages, leakages and inefficiencies of all departments may be detected and prevented.

8) Reveals causes of increase or decrease in profit : The exact cause of a decrease or an increase in profit or loss can be detected. A concern may suffer not because of cost of production is high or prices are low but also because of output is much below the capacity of the concern. This fact is revealed by cost accounts only.

9) It facilitates planning : Cost accounting explains the cost incurred and profit made in the various lines of business and processes and thereby provides data on the basis of which production can be appropriately planned.

10) Helps in cost reduction : It helps in the introduction of cost reduction programme and finding out new and improved ways to reduce the cost.

11) Helps in lowering prices : An efficient cost system is bound to lower the cost of production, the benefit of which is passed on to the public at large in the form of lower prices of product or services.

12) Reveals idle capacity : A manufacturing unit may not be working to full capacity due to reasons such as shortage of demand, machine breakdown or other difficulties in production. A cost accounting system can easily workout the cost of idle capacity so that the management may take immediate steps to improve the position.

13) Checks the accuracy of financial accounts : The results given by profit and loss account and statement of cost are reconciled at the end of a particular period. Thus, cost accounts provide reliable check on the accuracy of financial accounts.

14) Prevention of fraud and manipulation : The operation of a system of cost audit in the organisation prevents manipulation and fraud.

b) Advantages to the Investors / Owners.
 i) Due to higher profits, the shareholders i.e. owners can get higher rate of dividend.
 ii) Due to higher profits, some portion of the profit is transferred to reserve and thereby the financial position of concern is strengthened. The owners or investors feel that their investments are safe and secured.
 iii) The market value of shares of investors is increased due to higher profits and dividends and thereby they are benefited.

c) Advantages to Creditors :
 i) Due to higher profits, creditors get interest on loan regularly and their investment is also safe.
 ii) The creditors can verify the creditworthiness of the firm and if they feel that the firm is continuously progressing, they can extend more credit facilities to the firm.

d) Advantages to Workers :
 i) Proper costing methods and techniques increase the profitability and thereby workers get proper remuneration.
 ii) The efficient workers are rewarded and slow workers are given more incentives if they come up to certain level of efficiency.
 iii) Incentive plan is the integral part of costing system. This results not only in higher earnings to workers but also higher productivity.

iv) A sound costing system increases the profitability. The workers get bonus and incentives in various forms. This reduces labour turnover as the workers are getting security about their employment.

e) Advantages to Consumers / Customers :

i) An efficient system of costing is bound to lower the cost of production, the benefit of which is passed on to the customer or public at large in the form of lower prices of product or services. Thus, consumers get good quality products or services at reasonable rates or lower rates.

ii) As development through cost accounting is possible, it helps to generate more employment opportunities.

iii) The installation of costing system will infuse confidence in the minds of public about the fairness of the prices charged.

f) Advantages to the Government :

i) Cost accounts provide a sound base for the assessment of Excise Duty and Income Tax and the formulation of policies regarding industry, export and import, taxation etc.

ii) It provides the facilities for preparation of national plans for economic development of the country.

iii) It provides ready figures for the use by government for application to problems like price fixation, price control, tariff protection, wage level fixation, payment of dividends or settlement of disputes.

g) Advantages to Public Enterprises :

Costing has to play more important role in public enterprises than the private enterprises. The prime aim of public enterprises is to provide quality goods or services at lower rates. The efficiency of public sector can, therefore, be best judged by comparing its cost of production with the cost of production in the private sector. A good system of costing ensures an effective control through a proper analysis of their working. In short, costing measures the efficiency of public enterprises and it helps the management in fixing reasonable price of products or services.

B) Limitations of Cost Accounting :

Cost accounting is an important tool of management which is often used to improve the overall performance of the industry. But it suffers from certain limitations. These are as follows.

1) It is expensive : Cost accounting system is highly expensive. Its installation is quite expensive. So, only large scale industries can afford this system. It is argued that installation of the system will involve additional expenditure which will lead to a diminution of profit.

2) It is unnecessary : It is argued that costing is of recent origin and that industries which prospered in the past are still prospering without the aid of costing and therefore, expenditure incurred in installing a costing system would be unnecessary expenditure.

3) Lack of uniformity : Cost accounting lacks a uniform procedure. Lack of uniformity is the greatest limitation of cost accounting. It is possible that two equally competent cost accountants may arrive at different results from same information. Hence, all cost accounting results are considered as mere estimates.

4) It is based on conventions, estimation and arbitrariness : There are large number of conventions, estimates and flexible factors such as classification of costs into elements, issue of materials on average or standard price, apportionment of expenses, division of overheads into fixed and variable cost, controllable and uncontrollable costs etc. which are based on conventions, estimation and arbitrariness. Hence, the information provided by cost accounting may not be true and reliable.

5) Limited applicability : Modern methods of costing cannot be applied to all industries. For example, it is true that costing cannot be applied with advantage to trading concerns and concerns of small size. There is no single method or technique which may be used in all types of industries. The application of costing system is dependent upon the nature of business and the type of product manufactured by it.

6) More complex method : For ascertaining the cost of product, number of steps are to be taken into account. For example, collection and classification of expenses, allocation and apportionment of expenses, different methods of valuation of stock, different methods of issue of material etc. These steps are considered as complicated. Moveover, various documents and reports are to be prepared for the application of costing system. This results in delaying the preparation of final accounts.

7) Failure in many cases : It is argued that the adoption of costing system failed to produce desired results in many cases and therefore, the system is defective. The failure of the system may be due to several causes such as apathy or indifference of management, lack of adequate facilities, non-co-operation or opposition from employees etc. It is very difficult to find out the exact fault of costing system.

8) Not useful for handling futuristic situations : The contribution of cost accounting for handling futuristic situations has not been much. For example, it has not evolved so far any tool for handling inflationary situation.

9) It fails in considering social obligations : Social responsibility of business is gaining importance day-by-day. But social responsibility is out of preview of cost accounts. Thus, cost accounting fails to consider the social obligations of business.

10) Confusion regarding non-cost items : There are many items of incomes and expenses which are indirectly related to the business or concerns. These are called non-cost items. For example - interest on capital, income tax, provisions for reserves, dividend received, cash discount etc. There is always confusion, whether these items should be included or to be excluded from the cost accounts.

Apart from the above limitations, cost accounting is helping management in taking various decisions which help to solve the complicated business problems. Cost accounting like other branches of accountancy is not an exact science but an art which has developed through the theories and accounting practices based on reasoning and common sense. Many theories can be proved or disproved in the light of conventions and basic principles of cost accounting. These principles are not static but changing with the change of time and circumstances. In short, though certain objections are raised against cost accounting, it has been proved that the development of cost accounting is one of the most significant step to improve the performance of various business undertakings.

1.6 DIFFERENCE BETWEEN FINANCIAL ACCOUNTING AND COST ACCOUNTING.

Financial Accounting and Cost Accounting both are concerned with systematic recording and presentation of financial data. Both are based on double entry system and their roles are supplementary. Both are the branches of accounting and their objective is to provide information to management by recording the business transactions systematically and scientifically. But still there is a difference between financial accounting and cost accounting. The main differences between financial and cost accounting are as follows.

Point of Distinction	Financial Accounting	Cost Accounting
1. Meaning	Financial accounting is concerned with classifying, recording and analysing the transactions of business according to its nature and prepares financial statements like trading account, profit and loss account and balance sheet.	Cost accounting is concerned with the classification, allocations, recording, reporting and control of costs. It ascertains the cost of product or service by preparing cost sheet.
2. Purpose	The Main purpose of financial accounting is to prepare profit and loss account and Balance sheet for reporting to owners or shareholders, creditors and other outside agencies: i.e external users.	The main purpose of cost accounting is to provide detailed cost information to management : i.e internal users.

Point of Distinction	Financial Accounting	Cost Accounting
3. Statutory Requirement	Financial accounts are kept to fulfil the statutory requirements of Companies Act and Income Tax Act.	Cost accounts are generally kept voluntarily to meet the requirements of management. But now Companies Act has made it obligatory to keep cost records in big manufacturing industries.
4. Recording of Transaction	It classifies, record and analyses the transaction in the subjective manner i.e. according to the nature of expenses.	It records the expenditure in objective manner i.e. according to the purpose for which costs are incurred.
5. Control Aspect	It lays emphasis on the recording of financial transactions and does not attach any importance to control aspect.	It provides for a detailed system of control with the help of certain special techniques like standard costing, marginal costing and budgetory control.
6. Stock Valuation	In financial accounts, stocks are valued at cost or market price whichever is less.	In cost accounting, stocks are always valued at cost.
7. Coverage	It covers accounts of whole business relating to all commercial transactions. They disclose the profit or loss of business as a whole.	It covers the transaction relating to certain specific activities only e.g. production, sales, services etc. hence department-wise profit or loss is disclosed.
8. Accounting Period	Financial accounts are prepared at the end of financial year, so they disclose operating results at the end of year.	Cost reports or accounts can be prepared as and when desired and hence they can provide information to management at any time.

Point of Distinction	Financial Accounting	Cost Accounting
9. Nature of Cost	Financial accounts record only historical cost.	Cost accounts record both historical and predetermined cost.
10. Information	It records only monetary transactions.	It records monetary as well as non-monetary information.
11. Relative Efficiency	Financial accounts do not provide information on the relative efficiencies of various workers, plant and machinery.	Cost accounts provide valuable information on the relative efficiencies of various workers, plant and machinery.
12. Fixation of Selling Price	The objective of financial accounts is not to determine the selling price.	Cost accounting helps in determining appropriate selling price of various producs of the firm under different situations.
13. Figures	Financial accounts deal mainly with the actual facts and figures.	Cost accounts deal partly with facts and figures and partly with estimates.
14. Types of Transactions Recorded	Financial accounting records only external transactions like sales, purchases, receipts etc. with outside parties.	Cost accounting not only records external transactions but also internal or inter depart-mental transactions like issue of materials by store keeper to production departments.
15. Break up of Cost	The costs are reported in aggregate in financial accounting. They are not broken according to nature and functions.	The costs are broken down on unit basis in cost accounts. They are analysed according to nature and functions.
16. Inter-firm comparison	Inter or Intra-firm comparison is not possible in financial accounting.	Inter or Intra firm comparison is possible in cost accounting.

Point of Distinction	Financial Accounting	Cost Accounting
17. Classi-fication of Cost	It does not classify cost into fixed and variable or controllable and uncontrollable.	It makes clear classification into fixed and variable or controllable and uncontrollable. The classi fication helps manage- ment to take various decisions.
18. Reference	In financial accounting reference can be made in case of difficulty to company law and to business ethics.	No such reference is possible. Guidance can be had only from a body of conventions followed by cost accountants.
19. Material Control	It does not provide for material control.	It provides for material control.
20. Safeguard of Interest	Financial accounting aims at safeguarding the interest of the business and its proprietors and others concerned with it.	Cost accounting, on the other hand, renders information for the guidance of management for proper planning, operation, control and decision-making

1.7 CRITICISMS AGAINST COST ACCOUNTING

Cost Accounting is criticised by different sections of only society for several reasons which are enumerated as follows -

a) **Duplication of efforts** - Cost Accounting is only repetition. It uses as a basis, financial accounting data. Thus, it involves only rearrangement of data and change in terminology. To a great extent, expenses and cost means the same thing. Thus, this involves only duplication of efforts.

b) **Expensive** - Cost Accounting adds to the expenditure due to maintenance of registers, records and staff for cost ascertainment. This adds to the expenses.

c) **Unnecessary** - Quite often, production volume and prices are determined by market forces, competition and regulatory government authority. In such cases enterprise management is not free to enterprise management is not free to take effective decision. This reduces considerably utilisation of costing information. Therefore, the system is unnecessary.

d) Not useful for decision making - Many management decisions are effected by considerations or factors other than cost. The impact of such factors outweigh cost consideration. This reduces utility value of Cost Accounts.

e) Failure of the system - It is argued that costing system has failed to bring the desired results. Therefore, it is defective.

f) Limited applicability - Modern methods of costing can not be readily applied to certain industries. There is no ready made system which can be applied to all the concerns.

g) Not reliable - Cost Accounting is based on estimates and hence it is not reliable.

1.8 Cost Unit and Cost Centre

A) Cost Unit

Cost unit is the quantity of product, service or time in relation to which cost may be ascertained or expressed. The forms of measurement used as unit cost are the physical measurements like number, weight, volume, length, time and value. The selection of suitable cost unit depends upon several factors such as organisation of the factory, nature of business, availability of information, requirments of the costing system, methods of production, trade practices, management policy for decision-making out of alternative choices and conditions of incidence of cost. The unit selected must be one with which expenditure can be closely associated and is generally the unit clearly appropriate to business. It must be clearly defined and selected before the process of cost finding can be started. It must not be too big or too small and must be so selected that expenditure can be associated with it and is appropriate to the needs of business. For example, in case of brick kiln, the unit should not be each brick but 1000 bricks normally.

In case of industries rendering services, usually the unit is a compound of two measures since the single measure may be meaningless. For example, in case of transport industry determination of exact cost unit is very difficult. Transport industry provides transport service to the society and hence service provided by transport industry is to be measured in terms of money. Transport industry carries passengers and goods. So in case of transport industry the cost unit will be per passenger per kilometer or per ton per kilometer.

A cost unit is the unit of product or unit of service to which costs are ascertained by means of allocation, apportionment and absorption. It is the device for the purpose of breaking up or separating cost into smaller sub-divisions attributable to product or services. A cost unit is defined by CIMA London as a "unit of product, service or time in relation to which cost may be ascertained or expressed." Cost units are the "things' that the business is set up to provide of which cost is ascertained. For example, in sugar mill, the cost per tonne of sugar may be asecrtained or in a textile mill the cost per metre of cloth may be ascertained. Thus "a tonne' of sugar and "a meter' of cloth are cost units. Cost units may be related to production or service, hence cost unit may be classified as under.

i) **Unit of production -** It is related to the production. For example, a tonne of steel, a metre of cable.

ii) **Unit of service -** It is related to service. For example passenger mile, consulting hours, cinema seats etc. A few examples of cost units in various industries are given below.

Industry or product	Cost Unit	Production or Service
1) Automobile	Number / per number	Production
2) Cement	Per tonne	Production
3) Chemicals	Tonne, kilogram, liter	Production
4) Coal	per tonne	Production
5) Brick works	per 1000 bricks	Production
6) Printing press	per 1000 copies	Production
7) Pencils	Dozen or gross	Production
8) Gas	cubic feet or cubic metre	Production and Service
9) Hospital	per patient per day	Service
10) Hotel	Room per day, per plate meal, per guest per day.	Service Service
11) Mines and Quarries	per tonne produced.	production.
12) Nikel plating	per square metre.	Service
13) Cotton or Jute	per bale	Production.
14) Paper Mill	per tonne.	Production.
15) Power and Electricity	Kilowatt hours (KWH)	Service
16) Transport	per passenger per kilometer or per tonne per kilometer	Service
17) Nuts and Bolts	Tonne, number, per gross, per bag of standard weight of 100 kgs.	production
18) Timber	Cubic feet	Production
19) Carpets	Square feet	Production
20) Soft drinks	Crate of 24 bottles or 12 bottles	production

B) Cost Centre :

Cost are ascertained by cost centres and cost units or both. the Institute of Cost and Works Accountants, England defines the cost centre as "a location, person, or item of equipment (or group of these) in or connected with the undertaking, in relation to which costs may be ascertained and used for the purpose of cost control." Cost centre is the smallest segment of activity or area of responsibility for which costs are collected. Thus, cost centre may be :

a) **Location :** an area like sales area or production area.
b) **Equipment :** a lathe machine, drilling machine, a delivery van.
c) **A person :** a salesman, a machine operator, foreman etc.

By analysing the definition, it can be known that cost centres are of two kinds. Viz impersonal cost centre consists of a location or items of equipments and a personal cost centre consists of person or group of persons. In manufacturing concern, cost centre may be production cost centre or service cost centre.

ICMA defines cost centre as "a production or service, function, activity or item of equipment whose cost may be attributed to cost units. A cost centre is the smallest organisational sub-unit for which separate cost allocation is attempted."

From the functional point of view, a cost centre may be relatively easy to establish, because a cost centre is any unit of the organisation to which cost can be separately attributed. A cost centre is an individual activity or group of similar activities for which costs are accumulated. For example, production department, advertisement department, machine, a work group or a worker, foreman, etc. is considered as a cost centre.

In short a cost centre may be determined according to location, which may be a division, department, sales area, stockyard, tool room, administrative office, workshop etc. Further costs are accumulated in respect of a person who may be a Works Manager, Sales Manager, Purchase Manager, Personnel Manager, Finance Manager, or that of Foreman, Storekeeper, Salesman, Section Officer, Clerk etc.

The purposes of cost centre are as follows.

i) Recovery of costs : Cost are accumulated in respect of location, person, or an item of equipment and then distributed over the product for recovery of cost which has been incurred.

ii) Control of costs : Cost centres are helpful for control of cost in such a way that they try to locate responsibility by location, person, or equipment. Thus, manager of a cost centre will try to control costs in respect of his area of responsibility. Hence, cost centres are also called "Responsibility Centres.'

Types of Cost Centres :

1) Production cost centre : Production centres are engaged in manufacturing some products. Raw material is converted into finished product by the help of various departments which are connected with each other. In production cost centre, there may be operation and process cost centres. Operation cost centre is a cost centre which consists of those machines or persons which carry out the same operation. Process cost centre consists of a continuous sequence of operation.

2) Service cost centre : The service cost centres are supplementary to production and other departments. They provide services to production and other departments. For example, Labour canteen provides services to labour, Material handling department provides material handling services to production departments. Only non-manufacturing costs are charged to service cost centre.

3) Personal cost centre : A cost centre which consists of a person or group of persons is called personal cost centre. Under this type of cost centre, costs are analysed and accumulated by sales manager, works manager, storekeeper, foreman etc.

4) Impersonal cost centre : An impersonal cost centre consists of a location or item of equipment, production departments, a machine or group of machines.

5) Operation cost centre : It consists of machines or persons carrying out similar operations. For example, machines and operations engaged in turning, welding, moulding etc.

6) Process cost centre : A cost centre in which a specific process or a continuous sequence of operations is carried out is called a process cost centre. For example, Sugar industry, Cotton textile industry etc.

The principle of costing by cost centres may be applied to almost all industries. The number of cost centres and the size of each vary from organisation to organisation. It all depends upon the expenditure involved and the requirements of management for the purpose of cost control. The selection of cost centre generally depends upon the following factors. (a) layout and organisation of the factory, (b) Available information, (c) policy of management regarding the selection of cost centre. etc.

1.9 EXERCISES :

Objective Type Questions.

a) Indicate which of the following statements are true or false.

1) Cost accounting is the branch of financial accounting.
2) The application of cost accounting system is restricted only to manufacturing concern.
3) Cost control is the part of cost accountancy.
4) Costing is exactly the same thing as cost accounting.
5) A prosperous business does not need a costing system.
6) Main purpose of cost accounting is to maximise profit.
7) Cost accounting helps in the ascertainment of cost beforehand.

8) The scope of cost accounting includes cost ascertainment, cost presentation and cost control.
9) Cost accounting is nothing but a post-mortem of past costs.
10) Cost accounting is an instrument of management control.
11) Cost accounting is nothing more than a detailed analysis of expenditure.
12) Cost accounting aids in price fixation.
13) Cost accounting is the oldest branch of accounting.
14) Cost accounting and financial accounting are complementary to each other.
15) General principle of ascertaining cost is the same in every method of costing.
16) Cost accounting is nothing more than a detailed analysis of expenditure.
17) Costing, cost accounting and cost accountancy are synonymous.
18) Cost accounting can replace Financial Accounting.

Answers : 1 - False, 2 - False, 3 - True, 4 - False, 5 - False, 6 - False, 7 - True, 8 - True, 9 - False, 10 - True, 11 - False, 12 - True, 13 - False, 14 - True, 15 - True, 16 - False, 17 - False, 18 - False

b) Fill in the blanks.

1) Cost accounting is a technique of .....
2) Cost accounting has been developed because of ..... of financial accounting.
3) Cost accounting is a science, art and ...... of cost accountant.
4) Cost accounts deal partly with facts and figures and partly with ....
5) Cost accounting provides data for managerial ....
6) Cost accounting is a separate .... of accounting.
7) Cost accounting serves the information need of ......
8) Cost accounting is based on ...... figures.
9) Cost accounting records both monetary and ...... units.
10) Cost unit in a college may be a ......
11) The primary objective of cost accounting is to ......
12) The technique and process of ascertaining cost is termed as ....
13) A sound costing system must place the same emphasis on cost control as on ....
14) The meaning of cost and costing is ....
15) Cost accounting is ...... as well as ....
16) In antomobile industry, cost unit is .... (P. U. April 2014)

Answers : 1 - ascertaining cost, 2 - limitations, 3 - Practice, 4 - estimates, 5 - decision making, 6 - branch, 7 - management, 8 - estimated, 9 - physical, 10 - student, 11 - control cost, 12 - costing, 13 - cost ascertainment, 14 - different, 15 - Science, Art, 16 - Number

Essay type questions :

1) Distinguish between "costing" and "cost accounting'. Discuss the objectives of cost accounting.
2) State and explain the main differences between financial accounting and cost accounting.
3) What are the limitations of accounting? How far cost accounting has contributed in removing the defects of financial accounting?
4) What is cost accounting? Discuss the advantages of cost accounting.
5) "Cost accounting has come to be an essential tool of the management" Comment.
6) What is cost accountancy? Discuss the advantages and disadvantages of cost accounting.
7) State the advantages of cost accounting to
   i) Management   ii) Workers   iii) Creditors
   iv) Government   v) General public.
8) Distinguish between cost unit and cost centre.
9) Trace the origin of cost accounting and explain in brief how it emerged in the past.
10) What is cost centre? Explain the different types of cost centres.
11) Define 'Cost Accounting?' State the objectives of Cost Accounting.
12) Explain the concept 'Cost Accounting'. State the advantages and limitations of Cost Accounting.
13) (A) Explain the basic concepts of Cost, Costing and Cost Accounting.
    (B) State the limitations of Financial Accounting. (P. U. April 2014)
14) Define Cost Accounting. Explain the benefits of Cost Accounting. Also explain the criticisms against Cost Accounting.
15) Explain the basic concepts of Cost, Costing and Cost Accounting.
16) State the limitations of Financial Accounting.
17) Differentiate between Fincancial Accounting and Cost Accounting.

2:1 MATERIAL, LABOUR AND OTHER EXPENSES

2:1:1 Elements of Cost

The management must know the details of cost incurred in order to fix the selling price and to ascertain the profit or loss. But only the knowledge of cost cannot satisfy the needs of management. For proper control and managerial decisions, management must be provided with necessary data to analyse and classify cost. For this purpose total cost is to be analysed by nature of expenses i.e. elements of cost must be considered. Basically, there are three elements of cost. viz material, labour and other expenses. Further, they are classified as direct and indirect material, direct and indirect labour and direct and indirect expenses.

According to Dictionary meaning " Practically in all cases, a cost is the sum of three groups or components – the purchase or transfer price of material, the cost of hire of labour and the value of other disbursements made or expenditure incurred in achieving the desired product or result." Thus, the total cost is the aggregate of materials, labour cost and overheads i.e. all other expenses.

According to ICMA London, Elements of cost means "the primary classification of costs according to the factors upon which expenditure is incurred viz material cost, labour cost and expenses."

The element of cost can be analysed into different elements of cost as shown in the following chart.

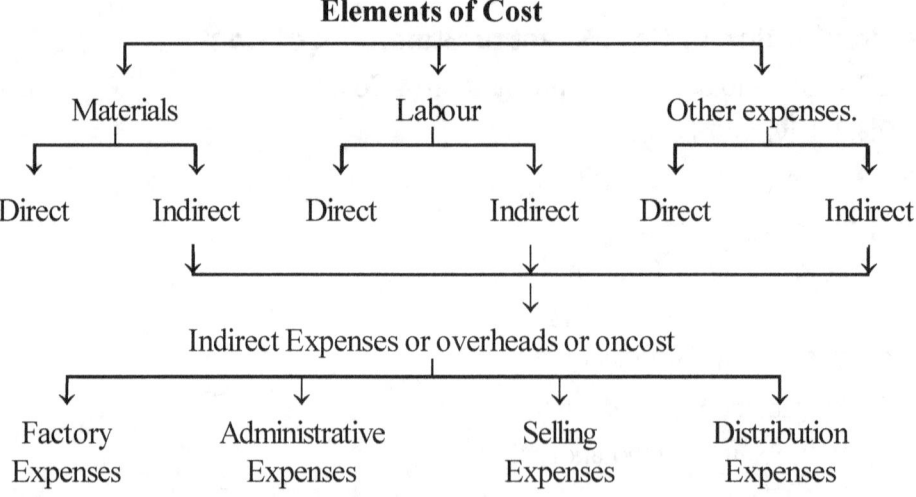

The aggregate of direct material, direct wages and direct expense is called as Direct cost or Prime cost. Overhead is the aggregate of indirect material, indirect labour and indirect expenses. The overheads are also termed as on cost or indirect cost. The overhead can be divided into factory, administration, selling and distribution overheads, depending on the department in which the expenses are incurred. Thus, the total cost is the sum of prime cost and all four kinds of overheads. The difference between the sales and total cost is the profit made or loss incurred. If the total cost is less than sales, the difference is the profit and if the total cost is more than sales the difference is the loss. If both are equal, there is no profit or no loss.

Thus, the total cost of product consists of various elements of cost. These elements are as follows.

2:1:2 Material Costs

Material cost is defined by ICMA, London as under. "The cost of commodities supplied to undertaking." Materials may be direct of Indirect.

Direct Materials : Direct materials are those materials which can be identified in the product and can be conveniently measured and directly charged to the product. It becomes the part of product. Finished product can be manufactured by using direct material.

For example : timber in furniture making, leather used in shoe making, cloth used in garments, steel used is machines. These are called as direct material or direct material cost.

a) Direct Materials

Direct material is classified as under.
i) All raw material, semi finished parts and components purchased for a particular job, order.
ii) Material passing from one process to another.
iii) All materials requisitioned from stores for production order.
iv) Primary packing materials e.g. cartons, wrappings, cardboard boxes, etc.

However, in many cases, though the direct materials become the part of finished product, yet it is not treated as direct materials, e.g. thread used in stitching cloth, nails used in furniture etc. This is because value of such material is so small that it is quite difficult and futile to measure it. Therefore, such material is called indirect material.

b) Indirect Materials :

The materials which cannot be identified with individual cost of a unit is called indirect materials. These are minor in importance. They cannot be separately allocated to the finish product. Examples of indirect materials are : consumable like cotton waste, lubricants, brooms, rags, cleaning materials, oil, grease, sand paper used in polishing, high speed diesel used in power generation, pins, nutbolts, screws, thread etc.

Classification of materials into direct and indirect facilitates material control. Direct materials are usually high value items as compared to indirect materials and need strict control. On the other hand indirect material cost is comparatively low and needs moderate control.

2:1:3 Labour Costs :

ICMA defines labour cost as,"the cost of remuneration (wages, salaries, commission, bonus etc.) of the employees of an undertaking."

Generally, for converting raw materials into finished product, workers efforts are necessary. In service sector, workers provide services to society. For producing product or providing services, workers are paid wages or remuneration and this is called labour cost.

Labour cost is divided into direct labour and indirect labour.

a) Direct Labour / (Direct wages) :

The labour cost which is expended in altering the construction, composition, confirmation or condition of the product is called direct labour. It is conveniently identified with a product and easily allocated to the product. Generally, direct labour cost consists of wages paid to workers directly engaged in converting raw materials into finished product. Direct labour includes the payment made to the following groups or labour.

    a) Labour engaged on actual production of the product.

    b) Labour engaged in aiding the manufacture by way of supervision, maintenance, tool setting, transportation of materials etc.

    c) Inspectors, analysts, etc. specially required for such production. The wages paid to supervisor, inspector etc. though not direct labour, can be treated as direct labour if they are directly engaged on a specific product or process, where labour cost is easily measured without much efforts.

b) Indirect Labour / Indirect Wages

The wages paid to the workers who are indirectly engaged in the manufacturing products are called indirect wages. They are of general character and cannot be conveniently identified with a particular cost unit or cost centre, but they are apportioned or absorbed by cost centres or cost units. In simple words, indirect labour is not directly engaged in the production operation but only assists or helps in production process. For example, wages of worker in administrative department, watch and ward department, sales department, general supervision, wages of foreman, supervisor, chargeman, inspector, clerical staff. etc.

2:1:4 Other Expenses or Expenses.

ICMA defines expenses as "the cost of services provided to an undertaking and the notional cost of use of owned assets." In other words all costs other than material and labour are termed as other expenses or expenses.

Other expenses or expenses can be classified as under :

a) Direct Expenses or Chargeable Expenses

Direct expenses are also known as chargeable expenses. It includes all types of expenses other than direct materials and direct labour which are incurred specifically for a particular product or process. ICMA London defines direct expenses as "direct expenses are those expenses which can be conveniently identified with and allocated to cost centres or cost units." These expenses are incurred in connection with a particular job or process. For example : Hire charges paid in respect of special plant and machinary or single purpose tools for a particular job, travelling expenses to site for the purpose of erection, cost of special tools, cores, patterns, designs, components and special parts purchased for special job, Inward charges, insurance and freight charges on special material chargeable to a job, Depreciation or hire of plant used on a contract at site, pilot scheme, royalty, licence fees, cost of special drawings or designs etc.

b) Indirect Expenses

All indirect costs other than indirect material and indirect labour cost are termed as indirect expenses. These cannot be directly identified with a particular product or process, or work order and are common to cost unit or cost centres. It is the cost of giving service to the production department. It includes factory expenses, administrative expenses, selling and distribution expenses. for example Rent and Rates, Factory Expenses, Depreciation, Lighting and Power, Advertising, Distribution Expenses, Office salaries.

Prime Cost / Direct Cost : The aggregate of direct materials, direct labour / wages and direct expenses is called as prime cost.

Overheads or oncost or supplementary cost : The aggregate of indirect materials, indirect labour and indirect expenses are called as overheads or oncost or supplementary cost. It arises as the result of overall operation of the production or business. It cannot be identified with a particular unit of output but can be apportioned or absorbed by cost centres or cost units. It is the cost of operating supplies and services used by the undertaking. It also includes maintenance of capital assets. According to **Wheldon**, overhead means "the cost of indirect material, indirect labour and such other expenses including services that cannot be conveniently charged direct to specific cost units. It includes all manufacturing and non manufacturing supplies and services."

Overheads are divided into three groups as under.

1) Factory Overheads :

Factory overheads are also called as production expenses or manufacturing expenses or works overheads. These expenses are concerned with the production. It includes indirect materials, indirect wages and indirect expenses in producing goods or providing services. In simple words, factory overheads is the aggregate of all the factory expenses incurred in connection with manufacture of a product. Examples of factory expenses are as under,

   a) **Indirect Materials -** coal, oil, grease, cotton waste, brush, sweeping broom, stationery in factory office, etc.

   b) **Indirect Labour or Wages -** Salary of foreman, supervisor, inspector, work's manager salary, salary of factory office staff, wages of factory sweeper, wages of factory watchman etc.

c) **Indirect Expenses** - Factory rent, rates and taxes, Depreciation of plant, Repairs and maintenance of plant, Factory lighting and power, Internal transport expenses Insurance of factory building etc.

2) Office and Administrative Expenses / Overheads

As per the ICMA definition, administration overhead is the cost of formulating the policy, directing the organisation and controlling the operation of an undertaking. These overheads are of general character and mainly related to office and administration of undertaking. These are not directly connected with production or selling and distribution activities. Examples of these expenses are as under.

1) **Indirect Material**
   a) Stationary used in general administrative office, postage, sweeping broom, brush etc.
   b) **Indirect Labour :** Salary of office staff, salary of Manager, salary of Managing Director, Remuneration of the director of a company.
   c) **Indirect Expenses :** Establishment charges, Telephone charges, Rent of office building, office lighting and power, Depreciation of office furniture, office air conditioning, Sundry expenses etc.

3) Selling and Distribution Overheads / Expenses

According to ICMA, "selling overhead is the cost incurred in promoting sales and retaining customers." It is also definied as "the cost of seeking to create and stimulate demand and of securing orders." Selling expenses are incurred to increase new as well as old customers. The expansion of any business is depended on the selling expenses, which are incurred by the concerned unit. New industrial unit has to promote sales by distributing free samples or gifts to customers.

Distribution expenses include all expenditure incurred from the time of completion of a product until it reaches to its destination. It is the cost of the process which begins with making the packed product available for dispatch and ends with making the reconditioned returned empty package available for reuse. for example– carriage outwards, delivery van expenses, insurance of goods in transit, warehousing etc. Examples of selling and distribution expenses are as under.

   a) **Indirect Materials :** Stationery used in sales office, cost of samples, packing materials, price-list, catalogues, oil, grease etc. for delivery vans etc.
   b) **Indirect Labour :** Salary of sales office staff, salary of godown staff, salary and commission of salesmen, salary of drivers and cleaners, salary of sales manager.
   c) **Indirect Expenses :** Carriage outwards, showroom expenses, Rent of godown, Bad debts, Travelling expenses, Advertising, Upkeep of delivery vans, Loading and Unloading charges, Sales Office expenses etc.

2:2 CLASSIFICATION OF COSTS AND TYPES OF COSTS

2:2:1 Classification of Costs

Classification is the process of grouping costs according to their common characteristics. It is a system of placement of like items together according to their common features. Costs are classified or grouped according to their nature i.e. materials, labour, overheads and a number of other characteristics, such as function, variability, controllability and normality. This classfication is very essential for identifying the costs with cost centers or cost units.

Classification of cost is defined by various authors as under.

1) According to **Dickey,** "Classification is the process of grouping like facts under a common designation on the basis of similarities of nature, attributes or relations."

2) The committee of National Association of Accountants defines classification as, "The identification of each item and the systematic placement of like items together according to their common features."

In short, cost classification is the process of grouping costs according to their common features.

There are various ways of classification of costs. Each classification serves a different purpose. The cost may be the same, but the classification of costs are made in different ways depending upon the need and objects to be achieved in a particular organisation. The chart given on **next page** shows the classification of cost.

Each classification is discussed in detail as follows.

1) By Elements or Nature or Analytical Classification.

According to this classification, costs are divided into three main categories e.g. Material, Labour and Expenses.

a) Materials : Material cost is defined by ICMA, London as under "the cost of commodities supplied to undertaking. Materials may be direct material and indirect material."

Direct materials are theose materials which can be identified in the product and can be conveniently measured and directly charged to product. It becomes the part of product. Finished product can be manufactured by using direct materials. For example, timber used in furniture, leather used is shoe making industry, component parts packing materials etc.

Indirect material cost has been defined as "material cost other than direct material cost." In other words, materials which cannot be identified with individual cost of a unit is called indirect material. These are minor in importance. They cannot be separately allocated to the finish product but they are apportioned on the product. Examples of indirect materials are : Consumables like cotton waste lubricants, brooms, rags, cleaning materials, pins, nutbolts, screws, thread etc.

b) Labour : ICMA defines labour cost as "the cost of remuneration (wages, salaries, commission, bonus etc) of the employees of an undertaking." Workers efforts are necessary for converting raw materials into finished products.In service industry workers provide services to society. Thus, for producing product or providing services, the workers are paid wages or remuneration. This is called labour cost. Labour cost may be direct labour cost or indirect labour cost.

The labour cost which is expended in altering the construction, composition, condition of the product is called **direct labour cost.** Direct labour cost is conveniently identified with the product and can be easily allocated to the product. For example, wages paid to shoemaker, weaver, machine operator etc.

The wages paid to workers, who are not directly engaged in the manufacturing process is called **indirect labour.** It is of general character and cannot be identified with the product or cost unit. For example, wages paid to Foreman, Supervisor, Inspector, Clerk, Peon etc.

c) Expenses : ICMA defines expenses as "the cost of services provided to an undertaking and the notional cost of use of own assets." In other words all costs other than material and labour are termed as other expenses or expenses. Expenses are classified into direct and indirect expenses.

Direct expenses are also called chargeables expenses. It includes all types of expenses other than direct material and direct labour. ICMA defined direct expenses as, "direct expenses are those expenses which can be conveniently identified with and allocated to cost centres or cost units." These are incurred for particular job or process. For example, Hire charges paid in respect of special plant, royalties, cost of patents, cost of experiments, architects fees etc.

All indirect costs other than indirect materials and indirect labour are termed as indirect expenses. These expenses cannot be directly charged to production. It is the cost of giving service to the production department. It includes factory expenses, administrative expenses and selling and distribution expenses.

2) By Degree of Traceability to the Product :

According to this classification, total cost is divided into direct cost and indirect cost.

Direct Costs are those costs which are incurred for and can be conveniently identified with a particular cost unit or process or department. In other words the aggregate of direct material, direct labour and direct expenses is called direct cost. It is also known as prime cost. Cost of raw materials used and wages of machine operator are the common examples of direct cost. Similarly, wages paid to a tailor in readymade garments company for stitching shirt or trouser is also a direct cost.

Indirect Cost are those costs which are general costs and are incurred for the benefit of a number of cost centres or cost units or departments. These cost cannot be conveniently identified with a particular product or cost unit or cost centre. In other words, the aggregate of indirect material, indirect labour and indirect expenses is known as indirect cost. Depreciation of machinery, insurance, lighting, power, managerial salaries, materials used in repairs, rent of building etc. are the common examples of indirect costs. Indirect cost is not traced or identified directly with a cost unit, because of the following reasons.

Classification of Costs

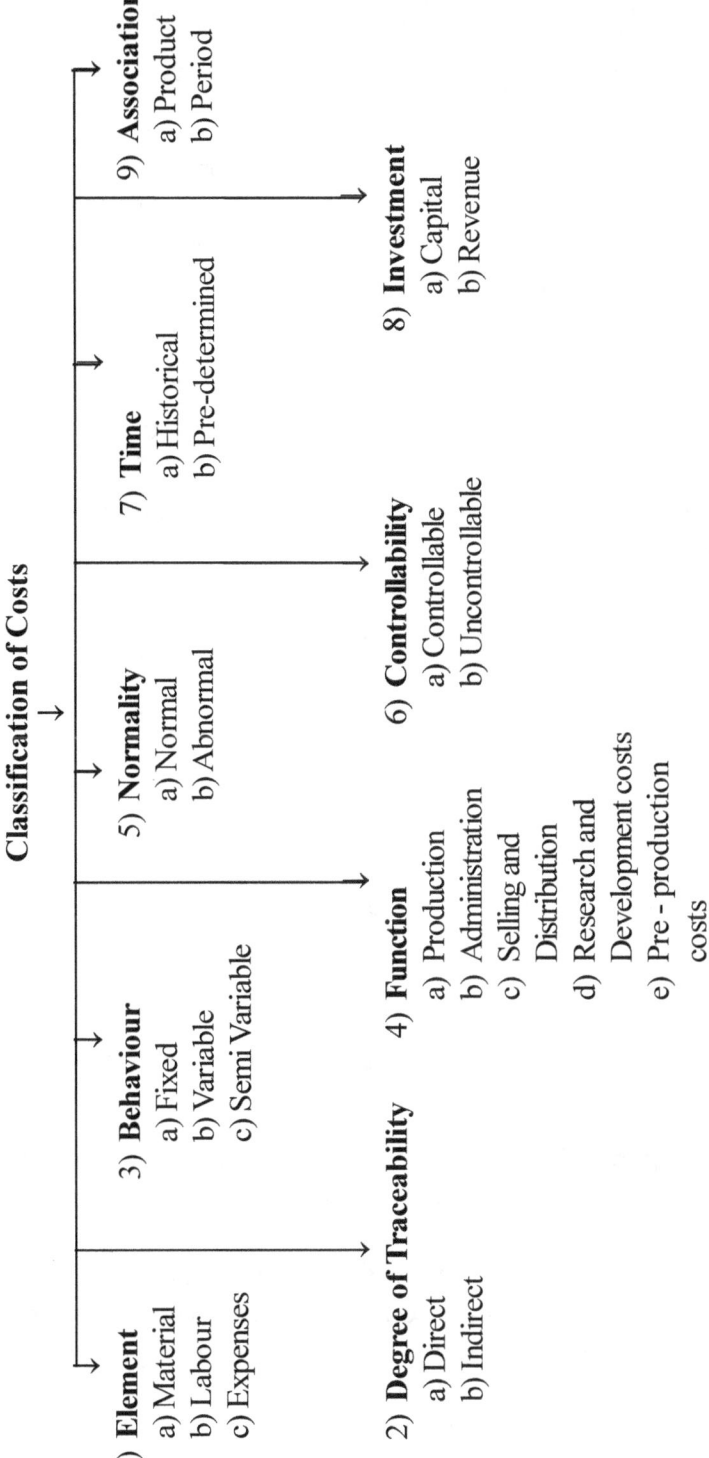

1) **Element**
a) Material
b) Labour
c) Expenses

2) **Degree of Traceability**
a) Direct
b) Indirect

3) **Behaviour**
a) Fixed
b) Variable
c) Semi Variable

4) **Function**
a) Production
b) Administration
c) Selling and
   Distribution
d) Research and
   Development costs
e) Pre - production
   costs

5) **Normality**
a) Normal
b) Abnormal

6) **Controllability**
a) Controllable
b) Uncontrollable

7) **Time**
a) Historical
b) Pre-determined

8) **Investment**
a) Capital
b) Revenue

9) **Association**
a) Product
b) Period

i) It is not possible to do so, e.g. rent of building.
ii) It is not feasible or convenient to do so, e.g. nails or screws used in furniture, thread used in stitching readymade clothes etc.
iii) Management chooses not to do so because of old customs which are in vogue.

Further the nature of business and the cost unit chosen will determine which costs are direct and which costs are indirect. Sometimes, an item of cost may be direct cost in one case and the same may be indirect in another case. For example, the hire of mobile crane for use by contractor at site would be regarded as direct cost but if the crane is used as a part of services of the factory, the hire charges would be regarded as indirect cost. In short, the nature and objective of cost determine whether the cost is direct or indirect.

3) Behaviourwise Classification or By changes in Activity or Volume :

Behaviour means changes in cost are classified into three groups. viz Fixed, Variable and Semi-variable.

i) Fixed Costs - Fixed cost is a cost which tends to be unaffected by variations in the volume of output. Fixed costs remain fixed in total amount for a specified period of time. Fixed costs do not increase or decrease, when the volume of production changes. For example, Rent or Insurance of building remains constant and do not change with the change in production level. But Fixed cost "per unit' increases when the volume of production decreases and decreases when the volume of production increases. For example, if total fixed cost is Rs. 1,00,000 per month, per unit fixed cost may be as under.

No of units produced	Fixed cost per unit
1,000	100
2,000	50
5,000	20
10,000	10

In short, if the production increases, fixed cost per unit is decreased according to the volume of production.

According to ICMA London - Fixed Cost is defined as, a cost which accrues in relation to the passage of time and which within certain output or turnover limits tends to be unaffected by fluctuations in volume of output or turnover. In other words, fixed costs remain fixed in total amount and do not increase or decrease with volume of production. But the fixed cost per unit increases when volume of production decreases and decreases when the volume of production increases. Thus, fixed costs are constant in total amount but fluctuate per unit as production changes. The characteristics of fixed cost are :

(a) Fixed total amount within a relevant output range.

(b) Increase or decrease in per unit fixed cost when volume of production changes.

(c) Fixed costs are apportioned to departments on some equitable basis.

(d) Fixed cost can be controlled mostly by the top level management.

Examples of fixed costs are : Rent, Rates, Taxes, Insurance of factory building, Manager's salary, Office staff salaries, Municipal taxes, etc.

The following is the graph indicating the behaviours of Fixed Cost- Which remains constant.

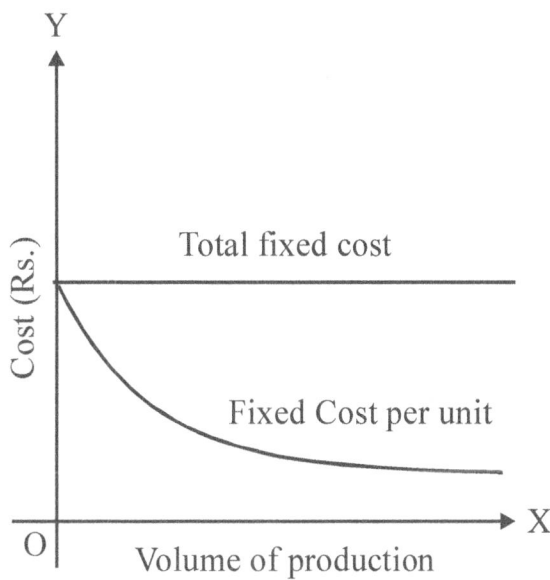

Behaviour of Fixed Cost

ii) Variable Costs - Variable cost is a cost which tends to vary directly with the variations in the volume of output. In other words, when the volume of production increases, total variable cost also increases and when volume of output decreases, total variable cost also decreases. But the variable cost **per unit** remains fixed or constant, if the production is increased or decreased. Thus, variable costs fluctuate in total amount but tend to remain constant per unit as production activity changes. Direct material cost, Direct labour cost, Direct expenses, power, repairs etc. are the examples of variable cost. The features of variables costs are as follows.

1) The variable cost per unit remains constant.
2) Total variable cost vary in direct proportion of output.
3) Variable cost can be controlled by department heads.
4) It is easy to allocate and apportion variable cost to department.

The nature of variable cost will be clear from the following example. Suppose that per unit variable cost is Rs. 10,s the total cost will change, as per the volume of output as under.

Per unit cost (Rs)	Total output (units)	Total variable cost (Rs)
10	10,000	1,00,000
10	8,000	80,000
10	12,000	1,20,000
10	16,000	1,60,000

Variable cost is also called product cost because it depends on the quantum of output rather than on time.

ICMA, London-defines Variable Cost as, a cost which in aggregate tends to vary in direct proportions to changes in the volume of output or turnover. In other words, when volume of output increases, total variable cost also increases and vice-versa, when volume of output decreases, total variable cost also decreases. But the variable cost per unit remains fixed.

The following is the graph indicating the behaviour of variable cost. - Which changes according to changes in output.

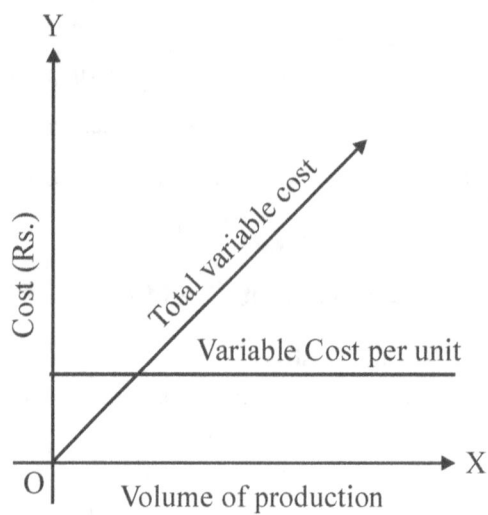

Behaviour of Variable Cost

Thus, variable costs, in general, indicate the following characteristics.
1. They vary in direct proportion to volume of output or turnover.
2. The variable cost per unit of product remains constant.
3. It is easy for allocatiobn and apportionment to departments.
4. Such costs can be controlled by departmental heads.

Examples of variable costs are : direct material cost, direct labour cost, direct expenses power, repairs, royalties, commission of salesman, normal spoilage, etc.

iii) Semi-variable or Semi fixed Cost : ICMA, London defines semi variable cost as, "a cost containing both fixed and variable elements, which is therefore partly affected by fluctuations in the volume of output or turnover." These costs include both partly fixed and partly variable. A semi-variable cost has fixed or constant element, below which it will never fall at any level of output. But the variable element in semi-variable cost changes as per volume of production. For example, Telephone expenses include a fixed portion of annual / monthly charge (Minimum Rent) plus variable according to calls made. Thus, total telephone expenses are semi-variable. Other examples of such costs are depreciation, repairs and maintenance of building and plant, supervision, profession tax etc.

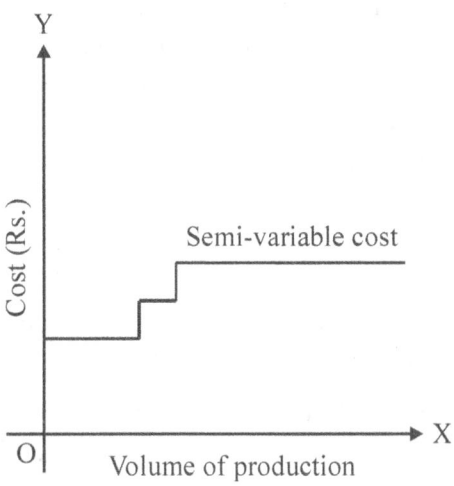

Following is the graph indicating the behaviour of fixed, variable and semi-variale costs.

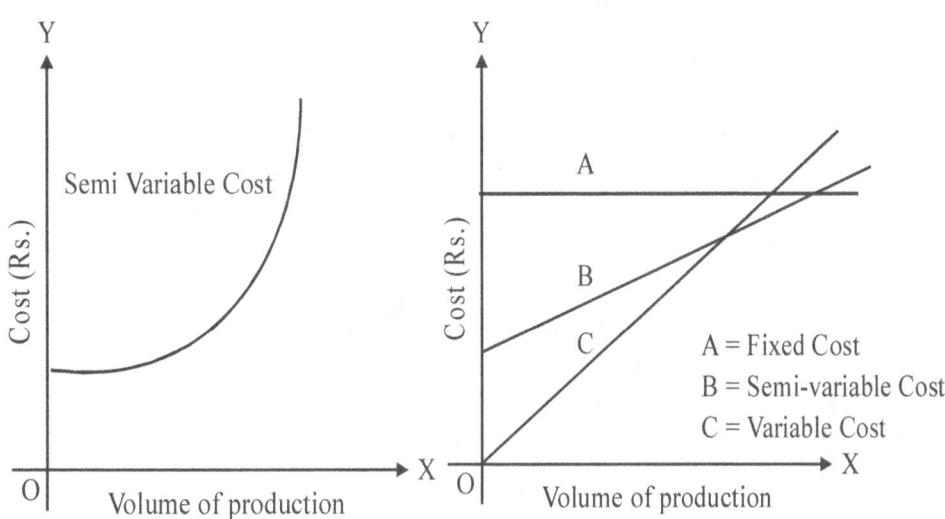

Examples of semi-variable costs are : Telephone charges, depreciation, repairs and maintenance of plant and machinery, building, supervision, compensation for accidents, light and power etc.

4) Functionwise / Functional Classification

According to this classification, the costs are divided in the light of different aspect of basic management activities involved in the operation of business undertaking. Cost are classified according to function such as production cost and commercial cost.

a) Manufacturing or Production Cost : This is the total of costs involved in the manufacture, construction and fabrication of unit of production. It is an operating cost of manufacturing department of an organisation. Production cost is the cost of process which begins with supplying materials, labour and services and ends with the packing of products. Thus, the materials, labour and expenses, both direct and indirect, constitute the cost of production. Examples of production cost are as under. Direct and indirect materials, Direct and indirect labour, Direct and indirect expenses, Depreciation of factory building and plant and machinery, factory heating and lighting, Insurance of factory building etc.

Commercial Cost : This is the total of costs incurred in the operation of business undertaking other than the cost of manufacturing and production.It is subdivided into administrative cost,selling & distribution cost and research and development cost.

b) Administrative Cost : ICMA defines administrative cost as, "the sum of the costs of general and management and of secretarial, accounting and administrative services which can not be directly related to production, marketing, research and development functions of the enterprise." In other words, administrative cost is the cost of formulating the policy, directing the organisation and controlling the operations of an undertaking. It is not related directly to research, development, production and selling and distribution activity or function. Directors fees, legal expenes, Audit fee, salaries of office staff, expenses of secretarial and accounting department, postage and telegram etc. are the examples of administrative expenses.

c) Selling Expenses : Selling cost is the cost incurred in promoting sales and retaining customers. Selling cost creates demand for product by advertising goods in the market. Examples of selling costs are : salaries and commission of salesmen and sales staff, Advertisement expenses, showrooms expenses, cost of free samples, travelling expenses of salesmen etc.

Distribution Expenses : Distribution expenses include all expenditure incurred from the time product is completed until it reaches its destination. It is the cost of the process which begins with making the packed product available for dispatch and ends with making the reconditioned returned empty package available for reuse. In short, expenses incurred for the distribution of product to ultimate customers are called as distribution expenses. Examples of distribution expenses are, salary of godown staff, expenses of delivery vans, carriage outwards, warehouse expenses, packing cost etc.

d) Research and Development Costs : According to ICMA "Research cost is the cost of searching for new and improved products, new application of materials or new or improved methods." It is carried out by the research staff of the organisation. Such costs include the cost of initial experimentation, all types of tests and subsequent small trial runs in order to prove the results of research.

Development Cost is the cost of the process which begins with the implementation of the decision to produce a new or improved products or to employ a new or improved methods and ends with the commencement of formal production of that product or by that method.

e) Pre-production Costs : These costs are incurred when a new product is introduced. These costs are incurred for trial run. They are treated as deferred revenue expenditure. They are charged to the cost of future production.

5) Normality :

The costs can be classified as Normal costs and Abnormal costs according to whether they are incurred normally at a given level of output in the conditions in which level of activity is normally attained.

a) Normal Costs : Normal cost is a cost which is normally incurred at a given level of output in the condition in which that level of output is normally attained. Normal costs are usual costs under given circumstances. Hence, it forms a part of cost of production.

b) Abnormal Costs : Abnormal cost is that which is not normally incurred at a given level of output. Such cost is over and above the normal cost. It is not treated as a part of cost of production. Hence, it is charged to costing Profit and Loss Account.

6) Controllability :

The concept of responsibility accounting leads directly to the classification of costs as controllable and uncontrollable cost. Under this, costs are classified according to whether or not they are influenced by the action of a given member of undertaking.

a) Controllable Cost : the controllable cost is a cost chargeable to a budget or cost centre, which can be influenced by the action of the person in whom control of centre is vested. These costs are generally regulated at a given level of management authority. Variable cost are generally controlled by department heads. For example, cost of raw material may be controlled by purchasing in larger quantities. But sometimes, cost can not be controlled by concerned authorities due to variations in budged and actual performance. For example, excessive scrap may arise from inadequate supervision or from latent defect in purchased material.

b) Uncontrollable Costs : Uncontrollable cost is the cost which is not influenced by the action of a given member of undertaking. For example, it is very difficult to control costs like managerial salaries, factory rent, factory insurance. Generally, all fixed cost are not controllable. These costs are beyond the control of management.

The distinction between controllable and uncontrollable costs is not very clear and may be left to individual judgement. Some expenditure which may be uncontrollable on short term basis can be controllable on long term basis. In short, it is practically very difficult to make difference in cost as controllable and uncontrollable.

7) Time :

On the basis of time of computation, costs are classified as historical cost and pre-determined costs.

a) Historical Costs : Historical costs are the costs which are ascertained, after these have been incurred. These are actual costs of production. Such costs are available only when the production of a particular thing has already been done. Such costs are only of historical value and not at all helpful for the control purpose.

b) Predetermined Costs : Predetermined costs are future costs, which are ascertained in advance of production on the basis of specification of all factors affecting cost. Predetermined costs help the management in taking various decisions. Predetermined cost determined on the scientific basis becomes standard cost. Such cost when compared with actual costs will give the reasons of variance and will help the management to fix the responsibility and to take remedial action to avoid future recurrence. Thus, future or predetermined cost are relevant for managerial decision making in cost control, profit projections, appraisal of capital expenditure, introduction of new products, expansion programme and pricing etc.

8) Investment :

Every industrial undertaking has to invest money in the business. Cost can be classified into capital cost and revenue cost.

a) Capital Cost : The cost which is incurred in purchasing an asset either to earn income or increasing the earning capacity of the business is called capital cost. For example, purchase of plant and machinery, cost of construction of factory building etc.

b) Revenue Cost : The cost which is incurred to maintain the earning capacity of the concern or running a business, is called revenue cost. For example, cost of material used in production, labour charges paid to convert raw material into finished product, salaries, repairs, maintenance, selling and distribution expenses etc. For calculating the profit or loss of the business, revenue expenses are to be considered.

9) Association of Product :

On the basis of association of product, cost can be divided into product cost and period cost.

a) Product Costs : Product costs are those costs which are necessary for production. If there is no production, product cost will not be incurred. It is traceable in the product and is included in the inventory valuation. It includes direct material and direct labour but may or may not include an element of overheads depending upon the type of costing system in force. Product costs are related to goods produced or purchased for resale and are intially indetifiable as the part of inventory. These product or inventory costs become expenses in the form of cost of goods sold only when inventory is sold.

b) Period Costs : Period costs are those which are not necessary for production. These are written off as expenses in the period in which these are incurred. These costs are incurred on the basis of time, such as rent, salaries, depreciation etc. These are related to administration and selling of goods. Such costs are essential to keep the business running. Such costs are of revenue in nature and therefore they are charged to profit and loss account.

2:2:2 Types of Costs

The word cost has different meanings in different situations. The clear understanding of various cost concepts, various types of costs are explained as follows.

1) Marginal Cost : Marginal cost is the total of variable cost i.e. prime cost plus variable expenses. It is the variable cost of one unit of product or a service i.e. cost which would be avoided, if the unit was not produced or provided. In short, in marginal cost, fixed cost is not considered and only variable costs are considered.

2) Notional Cost or Imputed Cost : The notional cost is hypothetical cost taken into account in a particular situation to represent the benefit enjoyed by an entity in respect of which no actual expenses are incurred. For example, Interest on own capital, rent on own building.

3) Opportunity Cost : The opportunity cost is the value of a benefit sacrificed in favour of an alternative course of action. It is the maximum amount that could be obtained at any given point of time if a resource was sold or put to the most valuable alternative use that would be practicable. In short, it can be defined as the revenue forgone by not making the best alternative use.

4) Out of pocket Costs : These are cash costs as opposed to cost such as depreciation which do not require any cash outlay.

5) Replacement Costs : It is the cost at which there could be purchase of an asset or material identical to that which is being replaced or revalued. It is the cost of replacement at current market price.

6) Total Cost : The aggregate of all expenses related to the production or services rendered, whether actually incurred or not is called total cost. In other words, it is an aggregate of material labour and overheads, which are incurred while producing things or commodities.

7) Standard Cost : The words standard "means" norm or a criterion. Standard cost is thus a criterion cost which may be used as yardstick to measure the efficiency with which actual cost has been incurred. In other words, standard costs are predetermined costs that should be incurred under efficient operating system. In the words of Brown and Howard, "the standard cost is a predetermined cost which determines what each product or service should cost under given circumstances."

8) Conversion Cost : The conversion cost is the cost incurred for converting the raw material into finished products. It consists of only direct wages paid and the production expenses incurred but excludes the cost of raw materials.

9) Sunk Cost : The sunk costs are those costs that have been invested in a project and which will not be recovered, if the project is terminated. The sunk cost is one for which the expenditure has taken place in past. For example, depreciation. This cost is not affected by a particular decision under consideration. Sunk cost is calculated when an old asset is replaced by a new one.

10) Joint Cost : The joint costs are the cost of either a single process or series of processes that simultaneously produce two or more products of significant relative sales value. In other words, when two or more products are produced from single raw material, we may get main product and by product, but their cost is a combined cost. This cost is called joint cost.

11) Common Cost : The common cost is an indirect cost that is incurred for the general benefit of number of departments or for the whole enterprise and which is necessary for present and future operation.

12) Differential Cost : The change in costs due to change in the level of activity or method of production is known as differential cost.

13) Avoidable Cost : Avoidable costs are those costs which can be avoided or eliminated, if a particular product or department is discontinued.

14) Unavoidable Cost : Unavoidable costs are those costs which can not be avoided if a particular department or product is discontinued. For example, Salary of General Manager.

15) Traceable Cost : Traceable cost is the cost which can be easily identified with a cost centre or cost unit or product. This is opposite to common cost.

16) Discretionary Cost : Fixed cost is classified into committed cost and discretionary cost. Committed cost cannot be avoided whereas discretionary cost can be avoided. For example, Research and development costs or Advertisement expenses can be avoided but depreciation or insurance premium cannot be avoided.

17) Urgent Cost : The urgent costs are those costs which must be incurred in order to continue operations of the firm or undertaking. For example, cost of materials, cost of labour.

18) Postponable Cost : The cost which can be shifted to future with little or no effect on the current efficiency is called postponable cost. For example, maintenance of building or machinery.

19) Setting up Cost : Setting up cost is the cost of process which begins after the production of one product is completed and ends when the production of another product is begun which requires a change of material, jigs, dies etc.

2:3 PREPARATION OF COST SHEET OR STATEMENT OF COST

A cost sheet is a statement which shows the total cost of a product or job. It is a statement of expenditure incurred on a particular product. The data required for the preparation of cost- sheet are collected from various statement of accounts, which have been written in cost accounts regularly.

A cost sheet is a memorandum statement, hence there is no fixed format for its preparation. There is no need to follow the principles of double entry system while preparing a cost sheet or statement of cost. It is generally presented in a columnar form and includes as many columns as is desired to show the necessary details. For example, cost per unit of product, total cost of all units produced, per unit and total cost for the previous year, estimated cost for future period etc. A cost sheet may be prepared periodically and the period covered may be a year, a month or a week. It shows the total cost as well as various components of total cost. The purposes and advantages of a cost sheet are as follows.

1) It discloses the total cost as well as cost per unit.
2) It discloses the various stages of production and expenses incurred at every stage of production.
3) It enables the manufacturer to keep a close watch and control over the cost of production and help to frame suitable production policy.
4) It helps in fixing selling price more accurately after considering the relevant Government regulations and directives.
5) It helps the businessman to minimise the cost of production,
6) It enables to compare the standard cost and help to correct the negative variances if any in time.

2:3:1 Steps to be taken for preparation of Cost Sheet

1) Calculate the materials consumed with the help of opening stock of materials, purchases of raw materials, expenses paid for purchases and closing stock.
2) Calculate the prime cost by adding direct labour and direct expenses to materials consumed.
3) Calculate the factory cost, by adding various factory expenses incurred in the premises of the factory to prime cost.
4) Calcuate the cost of production by adding various office and administrative expenses and selling and distribution expenses to factory cost.
5) Finally, add profit to the cost of production, in order to calculate the selling price.

2:3:2 Division of Cost

In short, the total cost is calculated as under :
1) Materials consumed = Opening stock of raw materials + Purchase + Expenses on purchases - Closing stock of raw materials

2) Prime cost = Materials consumed + Direct labour + Direct expenses.
3) Factory cost = Prime cost + Factory overheads or expenses.
4) Cost of production = Factory cost + Office and Administration expenses.
5) Total cost (cost of sales) = Cost of production + Selling and Distribution expenses
6) Sales = Cost of sale or total cost + profit.

Specimen of a simple Cost Sheet
In the books of a company.
Cost Sheet for the period ended .....

Units Produced .....
Units sold ......

Particulars	Total Cost (Rs)	Cost per Unit (Rs)
Direct Materials	- - -	- - -
Add : Direct labour / wages	- - -	- - -
Add : Direct Expenses PRIME COST	- - -	- - -
Add : Factory overheads / oncost / Expenses FACTORY COST / WORKS COST	- - -	- - -
Add : Office and Administrative expenses / Overheads COST OF PRODUCTION	- - -	- - -
Add : Selling and Distribution expenses COST OF SALES / TOTAL COST	- - -	- - -
Add : Profit TOTAL SALES	- - -	- - -

Notes
1) Expenses are also called as overheads or oncost.
2) Cost Sheet is also known as Statement of Cost.
3) Factory Cost is also called as Production Cost or Manufacturing Cost or Works Cost.

2:3:3 Specimen of Cost Sheet with Stock Adjustments and details of Overheads.

In the books of a company

Cost Sheet for the period ended ....

Units produced ....

Units sold ....

Particulars	Total Cost (Rs)	Cost per Unit (Rs)
Opening stock of materials Add : Purchases during the year Expenses on Purchases e.g. carriage / carriage inward, Octroi, Customs duty, Excise, Freight on purchases, Royalties etc. Less : Closing stock of materials. Purchases returns of raw materials, Scrap of raw materials sold, Defective raw materials returned, Value of by-product etc.		
COST OF MATERIALS CONSUMED	X X X X	X X X X
Add : Direct labour or Direct wages or Productive wages, Direct expenses.		
PRIME COST	X X X X	X X X X
Add : Factory Expenses / Factory Overheads or Factory oncost Indirect Materials Indirect Wages Indirect Expenses Factory Heating and Lighting, Power, Coal, Gas, Fuel etc. Factory Rent, Rates and Taxes Factory Insurance Factory water charges Repairs and Maintenance of Plant and Machinery, Tools and Equipments Depreciation on Factory Building Patterns, Equipments etc. Works Stationery		

Particulars	Total Cost (Rs)	Cost per Unit (Rs)

Lubricant, Cotton waste etc.
    Haulage
    Factory Supervision cost
    Salary of Works Manager, Foreman, Supervisor.
    Technical Directors fee
    Belting and shifting repairs and renewals.
    Amenities to Factory workers.
    Works Office expenses
    Internal Transport
    Drawing Office expenses
    Laboratory expenses
    Workmen's compensation
Less :   Scrap value of defective work
Add :   Opening stock of work-in-progress
Less : Closing stock of work-in-progress		

FACTORY OR WORKS COST	X X X X	X X X X

Office and Administrative Overheads / oncost or Expenses
Add :   Office salary and wages,
    Office Rent, Rates and Insurance
    Office Cleaning Expenses
    Electrical Expenses
    Postage, Telegram, Telephone Charges
    Printing and Stationery
    Director's fees (remuneration)
    General Manager's Salary
    Director's Travelling expenses
    Repairs and Maintenance of Office
    Building / Equipments
    Audit fee, Accountancy charges
    Legal fee, Sundry expenses
    Establishment charges
    Bank charges, Subscrip-tions to Journals
    Depreciation on office furniture, Equipments, building etc.
    Counting House salaries.		

Particulars	Total Cost (Rs)	Cost per Unit (Rs)
TOTAL COST OF PRODUCTION	X X X X	X X X X
Add : Opening stock of Finished product Less : Closing stock of Finished product		
COST OF GOODS SOLD	X X X X	X X X X
Add : **Selling and Distribution Overheads / onost / Expenses.** Salaries of Sales Manager Salaries and Commission of Salesmen Carriage Outwards, Freight Outwards Warehouse Rent and Other expenses Advertisement expenses Delivery Van expenses Showroom expenses Packing charges Free samples and Gifts. Export Duty Discount allowed Bad debts allowed Travelling expenses of Salesmen Depreciation of Delivery Van Driver's Wages and Other Distribution expenses. Selling price list, catalogue Stationery for sales office Commission on sales Loading charges Distribution expenses Printing and Stationery for Sales Dept. Debt collection charges Warehouse / Godown expenses Tender expenses		
TOTAL COST / COST OF SALES		
Add : **Profit**		
Less : **Loss**		
SALES / SELLING PRICE		

2:3:4 Non-Cost Items / Items to be excluded from the Cost Sheet

There are many items which are not directly related to the cost of a product. Such items are called as Non-Cost items. Such items are not to be considered while ascertaining the cost of a product. These items are as follows :

1) Interest paid or received.
2) Dividend paid or received.
3) Rent received.
4) Profit or loss on sale of asset or investment.
5) Share transfer fee
6) Income tax paid / provision for income tax
7) Transfer to reserves.
8) Abnormal wastage of material.
9) Abnormal idle time of men or machines.
10) Expenses incurred for raising capital
11) Discount allowed on shares or debentures.
12) Goodwill written off
13) Preliminary expenses written off.
14) Underwriting Commission
15) Salary or Commission to partner / managing director.
16) Interest on debentures or bank loan.
17) Donations, Charity, Damages paid under court decree.
18) Losses due to strikes and lockouts.
19) Capital expenditure like purchases of asset
20) Bonus to share holders / directors and employees.
21) Wealth tax
22) Penalties and fines.
23) Any other capital exenditure.
24) Trade discount
25) Cash discount

2:3:5 Problems on Cost Sheet

Problem No. : 1

The summary of expenses incurred during the year ended 31st March,2014 by a manufacturer is given below :

Particulars	Amount
Direct Wages	25,000
Materials issued to jobs	38,000
Hire of Cranes on jobs	1,000
Power	4,500

Rent and Rates (Factory)	3,000
Works Salaries	4,400
Salaries to Maintenance Workers	6,000
Office Rent	4,800
Salaries to Salesmen	7,500
Postage and Stationery	1,500
Salesmen's Commission	2,500
Travelling Expenses	4,000
Machine Repairs	2,100
Machine Depreciation	8,600
Director's Fees	3,000
Auditor's Fees	1,500
Up-keep of Delivery Vans	1,200
Warehouse Wages	2,400
Lighting (Factory)	1,800
Lighting (Office)	600
Interest on Loan	2,500
Bank Charges	200
Donations	500
Bad Debts	1,200
Cash Discount Allowed	600
Legal Expenses	300
Drawing Office Expenses	1,000
Dividends Paid	4,000
Royalty Paid	6,000
Market Research Expenses	600
Transfer to Reserve	2,000
Free Samples Distributed	300
Sales	1,60,000

Prepare a statement of cost, showing profits earned during the year.

(P.U.Oct 2011)

Solution :

Statement of Total Cost & Profit
for the year ended 31-3-2014

Particulars	Rs.	Total cost Rs.
Direct Materials	38,000	
Direct Wages	25,000	
Direct Expenses -		
(i) Hire of cranes 1000		
(ii) Royalty 6000	7,000	
PRIME COST		**70,000**
Add : Factory Overheads / Expenses		
Power	4500	
Rent & Rates (Factory)	3000	
Indirect Wages (6000+4400)	10400	
Machine Repairs	2100	
Machine Depreciation	8600	
Lighting (Factory)	1800	
Drawing Office Expenses	1000	31400
FACTORY / WORK COST		**1,01,400**
Office and Administrative Overheads.		
Rent (Office)	4800	
Postage of Stationery	1500	
Directors Fees	3000	
Auditors Fees	1500	
Lighting (Office)	600	
Bank Charges	200	
Legal Expenses	300	11,900
COST OF PRODUCTION		**1,13,300**
Selling and Distribution Overheds		
Salary - Salesmen	7500	
Commission to Salesmen	2500	
Travelling Expenses	4000	
Bad-debts	1200	
Market Research Expenses	600	
Free Samples	300	
TOTOL COST		**1,33,000**
PROFIT		**27,000**
Sales		1,60,000

Note : 1) Following items are not included in cost. Interest on Loan, Donations, Cash Discount allowed, Dividend, --- Transfer to Reserve.

Problem No. : 2   Prepare a Cost Sheet from the following information of Relic India Ltd. for the year ending 31-3-2014.

Particulars	Amount
Purchase of raw materials	1,55,000
Freight paid on raw material purchase	4,000
Productive Wages paid	75,000
Unproductive Wages	22,000
Productive Wages outstanding	7,000
Royalty on production	18,000
Fuel and power	4,500
Factory Rent	6,300
Insurance of machinery	1,700
Loading and unloading charges on	
Purchase of raw materials	3,500
Depreciation of machinery	8,300
Lighting - Factory	700
- Office	300
Factory cleaning	400
Advertising	3,700
Carriage outwards	1,300
Income Tax	6,040
Factory telephone	890
Plant repairs and maintenance	2500
Office computer depreciation	12,000
Office stationery	2,100
Travelling expenses - Salesmen	3,500
- Office Staff	1,800
Donations	1,350
Salaries of sales staff	7,000
Marketing research expenses	1,400
Bank charges and interest	340
Expenses on office cars	3,500
Office manager's salary	5,400
Bad debts	700
Sales	3,50,000

(P.U.March 2010)

Solution :

Statement of Cost Sheet for the year ended 31-3-2014

Particulars	Rs.	Total cost Rs.
Purchases of Raw Materials	1,55,000	
Add : Freight paid	4,000	
Loading and unloading charges	3,500	
(1) Cost of Materials Consumed		**1,62,500**
Production wages paid	75,000	
Add : Outstanding	7,000	82,000
Direct expenses (royalty)		18,000
(2) PRIME COST		**2,62,500**
Factory Overheads / Expenses		
Unproductive wages	22,000	
Fuel and Power	4,500	
Factory rent	6,300	
Insurance of machinery	1,700	
Depreciation on machinery	8,300	
Lighting 700		
Factory cleaning	400	
Telephone 890		
Plant, repairs and maintenance	2500	47,290
(3) FACTORY COST		**3,09,790**
Office and Administrative Overheads.		
Depreciation of office computers	12,000	
Office stationery	2,100	
Travelling exps of office staff	1,800	
Expenses on office cars	3,500	
Office managers salary	5,400	
Office lighting	300	25,100
(4) COST OF PRODUCTION		**3,34,890**
Selling and Distribution Overheads		
Advertising	3,700	
Carriage Outwards	1,300	
Travelling exps	3,500	
Salaries of Staff	7,000	

Particulars	Rs.	Total cost Rs.
Marketing research exps	1,400	
Bad-debts	700	17,600
(5) COST OF SALES		**3,52,490**
(6) LOSS		**2,490**
Sales		3,50,000

Note : 1) The following items are not included is being of purely financial nature.

1) Income Tax 2) Bank charges and interest 3) Donations

Problem No. : 3 The following information have been taken from the books of H.K. Manufacturing Company. Prepare a Cost Sheet of the manufacturer :

Particulars	Amount
Direct Materials used	1,50,000
Direct Wages	1,30,000
Depreciation of Factory Buildings	5,000
Insurance - Staff Car	1,000
- Office Building	800
- Factory Building	700
Expenses of Delivery Vans	1,500
Depreciation - Office Building	2,000
- Staff Car	500
Salaries - Sales Manager	10,000
- Chief Engineer	11,000
- Office Staff	2,500
Warehouse Expenses	2,500
Electricity (Including Rs.2,000 for office and Rs.500 for Showroom)	8,000
Showroom Expenses	3,500
Cost of Printing of Price Lists	1,000
Advertisement	2,700
Sundry Factory Expenses	20,000
Sales Promotion Expenses	2,000
Expenses for Participation in Industrial Exhibition	5,000
Opening Stock of Finished Goods	40,000
Closing Stock of Finished Goods	25,000
Sales	5,00,000

(P.U.March 2011)

Solution :

Statement of Total Cost & Profit

Particulars	Rs.	Total cost Rs.
Direct Materials	1,50,000	
Direct Wages	1,30,000	
(1) PRIME COST		**2,80,000**
Add : Factory Overheads / Expenses		
Depreciation of Factory Building	5,000	
Insurance of Factory Building	700	
Salary of Chief Engineer	11,000	
Sundry Factory Expenses	20,000	
Electricity	5,500	42,200
(2) FACTORY COST		**3,22,200**
Office and Administrative Overheads.		
Insurance of Staff Car	1,000	
Insurance of Office Building	800	
Depreciation of Office Building	2,000	
Depreciation of Staff Car	500	
Salaries (Others)	25,000	
Office Electricity	2,000	31,300
(3) COST OF PRODUCTION		**3,53,500**
Add : Opening Stock of Finished Goods		40,000
		3,93,500
Less : Closing Stock of Finished Goods		25,000
(4) COST OF GOODS SOLD		**3,68,500**
Selling and Distribution Expenses		
Expenses of Delivery Vans	1,500	
Salary of Sales Manager	10,000	
Warehouse Expenses	2,500	
Showroom Electricity	500	
Showroom Expenses	3,500	
Cost of Price Lists	1,000	
Advertisement	2,700	
Sales Promotion Expenses	2,000	
Exhibition Expenses	5,000	28,700
(5) COST OF SALES		**3,97,200**
(6) PROFIT		**1,02,800**
Sales		5,00,000

Problem No. : 4

From the following particulars, prepare a cost sheet showing the components of total cost and profit for the year ended 31st March, 2014.

Particulars	Amount
Stock of finished goods on 1-4-2013	6,000
Stock of finished goods on 31-3-2014	15,000
Stock of raw materials on 1-4-2013	40,000
Stock of raw materials on 31-3-2014	50,000
Work-in-progress on 1-4-2013	15,000
Work-in-progress on 31-3-2014	10,000
Purchase of raw materials	4,75,000
Income Tax	5,000
Carriage Inward	12,500
Dividend received	2,500
Wages	1,75,000
Works manager's salary	30,000
Interest on debentures	10,000
Factory employees' salaries	60,000
Transfer to Sinking Fund	20,000
Factory Rent, Taxes & Insurance	7,250
Preliminary Expenses	10,500
Power Expenses	9,500
Other production expenses	43,000
Sales for the year	8,60,000
Selling Expenses	16,000
General Expenses	32,500

Solution :

Statement of Cost Sheet for the year ended 31-3-2014

Particulars	Rs.	Total cost Rs.
Direct Materials :		
Opening Stock of Raw Materials 40,000		
Add : Purchase 4,75,000		
Add : Carriage Inward 12,500		
5,27,500		
Less : Closing Stock of Raw Materials 50,000	4,77,500	
Direct Wages	1,75,000	

Particulars	Rs.	Total cost Rs.
Direct Expenses		-
(1) PRIME COST		**6,52,500**
Factory Overheads / Expenses		
Works Manager's Salary	30,000	
Factory Employees's Salary	60,000	
Factory Rent, Taxes and Insurance	7,250	
Power Expenses	9,500	
Other Production Expenses	43,000	
	1,49,750	
Add : Opening Stock of Work in Progress	15,000	
	1,64,750	
Less : Closing Stock of Work in Progress	10,000	1,54,750
(2) FACTORY COST		**8,07,250**
Office and Administrative Overheads.		
General Expenses	32,500	32,500
(3) COST OF PRODUCTION		**8,39,750**
Add : Opening Stock of Finished Goods		6,000
		8,45,750
Less : Closing Stock of Finished Goods		15,000
(4) COST OF GOODS SOLD		**8,30,750**
Selling and Distribution Overheads		
Selling Expenses	16,000	16,000
(5) COST OF SALES		**8,46,750**
(6) PROFIT		**13,250**
Sales		8,60,000

Note : 1) The following items are excluded from Cost Sheet.

    1) Income Tax   2) Dividend Received

    3) Interest on Debentures   4) Transfer to Sinking Fund

    5) Preliminary Expenses

Problem No. : 5

From the following information of Artistic Manufacturing Ltd, Prepare a Cost Sheet for the year ended 31-3-2014. showing (1) Prime Cost (2) Factory Cost (3) Cost of Production (4) Cost of goods sold and Net profit. Also calculate the percentage of profit earned to Sales.

	Rs.
Opening Stock of Raw Materials	25,000
Purchases of Raw Materials	85,000
Carriage Inward	3,000
Hire of Special Plant	2,000
Wages - Direct	75,000
Indirect	10,000
Other Direct charges	15,000
Rent and Rates - Factory	5,000
Office	500
Depreciation - Plant and Machinery	1,500
Office Furniture	100
Salary - Office	2,500
Salesmen	2,000
Other Factory expenses	5,700
Other Office expenses	900
Managing Director's remuneration	12,000
Other Selling expenses	1,000
Travelling expenses of Salesmen	300
Carriage and Freight Outward	1,000
Provision for General Reserve	4,000
Interest on loan	3,000
Sales	2,50,000
Advance Income Tax Paid	15,000
Advertisement	2,000
Closing stock of Raw Materials.	40,000

Managing Director's remuneration is to be allocated Rs. 4,000 to factory, Rs. 2,000 to office, and Rs. 6,000 to selling departments.

Solution :

In the books of Artistic Manufacturing Ltd,
Statement of Cost for the year ended 31-3-2014

Particulars	Rs.	Total cost Rs.
Opening Stock of Raw Materials	25,000	
Add : Purchases of Raw Materials	85,000	
	1,10,000	
Less : Closing Stock of Raw Materials	40,000	
	70,000	
Add : Carriage Inward	3000	
(1) MATERIAL CONSUMED		**73,000**
Add : Direct wages	75,000	
Other Direct charges	15,000	
Hire of Special Plant	2,000	92,000
(2) PRIME COST		**1,65,000**
Factory Overheads / Expenses		
Indirect wages	10,000	
Rent and Rates	5,000	
Indirect Materials	500	
Depreciation of Plant & Machinery	1,500	
Other Factory expenses	5,700	
Managing Director's remuneration	4,000	26,700
(3) FACTORY COST		**1,91,700**
Office and Administrative Overheads.		
Rent and Rates	500	
Depreciation of Office furniture	100	
Office Salary	2,500	
Other Office expenses	900	
Managing Director's remuneration	2,000	6,000
(4) COST OF PRODUCTION		**1,97,700**
Selling and Distribution Expenses		
Salary - Salesmen	2,000	
Other Selling expenses	1,000	
Advertisement	2,000	
Travelling expenses	300	
Carriage and Freight outward	1,000	

Managing Director's remuneration	6,000	12,300
(5) COST OF SALES		**2,10,000**
(6) PROFIT		**40,000**
Sales		2,50,000

Note : 1) Provision for General Reserve, Interest on loan, Advance Income tax paid are non-cost items. Hence, they are excluded from cost sheet.

2) Calculation of percentage of profit to sales.

For Rs. sales 2,50,000 = 40,000 profit

for Rs. 100 = ?

$$\frac{40,000 \times 100}{2,50,000} = 16\%$$

Answers :
1) Materials consumed   73,000
2) Prime cost   1,65,000
3) Factory cost   1,91,700
4) Cost of production   1,97,700
5) Cost of sales   2,10,000
6) Profit   40,000
7) Percentage of Profit to sales   16%

Problem No. : 6

Calculate prime cost, manufacturing cost, cost of production, cost of sales and profit from the following particulars.

	Rs.
Direct Materials	1,00,000
Direct Wages	30,000
Wages of Foreman	2,500
Electric Power	500
Lighting : Factory	1,500
Office	500
Store Keeper's Wages	1,000
Oil and Water	500
Rent : Factory	5,000
Office	2,500
Repairs and Renewals :	
Factory plant	3,500
Office premises	500

Particulars		Rs.
Transfer to Reserve		1,000
Discount on Shares written off		500
Dividend		2,000
Depreciation :		
Factory plant		500
Office premises		1,250
Consumable stores		2,500
Manager's salary		5,000
Director's fees		1,250
Office Stationery		500
Telephone charges		125
Postage and telegrams		250
Salesmen's salaries		1,250
Travelling expenses		500
Advertising		1,250
Warehouse charges		500
Carriage Outward		375
Goodwill written off		10,000
Sales		1,89,500

Solution :

<h3 style="text-align:center">STATEMENT OF COST AND PROFIT</h3>

Particulars	Rs.	Total cost Rs.
Direct materials		1,00,000
Direct Wages		30,000
(1) PRIME COST		**1,30,000**
Add : Factory Overheads /		
Cost / Expenses		
Wages of Foreman	2,500	
Electric power	500	
Storekeeper's wages	1,000	
Oil and water	500	
Factory rent	5,000	
Repairs and renewals of Factory plant	3,500	
Factory lighting	1,500	
Depreciation - Factory plant	500	
Consumable stores	2,500	17,500

Particulars	Rs.	Total cost Rs.
(2) MANUFACTURING / FACTORY COST		**1,47,500**
Add : Office and Administrative Overheads		
Office rent	2,500	
Repairs and renewals -		
Office premises	500	
Office lighting	500	
Depreciation - Office premises	1,250	
Manager's salary	5,000	
Director's fees	1,250	
Office stationery	500	
Telephone charges	125	
Postage and Telegrams	250	11,875
(3) COST OF PRODUCTION		**1,59,375**
Add : Selling and Distribution expenses		
Carriage outward	375	
Salesmen's salaries	1,250	
Travelling expenses	500	
Advertising	1,250	
Warehouse charges	500	3,875
(4) TOTAL COST / COST OF SALES		**1,63,250**
(5) Add : PROFIT		**26,250**
Sales		1,89,500

Answers :
1) Prime cost Rs. 1,30,000
2) Manufacturing cost Rs. 1,47,500
3) Cost of production Rs. 1,59,375
4) Cost of sales Rs. 1,63,250
5) Profit Rs. 26,250

Notes : 1) Transfer to reserve and dividend are excluded from cost accounts being items of appropriation of profit.

2) Discount on Shares written off and Goodwill written off, being items of non-operating in nature are also excluded from cost.

Problem No. : 7

The following figures are extracted from the books of Apollo Co. Ltd. for the year ended 31-12-2013. Prepare a cost sheet showing clearly the cost per unit under various elements, direct and indirect cost and also the profit or loss per unit.

Direct materials	2,00,000
Material used in primary packing	20,000
Loading and unloading expenses on purchases	15,000
Direct wages	38,000
Cost of special drawing	4,000
Freight inward	11,000
Architect's fees	8,000
Sale of scrap raw materials	6,000
Depreciation of Factory building	1,500
Branch Office expenses	4,000
Depreciation of Office building	800
Salaries (including Sales Manager Rs. 2,500 and	
Factory Chief Engineer Rs. 2,500)	30,000
Finished goods warehouse expenses	2,000
Electricity	
(including Rs. 400 for administrative office)	4,000
Advertisement	1,000
Delivery van expenses	200
Materials purchased for Selling and	
Distribution department	800
Technical directors fees	10,000
Works stationery	4,000
Lubricants and cotton waste	5,000
Repairs and maintenance of plant and machinery	15,000
Director's fees	1,000
Counting house salaries	2,000
Auditor's fees	1,500
Bank charges	500
Sales promotion expenses	500
Exhibition expenses	500
Debt collection charges	1,200
Profit 20% on cost	
Units produced - 1,000 Nos.	

Solution :

In the books of Apollo Co. Ltd,
Cost Sheet showing cost and profit
for the year ended 31-12-2013

Units Produced. 1,000.

Particulars	Total Cost (Rs.)	Per Unit Cost (Rs.)
Direct Materials	2,00,000	200.00
Add : Materials used in primary packing	20,000	20.00
Loading & unloading expenses on purchases	15,000	15.00
Freight inward	11,000	11.00
	2,46,000	246.00
Less : Sale of scrap raw materials	6,000	6.00
(1) Material consumed / Direct material cost	2,40,000	240.00
Add : Direct wages	38,000	38.00
Add : Direct Expenses :		
Cost of special drawings	4,000	4.00
Architect's fees	8,000	8.00
PRIME COST	**2,90,000**	**290.00**
Add : Factory overheads (Indirect cost)		
Depreciation on Factory building	1,500	1.50
Salary factory chief Engineer	2,500	2.50
Indirect salary 30,000 - (2,500 Chief Engr. + 2,500 Sales Manager)	25,000	25.00
Electricity (4,000 - 400)	3,600	3.60
Technical director's fee	10,000	10.00
Works stationery	4,000	4.00
Repair and maintenance of Plant and Machinery	15,000	15.00
Lubricants and Cotton waste	5,000	5.00
FACTORY COST / WORKS COST	**3,56,600**	**356.60**
Add : Office and Administrative Expenses or overheads (Indirect cost)		

Particulars	Rs.	Total cost Rs.
Branch Office expenses	4,000	4.00
Depreciation of Office building	800	0.80
Electricity	400	0.40
Director's fees	1,000	1.00
Counting house salaries	2,000	2.00
Auditor's fees	1,500	1.50
Bank charges	500	0.50
COST OF PRODUCTION	**3,66,800**	**366.80**
Add : Selling and Distribution Expenses (Indirect cost)		
Sales Manager's salary	2,500	2.50
Finished goods warehouse expenses	2,000	2.00
Advertisement	1,000	1.00
Delivery van expenses	200	0.20
Material purchased for selling Dept.	800	0.80
Sales promotion expenses	500	0.50
Exhibition expenses	1,000	1.00
Debt. collection charges	1,200	1.20
TOTAL COST / COST OF SALES	**3,76,000**	**376.00**
Add : Profit 20% on cost **(i.e. 20% on 3,76,000)**	**75,200**	**75.20**
Selling price / sales	4,51,200	451.20

Answers :	Total units (Rs.)	Per unit (Rs.)
1) Direct cost	2,90,000	290.00
2) Indirect cost		
a) Factory overheads	66,600	66.60
b) Office and Administrative overheads	10,200	10.20
c) Selling and Distribution overheads	9,200	9.20
Total Indirect overheads	86,000	86.00
Total cost (Direct + Total indirect overheads)	3,76,000	376.00
Profit	75,200	75.20
Sales / selling price	4,51,200	451.20

Problem No. : 8

The following information has been obtained from the records of a manufacturing Company as on 31-12-2013.

	1-1-2013 (Rs.)	31-12-2013 (Rs.)
Stock of raw materials	40,000	50,000
stock of Finished goods	1,00,000	1,50,000
Stock of work-in-progress	10,000	14,000

Other particulars	Rs.
Indirect labour	50,000
Lubricants	10,000
Loss on sale of asset	5,000
Insurance on Plant	3,000
Purchase of raw materials	4,00,000
Sales commission	60,000
Salaries of Salesmen	1,00,000
Administrative expenses	1,00,000
Carriage outward	20,000
Undertwriting commission	10,000
Power	30,000
Direct labour	3,00,000
Depreciation on machinery	50,000
Interest on Investment	8,000
Factory Rent	60,000
Property Tax on Factory building	11,000
Sales	12,00,000

Prepare a statement of cost and profit showing (i) Value of materials consumed (ii) Prime cost (iii) Factory cost (iv) Cost of production (v) Cost of sales (vi) Profit.

Solution :

In the books of a Manufacturing Company
STATEMENT OF COST
For the year ended 31-12-2013

Particulars	Rs.	Total cost Rs.
Stock of Raw materials as on 1-1-2013	40,000	
Add : Purchases of Raw materials	4,00,000	
	4,40,000	
Less : Stock of materials as on	50,000	
31-12-2008	3,90,000	

Particulars	Rs.	Total cost Rs.
(1) VALUE OF MATERIALS CONSUMED		**3,90,000**
Add : Direct labour	3,00,000	3,00,000
(2) PRIME COST	**6,90,000**	**6,90,000**
Add : Factory overheads		
Indirect labour	50,000	
Lubricants	10,000	
Insurance on Plant	3,000	
Power	30,000	
Depreciation on Machinery	50,000	
Factory rent	60,000	
Property tax on Factory building	11,000	
Add : Stock of work-in-progress as on 1-1-2008	10,000 9,14,000	
Less : Stock of work-in-progress as on 31-12-2008	14,000	
(3) FACTORY COST	**9,00,000**	**9,00,000**
Add : Administrative Expenses	1,00,000	1,00,000
(4) COST OF PRODUCTION	**10,00,000**	**10,00,000**
Add : Stock of Finished Goods as on 1-1-2013	1,00,000	
	11,00,000	
Less : Stock of Finished Goods as on 31-12-2013	1,50,000	
COST OF GOODS SOLD	**9,50,000**	**9,50,000**
Add : Selling and Distribution Expenses		
Sales commission	60,000	
Salaries of Salesmen	1,00,000	
Carriage outwards	20,000	
(5) COST OF SALES	**11,30,000**	**11,30,000**
Add : Profit	**70,000**	**70,000**
SALES	12,00,000	12,00,000

Answers :

i) Value of Raw materials consumed   3,90,000
ii) Prime cost   6,90,000
iii) Factory cost   9,00,000
iv) Cost of production   10,00,000
v) Cost of sales   11,30,000
vi) Profit   70,000

Note : Loss on sale of asset, underwriting commission and interest on investment etc. are non-cost items, hence they are not considered in cost sheet.

Problem No. : 9

The accounts of Bharati Manufacturing Ltd. for the year ended 31-3-2014 shows the following :

Stock of Raw materials as on 1-4-2013	67,000
Bad debts written off	5,000
Raw materials purchased	2,60,000
Motive power	10,000
Traveller's commission	15,000
Depreciation on Office equipments	400
Carriage Inwards	1,000
Interest on Bank loan	580
Factory taxes	12,000
Productive wages	1,76,000
Director's Travelling expenses	8,000
Coal and coke	2,000
General Overheads	4,000
Gas and water - Factory	3,000
Packing charges	2,000
Interim dividend paid	8,000
Manager's salary (Factory 2/3, Office 1/3)	15,000
Legal charges	4,050
Delivery van expenses	4,000
Depreciation on Factory Building	12,000
Publicity charges	2,000
Repairs to Plant	6,000
Carriage Outward	7,000
Hire charges of special machinery	8,000
Share transfer fee	1,000
Office rent	2,600

Particulars		
Surveyor's fees		1,000
Stock of Raw materials as on 31-3-2014		87,000
Sales		6,00,000

Prepare a Cost Sheet showing :
1) Cost of materials consumed
2) Prime cost
3) Production cost
4) Cost of production
5) Total cost
6) Profit for the year
7) Selling price

Also calculate the percentage of :
i) Factory overheads to direct wages
ii) Office oncost to Works cost
iii) Selling and distribution to cost of production

Solution :

In the books of Bharati Manufacturing Ltd.
Cost sheet for the year ended 31-3-2014

Particulars	Rs.	Total cost Rs.
Stock of Raw materials as on 1-4-2013	67,000	
Add : Raw material purchased	2,60,000	
Carriage Inward	1,000	
	3,28,000	
Less : Stock of Raw material		
as on 31-3-2014	87,000	
COST OF MATERIAL CONSUMED	2,41,000	2,41,000
Add : Productive wages	1,76,000	
Direct expenses		
Hire charges of special machinery	8,000	
Surveyor's fees	1,000	1,85,000
PRIME COST		**4,26,000**
Add : Factory overheads /expenses		
Motive power	10,000	
Factory taxes	12,000	
Coal and coke	2,000	
Gas and water -Factory	3,000	

Particulars	Rs.	Total cost Rs.
Manager's salary (2/3 of 15,000)	10,000	
Depreciation of Factory building	12,000	
Repairs to Plant	6,000	55,000
WORKS COST		**4,81,000**
Office and Administrative Expenses		
Depreciation on Equipments	400	
Director's travelling expenses	8,000	
General Overheads	4,000	
Manager's salary ($\frac{1}{3}$ of Rs.15,000)	5,000	
Office rent	2,600	
Legal charges	4,050	24,050
COST OF PRODUCTION		**5,05,050**
Selling and Distribution Expenses		
Bad debts written off	5,000	
Traveller's commission	15,000	
Packing charges	2,000	
Delivery van expenses	4,000	
Publicity charges	2,000	
Carriage Outward	7,000	35,000
COST OF SALES / TOTAL COST		**5,40,050**
Profit		**59,950**
Sales		6,00,000

Answers :

i) Material Consumed   2,41,000
ii) Prime cost   4,26,000
iii) Works cost   4,81,000
iv) Cost of production   5,05,050
v) Total cost   5,40,050
vi) Profit   59,950
vii) Sales   6,00,000

Note : Interest on bank loan, Interim dividend paid, Share transfer fee etc. are non cost items, hence they are excluded from cost sheet.

Calculations of various percentages.

1) Percentage of Factory overhead to Direct wages.
   If Direct wages are Rs. 1,76,000 = Rs. 55,000 Factory overheads
   For Rs. 100 = ?

   $$\frac{100 \times 55,000}{1,76,000} = 31.25\%$$

2) Percentage of Office oncost to Works cost.
   If Rs. 4,81,000 works cost = Rs. 24,050 Office oncost
   For Rs. 100 = ?

   $$\frac{24,050 \times 100}{4,81,000} = 5\%$$

3) Percentage of Selling and Distribution expenses to Cost of production.
   If Rs. 5,05,050 cost of Production = Rs. 35,000 Selling and Dis. exp.
   For Rs. 100 = ?

   $$\frac{35,000 \times 100}{5,05,050} = 6.93\%$$

Problem No. : 10

The following details have been obtained from the cost records of A.C.C. Ltd for the month of March 2014

	Rs.
Stock of Raw Materials on 1st March 2014	75,000
Stock of Raw Materials on 30th March 2014	91,500
Direct wages	50,000
Indirect wages	2,750
Wages payable	2,500
Work-in-progress 1st March 2014	28,000
Work-in-progress 31st March 2014	35,000
Purchases of Raw Materials	66,000
Factory rent, rates, power	15,000
Depreciation on Plant and machinery	3,500
Travellers wages and Commission	7000
Expenses on Purchases	1,500
Carriage Outward	4,750
Advertising	5,000
Office rent and taxes	2,500
Stock of finished goods 1st March 2014	54,000
Stock of finished goods 31st March 2014	31,000

Assuming that all goods manufactured are sold, what should be the selling price to obtain 20% profit on selling price i.e. on turnover?

Prepare a cost sheet, showing;

1) Materials Consumed   2) Prime cost   3) Works cost
4) Cost of Production   5) Profit   6) Sales

Solution

In the books of A.C.C. Ltd,
Cost sheet for the month ended 31st March 2014

Particulars	Rs.	Total cost Rs.
Stock of Raw Materials on		
1st March 2014	75,000	
Add : Purchases of Raw Materials	66,000	
Expenses on purchases	1,500	
	1,42,500	
Less : Closing stock of Raw materials	91,500	
MATERIALS CONSUMED		**51,000**
Add : Direct wages. 50,000		
+ Wages Payable 2,500		52,500
PRIME COST		**1,03,500**
Add : Factory overheads		
Indirect wages	2,750	
Factory rent, rates & power	15,000	
Depreciation on plant & Machinery	3,500	21,250
Add : Work-in-progress on		
1st March 2014		28,000
		1,52,750
Less : Work-in-progress		
30thMarch 2014		35,000
FACTORY COST / WORKS COST		**1,17,750**
Office and Administrative Overhead		
Add : Office rent and taxes		2,500
COST OF PRODUCTION		**1,20,250**
Add : Stock of Finished goods		
on 1st March 2014.		54,000
		1,74,250

Particulars	Rs.	Total cost Rs.
Less : Stock of Finished goods on 1st March 2014.		31,000
COST OF GOODS SOLD		**1,43,250**
Add : Selling and Distribution Expenses		
Carriage Outward	4,750	
Advertising	5,000	
Traveller's Wages and Commission	7,000	16,750
COST OF SALES		**1,60,000**
PROFIT 20% on sales i.e. 25% on cost of sales		40,000
SELLING PRICE		2,00,000

Note : Calculation of profit on sales i.e. 20% on turnover.

For calculation of Profit on Sales or turn over following formula should be used.

$$\text{Profit} = \frac{\text{Rate percentage on sales} \times \text{Total cost}}{100 - \text{Rate percentage on sales}}$$

$$= \frac{1,60,000 \times 20}{80} = 40,000$$

Profit Rs. 40,000

Answers :
1) Materials consumed   51,000
2) Prime cost   1,03,500
3) Factory cost   1,17,500
4) Cost of production   1,20,250
5) Total cost   1,60,000
6) Profit   40,000
7) Selling price   2,00,000

Problem No. : 11

The Lucky Manufacturing Company furnished the following data relating to the manufacture of a standard product during the month of March 2014

	Rs.
Closing Stock of Raw Materials	5,700
Sale of scrap Raw Materials	300
Customs duty paid	400
Operating wages payable	1,200
Royalty	3,000
Opening stock of Raw Materials	2,400
Machine hour rate	5
Purchases of Raw Materials	29,200
Administration Overheads : 10% of Works Cost	
Selling and Distribution expenses Rs. 7 per unit	
Direct Labour charges	8,800
Cost of Layout	1,000
Operation of machine hours 1600	
Monthly production 200 units	
Units sold - 1800 at Rs. 40 per unit.	

You are required to prepare a cost sheet showing the total cost and cost per unit for the month ended 31st March 2014. Also calculate profit for the month and profit per unit sold.

Solution :

In the books of Lucky Manufacturing Company
Cost Sheet / Statement of Cost
for the month ended 31st March 2014

Units Produced 2,000
Units Sold 1,800

Particulars	Rs.	Total Cost Cost Rs.	Per Unit Cost Rs.
Opening stock of Raw Materials		2,400	
Add : Purchases of Raw Materials		29,200	
Custom Duty paid		400	
		32,000	
Less : Scrap of Raw Materials	300		
Closing stock of Raw Materials	5,700	6,000	

Particulars	Rs.	Total Cost Cost Rs.	Per Unit Cost Rs.
COST OF MATERIAL CONSUMED		**26,000**	**13.00**
Add : Direct labour charges	8,800		
Operating wages payable	1,200	10,000	
Add : Direct Expenses			
Royalty	3,000		
Cost of layout	1,000	4,000	
PRIME COST		**40,000**	**20.00**
Add : Factory overheads (1600 hours at Rs. 5 per hour)		8,000	4.00
FACTORY COST		**48,000**	**24.00**
Add : Administrative overheads (10% of Rs. 48,000)		4,800	2.40
COST OF PRODUCTION		**52,800**	**26.40**
Add : Opening stock of Finished goods		-	-
Less : Closing stock of finished goods.		5,280	-
COST OR GOOD SOLD		**47,520**	-
Add : Selling and Distribution expenses (1800 unit at Rs. 7 each)		12,600	7.00
Cost of Sales		**60,120**	**33.40**
Add : PROFIT		**11,880**	**6.60**
Sales (1800 units at Rs. 40 each)		72,000	40.00

Answers :

	Total (Rs.)	Per Unit (Rs.)
1) Materials Consumed	26,000	13.00
2) Prime Cost	40,000	20.00
3) Factory Cost	48,000	24.00
4) Cost of Production	52,800	26.40
5) Cost of sales	60,120	33.40
6) Profit	11,880	6.60

Notes :

1) Calculation of Factory expenses.
   Machine hour rate x Machine hours operated
   Rs. 5 x 1,600 = Rs. 8,000

2) Valuation of closing stock of Finished goods.
   Units produced - Units sold = Closing stock
   2000 - 1800 = 200 units
   For 2000 units = Rs. 52,800 Total cost
   For 200 units = ?

   $$\frac{52,800 \times 200}{2,000} = \text{Rs. } 5,280$$

Problem No. : 12

The following is the Trading and Profit and Loss Account of Sudarshan Chemicals Ltd., Pune for the year ended 31-3-2014

Dr.   Cr.

Particulars	Rs.	Particulars	Rs.
To Opening stock of Raw Materials	9,000	By sales 2,55,000 Less Returns Inwards 5,000	2,50,000
To purchases 1,26,000 - Return outwards 1,000	1,25,000	By sale of scrap Raw Materials	500
To Direct wages	51,000	By Closing stock of Raw Materials	5,000
To Carriage	12,500		
To Royalty	3,600		
T Gas & Water	9,500		
To Wages payable	4,000		
To Custom charges	4,000		
To Chargeable expenses	1,400		
To Heating & Lighting	5,500		
To Gross Profit c/d	30,000		
	2,55,500		2,55,500
To Carriage	2,500	By Gross Profit	30,000
To Preliminary expenses	3,000	By Discount received	5,000
To Underwriting Commission	2,000	By Interest on Investment	6,000
To Commission on sales	3,800	By Commission	4,000
To Sales expenses	1,200		

Particulars	Rs.	Particulars	Rs.
To Discount on issue of shares	3,000		
To Salaries	8,000		
To Bad debts provision	500		
To Property Tax on Office Building	1,000		
To Income Tax	2,500		
To Depreciation on furniture	1,000		
To Donations	2,000		
To Net profit c/d	14,500		
	45,000		**45,000**

You are required to prepare a cost sheet for the year ended 31-3-2014.
1) Materials consumed 2) Prime cost 3) Factory cost 4) Total cost.
Also calculate the precentage of profit on sales.

Solution :

In the books of Sudarshan Chemicals Ltd.
Cost Sheet for the year ended 31-3-2014

Particulars	Rs.	Rs.	Total Cost Rs.
Opening stock of Raw Materials		9,000	
Add Purchase of Raw Materials		1,26,000	
Expenses on Purchases			
Carriage	12,500		
Custom Charges	4,000	16,500	
Less :		1,51,500	
1) Closing stock of Materials	5,000		
2) Sales of scrap of Raw Materials	500		
3) Returns outward	1,000	6,500	
MATERIALS CONSUMED		**1,45,000**	**1,45,000**
Add: Direct Labour			
Direct wages	51,000		
Wages payable	4,000	55,000	
Add : Direct Expenses			
Royalty	3,600		

Particulars	Rs.	Rs.	Total Cost Rs.
Chargeable expenses	1,400	5,000	
PRIME COST		**2,05,000**	**2,05,000**
Add : Factory overheads			
Gas and water	9,500		
Heating and Lighting	5,500	15,000	
FACTORY COST		**2,20,000**	**2,20,000**
Add : Office & Administrative			
expenses			
Salaries	8,000		
Property Tax on Factory			
office building	1,000		
Dep. on Office Furniture	1,000	10,000	
COST OF PRODUCTION		**2,30,000**	**2,30,000**
Add : Selling and Distribution			
expenses			
Carriage	2,500		
Commission on Sales	3,800		
Sales expenses	1,200	7,500	
TOTAL COST		2,37,500	2,37,500
Add : PROFIT		**12,500**	**12,500**
SALES		2,50,000	2,50,000

Answers	Rs.
Materials Consumed	1,45,000
Prime Cost	2,05,000
Factory Cost	2,20,000
Total Cost	2,30,000
Percentage of profit to Sales = 5%	

Note : 1) Preliminary expenses, Underwriting commission, Discount on issue of Shares, Bad debts provision, Income Tax, Donations given, Discount received, Interest on Investment, Commission received etc. are the non cost items. hence, they are excluded from the cost sheet.

2) Calculation of percentage of profit on Sales.
   If sales Rs. 2,50,000 = Rs. 12,500 profit

For Rs. 100 = ?

$$\frac{100 \times 12,500}{2,50,000} = 5\%$$

Problem No. : 13

The following extract of costing information relates to commodity 'X' for the half year ending 31st December, 2013

Particulars	Rs.	Particulars	Rs.
Purchases of Raw Materials	1,20,000	Stock (31st Dec. 2013) Raw Materials	22,240
Works Overheads	48,000	Finished Products	
Direct Wages	1,00,000	(2,000 tons)	32,000
Carriage on Purchases	1,440	Work-in-Progress	
Stock (1st July, 2013)		(1st July 2013)	4,800
Raw Materials	20,000	Work-in-Progress	
Finished Products		(31st Dec. 2013)	16,000
(1,000 tons)	16,000	Sales-Finished Products	3,00,000

Selling and Distribution Overheads are Re. 1 per ton sold. 16,000 tons of commodity were produced during the period.

You are to ascertain (*i*) Cost of Raw Materials used, (*ii*) Cost of Output for the period, (*iii*) Cost of Sales, (*iv*) Net Profit for the period, (*v*) Net Profit per ton of the commodity.

Solution

Statement of Cost and Profit
for the half year ending 31 st December 2013

Particulars	Units (Tons)	Total Cost Rs.
Opening Stock of Raw Materials		20,000
Add : Purchases of Raw Materials		1,20,000
Add : Carriage on Purchases		1,440
		1,41,440
Less : Closing Stock of Raw Materials		22,240
(i) Value of Raw Materials Used		**1,19,200**
Add : Direct Wages		1,00,000
Prime Cost		**2,19,200**
Add : Works Overhead		48,000
Add : Opening Stock of Work-in-Progress		4,800

Particulars	Units (Tons)	Total Cost Rs.
		2,72,000
Less : Closing Stock of Work-in-Progress		16,000
(ii) Cost of Output for the period	**16,000**	**2,56,000**
Add : Opening Stock of Finished Products	1,000	16,000
	17,000	2,72,000
Less : Closing Stock of Finished Products	2,000	32,000
Cost of Goods Sold	15,000	2,40,000
Selling and Distribution Overheads		
on 15,000 tons @ Rs. 1 per ton		15,000
(iii) Cost of Sales		**2,55,000**
(iv) Net Profit for the Period		**45,000**
Sales		3,00,000
(v) Net Profit per ton = $\dfrac{Rs.45,000}{15,000}$ = Rs. 3		

Answers :
i) Cost of raw materials used Rs. 1,19,200
ii) Cost of out put for the period Rs. 2,56,000
iii) Cost of sales Rs. 2,55,000
iv) Net Profit for the period Rs. 45,000
v) Net Profit per ton Rs. 3

Problem No. : 14

The following figures are extracted from the Trial Balance of Goldstar co. on 31st March 2014

Debit Balances	Rs.	Debit Balances	Rs.
Opening Inventories		Repairs and	
Finished Stock	80,000	Upkeep-Factory	14,000
Raw Materials	1,40,000	Heat, Light and Power	65,000
Work-in-Progress	2,00,000	Rates and Taxes	6,300
Office Appliances	17,4000	Miscellaneous Factory	
Plant and Machinery	4,60,500	Expenses	18,700
Building	2,00,000	Sales Commission	33,600
Sales Return and Rebates	14,000	Sales Travelling	11,000
Materials Purchased	3,20,000	Sales Promotion	22,500
Freight incurred on		Distribution Dept.	
Materials	16,000	Salaries and Expenses	18,000

Debit Balances	Rs.	Debit Balances	Rs.
Direct Labour	1,60,000	Office Salaries and	
Indirect Labour	18,000	Expenses	8,600
Factory Supervision	10,000	Interest on Borrowed	
		Funds	2,000
		Credit Balances	
		Sales	7,68,000
		Purchase Returns	4,800

Further details are available as follows :

(i) Closing Inventories :
   Finished Goods Rs. 1,15,000 ; Raw Materials Rs. 1,80,000; Work-in-Progress Rs. 1,92,000.
(ii) Accrued expenses on :
   Direct Labour Rs. 8,000; Indirect Labour Rs. 1,200; Interest on Borrowed Funds Rs. 2,000.
(iii) Depreciation to be provided on :
   Office Appliances 5%, Plant and Machinery 10%; Buildings 4%
(iv) Distribution of the following costs :
   Heat, Light and Power to Factory, Office and Distribution in the ratio of 8 : 1 : 1.
   Rates and Taxes two-thirds to Factory and one-third to Office.
   Depreciation on Building to Factory, Office and Selling in the ratio of 8 : 1 : 1.

With the help of the above information, you are required to prepare:

(i) a statement of cost showing various elements of cost, and
(ii) a statement of Profit.

Solution

In the books of Goldstar Co.
Statement of Cost

Particulars	Rs.	Rs.
Opening Raw Materials Inventory	1,40,000	
Add : Materials Purchased	3,20,000	
Freight on Material	16,000	
	4,76,000	
Less : Purchases Returns 4,800		
Closing Raw Materials 1,80,000		
Inventory	1,84,800	

Particulars	Rs.	Rs.
MATERIAL CONSUMED		2,91,200
Direct Labour (Rs. 1,60,000 + Rs.8,000)		1,68,000
Prime Cost		4,59,200
Add : Factory Overheads :		
Indirect Labour (Rs. 18,000 + Rs. 1,200)	19,200	
Factory Supervision	10,000	
Repairs and upkeep - Factory	14,000	
Heat, Light and Power $\left(\dfrac{4}{5}\text{of Rs.}65,000\right)$	52,000	
Rates and Taxes $\left(\dfrac{2}{3}\text{of Rs.}6,300\right)$	4,200	
Misc. Factory Expenses	18,700	
Depreciation of Plant (10% of Rs. 4,60,500)	46,050	
Depreciation on Building $\left(\dfrac{4}{100}\times\text{Rs.}2,00,000\times\dfrac{4}{5}\right)$	6,400	
		1,70,550
Gross Works oncost		6,29,750
Add : Opening Work-in-Progress Inventory		2,00,000
		8,29,750
Less : Closing Work-in-Progress Inventory		1,92,000
WORKS COST		6,37,750
Add : Administration Expenses :		
Office Salaries and Expenses	8,600	
Depreciation on Office Appliances (5% of Rs. 17,400)	870	
Depreciation on Building	800	
Heat, Light and Power $\left(\dfrac{1}{10}\text{of Rs.}65,000\right)$	6,500	
Rates and Taxes	2,100	

Particulars	Rs.	Rs.
		18,870
COST OF PRODUCTION		6,56,620
Add : Opening Finished Goods Inventory		80,000
		7,36,620
Less : Closing Finished Goods Inventory		1,15,000
COST OF GOODS SOLD		6,21,620
Add : Selling and Distribution Expenses		
Sales Commission	33,600	
Sales Travelling	11,000	
Sales Promotion	22,500	
Distribution Department -		
Salaries and Expenses	18,000	
Heat, Light and Power $\left(\dfrac{1}{10} \text{ of Rs.} 65,000\right)$	6,500	
Depreciation on Building	800	
COST OF SALES		92,400
		7,14,020

STATEMENT OF PROFIT

Particulars	Rs.	Rs.
Sales	7,68,000	
Less : Returns	14,000	
		7,54,000
Less : Cost of Sales		7,14,020
Net Operating Profit		39,980
Less : Interest on Borrowed Funds		4,000
Net Profit		**35,980**

Problem No. : 15

From the following particulars, prepare a cost sheet showing the components of the total sales and the profit for the years ended 31st December 2011 :

Particulars		Amount
Stock of finished goods (1st January, 2011)		6,000
Stock of raw materials (1st January, 2011)		40,000
Work-in-progress (1st January, 2011)		15,000
Purchase of raw materials		4,75,000
Carriage inwards		12,500
Factory rent, taxes		7,250
Other production expenses		43,000
Stock of finished goods (31st December, 2011)		15,000
Income Tax		5,000
Wages		1,75,000
Works manager's salary		30,000
Donations		10,000
Factory employees' salary		60,000
Interest on Bank Loan		20,000
Power expenses		9,500
General expenses		32,500
Sale for the year		8,60,000
Stock of raw materials (31st December, 2011)		50,000
Work-in-progress (31st December, 2011)		10,000
Trade Discount		2,000

(P.U. Oct.2012)

Solution

Cost Sheet for the year 31-12

Particulars	Rs.	Rs.
Stock of Raw Materials on 1st Jan	40,000	
+ Purchases during the year	4,75,000	
+ Carriage Inward	12,500	
	527500	
- Stock of raw materials on 31st Dec.	50,000	
Cost of Material Consumed		4,77,500
Wages		1,75,000
PRIME COST		652500
FACTORY OVERHEAD		
Works Managers Salary	30,000	
Factory employee's Salary	60,000	
Factory Rent, Taxes & Insurance	7,250	
Power Expenses	9,500	
Other production expenses	43,000	
	1,49,750	
+ Work in Progress on 1st Jan	15,000	
	1,64,750	
- Work in Progress on 31st Dec	10,000	1,54,750
FACTORY COST		8,07,250
OFFICE & ADMIN OVERHEADS		
General Expenses		32,500
COST OF PRODUCTION		8,39,750
+ Stock of Finished Goods on 1st Jan		6,000
		8,45,750
- Stock of Finished Goods on 31st Dec.		15,000
COST OF GOODS SOLD		8,30,750
PROFIT	29,250	
SALES		8,60,000

Problem No. : 16

The following date have been extracted from the books of Ashok Industries Ltd. for the year 2014:

Particulars	Amount Rs.
Opening Stock of Raw Materials	25,000
Purchase of Raw Materials	85,000
Closing Stock of Raw Materials	40,000
Carriage Inward	5,000
Wages Direct	90,000
Wages Indirect	10,000
Rent and Rates :	
Factory	5,000
Office	500
Depreciation :	
Plant and Machinery	1,500
Office Furniture	100
Indirect Consumption of Materials	500
Salary :	
Office	2,500
Salesmen	2,000
Other Factory expenses	5,700
Other office expenses	900
Manager's Remuneration	12,000
Bad Debts	1,000
Advertisement Expenses	2,000
Travelling Expenses of Salesmen	1,100
Carriage and Freight Outward	1,000
Sales	2,50,000
Advance Income tax paid	15,000
Cash Discount	5,000

The manager has the overall charge of the company and his remuneration is to be allocated as Rs. 4,000 to the factory, Rs. 2,000 to the office and Rs. 6,000 to the selling operations. From the above particulars prepare a statement showing
(a) Prime Cost (b) Factory cost (c) Cost of Production (d) Cost of sales and (e) Net Profit.

(P. U. April, 2014)

Solution

Cost Sheet for the year 31-12-2014

Particulars	Rs.	Rs.
Stock of Raw Materials on 1st Jan	25,000	
+ Purchases of Raw Material	85,000	
	1,10,000	
- Stock of raw materials on 31st Dec.	40,000	
	70,000	
+ Carriage Inward	5,000	
Cost of Material Consumed		75,000
Direct Wages		90,000
PRIME COST		**1,65,000**
FACTORY OVERHEAD		
Indirect Wages	10,000	
Rent & Rates (Factory)	5,000	
Indirect consumption of materials	500	
Depreciation on plant & machinery	1,500	
Other factory expenses	5,700	
Managers Remuneration	4,000	26,700
FACTORY COST		**1,91,700**
Administrative Overheads		
Rent & Rates (Office)	500	
Depreciation on office furniture	100	
Salary office 2,500		
Other Office expenses	900	
Managerial Remuneration	2,000	6,000
COST OF PRODUCTION		**1,97,700**
Selling & Distribution Overheads -		
Bad debts 1,000		
Advertisement expenses	2,000	
Travelling expenses of Salesman	1,100	
Carriage & Freight outward	1,000	
Manager's remunaration	6,000	
Salary of Salesman	2,000	13,100
COST OF SALES		**2,10,800**
PROFIT		39,200
SALES		**2,50,000**

Note :

1) Advance Payment of Income Tax is excluded from cost accounts being item of appropriation of profit.

2) Discount - Trade & Cash-both are excluded from cost accounts. Trade discount is reducted from sales price & entries are made for net price in the cost books. Cash discount being financial item is excluded from cost accounts.

2:3:6 Preparation of Tenders.

Very often the manufacturers, Government Undertakings, banks, Insurance companies, etc. give the advertisement in leading newspapers for the completion of specific work, like for e.g. construction of roads, bridges, dams, buildings, supply of materials or machines etc. For this purpose, tenders are invited from contractors. A tender may be national or international. National tender is invited from the public of a specific nation and international tenders are invited from foreign countries. Thus, a tender is an advertisement published in national or international newspapers inviting the quotations for purchase of some materials or machinery or for carrying out some huge construction work, so that the most competitive price can be fixed which will reduce the cost of project.

A tender has no specific form but a tender generally includes the following particulars :

1) Full particulars regarding the job or product.
2) The price of tender, taxes, duties to be paid to the government should be included in tender.
3) Transportation arrangement
4) Terms relating to delivery period or date of completion of the contract.
5) Bank guarantee, if required, for the completion of project.
6) After sales services offered etc.

2:3:7 Problems on Tenders

Problem No. 1

	Rs.
Stock of Finished goods 31-12-2013	28,000
Stock of Raw Materials 31-12-2013	12,800
Purchase of Raw Materials	2,92,000
Productive wages	1,98,800
Sales of Finished Goods	5,92,000
Stock of Finished Goods 31-12-2014	30,000
Stock of Raw Materials 31-12-2014	13,600
Works Overhead	43,736
Office Expenses	35,524

Prepare a cost sheet. The company wants to send a tender. It is estimated that material required would cost Rs. 40,000 and Labour Rs. 24,000. Tender is to be made at a profit of 20% on selling price. The percentage of Works overhead to wages and to General overheads to Works cost remain same.

Cost Sheet

Particulars	Rs.	Rs.
Stock of Raw Materials 31-12-2013 (opening stock)	12,800	
Add : Purchase of Raw Material	2,92,000	
	3,04,800	
Less : Stock Raw Materials 31-12-2014 (Closing stock)	13,600	
MATERIAL CONSUMED		2,91,200
Add : Productive wages		1,98,800
PRIME COST		4,90,000
Add : Works Overhead		43,736
WORKS COST		5,33,736
Add : Office expenses		35,524
COST OF PRODUCTION		5,69,260
Add : Opening stock of finished goods		28,000
		5,97,260
Less : Closing Stock of finished goods		30,000
COST OF GOODS SOLD		5,67,260
PROFIT		24,740
SALES		5,92,000

Notes :

1) Calculation of percentage of Works oncost to wages

$$= \frac{\text{Works overhead}}{\text{Productive wages}} \times 100$$

$$= \frac{43,736}{1,98,800} \times 100$$

$$= 22\%$$

2) Percentage of General overhead (Office expenses)

$$\text{to Works cost} = \frac{\text{Office expenses}}{\text{Works cost}} \times 100$$

$$= \frac{35,524}{5,33,736} \times 100$$

$$= 6.66\%$$

Statement showing Tender Price

Particulars	Rs.	Rs.
Direct Material	40,000	
Add : Direct Labour	24,000	
PRIME COST		64,000
Add : Works overhead (22% of 24,000)		5,280
WORKS COST		69,280
Add : Office Expenses (6.66% of 69,280)		4,614
TOTAL COST		73,894
PROFIT		
20% on selling price i.e. 25% on cost		18,473
TENDER PRICE		92,367

Note : Calculation of profit 20% on selling price or turnover
Formula for calculation of Profit on Sales

$$\text{Profit} = \frac{\text{Rate percentage on sales} \times \text{Total cost}}{100 - \text{Rate percentage on sales}}$$

$$= \frac{20 \times 73894}{100 - 20}$$

$$= \text{Rs. } 18,473$$

Problem No. 2

ABC Co.Ltd intends to submit a tender. You are given the following particulars for the year ended 31st March 2014.

Opening stock of Finished goods.	72,800
Opening stock of Raw Materials	33,280
Purchase of Raw Material	7,59,200
Direct wages	5,16,880
Sale of Finished goods	15,39,200

Particulars	Rs.
Works overhead expenses	1,29,220
Office overhead expenses	70,161
Closing stock of finished goods	78,000
Closing stock of Raw Material	35,360

From the above details prepare a statement showing :

- (a) Prime cost (b) Works cost (c) Total cost (d) the percentage of Factory overhead to Direct wages, and (e) the percentage of Office overhead to Works cost.
- b) Based on the above mentioned percentages, prepare a statement showing the amount of tender for manufacturing a plant considering the following further information. (i) Cost of Raw Material to be consumed Rs. 52,000. (ii) Wages to be paid to workmen for, making this plant Rs. 31,200 (iii) the company must earn a net profit of 25% on cost.

In the books of ABC Ltd
Cost Sheet

Particulars	Rs.	Rs.
Opening stock of Raw Materials	33,280	
Add : Purchases of Raw Materials	7,59,200	
	7,92,480	
Less : Closing stock of Raw Materials	35,360	
MATERIAL CONSUMED		7,57,120
Add : Direct wages		5,16,880
PRIME COST		12,74,000
Add : Works overhead expenses		1,29,220
WORKS / FACTORY COST		14,03,220
Add : Office overhead expenses		70,161
COST OF PRODUCTION		14,73,381
Add : Opening stock of Finished goods		72,800
		15,46,181
Less : Closing stock of Finished goods		78,000
COST OF SALES		14,68,181
PROFIT		71,019
SALES OF FINISHED GOODS		15,39,200

Notes :

1) Calculation of Works overhead to Wages

$$= \frac{\text{Works overhead}}{\text{Direct wages}} \times 100$$

$$= \frac{1,29,220}{5,16,880} \times 100$$

$$= 25\%$$

2) Calculation of Office overhead to Works cost

$$= \frac{\text{Office overheads}}{\text{Works cost}} \times 100$$

$$= \frac{70,161}{14,03,220} \times 100$$

$$= 5\%$$

Statement Showing Tender Price

Particulars	Rs
Direct Material	52,000
Add : Direct wages	31,200
PRIME COST	83,200
Add : Factory expenses (Works overheads)	
(25% on 31,200)	7,800
WORKS COST	91,000
Add : Office overhead	
(5% on 91,000)	4,550
TOTAL COST	95,550
PROFIT	23,887.50
SELLING PRICE	1,19,437.50

Problem No. 3

	Rs.
Opening stock of Materials	30,000
Purchases	50,000
Closing stock of Materials	10,000
Productive wages	30,000
Factory expenses	10,000
Office expenses	11,000
Selling & Distribution expenses	16,500

Prepare a Cost sheet and also calculate (1) Percentage of factory expenses to wages (2) Percentage of Office expenses to Factory cost and (3) Percentage of Selling expenses to Factory cost.

The firm has to send a tender. It is estimated that material required will cost Rs. 20,000/- and wages Rs. 9,000. The tender is to be made at 10% profit on cost.

Solution :

Preparation of Cost Sheet

Particulars	Rs.	Rs.
Opening stock of Materials	30,000	
Add : Purchases	50,000	
	80,000	
Less : Closing stock of Materials	10,000	
MATERIALS CONSUMED		70,000
Add : Productive wages		30,000
PRIME COST		1,00,000
Add : Factory Overheads		10,000
WORKS COST		1,10,000
Add : Office Overheads		11,000
COST OF PRODUCTION		1,21,000
Add Selling & Distribution expenses		16,500
TOTAL COST		1,37,500

1) Percentage of Factory expenses to Wages.

$$= \frac{\text{Factory expenses}}{\text{Wages}} \times 100$$

$$= \frac{10,000}{30,000} \times 100$$

$$= 33.33 \text{ or } 1/3$$

2) Percentage of Office expenses to Factory cost

$$= \frac{\text{Office expenses}}{\text{Factory cost}} \times 100$$

$$= \frac{11,000}{1,10,000} \times 100$$

$$= 10\%$$

3) Percentage of selling expenses to Factory cost.

$$= \frac{\text{Selling expenses}}{\text{Factory cost}} \times 100$$

$$= \frac{16,500}{1,10,000} \times 100$$

$$= 15\%$$

Statement showing Tender Price

Particulars	Rs.	Rs.
Direct Materials	20,000	
Add Direct wages	9,000	
PRIME COST		29,000
Add Factory expenses 33.33% of wages $\left(9000 \times \dfrac{1}{3} \right)$		3,000
WORKS COST		32,000
Add : Office overheads (10% of 32,000)		3,200
COST OF PRODUCTION		35,200
Add : Selling and Distribution expenses (15% of 32,000)		4,800
Add : Profit (10% of cost)		40,000
i.e (10% of 40000)		4,000
TENDER PRICE		44,000

Problem No. 4

From the following Particulars prepare a cost sheet for the year 2013-2014

	Rs.
Stock of Raw Materials (1-4-2013)	40,000
Selling & Distribution expenses	71,500
Wages due but not paid	4,500
Customs Duty	5,500
Share transfer fee	1,500
Purchases of Raw Materials	1,50,000

	Rs.
Sale of Scrap Raw Materials	500
Works overheads	45,000
Office oncost	32,500
Stock of Raw Materials (31-3-2014)	15,000
Direct wages	95,500

The company has to submit a tender for manufacturing a machine in the year 2014-2015. As per judgement of costing department, materials of Rs. 80,000 will be required and wages will be Rs. 50,000. The factory expenses bear the same percentage on direct wages office expenses on Works cost and Selling and Distribution expenses on the cost of production for the year 2013-14. The tender is to be made at a profit of 25% on the market price.

Solution

Preparation of Cost sheet for the year ended 31-3-2014

Particulars	Rs.	Rs.
Stock of Raw Materials on 1-4-2013	40,000	
Add : Purchases of Raw Materials	1,50,000	
Add : Customs duty	5,500	
Less : Stock of Raw Materials	1,95,500	
as on 31-3-2014	15,000	
Less : Scrap of Raw Materials.	500	
COST OF MATERIALS CONSUMED		1,80,000
Add : 1) Direct Labour	95,500	
2) Wage due but not paid	4,500	1,00,000
PRIME COST		2,80,000
Add : Works Overhead		45,000
Factory cost		3,25,000
Add : Office oncost		32,500
COST OF PRODUCTION		3,57,500
Add : Selling & Distribution expenses		71,500
Total Cost		4,29,000

Note : Share transfer is the item to be excluded form cost sheet.

Calculation of various percentages.

1) Percentage of Factory expenses to Wages.

$$= \frac{\text{Factory expenses}}{\text{Wages}} \times 100$$

$$= \frac{45,000}{1,00,000} \times 100 = 45\%$$

2) Percentage of Office expenses to Works cost.

$$= \frac{\text{Office expenses}}{\text{Works Cost}} \times 100$$

$$= \frac{32,500}{3,25,000} \times 100$$

$$= 10\%$$

3) Percentage of Selling and Distribution expenses to cost of Production.

$$= \frac{\text{Selling and Distribution expenses}}{\text{Cost of Production}} \times 100$$

$$= \frac{71,500}{3,57,000} \times 100$$

$$= 20\%$$

A) Statement Showing Tender Price for the year 2014-2015

Particulars	Rs.	Rs.
Materials	80,000	
Add : Wages	50,000	
PRIME COST		1,30,000
Add : Works Overheads		
(45% of Wages i.e. Rs. 50,000)		22,500
WORKS COST		1,52,500
Add : Office oncost		
(10% of Works cost i.e. Rs. 1,52,500)		15,250
COST OF PRODUCTION		1,67,750
Add : Selling and Distribution expenses		
(20% of cost of Production i.e.		
Rs. 1,67,750)		33,550
TOTAL COST		2,01,300
Add Profit (25% on Market price		
i.e. Selling or Tender price)		67,100
TENDER PRICE		2,68,400

Note :

1) Calculation of Profit

25% on Market or Selling Price.

Selling price = Cost Price + Profit.

If selling price is Rs. 100 = 75 + 25

(Now cost price is Rs. 75)

If Rs. 75 Cost price = Rs. 25 profit

for Rs. 2,01, 300 = ?

$$= \frac{2,01,300 \times 25}{75}$$

= Rs. 67,000

Problem No. 5

Following figures are obtained from the books of Kirloskar Cable Company for the year 2013-2014.

Cost of materials	2,50,000
Direct wages	2,00,000
Factory overheads	1,00,000
Administrative expenses	60,000
Chargeable expenses	50,000
Selling & Distribution expenses	33,000
Profit	69,300

A Work order has been executed in the year 2014-2015 and following expenses have to be incurred.

Materials	22,000
Wages	10,000
Direct expenses	2,000

Assuming that in the year 2014-2015 the Factory overheads have increased by 15%, Administrative cost have gone up by 20% and Selling and Distribution expenses have gone down by 10%.

What estimated price should the product be sold so as to earn 20% profit on selling price?

Solution :

In the books of Kirloskar Cable Co. Ltd.

Particulars	Rs.	Rs.
Cost of materials	2,50,000	
Add : Direct wages	2,00,000	
Chargeable expenses	50,000	
PRIME COST		5,00,000
Add : Factory expenses		1,00,000
FACTORY COST / WORKS COST		6,00,000
Add : Administrative expenses		60,000
COST OF PRODUCTION		6,60,000
Add : Selling and Distribution expenses		33,000
TOTAL COST		6,93,000
PROFIT		69,300
SALES		7,62,300

Notes and Calculations

1) Calculation of percentage of Factory overheads to Wages.

$$= \frac{\text{Factory expenses}}{\text{Direct wages}} \times 100$$

$$= \frac{1,00,000}{2,00,000} \times 100$$

$$= 50\%$$

2) Calculation of percentage of Administrative expenses to Factory cost.

$$= \frac{\text{Administrative expenses}}{\text{Works cost}} \times 100$$

$$= \frac{60,000}{6,60,000} \times 100$$

$$= 10\%$$

3) Calculation of Selling and Distribution expenses to cost of Production

$$= \frac{\text{Selling and Distribution expenses}}{\text{Cost of Production}} \times 100$$

$$= \frac{33,000}{6,60,000} \times 100 = 5\%$$

In the books of Kirloskar Cable Co. Ltd.
Estimated Cost Statement
of the work order for the year 2014-2015

Particulars	Rs
Direct Materials	22,000
Add : Direct wages	10,000
Direct expenses	2,000
PRIME COST	**34,000**
Add : Factory expenses	
50% wages i.e. 50% of	
10,000 = 5,000 + 750 (15% increase)	5,750
FACTORY COST	**39,750**
Add : Administrative expenses	
10% of Factory cost i.e.	
10% of 39,750 = 3,975	
+ 20% increase = 795	4,770
COST OF PRODUCTION	**44,520**
Add : Selling & Distribution expenses	
5% of 44,520 = 2,226 - 223 (10% decrease)	2,003
TOTAL COST	**46,523**
Add : Profit 20% on Selling price i.e. 25% on cost	11,631
ESTIMATED SELLING PRICE	**58,154**

1) Calculation of profit, 20% on selling price
   Selling price = Cost + Profit
   100 = 80 + 20
   If Rs. 80 cost = Rs.20 profit
   For Rs. 46,523 = ?

   $$\frac{20 \times 46,523}{80} = 11630.75 = Rs.11,631$$

Problem No. 6

Raviraj Electronics Ltd. furnishes the following information for 10,000 machine bearings manufactured during the year 2011-12.

Materials	4,50,000
Direct Wages	3,00,000
Factory Indirect Wages	75,000
Power and stores	60,000
Lighting of factory	27,500
Defective works (Cost of rectification)	15,000
Clerical Salaries and Management Expenses	1,67,500
Selling Expenses	27,500
Sales proceeds of scrap	10,000
Plant Repairs and Depreciation	57,500

The net selling price was Rs.158.00 per bearing and all bearing were sold.

As from 1st July, 2012 the selling price was reduced to Rs.155.00 per bearing and it was estimated that production could be increased in 2012-2013 by 50% due to spare capacity.

Rates for materials and Direct Wages will increase by 10%.

You are required to prepare :

(a) Cost Sheet for the year 2011-12 showing various elements of cost per unit, and

(b) Estimated cost (Tender) and profit for 2012-2013. Assuming that 15,000 bearing will be produced and sold during the year, and factory overheads will be recovered as a percentage of direct wages and office and selling expenses as a percentage of works cost.

(P.U.Oct.2000)

Solution :

Raviraj Electronics Ltd.
Cost Sheet for the year 2011-12
Output : 10,000 Bearings

Particulars		Rs. Total Cost	Rs.Cost per unit
Materials	4,50,000		45.00
Wages	3,00,000		30.00
PRIME COST		7,50,000	75.00
Add : Works overhead expenses			
WORKS / FACTORY COST			
Factory Ind. Wages	75,000		

Particulars		Rs. Total Cost	Rs.Cost per unit
Power for stores	60,000		
Light of factory	27,500		
Defective Works	15,000		
Plant Rep and Dep.	57,500		
	2,35,000		
Less sale of Scrap	-10,000	2,25,000	22.50
WORKS COST		9,75,000	97.50
OFFICE & SELLING OVERHEADS			
Clerk Salary & Mgt.Exp	1,67,500		
Selling Exps.	27,500	1,95,000	19.50
COST OF SALES		11,70,000	117.00
PROFIT		4,10,000	41.00
SALES		15,80,000	158.00

ESTIMATED COST SHEET FOR 2012-2013

Particulars	Rs.	Rs.
Materials (10% increase)	7,42,500	49.50
Wages (10% increase)	4,95,000	33.00
PRIME COST	12,37,500	82.50
Factory Overheads (75% of wages)	3,71,250	24.75
WORKS COST	16,08,750	107.25
Office & Sell Exps. (20% of Works Cost)	3,21,750	21.45
Cost of Sales	19,30,500	128.70
PROFIT	3,94,500	26.30
SALES	23,25,000	155.00

Problem No. 7

From the following particulars relating to Dunlop Ltd.Delhi, prepare a cost-sheet for the year 2013-2014.

Sale of scrap of raw material	500
Works overheads	45,000
Stock of raw materials as on 1-4-2013	40,000
Selling and Distribution expenses	71,500
Wages due but not paid	4,500
Custom Duty on purchase	5,500
Share transfer fees paid	1,500
Purchase of raw materials	1,50,000
Office on cost	32,500
Share transfer fees received	2,500
Stock of raw materials as on 31-03-2014	15,000
Direct wages	95,500

The company has to submit a tender for the manufacture of a machine in the year 2014-2015. As per the judgements of costing department materials of Rs. 80,000 will be required and wages will be Rs.50,000. The factory expenses bears the same percentage on direct wages, office expenses bears the same percentage on works cost and selling and distribution expenses bear the same percentage on the cost of production as that of the year 2013-2014. The tender is to be made at a profit of 25% on market price.

Calculate the tender price.

Solution :

In the books of Dunlop Ltd., Delhi
Cost Sheet for the year ended 31-3-2014

Particulars	Rs.	Rs.
Stock of Raw Materials as on 1-4-2013	40,000	
Add : Purchases of Raw Materials	1,50,000	
Add : Custom duty on purchases	5,500	
	1,95,500	
Less : Stock of Raw Materials as on 31-3-2014	15,000	
Less : Sale of scrap of raw materials	500	
COST OF MATERIALS CONSUMED	1,80,000	1,80,000
Add : Direct Labour	1,00,000	

Particulars	Rs.	Rs.
(1) Direct wages 95,500 (2) Wages due but not paid 4,500		
PRIME COST Add : Works overhead expenses	2,80,000 45,000	2,80,000
WORKS / FACTORY COST Add : Office on Cost	3,25,000 32,500	3,25,000
COST OF PRODUCTION Add : Selling and Distribution Expenses	3,57,500 71,500	3,57,500
TOTAL COST	**4,29,000**	**4,29,000**

Calculation and Notes :

1. Calculation of percentage of factory expenses to direct wages:

   If Rs.1,00,000 D.W. = Rs.45,000 F.E.

   $$100 = ?$$

   $$\frac{100 \times 45,000}{1,00,000}$$

   $$= 45\%$$

2. Calculation of percentage of office expenses of works cost :

   If Rs.3,25,000 W.C. = Rs.32,500 O.E.

   $$100 = ?$$

   $$\frac{100 \times 32,500}{3,25,000}$$

   $$= 10\%$$

3. Calculation of percentage of selling and distribution expenses to cost of production :

   If Rs.3,57,000 C.O.P. = Rs.71,500 S & D.E.

   $$100 = ?$$

   $$\frac{100 \times 71,500}{3,57,500}$$

   $$= 20\%$$

4. Calculation of profits i.e.25% on market price

   $$SP = CP + P$$

   (i.e.market price) $100 = 75 + 25$

   If 75 CP = 25 P

   Rs.2,01,300 TC= ?

$$\frac{2,01,300 \times 25}{75}$$
$$= Rs. 67,100.$$

Note : Share transfer fees paid, share transfer fees received etc.are the items to be excluded from cost.

In the books of Dunlop Ltd.Delhi
Statement showing Tender Price for the manufacture of
a machine for the year 2014-2015

Particulars	Rs.	Rs.
Materials		80,000
Add : Wages		50,000
PRIME COST		**1,30,000**
Add : Works Overheads (45% of wages i.e.Rs.50,000)		22,500
WORKS COST		**1,52,250**
Add : Office on Cost (10% of Works cost i.e.Rs.1,52,500)		15,250
COST of PRODUCTION		**1,67,750**
Add : Selling and Distribution Expenses (20% of cost of production i.e.Rs.1,67,750)		33,550
TOTAL COST		2,01,300
Add : Profits (25% on market price i.e.Tender Price)		67,100
TENDER PRICE		**2,68,400**

Problem No. 8
Following details have been obtained from the cost records of M/s Maharashtra Traders, Pune for the year 2013-2014

Purchase of Materials	68,500
Productive Wages	28,000
Stock of Materials on 31-3-2014	15,000
Works on cost	10,000
Stock of Materials on 1-4-2013	12,000
Administrative Overheads	11,000

Particulars	Rs.
Trade Discount	1,000
Dock charges on purchases of materials	4,500
Wages payable	2,000
Selling and Distribution Expenses	16,500

Prepare a Simple Cost-Sheet and also calculate percentage of-

(i) Factory expenses to direct wages.

(ii) Office expenses to factory cost.

(iii) Selling and distribution expenses to factory cost.

The firm has to send a tender for 2014-2015. It is estimated that material required costs Rs.20,000 and wages Rs.9,000. Tender is to be made at a profit of 20% on tender price.

Solution :

In the books M/s Maharashtra Traders, Pune

Cost - Sheet for the year ended 31-3-2014

Particulars		Rs.	Rs.
Stock of Materials as on 1-4-2013		12,000	
Add : Purchase of Materials		68,500	
Add : Dock charges on purchases of materials		4500	
		85000	
Less : Stock of Materials as on 31-3-2014		15000	
COST OF MATERIALS CONSUMED		70,000	70,000
Add : Direct Labour			
(1) Productive wages	28,000		
(2) Wages payable	2,000	30,000	
PRIME COST		1,00,000	1,00,000
Add : Works on Cost		10,000	
FACTORY COST		1,10,000	
Add : Administrative Overheads		11,000	
COST OF PRODUCTION		1,21,000	1,21,000
Add : Selling and Distribution Expenses		16,500	
TOTAL COST		1,37,500	1,37,500

Calculation and Notes :

1. Calculation of percentage of factory expenses to direct wages:

If Rs.30,000 D.W. = Rs.10,000 F.E.

$$100 = ?$$

$$\frac{100 \times 10,000}{30,000}$$

$$= 33\frac{1}{3}\%$$

2. Calculation of percentage of office expenses of factory cost :

If Rs.1,10,000 F.C. = Rs.11,000 O.E.

$$100 = ?$$

$$\frac{100 \times 11,000}{1,10,000}$$

$$= 10\%$$

3. Calculation of percentage of selling and distribution expenses to factory cost :

If Rs.1,10,00 F.C. = Rs.16,500 S & D.E.

$$100 = ?$$

$$\frac{100 \times 16,500}{1,10,000}$$

$$= 15\%$$

4. Calculation of profits i.e.20% on Tender price

SP   = CP + P

(i.e. Tender price) 100 = 80 + 20

If 80 CP = 20 P

Rs.40,000 TC = ?

$$\frac{40,000 \times 20}{80}$$

$$= \text{Rs. } 10,000$$

In the books of M/s Maharashtra Traders, Pune
Statement showing Tender Price for the year 2014-2015

Particulars	Rs.	Rs.
Materials		20,000
Add : Wages		9,000
PRIME COST		29,000
Add : Works on Cost ($33\frac{1}{3}\%$ of wages i.e.Rs.9,000)		3,000

Particulars	Rs.	Rs.
FACTORY COST Add : Administrative Overheads (10% of Works cost i.e.Rs.32,000)		32,000 3,200
COST OF PRODUCTION Add : Selling and Distribution Expenses (15% of factory cost i.e.Rs.32,000		35,200 4,800
TOTAL COST Add : Profits (20% on Tender Price)		40,000 10,000
TENDER PRICE		**50,000**

Note : Trade discount is an item to be excluded from cost.

2:3:8 Quotations -

Quotations are required to be given by the suppliers to the purchaser for supply of small quantities. Even if an individual person wants to buy a consumer durable e.g. a T.V., he needs a quotation from the supplier or dealer. Thus, there is a difference between a Tender and a Quotation. A Tender is usually given for undertaking huge contracts while a quotation is given for small quantities. Again tender can be with the country or they can be invited from abroad also (Global tender), but quotations are usually given for customers who are within the country.

The preparation of the cost statement is done in the same way as in the case of a tender and a separate estimate for quotation is prepared wherein the sales price is quoted if there is severe competition in the market for that goods. But in case of standardized items or having similar functions or output etc., the quotation price does not differ much from company to company. Hence, quotation prices are the open prices which can be obtained freely from any supplier in the market, but tender prices are secret prices which are known only on a particular day, date and time fixed for opening the tenders. Thus, no one knows what price has been quoted in the tender.

While giving the quotations, the following points should be considered :

1. Full description of the product should be given e.g.size, shape, colour,etc.with technical specifications.

2. The price quoted should clearly mention whether it includes all taxes or the exclusive of all taxes.

3. The quotation should indicate clearly the period for which it will remain valid.

4. The price quoted should be subjected to change, if any.

5. The terms of delivery i.e.whether ex-factroy price is quoted or delivery to be given free or how much to be charged for transportation.

6. Guarantee/Warrantee period,if any.

7. After sales service provided if any and the term for it.

8. Payment term/discount,etc.

2:3:9 Problems on Quotations -

Problem No.1

Mahendra Co.showed the following records for the year 2013-2014

Office on Cost	6,000
Direct Expenses	1,000
Factory Overheads	4,000
Direct Material used	11,000
Direct wages	8,000
Sales	40,000

From the above mentioned information prepare a Simple Cost Sheet showing :

(a) Prime Cost (b) Factory Cost (c) Total Cost and (d) Profits for the year 2013-2014

The company wants to quote for a specific job for the year 2014-2015 which will require Direct materials of Rs.2,500, Direct wages of Rs.2,000 and Direct expenses of Rs.500.

What should be the quotation price if a profit of 25% on selling price is desired?

Solution :

In the books of Mahendra Company Cost-Sheet
for the year 2013-2014

Particulars	Rs.	Rs.
Direct Materials used	11,000	
Add : Direct Wages	+ 8,000	
Add : Direct Expenses	+ 1,000	
PRIME COST	(a) 20,000	20,000
Add : Factory Overheads	+ 4,000	
FACTORY COST	(b) 24,000	24,000
Add : Office on Cost	+ 6,000	
TOTAL COST	(c) 30,000	30,000
Add : Profits for the year 2013-2014	(d) + 10,000	10,000
SALES 40,000	**40,000**	

Calculation and Notes :

1. Calculation of percentage of factory expenses to direct wages:

If Rs.8,000 D.W. = Rs.4,000 F.O.

$$100 = ?$$

$$= \frac{100 \times 4,000}{8,000}$$

$$= 50\%$$

2. Calculation of percentage of office on Cost to Factory Cost

If Rs.24,000 F.C. = Rs.6,000 O.O.C.

$$100 = ?$$

$$= \frac{100 \times 6,000}{24,000}$$

$$= 25\%$$

3. Calculation of profits i.e.25% on Selling Price

$$SP = CP + P$$

$$100 = 75 + 25$$

If 75 CP = 25 P

Rs.7,500 TC = ?

$$= \frac{7,500 \times 25}{75}$$

$$= Rs. 2,500$$

In the books of Mahendra Company
Statement showing Quotation Price for a job
for the year 2014 - 2015

Particulars	Rs.	Rs.
Direct Materials used		2,500
Add : Direct Wages		+ 2,000
Add : Direct Expenses		+ 500
PRIME COST		5,000
Add : Factory Overheads (50% of Direct Wages i.e.Rs.2,000)		+ 1,000
FACTORY COST		6,000
Add : Office on Cost (25% of Factory cost i.e.Rs.6,000)		+ 1,500
TOTAL COST		7,500
Add : Profits (25% on Selling Price)		+ 2,500
Quotation Price		**(a) 10,000**

Problem No.2

From the following particulars of Chitale Co.Pune for the year ended 31-3-2014. Prepare a statement of cost.

	Rs.
Units produced and sold	2,000
Stock of Raw Materials as on 1-4-2013	20,000
Stock of Raw Materials as on 31-3-2014	5,000
Finished Stock on 1-4-2013	NIL
Finished Stock on 31-3-2014	25,000
Direct Wages	80,000
Office overheads	6,000
Purchases of Raw Materials	45,000
Factory Overheads	15,000
Sales	1,49,600

The company has received an order for the supply of 4,000 units till 31-3-2015. During the period of executing the order, the material cost is expected to rise by 20% and the cost of wages has to be raised by 15%. However, the overhead rates will remain the same.

Assuming the same percentage of profit to be maintained as during the period ended 31-3-2014, state the price to be quoted for the supply of 4,000 units.

Solution :

In the books of Chitale Co.Pune

Statement of Cost for the year ended 31-3-2014

Units Produced : 2000 Units

Units Sold : 2,000 Units

Particulars	Rs.	Rs.
Stock of Raw materials as on 1-4-2013	20,000	
Add : Purchase of Raw Materials	+ 45,000	
	65,000	
Less: Stock of raw materials as on 31-3-2014	- 5,000	
COST OF MATERIALS CONSUMED	(1) 60,000	60,000
Add : Direct Wages	80,000	
PRIME COST	(2) 1,40,000	1,40,000
Add : Factory Overheads	15,000	

Particulars	Rs.	Rs.
FACTORY COST Add : Office overheads	(3) 1,55,000 6,000	1,55,000
COST OF PRODUCTION Add : Finished stock on 1-4-2013	(4) 1,61,000 NIL	1,61,000
  Less : Finished stock on 31-3-2014	1,61,000 - 25,000	1,61,000
TOTAL COST PROFITS + 13,600	(5) 1,36,000	1,36,000
SALES 1,49,600	**1,49,600**	

In the books of Chitale Co. Pune
Statement showing Quotation Price for the supply
of 4,000 units for the year ended 31-3-2015

Particulars	Rs.	Rs.
Material Cost (Rs.60,000 x 2 = Rs.1,20,000 +(20%) + Rs.24,000 = Rs.1,44,000)		1,44,000
Add : Cost of Wages (Rs.80,000 x 2 = Rs.1,60,000 + (15%) + Rs.24,000 = Rs.1,84,000)		+ 1,84,000
PRIME COST Add : Factory Overheads (Rs.15000 x 2 = Rs.30,000)		3,28,000 + 30,000
FACTORY COST Add : Office Overheads (Rs.6,000 x 2 = Rs.12,000)		3,58,000 + 12,000
TOTAL COST Add : Profits	 + 37,000	3,70,000
QUATATION PRICE		**4,07,000**

1. Calculation of Profit -
    If Rs.1,36,000 T.C. = Rs.13,600
    Rs.3,70,000 TC = ?
    = Rs.3,70,000 x Rs.13,600
    Rs.1,36,000
    = Rs.37,000

2.4 EXERCISES

A) Indicate which of the statements are true of False.

1) Total Variable cost do not increase in total production to output.
2) Variable cost per unit remains constant.
3) Fixed cost do not change, in the same proportion in which output changes.
4) Administration Expenses are mostly fixed.
5) Abnormal cost is controllable.
6) Direct cost is one which can be conveniently identified with and charged to a particular unit of cost.
7) Fixed cost per unit decreases with the rise in output and increases with the fall in output.
8) Fixed cost per unit remains fixed.
9) Cost of production is equal to prime cost plus works cost.
10) Direct cost is one which can be conveniently idientified with and charged to a particular unit of cost.

Answers : True : 2, 3, 4, 5, 6, 7,10   False : 1, 8,9

B) Fill in the blanks.

1) An item of cost that is direct for one business may be ..... for another business.
2) All cost are ..... controllable.
3) Variable cost change ..... with change in output.
4) An example of variable cost is ......
5) Fixed cost per unit .... with increase in out put.
6) .... costs are partly fixed and partly variable.
7) Per unit variable cost remains ....
8) Royalty payable is to be treated as .... expenses.

Answer : 1 - Indirect, 2 - Not, 3 - Proportionately, 4 - Direct Material, 5 - Decreases, 6) Semi-Variable, 7) Constant, 8) Direct

C) Essay type question.

1) Describe various elements of cost.
2) Distinguish between Fixed and Variable cost.
3) Distinguish between direct cost and indirect cost.
4) Explain the various methods of cost classification.
5) "The classification of cost as controllable and non controllable depends upon point of reference" Explain.
6) Prepare a chart showing the different elements of cost.
7) Explain fully the concept of 'Cost'. Distinguish between Direct cost and Indirect cost.

8) "Fixed cost are variable per unit while variable cost are fixed per unit." comment.
9) What is Cost? Explain the classification of cost in detail.

D) EXERCISES :

1) **The accounts of Govind Manufacturers for the year ending 31st Dec - 2013 shows the following.**

Stock of materials on 1-1-2013	16,720
Materials purchased	25,900
Bad debts written off	910
Travellers salaries and commission	1,078
Depreciation of Office furniture	42
Rent, rates and taxes (Factory)	1,190
Productive wages	17,640
Director's fees	840
General expenses	476
Gas and water (Factory)	168
Travelling expenses	294
Sales	70,000
Manager's salary ($\frac{2}{3}$ Factory, $\frac{1}{3}$ Office)	1,500
Depreciation of Plant Machinery	1,820
Repairs to Plant and Machinery	623
Carriage outwards	602
Direct expenses	1,001
Rents, Rates and Taxes (Office)	280
Gas and Water (Office)	56
Discount allowed	406
Stock of Materials as on 31-12-2013.	8,792

Prepare a statement of cost showing -
1) Cost of Materials Consumed
2) Prime cost
3) Factory cost
4) Cost of Production
5) Total cost

Ans : 1) Rs. 33,828, 2) Rs. 52,469, 3) Rs. 57,270, 4) Rs. 59,758,   5) Rs. 62,348

2) **The following information has been obtained from Samarth Company Ltd. for the quarter ending 31-3-2014.**

Stock of Raw Materials on 1-1-2014	1,00,000
Stock of Raw Materials on 31-3-2014	74,000

Purchases of Raw Materials	6,00,000
Travelling expenses	5,000
Carriage Inwards	10,000
Carriage Outwards	15,000
Depreciation on Plant	18,000
Factory rent	12,000
Office rent	10,000
Bad debts	7,000
Productive wages	20,000
Traveller's commission	4,000
Expenses on Purchases	4,000
Gas, water, fuel	8,000
Manager's salaries (2/3 for factory)	9,000
Sales	10,48,000

Prepare a cost sheet showing

1) Materials Consumed   2) Prime Cost
3) Works Cost   4) Cost of Production
5) Total cost   6) Profit

Ans. :   1) Rs. 6,40,000   2) Rs. 6,60,000   3) Rs. 7,04,000,
           4) Rs. 7,22,000   5) Rs. 7,48,000   6) Rs. 3,00,000

3) **Following information of XYZ Co. Ltd. relates to commodity for the year ending 31-3-2014**

Opening stock as on 1-4-2013	Rs.
Raw Materials	5,000
Work in progress	1,200
Finished goods (1,000 tons)	4,000
Closing stock as on 31-3-2014	
Work in progress	3,200
Finished goods	9,000
Purchases of Raw Material	35,000
Prime cost Labour	25,000
Excise duty	2,000
Administration overheads	8,000
Cost of Factory supervision	12,000
Income Tax	5,000
Carriage and Cartage	1,000
Management expenses	1,000
Accountancy charges	1,000

Preliminary expenses   3,200
Sales of Finished goods   1,17,500
Advertising, Bad debts and Selling on cost amounted to Rs. 50 paise per ton sold.
16,000 tons of commodities were produced during the year.
Prepare a cost sheet showing.
  1) Materials consumed   2) Prime cost
  3) Works cost   4) Cost of production
  5) Cost of goods sold   6) Profit for the period
  7) Profit per ton sold.

Ans. : 1) Rs. 40,000 2) Rs. 65,000 3) Rs. 75,000 4) Rs. 85,000 5) Rs. 80,000
        6) Rs. 3,000 7) Rs. 2 per ton

4) From the following particulars prepare a Cost Sheet showing the total cost per tonne for the period ended 31st Dec. 2014.

	Rs.		Rs.
Raw Materials	33,000	Rent and taxes (Office)	500
Productive wages	38,000	Water supply (Works)	1,200
Unproductive wages	10,500	Factory Insurance	1,100
Factory rent and taxes	7,500	Office Insurance	500
Factory lighting	2,200	Legal expenses	400
Factory heating	1,500	Rent of warehouse	300
Motive power	4,400	Depreciation of	
Haulage (Works)	3,000	–Plant and Machinery	2,000
Directors' fees (Works)	1,000	–Office Building	1,000
Directors' fees (Office)	2,000	– Delivery Vans	200
Factory cleaning	500	Bad debts	100
Sundry Office expenses	200	Advertising	300
Estimating expenses		Sales Department's	
(Works)	800	salaries	1,500
Factory Stationery	750	Upkeep of delivery vans	700
Office stationery	900	Bank charges	50
Loose tools written off	600	Commission on sales	1,500

        The total output for the period has been 14,775 tonnes.
Ans. Prime Cost Rs. 71,000; Factory Cost Rs. 1,08,050; Cost of Production Rs. 1,13,600;
      Total Cost Rs. 1,18,200
      cost per ton Rs. 8.

5) **The Accounts of 'A' Manufacturing Company for the year ended December, 2014 show the following :**

	Rs.		Rs.
Factory Office salaries	6,500	Travelling expenses	2,100
General Office salaries	12,600	Traveller's Salaries and	
Carriage Outward	4,300	commission	7,700
	Rs.		Rs.
Carriage on Purchases	7,150	Productive Wages	1,26,000
Bad Debts written off	6,500	Depreciation - Plant	
Repairs of Plant,		Machinery and Tools	6,500
Machinery and Tools	4,450	Depreciation Furniture	300
Rent, Rates, Taxes		Directors' Fees	6,000
and Insurance-Factory	8,500	Gas and Water - Factory	1,200
Office	2,000	Office	400
Sales	4,61,100	Manager's Salary (3/4th	
Stock of Materials		Factory and 1/4 Office)	10,000
31st Dec., 2013	62,800	General expenses	3,400
31st Dec., 2014	48,000	Income Tax	500
Materials Purchased	1,85,000	Dividend	1,000

Prepare statement giving the following information :

(a) Materials Consumed (b) Prime Cost (c) Factory cost (d) Cost of Production (e) Total Cost (f) Net Profit.

Ans. [(a) Rs. 2,06,950 (b) Rs. 3, 32, 950 (c) Rs. 3,67, 600 (d) Rs. 3,94,800 (e) Rs. 4,15,400 (f) Rs. 45,700]

6) **The following data have been extracted from the books of Moonlight Industries Ltd., for the year 2014.**

	Rs.		Rs.
Opening Stock of		Indirect consumption of	
Raw Material	25,000	Materials	500
Purchase of		Salary - Office	2,500
	Rs.		Rs.
Raw Material	85,000	Salesmen	2,000
Closing stock of		Other Factory Expenses	5,700
Raw Material	40,000	Other Office Expenses	900
Carriage Inward	5,000	Manager's	

Wages - Direct	90,000	Remuneration	12,000
Wages - Indirect	10,000	Bad Debts written off	1,000
Rent and Rates (Factory)	5,000	Advertisement Expenses	2,000
	Rs.		Rs.
(Office)	500	Travelling Expenses of	
Depreciation		Salesmen	1,100
Plant and Machinery	1,500	Carriage and Freight	
Office Furniture	100	Outward	1,000
Cash Discount	5,000	Sales	2,50,000
		Advance Income	
		Tax Paid	15,000

The manager has the overall charge of the company and his remuneration is to be allocated as Rs. 4,000 to the factory, Rs. 2,000 to the Office and Rs. 6,000 to the Selling operations.

From the above particulars prepare a statement showing (a) Prime cost (b) Factory cost (c) Cost of production (d) Cost of sales (e) Net Profit.

Ans. [(a) Rs. 1,65,000 (b) Rs. 1,91,700 (c) Rs. 1, 97,700 (d) Rs. 2, 10, 800; (e) Rs. 39, 200]

7) **A manufacturing concern requires a statment showing the result of its production operation for March, 2014 cost records give the following information.**

	1st Sep. 2014	30th Sep. 2014
Raw Materials	1,00,000	1, 23,500
Finished Goods	71,500	42,000
Work-in-Progress	31,000	34,500
Transactions during the month of September 2014 :		

	Rs.		Rs.
Purchase of		Sales of Factory	
Raw Materials	88,000	scrap	2,000
Direct Wages	70,000	Selling and	
Works Expenses	39,500	Distribution expenses	15,000
Administration Expenses	13,000	Sales	2,84,000

Ans. [Raw materials consumed Rs. 64,500; Prime cost Rs. 1,34,500; Factory cost Rs. 1,68,500; Cost of Production Rs. 1,81,500; Cost of goods sold Rs. 2,11,000; Cost of Sales Rs. 2,26,000; Profit Rs. 58,000]

8) The Modern Manufacturing Company submits the following information on 31st March, 2014 :

	Rs.	Rs.
Sales for the year		2, 75,000
Inventories at the beginning of the year :		
Finished goods	7,000	
Work-in-progress	4,000	
Purchase of Materials for the year		1,10,000
Materials Inventory :		
at the beginning of the year	3,000	
at the end of the year	4,000	
Direct Labour		65,000
Factory overhead @ 60% of the Direct Labour cost		
Inventories at the end of the year :		
Work-in-progress	6,000	
Finished goods	8,000	
Other expenses of the year :		
Selling expenses 10% of Sales		
Administrative expenses 5% of Sales		

Prepare a statement of cost and profit.

Ans. [Prime cost Rs. 1,74,000; Works cost Rs. 2,11,000; Cost of Production Rs. 2, 24, 750; Cost of Goods Sold Rs. 2,23,750; Cost of Sales Rs. 2,51,250; Profit Rs. 23,750]

9) Following information has been obtained from the records of a Manufacturing Company :

		1-1-2013	31-12-2013
		Rs.	Rs.
Stock of Raw Materials		40,000	50,000
Stock of Finished Goods		1,00,000	1,50,000
Stock of Work-in-Progress		10,000	14,000
	Rs.		Rs.
Indirect	50,000	Administration	
Lubricants	10,000	expenses	1,00,000
Insurance on Plant	3,000	Power	30,000
Purchase of		Direct Labour	3,00,000
Raw Materials	4,00,000	Depreciation on	
Sales Commission	60,000	Machinery	50,000
Salaries of Salesmen	1,00,000	Factory Rent	60,000
Carriage Outward	20,000	Property Tax on	
		Factory Building	11,000
		Sales	12,00,000

Prepare a Statement of Cost and Profit showing (a) Cost of Raw Materials consumed ; (b) Prime cost; (c) Total Manufacturing cost; (d) Factory Manufacturing cost; (e) Cost of Production; (f) Cost of Goods sold; (g) Cost of Sales; and (h) Profit.

Ans. [(a) Rs. 3,90,000 (b) Rs. 6,90,000 (c) 9,04,000 (d) Rs. 9,00,000 (e) Rs. 10,00,000 (f) Rs. 9,50,000 (g) Rs. 11,30,000 (h) Rs. 70,000]

10) Following information has been obtained from the records of a manufacturing concern :

		1-1-2013 Rs.	31-12-2013 Rs.
Stock of Raw Materials		30,000	35,000
Work-in-Progress		15,000	20,000
Stock of Finished Goods		43,700	54,000

	Rs.		Rs.
Indirect Wages	9,720	Purchase of	
Sales	3,25,000	Raw Materials	1,20,000
Factory Rent and Rates	7,830	Productive Wages	90,000
Office Salaries	15,030	Plant Repair	3,420
General Expenses	13,500	Depreciation on Plant	8,360
Office Rent	2,000	Factory Lighting	7,380
Rent of Show Room	1,200	Salesmen's salaries	7,650

Prepare : (i) Cost Sheet Showing cost of raw materials consumed, prime cost, and factory cost. (ii) Income statement in traditional form for the year showing gross profit and net profit.

Ans. [(i) Rs. 1,15,000; Rs. 2,05,000; Rs. 2,41,710; Rs. 2,36,710 (ii) Rs. 98,590; Rs. 59,210]

11) From the following particulars, prepare a Cost Statement showing the components of Total Cost and Profit for the year ended 31st December, 2013.

		1-1-20133 Rs.	1-12-2013 Rs.
Stock of Finished goods		6,000	15,000
Stock of Raw Materials		40,000	50,000
Work-in-progress		15,000	10,000

	Rs.		Rs.
Purchase of Raw		Sales for the year	8,60,000
Materials	4,75,000	Income Tax	500
Carriage Inward	12,500	Dividend	1,000
Wages	1,75,000	Debenture interest	5,000

Works Manager's salary 30,000 Fund for replacement		Transfer to Sinking	
Factory Employee's		of machinery	10,000
salaries	60,000	Goodwil written off	10,000
Factory rent, taxes			
and insurance	7,250	Payment of Sales Tax	16,000
Power expenses	9,500	Selling expenses	9,250
Other Production			
expenses	43,000		
General expenses	32,500		

Ans. [Prime cost Rs. 6,52,500; Works cost Rs. 8,07,250; Cost of Production Rs. 8,39,750; Cost of Goods sold Rs. 8,30,750; Cost of Sales Rs. 8,40,000; Profit Rs. 20,000]

12) **From the following particulars of a manufacturing firm, prepare a statement showing (a) Cost of materials used; (b) Works cost; (c) Cost of production; (d) Percentage of Works overhead to Productive wages; (e) Percentage of General overhead to Works cost.**

	Rs.		Rs.
Stock of Materials on 1-1-2014	40,000	Finished goods sold	24,00,000
Purchase of Materials in January 2014	11,00,000	Works overhead Office and	1,50,000
Stock of Finished goods on 1-1-2014	50,000	General expenses Stock of Materials	1,00,000
Productive Wages	5,00,000	on 31-1-2014	1,40,000
		Stock of finished goods on 31-1-2014	60,000

Ans. [(a) Rs.10,00,000 (b) Rs. 16,50,000 (c) Rs. 17,50,000 (d) 30%; (e) 6.06%]

13) **From the following particulars of a manufacturing firm**

	Rs.
Stock of Materials (1-1-2014)	3,500
Stock of Materials (31-12-2014)	5,000
Purchases of Materials	50,000
Direct wages	20,000
Factory expenses	5,000
Office expenses	14,700
Selling expenses	7,350

The firm has to send a tender. It is estimated that Materials required cost Rs. 10,000/- and wages Rs. 4,000/-. The Tender is to be made at 10% profit on Market price.

Ans :

1) Percentage of Works expenses to Wages   25%
2) Percentage of Office exps. to Works cost   20%
3) Percentage of Selling exps. to Works cost   10%
4) Tender Price   Rs. 21,667

14) **From the following particulars prepare a statement showing (i) Cost of Material used (ii) Prime cost (iii) Works cost (iv) Total cost (v) Percentage of Works overhead to Productive wages and percentage of Office expenses to Works cost.**

Stock on 1-1-2014	Rs.
Finished goods	1,45,600
Raw Materials	66,560
Purchases of Raw Materials	15,18,400
Productive wages	10,33,760
Sales	30,78,400
Stock on 31-12-2014	
Finished goods	1,56,000
Raw Materials	70,720
Works overheads	2,58,440
Office expenses	1,40,322

The Company is about to send a tender for a large Plant which, it is estimated, would required Rs. 52,000 towards Materials and Rs. 31,200 towards Wages. The tender is to be made at a net profit of 20% on Selling price.

Show what the amount of tender would be based on the above percentages.

Ans. :

1) Percentage of works overhead to Wages   25%
2) Percentage of Office expenses to Works cost   5%
3) Amount of tender   Rs. 1,19,437.50

Objective type questions.

A) Fill in the blanks.

1) The total of all direct expenses is known as .....
2) Works cost is the total of .....
3) Overhead is the aggregate of all ...... cost.
4) Total cost + profit = ...
5) Prime cost + Factory overhead =

6) Material, labour and other expenses are the.......of cost.
7) Timber used in furniture is.........material.
8) Wages paid to workers.............engaged in converting raw materials into finished products is a direct labout cost.
9) ....cost is a period cost.
10) Depreciation is an example of...............cost.
11) ....costs are partly fixed and partly variable in relation to output.
12) ....costs change proportionately with change in output.
13) Out of pocket costs involve payment to..........
14) The total of all direct expenses is known as.............cost.
15) ....cost is the sacrifice involved in accepting an alternative proposal.
16) Conversion cost is the factory cost minus..........cost.

Ans. : 1) Prime cost, 2) All Direct cost + Works overhead, 3) Indirect, 4) Sales, 5) Factory cost, 6) elements, 7) direct, 8) directly 9) fixed, 10) indirect, 11) semi-variable, 12) variable, 13) outsiders, 14) prime, 15) opportunity, 16) direct material.

B) Indicate whether each of the following statements are True or False. Give reason in brief.

1) Cost and Expenses are synonymous.
2) Rent of building is an overhead cost.
3) Abnormal losses are charged to costing Profit and Loss Account.
4) Supervisor's salary is a direct Labour cost.
5) Chargeable expenses are the total of Direct and Indirect expenses.
6) Cost of Production is equal to Prime cost plus Works cost.
7) The aggregate cost of indirect material, indirect labour and indirect other expenses are termed as prime cost.
8) Direct cost cannot be conveniently identified with individual cost units or cost centres.
9) Direct expenses are also known as chargeable expenses.
10) Variable cost per unit remains constant.
11) Normally, administrative cost is a fixed cost.
12) Fixed cost remains constant in total amount over a wide range of activity for a specified period of time.
13) The change in cost due to change in the pattern or method of production is known as marginal cost.
14) Abnormal cost is controllable.
15) Period costs are not assigned to products.
16) Standard costs tell us what the cost is.
17) Sunk costs are relevant for decision making.

Answers :

       True : 2,3,6,9,10,11,12,14,15   False : 1,4,5,7,8,13,16,17

C) Essay type questions.

a) Short Answer Questions :

1) Differentiate between direct and indirect cost.
2) What is fixed cost? Give three examples of fixed cost.
3) Total variable cost varies in direct proportion to the volume of output. Do you agree?
4) What are chargeable expenses? Give two examples.
5) What is the difference between direct and indirect material? Give two examples of each.
6) What are selling overheads? How these differ from distribution overheads?
7) Define and give examples of direct and indirect wages.

D) Long Answer / Essay type Questions :

1) What are the elements of cost? Explain the different elements of total cost of a product?
2) Explain and illustrate the various of cost.
3) Give the method of classification of cost according to their functional element.
4) Briefly describe the various bases available for classification of cost.
5) Write an explanatory note on element wise classification of cost.
6) "Cost may be classified in a variety of ways according to their nature and the information needs of management." Explain and discuss this statement giving examples of classification required for different purposes.
7) What is Cost? Explain the different elements of cost.

E) Write Short Notes on :

1) Elements of cost
2) Factory overheads
3) Conversion cost
4) Sunk cost
5) Opportunity cost
6) Out of pocket cost
7) Differential cost.

MATERIAL CONTROL

INTRODUCTION

In manufacturing process, various elements of cost play an important role. Among all the factors of production, material is very important. In many private and public organisations more than 60% of total cost is incurred for purchases or raw and other materials. According to the Indian Association of Material Management, 64 paise in a rupee are spent on materials by Indian industries, 16 paise on labour and the rest of one rupee of the cost is spent on overheads. This reveals the importance of material in production. If the cost of material is reduced, the cost of production is also decreased and thereby selling price can be reduced.

The term material may be defined as 'anything that can be stored, stocked or stockpiled.' It refers to all commodities that are consumed in the process of manufacture. It includes physical commodities used to manufacture the final product. It is stored and does not get wasted and exhausted with the passage of time. Secondly, it can be purchased in varying quantities as per requirements of industry, whereas other elements of cost like labour and other services can not be easily varied once they are established. In short, material is most flexible and controllable aspect of cost of production. Materials are classified as under.

1) **Direct materials :-** Materials which become the main part of finished product is generally known as direct material. The consumption of direct material can be easily identified with specific production unit. Direct materials not only include the materials entering into the process at the start of production but also all the materials following

a) Any material entering into production after the initial stage e.g. glazing in manufacture of crockery.

b) Any material used in production process e.g. fertilizers used for plants.

c) Any finished component assembled in the final product. e.g. T.V. or AC fitted in bus.

d) Any packing material. i.e. cans for oil, bottles of soft drinks etc.

2) **Indirect materials : -** The materials which do not physically become the part of final product and cannot be conveniently identified with individual cost unit, are known as indirect material. For example, nail used in manufacturing furniture, oil and grease used in motor car etc.

3) **Components :-** The manufactured or finished parts entering into products are called components. e.g. spark plug used in motor cycle. These parts may be manufactured by firm itself or purchased from outside.

4) **Consumable stores:-** Consumable stores are the items used in the product, but do not become the part of finished product. For example :- soap, sand paper, oil, grease etc.

5) **Stores :-** In simple words, stores means stock lying in godown. The term stores has wider meaning. It does not include only raw materials but also all other items held in stock in storeroom or godown. For example, Direct materials, indirect materials, component parts, finished product etc.

3:1 NEED AND ESSENTIALS OF MATERIAL CONTROL.

Material control is the system which ensures the availability of right quantity of materials of the right quality, at right time, with minimum amount of capital by purchasing them at right price from the right source. Material control is defined as, " A systematic control over purchasing, storing and consumption of materials and at the same time avoiding overstocking or understocking." In simple words, material control is a systematic control over the purchasing, storing and using of materials so as to have minimum possible cost of materials.

Materials are the main part of product and element of cost, hence every rupee spent for materials should be efficiently and effectively utilised. Proper control on materials ensure reduction in cost.

Aspects of material control.

There are two aspects of material control as given below

(i) **Accounting Aspect :** This aspect of material control is concerned with maintaining documentary evidence of movement of materials at every stage right from the time production budgets are approved to the point when materials are purchased and actually used in production operation.

(ii) **Operational Aspect :** This aspect of material control is concerned with the maintenance of material supplies at a level so as to ensure that material is available for use in production and production services as and when required by minimizing investment in materials.

3.1.1. Need of Material Control :

No cost accounting system can become effective without proper and efficient control of material, as materials constitute a major portion of cost of production. The following are the various objectives of material control.

1) **Availability of materials:-** As material constitutes a major part of production, there should be continuous availability of all types of materials in a factory, so that production may not be held up for want of materials.

2) **Minimum wastage :-** Loss of materials occurs due to deterioration, obsolescence, pilferage, theft and evaporation. So, proper storage condition must be provided, in order to minimize loss of materials.

3) **Moderate investment in materials :-** There should be no excessive investment in stocks. Material should be purchased as per requirements of production department. Overstocking of materials should be avoided.

4) **Reasonable price :-** While purchasing materials, it should be seen that it is purchased at a reasonably low price. Quality is not to be sacrificed at the cost of lower price. Management should purchase quality raw materials in order to maintain the quality of finished products.

5) **Risk of spoilage and obsolescence :** There may be a possibility of spoilage and obsolescences of materials in production process. For this purpose, a maximum quantity of each material is determined and proper method of issue of materials is followed.

6) **Checking of Invoices :** Invoices received from the suppliers should be approved for payment, only if the items of materials ordered have been received and properly checked to avoid excess payment to suppliers.

7) **No understocking :-** Understocking of materials should be avoided. The shortage of materials may held up the production. It may increase the cost of production and thereby profit may be reduced.

3.1.2 Essentials of Material Control

The material control must ensure that the following requirements are fully met.
1) There should be proper co-operation and co-ordination amongst the departments involved in purchasing and inspection, storage, sales, production and accounting department.
2) Centralization of purchasing under an efficient purchase department.
3) A good method of classification and codification, standardization and simplification should be followed.

4) Use of standard forms and documents in all the stages.
5) Material requirement should be properly planned.
6) There should be proper inspection of materials when they are received by receiving department.
7) Storage of material should be planned. The various stock levels like maximum, minimum etc. should be fixed for each item of materials.
8) There should be proper scheduling of materials.
9) A good method of issue of materials to various jobs, orders, processes should be followed.
10) A good system of internal check should be introduced to ensure that all transactions involving materials are checked by properly authorized independent persons.
11) There should be regular reporting to management regarding purchases, issues and stock of materials. Special reports should be prepared for obsolete items, spoilage, returns to suppliers etc.
12) Adequate record of materials during production should be maintained to ensure that there is a minimum possible wastage.
13) Perpetual inventory system and continuous physical stock verification should be operated to facilitate regular checking of stock.
14) Ordering quantity for each type of material should be fixed to reduce the ordering costs and carrying costs of materials.

3:2 FUNCTIONS OF PURCHASE DEPARTMENT:

Purchasing plays a vital role in material management and stock-keeping. Generally, a separate purchase department is established in the factory. The scope of purchase department depends upon the volume and nature of industry. If the purchase department is efficient, proper quantity of all types of material will be purchased at right time and at right price. It will reduce the cost of production of final product. In short, in order to attain the objectives of scientific purchasing, the purchase department has to perform the following functions.

1) **Purchase of Right Quality :** Before purchasing, the purchase department prepares a bill of materials which contains the schedule of component parts and raw materials required for particular job or work order. This enables purchase manager to purchase right quality of materials. Proper quality of raw material is necessary to produce quality product which further meets the requirements of markets.

2) **Purchase of Right Quantities :** Generally, 50% to 70% of the total cost is incurred for the purchase of raw materials. Hence, care should be taken that there should not be understocking or overstocking. The purchase department should purchase the raw materials strictly as per requisition of various departments. In short, it is important to note that, only the correct quantity of materials is to be purchased.

3) **Purchase at Right Price :** The purchase of material should be made at a right price. Right price does not mean lowest price. It should be most economical price. The purchase department must compare the quotations of various suppliers and then the suppliers who supply material at reasonable price should be selected.

4) **Purchase at Right Time :** The purchase department should consider the time factor, while making purchases. It is most important element in purchase procedure. The right time to purchase the material depends on the date of requirement of material and lead time involved in purchasing materials. Usually, the date of requirement is specified in the purchase requisition. In short, the purchase department should purchase materials in such a way that there may not be the stoppage of production for the want of material.

5) **Purchase from Right Source :** The procedure for inquiry, tenders and quotations decides the right source for purchase of materials. As far as possible purchases should be made from manufactures or their approved dealers in order to eliminate the middlemen. While selecting the supplier, various factors like reliability of supplier, terms of payments. date of delivery, technical assistance etc. should be taken into account.

6) **Placing of an Order :** The purchase department has to place a purchase order for the supply of materials to the supplier. It should purchase the materials at the lowest possible cost. Once the purchase order is placed to the supplier, it is obligatory on the part of purchase department to take the delivery of goods and arrange for payment of the materials purchased.

7) **Preparation of Purchase Budget :** Before making purchases, the purchase department has to prepare purchase budget. While preparing of this budget, requirements of various departments should be taken into consideration. This budget helps the purchase manager in purchasing the quantity and quality of materials.

8) **Follow up of Purchase Orders :** Once the purchase order is placed to supplier, the purchase manager has to remain in continuous contact with the supplier for receiving the delivery of materials in time.

9) **Verification of Quality and Quantity Received :** After the receipt of materials, the purchase department verifies the materials in respect of quality and quantity. The material received should tally with the order placed by purchase department.

10) **Checking Invoices :-** On receipt of materials, verification of invoices will be done by purchase department. The invoice contains the information regarding quantity of material, quality, price, method of packing, means of transportation of goods etc.

11) **Co-ordination with other Departments :** The purchase department co-ordinates with stores, accounts and industrial engineering departments on all matters relating to purchases. Co-ordination ensures smooth and efficient functioning of purchase department.

12) Maintenance of Record : Purchase department has to maintain upto date and reliable records about the best markets, best seasons, new and improved material, spare parts components, equipments etc. This is required for the efficient operation of purchase department.

Centralised and Decentralised Purchasing

Generally, all purchases are made by purchase department. The setup of purchase department varies from firm to firm. Purchase department may be centralized or decentralized.

1] Centralised Purchase Department :

Centralisation of purchasing means that, all purchases are made by a single or one purchase department. The head of purchase department is designated as purchase manager or chief buyer. He is efficient and competent in purchasing. The main objective of centralized purchasing is to avoid duplication, overlapping and non-uniform procurement. All departments of the industry send their purchase requisitions to purchase department for materials supplies, services and machines and tools.

Advantages of Centralised Purchasing.

Following are the advantages of centralised purchasing.
(1) Centralised purchasing ensures uniformity in purchasing policies, practices and procedures.
(2) It ensures timely and regular supply of materials to various departments.
(3) It ensures better control over purchases.
(4) Standardisation of quality raw material is facilitated.
(5) It avoids duplication, overlapping and non-uniform procurement.
(6) Purchases can be made on most favourable terms. e.g. More trade discount, easy terms of payments; or economies in transport can be obtained because of large purchases.
(7) The liason with production and service departments become more easier by centralised purchasing as other departments depend on purchase department for all types of material.
(8) Better control over purchasing is possible because reckless buying by various individuals is avoided.
(9) Free home delivery under this system may be available due to large or bulk purchasing.
(10) Expert and efficient staff is appointed in the purchase department thereby advantage of specialised knowledge and skill is available.

Disadvantages of Centralised Purchasing :

(1) It will lead to high initial cost because a separate purchase department is to be set up for purchases of materials.
(2) Centralised purchasing is not suitable for plants or branches located at different places which are far away from each other.

(3) Due to the bulk purchases, heavy capital is locked up in stores or materials.

(4) The branches can not enjoy the benefit of local purchases.

(5) There are chances of misunderstanding between the branch which requires the materials and the purchasing department. With the result that wrong purchases of materials may be made.

(6) The branches or department may not receive goods in time due to delay in purchases.

2) Decentralised Purchasing :

Under this system, the branch or department enjoys the freedom of purchases. Each branch or department is given authority to purchase required materials from local market. This system is more suitable, when the branches or plants are located at different places. In short, the purchases are made by branches or department instead of centralised purchasing.

The **advantages** of decentralised purchasing are as follows.

(1) Local branches make purchases as and when they require materials, hence delay in purchasing is avoided.

(2) This sytem is more flexible than centralised purchasing.

(3) Due to local purchasing, the cost of procurement of material is less, thus cost of production is reduced.

(4) It is more convenient for uncommon items which are specific to department or branches.

(5) Local suppliers extend liberal credit facility to branches or departments due to personal contacts.

Disadvantages of decentralised purchasing

The disadvantages of this system are as under.

(1) Local managers may not be specialised in purchasing, hence the department or unit may not get proper quality materials.

(2) The benefit of bulk purchasing is not available in dencentralised purchasing.

(3) Sometimes, the losses incurred may be more than saving effected due to this system.

(4) This system is inconvenient for big units having many branches at different places.

3:3 PURCHASE PROCEDURE.

The prime function of purchase department is to make purchases for various departments of the industry. While purchasing, the purchase manager has to consider the five basic qualities involved in purchase procedure, such as, purchase of right quality, purchase at right time, purchase of right quantity, purchase at right price and purchase from right sources. The purchase procedure starts with the initiation of purchase requisition and ends with the receipt of materials into stores and payment of bill for purchases. The purchase procedure varies from industry to industry depending upon the size, nature and conditions of industry. Generally, the following procedure is adopted by the purchase department, where purchases are centralised.

Steps in Purchase Procedure.

1) Receiving purchase requisition
2) Locating source of supply.
3) Selection of supplier.
4) Issue of enquiry letters and finalisation of quotations.
5) Placing and follow up of purchase order.
6) Receipt of materials.
7) Inspection and testing of materials.
8) Return of rejected materials.
9) Co-ordination with accounts department.
10) Passing invoices and payment of bills.

1) Receiving Purchase Requisition :

Generally, the materials are issued to production departments from the stores. When any production department requires specific material, an enquiry is made with the storekeeper. The storekeeper, after receiving the demand from production department, ensures whether the specific material is available in the stores or not. If the material is available, it is issued to the concerning production department. But if the material is not available in the stores, the storekeeper has to make the arrangement regarding the particular goods. The storekeeper prepares a request letter or indent for procuring the goods and sends it to the purchase department. This request form or indent is known as purchase requisition. Purchase requisition is a printed form to make formal request to purchase department for procuring the materials. In addition to storekeeper purchase requisition may be received from following authorised persons.

(a) The production department may directly send purchase requisition to purchase department for special materials.
(b) Plant engineer may send purchase requisition to purchase department for repairs and maintenance materials.
(c) Head of departments may send purchase requisition for special items such as cupboard, filing cabinet, office equipment etc. to purchase department.

Purposes : The purposes of purchase requisition are as under.

1) It initiates the purchase and sets the purchasing process in motion.
2) It provides date for reference e.g. date when materials are required.
3) It provides a written record of details like quantities, specifications etc. of materials to be purchased.

The purchase requisition contains the information like (i) serial number, (ii) name of the department initiating requisition, (iii) description of material required, (iv) date of delivery required, (v) date of issue, (vi) signature of responsible person etc.

The purchase requisition is generally prepared in triplicate in different shade of colours.

(1) The original copy is sent to purchasing department, (2) Second or duplicate copy is kept by storekeeper or the department which initiates the purchase requisition and (3) The third or triplicate copy is sent to the authorising executive.

2) Locating Sources of Materials :

Once the decision of purchases is taken, the purchase manager has to tap various sources of supply of materials. Generally, the important sources of supply of materials are as follows.

(1) Catalogues
(2) News papers and periodicals.
(3) Trade directories.
(4) Telephone directories.
(5) Quotations.
(6) Suppliers index files and past records.
(7) Market surveys
(8) Exhibitions and trade shows.

3) Selection of Supplier :

The purchase manager has to select the source of supply of materials, after the receipt of purchase requisition. The purchase manager usually maintains a list of suppliers for every group of materials which contain the names and addresses of suppliers. While selecting the supplier to whom order is to be given for purchase of materials, the purchase department should keep in mind the following factors. (i) Manufacturing capacities, (ii) Reliability of supplier, (iii) Financial condition of supplier, (iv) Price quoted, (v) Terms of payments, (vi) Terms of delivery, (vii) Quality of materials etc.

As a general rule the purchase manager should buy the best quality materials at the lowest possible price. The supplier from whom the material is to be purchased should be dependable and capable of supplying materials of uniform quality at right time and at reasonable price.

4) Issue of Enquiry Letters and Finalisation of Quotations :

After the selection of supplier, the purchase manager will take action for issue of enquiry letters and tender papers to various approved suppliers. The purchase manager receives quotations from the selected suppliers. Then all quotations for each material are to be tabulated and a comparative statement of quotations is to be prepared. This enables the purchase manager to know the lowest acceptable offer. Generally, lowest price quotation is accepted. But at the same time quality of material, reliability of the supplier and other terms and conditions of supplier should be given due consideration. Thus, the name of desirable supplier will be selected.

5) Placing and Follow up of Order :

After selecting the supplier, the purchase department prepares a purchase order for the supply of stores. The purchase order is a form used by purchase department authorising the supplier to supply the specified materials at a price and terms therein. It is a written contract between the buyer and supplier and binding on both the parties. The supplier is bound to supply materials according to the terms and conditions of purchase order and the purchaser is required to accept the delivery and make payment for materials as agreed upon. It authorises receiving department to receive the materials and to the accounts department to accept the bill from the supplier for payment.

The purchase order contains the following information.

1) Serial number of order
2) Name and address of supplier
3) Quantity and full description of goods.
4) Date of delivery.
5) The price per unit and total cost of the order.
6) Instructions for packing and dispatching.
7) Terms of payment.
8) Place of delivery.
9) Reference to purchase requisition.
10) Signature of responsible officer.

The number of copies of purchase orders to be prepared depends on the organisation of the concern and the routine adopted. In a large organisation five copies are prepared and each copy of purchase order is sent to following department.

(a) The supplier i.e. the seller.
(b) The receiving department.
(c) The person or department which initiates purchase requisition.
(d) The accounts department.
(e) The filing or purchase department for future reference.

It is very important to follow up purchase order so as to ensure timely delivery. Enquiries should be made at regular intervals of delivery dates agreed upon. If delivery date is expired, the supplier should be asked to indicate the date by which he would supply the materials. Extension of date for delivery should be exceptionally granted. In short, lack of follow up measures may cause delay in arrival of materials resulting in stoppage of production for the want of materials. Hence, for smooth running of factory, it is essential to follow up the purchase orders, which have been placed to suppliers.

6) Receipt of Materials :

In large concerns, a separate receipt and inspection department is established to receive and inspect the incoming materials. In a small concern, the receipt and inspection of material may be done by one person or goods receiving clerk. In large concern, a goods receiving department performs the functions of upkeeping the goods received and verifying their quantities and condition. The quantity received is checked against the purchase order and suppliers advice note which is generally received along with the materials. The goods receiving clerk is not expert in checking the quality of materials. He can just count weight or measure the quantity of material received and ensures that goods are received in safe condition. Shortage or breakage, if any, is intimated to the supplier. As soon as he receives the goods, he signs the note, which is called goods received note or material received note.

The material received note contains the following information.

(i) Serial number
(ii) Name and address of supplier.
(iii) Date of receipt of materials.
(iv) Description and quantity of goods.
(v) Suppliers advice note number
(vi) Order number, inspection report, bin no. etc.
(vii) Condition in which materials are received.
(viii) Mode of transportation.
(ix) Type of container.
(x) Signature of responsible person receiving the materials.

Goods or materials received note serves the following purposes.

(1) It informs the storekeeper or other requisitionist of the receipt of materials.
(2) It notifies the accounting department that the materials have been received and that the voucher can be prepared.
(3) When it includes columns of cost, it can serve as a source of entry in the store ledger.

Generally, six copies of goods received note are prepared and sent to various departments as follows.

(1) first copy is sent to supplier with remark whether the goods are received in perfect condition or not.
(2) Second copy is sent to purchase department, who placed a purchase order.
(3) Third copy is sent to store department who will make all the necessary entries in respect of receipt of materials in bin card and store ledger.
(4) The fourth copy is sent to accounts department, who will make the payment of goods received.
(5) The fifth copy is sent to the department who has initiated the purchases.
(6) Final or sixth copy is retained by goods receiving department for future reference.

7) Inspection and Testing of Materials :

In large manufacturing concern, there may be a separate inspection and testing department to test the quality of material purchased. The quality of material is checked by an engineer or chemist, where technical or laboratory inspection is necessary. He is to ensure that the quality is according to the purchase order. After checking the quality of material, an inspection report is prepared to show the results of inspection. The report is either prepared separately or incorporated in the goods received note by providing necessary coloums. In either case, the report is forwarded to the purchase department. On completion of inspection, the goods receiving clerk should enter details of materials received in stores or goods received note. In small factories or concerns inspection function is performed by receiving clerk or by the storekeeper.

Inspection report generally contains information like number and date of report, number and date of materials received note, purchase order number, name of supplier, details of goods accepted/rejected, signature of inspector and special remarks, if any etc. Inspection report is prepared in triplicate. The original copy is sent to the purchase department, second copy is sent to store or production department and the third copy is retained by inspection department for future reference.

8) Return of Rejected Materials :

When the material received is not in accordance with specification or is in damaged condition, it is returned to the supplier along with the debit note. The debit note informs the supplier that his account is debited with the value of material returned and the reasons for returned material are also stated in this note. The rejected materials may be returned to supplier or they may be held pending for the instructions of supplier. The debit note is prepared on the basis of inspection report, by the purchase department. Generally, three copies of debit note are prepared and they are sent to various departments as follows.

(a) Original copy is sent to supplier.
(b) Second copy is sent to accounts department for adjustment of entries and
(c) Third copy is retained by purchase department for filing purpose.

After receiving the debit note and material, the supplier accepts the claim and prepares a credit note. This credit note is sent to purchaser.

9) Co-ordination with Accounts Department :

Follow-up section in the purchase department should co-ordinate with the accounts department for the payment of suppliers invoices. Suppliers should be paid for the accepted quantities at the rates, terms and conditions specified in the purchase order. The deductions like freight, penalties, liquidated damages, wharfage and demurrage on account of suppliers fault etc, if any, are to be communicated to accounts department. This will help the accounts department to recover all these amount, before making payments.

10) Passing Invoices for Payment.

This is the last step in purchase procedure. Once the invoices are received by the purchase department, they are serially numbered and are entered in the invoice registered. The purchase department assembles the following documents in support of invoices. (a) Purchase order, (b) Goods received note, (c) Inspection report, (d) Debit or credit note etc. These documents are compared with the invoice and if there is no descrepancy, the purchase manager will sign it and send it to the accounts department for payment. All calculations are checked before a voucher authorising payment is prepared. Finally, payment of voucher is made by accounts department. Small amount of payment may be made by money order or postal orders. Huge amounts are generally remitted by crossed cheques or demand drafts. Thus, the supplier receives the payment of goods sent to purchaser.

Note : (Specimen of various forms used in purchase procedure are given in unit purchase documentation)

3.4 PURCHASE DOCUMENTATION.

Purchase procedure involves many documents. Each document is prepared by the respective department and copies of that document are given to concerned department. Each document is prepared with some specific objectives. Each document is written document, hence ambiguity, confusion and disputes are avoided. In purchase procedure, purchase requisition, quotation purchase order, Material received note, Material Inspection report, Debit Note, Invoices etc. are prepared. As these documents are related to the purchases, they are called as "Purchase Documents". These are as follows.

(1) Purchase Requisition
(2) Quotations
    (a) Tender (b) Quotation
(3) Schedule of Quotation or
    Comparative statement of quotation.
(4) Purchase order
(5) Goods / Material / Stores Received Note No.
(6) Inspection Report
(7) Debit Note
(8) Invoice

1) Purchase Requisition

A purchase requisition is a form used as formal request to the purchasing department to purchase material. Such requisitions are received from storekeeper or departmental heads or plant engineers or product planner by purchase department. A specimen form of purchase requisition is as under.

RELIANCE INDUSTRIES LTD.
Purchase Requisition
Regular / special

No................   Department.................................

Date................   To be delivered at......................

Date by which materials
are required................

Please order the items listed below.

Serial No	Description	Quantity Required	Code No	Purchase order No	Remarks

Requested by...   For use of purchase dept. only.

Checked by...   Purchase order No...

Approved by...   Date issued...

                                     Suppliers...

                                     Purchase officer/manager.

2) Quotation :

After receiving purchase requisition, the purchase department invites quotations from suppliers. For inviting quotations, the purchase department issues tender form to suppliers. The specimen of tender form and quotations are as follows.

RELIANCE INDUSTRIES LTD.
Tender Form

Indent No...   Tender No....................................

To...   Date ....

Dear sir,

Please let us have your best offer for the supply of following items. The items should be delivered F.O.R. Mumbai. The tender closes on January 15, 2009 at 1.00 P.M. and will be opened at 11.00 A.M. on the following day. The first copy of the tender should be despatched to us duly filled in

Serial No	Description the item	Quality	Quantity	Price	Terms of Delivery	Other terms terms
					Yours faithfully, XXXX Purchase officer (For Reliance Industries Ltd.)	

(b) Specimen of Quotation :

RELIANCE INDUSTRIES LTD.

Request For Quotation

This is not an Order...........

No....................................

Date ....

To,

Name of supplier.

Dear sir,

We are interested in purchasing the following materials. Please quote your terms and delivery date.

Serial No	Description	Quantity Grade	Quantity Required	Date of Delivery	Price	Remarks
				Yours faithfully, XXX Purchase manager (For Reliance Industries Ltd.)		

3) Schedule of Quotation

After the expiry of last date, the quotations are opened and a comparative statement of quotations received is prepared. In this statement, comparison in respect of price, terms of delivery, quality etc. is made with each other and a suitable source of supply is selected. This statement is also known as "Schedule of quotations." Its specimen is as under.

RELIANCE INDUSTRIES LTD.

Comparative statement of quotations.

Name of material.................

Date when material required...............

Serial No	Name of supplier	Description of materials	Quantity	Previous price Rs.	Quoted price Rs.	Terms of delivery	Time of deli-very	Remarks

Purchasing clerk

Purchase manger

4) Purchase Order

After choosing or selecting the name of supplier, the purchase manager prepares a purchase order for the supply of materials. Purchase order is a written contract between purchaser and supplier. A specimen form of purchase order is as under.

RELIANCE INDUSTRIES LTD.

Purchase Order

To.................   Order No......................

Name of supplier   Date.............................

Please supply the following materials subject to the terms and conditions given on the reverse side of this purchase order.

Serial No	Description	Quantity	Rate (Rs.)	Total cost (Rs.)	Remarks

Place of delivery........................
Date of delivery........................
Terms of payment........................
Packing and dispatch instructions........................
Discount allowed........................

Purchase officer/manager

5) Goods Received Note/Material Received Note.

As soon as the material is received, the goods receiving clerk enters particulars of goods received in material or goods or stores Received Note. The proforma of material received note is as under.

RELIANCE INDUSTRIES LTD.

Good Received Note

Supplier's Name...   No................................

Advice Note No...   Date.............................

                                                     Purchase order No..........

Serial No	Description	Code No	Quantity received	Advice Note/ Invoice Note	Amount Rs.	Inspection		Reason's for rejection
						Qty. passed	Qty. rejected	

Received by....................
Store ledger posted by....................   Inspected by....................
Costed by.......................   Storekeeper....................

6) Inspection Report :

In big concerns, the quality of goods received is checked by engineer or chemist. He is to ensure that the quality is according to purchase order. After checking the quality of material, the inspection department prepares inspection report and it is sent to stores and purchase department. The specimen of inspection report is as under.

RELIANCE INDUSTRIES LTD.						
Material Inspection Report.						

No...................
Date.................
Supplier's Name

Purchase order No......................
Goods Received Note No...........
Date..
Date of Receipt...........................

Serial No	Description of material	Code No	Quantity			Reasons for Rejections
			Received	Accepted	Rejected	

Special Remark...

Inspected by...
Date...

7) Debit Note :

When the materials received are not in accordance with the specification, these are returned to supplier. The debit note is prepared by the purchase department on the basis of inspection report and supplier is informed that his account is debited. The specimen of debit note is as follows.

RELIANCE INDUSTRIES LIMITED			
Debit Note			

No.......................
Date...................

To,
Name of supplier,

We are debiting your account with the value of under mentioned materials for the reason stated. Meanwhile we wait for your instructions.

Quantity	Description	Rate (Rs.)	Amount (Rs.)

Reason.......	Date of Receipt
Purchase order No...	Material Received Note No...
Supplier's Invoice No...	Signature...

8) Invoice :

The supplier prepares the invoice of goods supplied and sends it to the purchaser. It includes the particulars of material supplied to purchaser and amount receivable by supplier. the specimen of invoice is as under.

TAJ CO. LTD.

Invoice

To,
....
Customer
.....
Account No...

No................................
Date ....
Purchase Order No..........
Delivery Note No.............
Date of dispatch...............

Serial No.	Description of Materials	Code No	Quantity	Rate Rs.	Amount Rs.	Remarks

Terms of payment...
...

XXXX
Signature.

3:5 STOCK LEVELS :

The most important function of storekeeper is to receive and issue the goods to the production departments. While performing the functions, the storekeeper has to maintain various levels of stock. He has to regulate inflow and outflow of materials in such a way that neither production is adversely affected due to the want of materials nor there is unnecessary blocking of capital due to the overstocking of materials. In order to have a proper control on materials, the following levels are to be set by the management or storekeeper.

(1) Re-order level, (2) Minimum stock level, (3) Maximum stock level, (4) Average stock level, (5) Danger stock level.

(1) Reorder Level or Ordering Level

This is the level or point fixed between the maximum and minimum stock levels and at this time, it is essential to initiate purchase action for fresh supplies of materials. This level is fixed in such a way that the difference of quantity of materials between reordering level and minimum level will be sufficient to meet the requirements of production upto the time the fresh supply of the material is received. The following factors are taken into account while fixing the reorder level.

(a) Maximum consumption or usage of materials.
(b) The normal delivery time i.e. Maximum reorder period i.e. maximum lead time.
(c) Maximum stock level.
(d) Minimum stock level.
(e) Rate of consumption of material.
(f) Variations in delivery period i.e. emergencies like delay in supply, abnormal wastage etc.

Lead time : It is the time required to replenish the supply i.e. time required from order placed to the time to receive the materials or supplies.

Reorder level can be calculated by applying the following formula.

Reorder level = Maximum consumption or usage **x** Maximum reorder period

OR

Reorder level = Minimum stock level + Consumption during the lead time.

OR

Reorder level = Minimum stock + (Average usage **x** Average Re-order period)

Note : The choice of formula depends upon the information given in problem.

2) Minimum Stock Level or Safety Stock Level :

It is also known as safety stock or buffer stock. It is that level below which stock should not normally be allowed to fall. If stocks go below this level, there is a danger of stoppage of production due to the shortage of materials. In case the stock falls below this level, the purchase manager has to give topmost priority to acquire fresh or new supplies. In short, minimum stock level represents the minimum quantity of the materials which must be maintained in hand at all times. In fixing this level following factors are to be considered.

(a) Lead time i.e. normal delivery time
(b) Reordering level.
(c) Average rate of consumption of materials.
(d) Nature of materials.

(e) Stock-out cost.

(f) Source of supply.

Minimum stock level is calculated by the following formula.

Minimum stock = Re-ordering level - (Normal consumption
       level   x Normal re-order period.)

Normal consumption = Average Usage

Normal reorder period = Average delivery period or lead time.

OR

Minimum stock = Minimum rate – Average rate x Lead time
      level   of consumption   of consumption

3) Maximum Stock Level :

The maximum stock level is that quantity above which stocks should not normally be allowed to exceed. It is the upper limit of quantity which can be held in stock at any time. The quantity is fixed so that there may be no overstocking. Overstocking means unnecessarily blocking of working capital, hence it should be avoided as far as possible. While fixing the maximum stock level, following factors are to be taken into account.

1) Rate of consumption of material
2) Amount of capital available for maintaining stores.
3) Storage space available, cost of storage and insurance.
4) Lead time i.e. normal delivery time
5) Reorder level.
6) Risk of obsolescence and deterioration
7) Re-order quantity i.e. Economic order quantity.
8) Seasonal consideration.
9) Government or local authority restrictions.
10) Price fluctuations.

Maximum stock level is computed by the following formula.

$$\text{Maximum Stock Level} = \text{Reoder Level} + \text{Reoder quantity} - \left(\text{Minimum Consumption} \times \text{Minimum Reorder period} \right)$$

OR

$$\text{Maximum stock level} = \text{Re-order level} - \text{Consumption during the time required to get supplies at minimum rate} + \text{Economic order size/quantity}$$

4) Average Stock Level :

An average stock level takes into account the average of maximum stock level and minimum stock level. It is calculated as under.

$$\text{Average Stock Level} = \frac{\text{Maximum stock Level} + \text{Minimum Stock Level}}{2}$$

OR

Average stock level = Minimum stock level + 1/2 Re-order quantity

5) Danger Stock Level :

This is the level below the minimum stock level. When the stock reaches this level, immediate action is needed for replenishment of stock. As the normal delivery time is not available, regular purchase procedure cannot be followed. Hence, this level is useful for taking corrective action only. If it is fixed below the reorder level and above minimum level, it will be possible to take preventive action. In short, danger stock level indicates the danger and immediate action for purchasing of material at higher purchasing cost is necessary. It is calculated as under.

Danger Stock Level = Minimum Consumption × Minimum reorder period

OR

Danger Stock Level = Average Consumption × Maximum reorder period for emergency purchases.

3:6 RE-ORDER QUANTITY (ECONOMIC ORDER QUANTITY I.E. EOQ)

It is very important to note that only the correct quantity of materials is to be purchased. For this purpose, the factors such as maximum level, minimum level, re-order level, danger level, quantity reserved, availability of funds, quantity of discount, interest on capital, consumption and availability of storage etc. are to be kept in view. Overstocking and understocking is to be avoided. All these problems can be settled and solved by re-order quantity.

Re-order quantity is the quantity for which order is placed when stock reaches re-order level. By fixing this quantity the purchaser need not recalculate the quantity to be purchased each time he orders for materials. Economic order quantity is the quantity of materials purchased, where the cost of order to be placed is the minimum. Generally, when the carrying costs and ordering costs are equal, the cost of materials to be purchased is equal and this situation or point is called economic order quantity. The concepts of carrying cost and order cost are explained as under.

(i) Carrying Cost :

It is the cost of holding the materials in store and it includes:

(1) Cost of operating the stores (salaries, rent, stationery etc.)
(2) Cost of storage space which could have been utilised for some other purpose.
(3) Interest on capital locked up in store.
(4) Deterioration, spoilage, wastages, losses, obsolescence of material.
(5) Transportation cost in relation to stock.
(6) Cost of bins and racks that have been provided for storage of materials.
(7) Insurance cost.
(8) Clerical cost
(9) Any other cost for storing materials etc.

2) Ordering Cost :

Ordering cost is the cost of placing order for the purchase of materials. It mainly includes the cost of stationery, salaries of those engaged in receiving and inspection, salaries of those engaged in placing order, cost of postage and telephone, preparation of purchase order, cost of rejecting defective goods etc.

From the above information, we can say that economic order quantity (EOQ) is the quantity fixed at the point, where the total cost of ordering and the cost of carrying the inventory will be the minimum. If the quantity of purchases is increased, the cost of ordering decreases, while the cost of carrying increases. If the quantity of purchases is decreased, the cost of ordering increases, and the cost of carrying decreases. But in case of economic order quantity, the total of both costs should be kept at the minimum.

Methods of determination of EOQ.

Generally, following methods are used for the determination of economic order quantity.
1) Tabular method.
2) Formula method.

1) Tabular Method :

Under this method, economic order quantity is determined with the help of tables. Hence, it is called tabular method. Such tables are prepared to show the various costs for different ordering quantities thus, enabling to find out the most economic size of quantity to be ordered. When the ordering and carrying costs are equal, that lot is treated as economic order quantity. This is explained with the help of following illustration.

Annual consumption - 12,000 units.
Cost of ordering - Rs. 30. per order.
Cost of material - Rs. 2.50 per unit.
Carrying cost - 10% of average inventory.
The following table is prepared to determine the economic order quantity.

No of Orders Per year	Units per order (Rs.)	Value per order (Rs.) (Units per order × Rate)	Ordering cost (Rs.) (No. of order × Rate per order)	Carrying cost (Rs.) 10% value per order	Total cost (Rs.) (Ordering cost + Carrying cost)
1	12000÷1 = 12000	12000 × 2.5 = 30000	1 × 30 = 30	10% of 30000 = 3000	30 + 3000 = 3030
2	12000÷2 = 6000	6000 × 2.5 = 15000	2 × 30 = 60	10% of 15000 = 1500	60 + 1500 = 1560
3	12000÷3 = 4000	4000 × 2.5 = 10000	3 × 30 = 90	10% of 10000 = 1000	90 + 1000 = 1090
4	12000÷4 = 3000	3000 × 2.5 = 7500	4 × 30 = 120	10% of 7500 = 750	120 + 750 = 870
5	12000÷5 = 2400	2400 × 2.5 = 6000	5 × 30 = 150	10% of 6000 = 600	150 + 600 = 750
6	12000÷6 = 2000	2000 × 2.5 = 5000	6 × 30 = 180	10% of 5000 = 500	180 + 500 = 680
7	12000÷7 = 1714	1714 × 2.5 = 4284	7 × 30 = 210	10% of 4284 = 428	210 + 428 = 638
8	12000÷8 = 1500	1500 × 2.5 = 3750	8 × 30 = 240	10% of 3750 = 375	240 + 375 = 615
9	12000÷9 = 1333	1333 × 2.5 = 3334	9 × 30 = 270	10% of 3334 = 333	270 + 333 = 603
10	**12000÷10 = 1200**	**1200 × 2.5 = 3000**	**10 × 30 = 300**	**10% of 3000 = 300**	**300 + 300 = 600**
11	12000÷11 = 1091	1091 × 2.5 = 2728	11 × 30 = 330	10% of 2728 = 273	330 + 273 = 603
12	12000÷12 = 1000	1000 × 2.5 = 2500	12 × 30 = 360	10% of 2500 = 250	360 + 250 = 610
13	12000÷13 = 923	923 × 2.5 = 2308	13 × 30 = 390	10% of 2308 = 231	390 + 231 = 621
14	12000÷14 = 857	857 × 2.5 = 2142	14 × 30 = 420	10% of 2142 = 214	420 + 214 = 634
15	12000÷15 = 800	800 × 2.5 = 2000	15 × 30 = 450	10% of 2000 = 200	450 + 200 = 650

The above table shows that 1200 units is the ideal size of the order because total cost at this level is the least (i.e. Rs. 600) of all. This means the number of orders per year should be 10. Other quantities (i.e. more than or less than 1200 units) are not so economical because total cost is more than that of this level. Further for 1200 units the ordering cost and carrying cost is Rs. 300 and total cost is Rs. 600, which is the minimum. Hence, economic order quantity is 1200 units.

2) Formula Method :

In addition to tabular method, economic order quantity can be determined with the help of a mathematical formula. The formula is as under.

$$EOQ = \sqrt{\frac{2.A.B}{C.S}} \text{ or } \sqrt{\frac{2 \times A \times B}{C \times S}} \text{ or } \sqrt{\frac{2.A.O}{C}}$$

Where : EOQ = Economic Order Quantity
A = Annual consumption in units.
B = Buying or ordering cost per order.
C = Cost per unit
S = Storage or carrying cost as a percentage of average inventory.

Alternatively, $EOQ = \sqrt{\dfrac{2.A.B}{S}}$

Where S = Storage cost per unit per annum.
Calculation of No of orders to be placed in a year.

$$\text{No of orders} = \frac{\text{Annual Consumption}}{\text{Economic Order Quautity}}$$

Problems on Stock Levels and EOQ

Problem No.1

From the following information, find out the economic order quantity.

Annual consumption or usage	6000 units
Cost of material per unit	Rs. 20
Cost of placing and receiving one order	Rs. 60
Carrying cost per unit 10% of inventory value.	

Solution :

$$EOQ = \sqrt{\frac{2 \times A \times B}{C \times S}}$$

$$= \sqrt{\dfrac{2 \times 6000 \times 60}{20 \times \dfrac{10}{100}}} = \sqrt{\dfrac{7,20,000}{2}}$$

$$= \sqrt{3,60,000}$$

$$= \textbf{600 units.}$$

It is also possible to express EOQ in rupee value rather than in units. For this purpose the following formula is used.

$$EOQ = \sqrt{\dfrac{2.A.B.}{S}} \quad \text{or} \quad \sqrt{\dfrac{2 \times A \times B}{S}}$$

Where A = Annual consumption in rupees i.e. Units X Cost per unit.
B = Buying or Ordering cost per unit.
S = Storage or carrying cost. (in %)

Assuming the figures in above illustration EOQ in rupees will be computed as follows.

Annual consumption in Rs. = Units X Cost per unit
= 6000 X 20 = Rs. 1,20,000

$$EOQ = \sqrt{\dfrac{2 \times 1,20,000 \times 60}{10\% \text{ or } \dfrac{10}{100}}} = \sqrt{\dfrac{2 \times 1,20,000 \times 60 \times 100}{10}}$$

$$= \sqrt{14,40,00,000}$$

$$= \textbf{Rs. 12,000}$$

or 600 units (i.e. Rs. 12000)

Problem No.2

Calculate the maximum stock level, minimum stock level and reorder level from the following data.

1) Reorder quantity   -   1500 units
2) Re-order period   -   4 to 6 units
3) Maximum consumption -   400 units
4) Normal consumption   -   300 units
5) Minimum consumption   -   250 units

Solution :

1) Reorder level = Maximum consumption x Maximum Re-order period.
= 400 units x 6 weeks
= **2400 units**

2) **Maximum level** = Reorder level + Reorder quantity –

$\qquad$ (Minimum consumption - Minimum reorder period)

$\qquad$ = 2400 units + 1500 units - (250 units x 4 weeks)

$\qquad$ = 3900 units – 1000 units

$\qquad$ **= 2900 units**

3) **Minimum stock level** = Re-order level –

$\qquad$ (Normal consumption x Normal Re-order period)

$\qquad$ = 2400 units – (300 units x 5 week)

$\qquad$ = 2400 units – 1500 units

$\qquad$ **= 900 units**

Problem No.3

Calculate minimum stock level.

(1) Economic order quantity - 600 units

(2) Maximum stock level allowed for emergencies - 5 weeks

(3) Average lead time - 4 Weeks

(4) Average consumption per week - 500 units

(5) Minimum consumption in 4 weeks - 1600 units.

Solution :-

In this problem, neither re-order level nor maximum consumption and maximum re-order period are given, hence the following formula will be used to calculate minimum stock level.

Minimum stock level $\qquad$ = Average consumption x Minimum stock level to be allowed

$\qquad$ for emergencies.

$\qquad$ = 500 units x 5 weeks

$\qquad$ = 2500 units.

Problem No.4

In a manufacturing unit, material is used as follows.

Maximum consumption	-	12000 units per week.
Minimum consumption	-	4000 units per week.
Normal consumption	-	8000 units per week.
Re-order quantity	-	48000 units.

Time required for delivery - Minimum 4 weeks, Maximum 6 weeks.

Calculate (a) Re-order level, (b) Minimum level, (c) Maximum level, (d) Danger level and (e) Average stock level.

Solution :

Time required for delivery :

Minimum 4 weeks, Maximum 6 weeks.

So average will be 5 weeks. i.e. $\left(\dfrac{4+6}{2}\right)$

(a) **Re-order level** = Maximum consumption x Maximum Re-order period.

= 12000 units x 6 weeks

= **72000 units.**

(b) **Minimum stock level** = Re-order level - (Average consumption x Average re-order period)

= 72000 units - (8000 units x 5 weeks)

= 72000 units - 40000 units

= **32000 units.**

(c) **Maximum stock level** = Re-order level + Re-order quantity

− (Minimum consumption − Minimum re-order period)

= 72000 units + 48000 units - (4000 units x 4 weeks)

= 1,20,000 units - 16000 units

= **1,04,000 units.**

(d) **Danger stock level** = Minimum consumption x Minimum Re-order period

= 4000 units x 4 weeks

= **16000 units.**

(e) **Average stock level** $= \dfrac{\text{Maximum level} + \text{Minimum Level}}{2}$

$= \dfrac{1,04,000 \text{ units} + 32000 \text{ units}}{2}$

$= \dfrac{1,36,000}{2} = $ **68000 units.**

Problem No.5

Compute the minimum and maximum stock level from :

Minimum consumption	-	200 units per day
Maximum consumption	-	300 units per day.
Normal consumption	-	240 units per day
Re-order period	-	10-15 days
Re-order quantity	-	1500 units.
Normal re-order period- 12 days		

Solution

Re-order level is not given in the problem but we require re-order level to calculate minimum and maximum level, hence it is to be calculated first as under.

Time required for delivery :

a) Re-order level = Maximum consumption x Maximum Re-order period.

= 300 units x 15 days

= 4500 units.

b) Minimum level = Re-order level - (Normal consumption x

Normal re-order period)

= 4500 units - (240 units x 12.5 days)

= 4500 units - 3000 units

= 1500 units.

Normal or Average re-order period $= \dfrac{10+15}{2} = = 12.5$ days.

(c) Maximum level = Re-order level + Re-order quantity −

(Minimum consumption x Minimum re-order period)

= 4500 units + 1500 units - (200 units x 10 days)

= 6000 units − 2000 units

= 4000 units.

Problem No.6

M/s L.G limited a manufacturer of T.V's., gives the following information in respect of two components namely A and B in the manufacturing process.

Normal Usage   - 200 units per week each

Maximum Usage   - 300 units per week each

Minimum Usage   - 100 units per week each

Re-order Quantity   A - 1600 units

                           B - 2400 units

Re-order Period   A - 2 to 4 weeks

                           B - 1 to 2 weeks.

Calculate for each component -

(a) Re-order level, (b) Maximum stock level, (c) Minimum stock level and (d) Average stock level.

Solution.

             Component A   Component B

a) **Re - order Level** = Maximum Consumption × Maximum reorder period

= 300 units x 4 weeks   = 300 units x 2 weeks

= 1200 units.   **= 600 units**

	Component A	Component B

b) $\underset{\text{Stock Level}}{\textbf{Minimum}} = \underset{\text{Level}}{\text{Re order}} - \left(\underset{\text{Consumption}}{\text{Normal}} \times \underset{\text{delivery periold}}{\text{Normal}} \right)$

$= 1200 \text{ units} - (200 \times \dfrac{2+4}{2})$ $= 600 \text{ units} - (200 \times \dfrac{1+2}{2})$

$= 1200 \text{ units} - 600 \text{ units}$ $= 600 \text{ units} - 300 \text{ units}$

= 600 units.   **= 300 units.**

(c) $\underset{\text{Stock Level}}{\textbf{Maximum}} = \underset{\text{Level}}{\text{Re order}} + \underset{\text{quantity}}{\text{Re order}} \left(\underset{\text{Usage}}{\text{Minimum} \times} \underset{\text{delivery periold}}{\text{Minimum}} \right)$

$= 1200 \text{ units} + 1600 \text{ units} -$ $= 600 \text{ units} + 2400 \text{ units}$

$(100 \text{ units} \times 2 \text{ weeks})$ $- (100 \text{ units} \times 1 \text{ weeks})$

$= 2800 \text{ units} - 200 \text{ units}$ $= 3000 \text{ units} - 100 \text{ units}$

= 2600 units.   **= 2900 units**

(d) $\underset{\text{Stock Level}}{\textbf{Average}} = \dfrac{\text{Maximum stock level} + \text{Minimum stock level}}{2}$

$= \dfrac{2600 \text{ units} + 600 \text{ units}}{2}$ $= \dfrac{2900 \text{ units} + 300 \text{ units}}{2}$

$= \dfrac{3200}{2}$ $= \dfrac{3200}{2}$

= 1600 units.   **= 1600 units**

Problem No.7

From the following figures, calculate the Economic Order Quantity and number or orders to be placed in a year.

Annual demand or consumption of materials	4000 kgs.
Cost of buying per order	Rs. 5
Cost per unit	Rs. 2 per kg.

Storage and carrying cost 8% of the average inventory.

Solution :

$$EOQ = \sqrt{\dfrac{2 \times A \times B}{C \times S}}$$

$$= \sqrt{\dfrac{2 \times 4000 \times 5}{2 \times \dfrac{8}{100}}} = \sqrt{\dfrac{40000 \times 100}{16}}$$

$$= \sqrt{\dfrac{40,00,000}{16}}$$

$$= \sqrt{2,50,000}$$

$$\textbf{= 500 units}$$

Where :

EOQ = Economic Order Quantity

A = Annual consumption.

B = ordering cost.

C = Cost per unit

S = Storing cost per unit per year.

No. of orders to be placed in a year

$$\textbf{No. of orders} = \dfrac{\text{Annual consumption}}{\text{Economic order quantity}}$$

$$= \dfrac{4000}{500}$$

= 8 orders in a year.

Problem No.8

A factory requires 20,000 kgs of certain materials for the year. Cost of 1 kg of material is calculated to be Rs. 20 per year and it is estimated that expenses of placing an order and receiving would amount to Rs. 500.

Calculate EOQ and number of orders to be placed each year.

Solution :

$$\textbf{EOQ} = \sqrt{\dfrac{2 \times A \times B}{S}} \, ,$$

Where,

A = Annual consumption.

B = Buying cost per order.

S = Storing cost per unit.

$$= \sqrt{\dfrac{2 \times 20,000 \times 500}{20}}$$

$$= \sqrt{\frac{2,00,00,000}{20}}$$

= **1000 kgs.**

No. of orders to be placed in each year.

$$\textbf{No. of orders} = \frac{\text{Total Consumption}}{\text{EOQ}}$$

$$= \frac{20,000}{1,000}$$

= **20 orders per year.**

Problem No.9

A manufacturer buys certain equipments from outside suppliers at Rs. 30 per unit. The total annual needs are 1600 units. The following further data are available.

Annual return on investment 10%

Rent, Insurance, tax per unit per year Re. 1.

Cost of placing an order Rs. 50.

Determine the Economic Order Quantity.

Solution :

$$\textbf{EOQ} = \sqrt{\frac{2 \times A \times B}{S}}$$

Where,

EOQ = Economic order quantity

A = Annual requirement i.e. consumption

B = Buying cost per unit.

S = Inventory carrying cost per year per unit.

$$= \sqrt{\frac{2 \times 1600 \times Rs. 50}{4}}$$

$$= \sqrt{\frac{1,60,000}{4}}$$

$$= \sqrt{40,000}$$

= **200 units.**

Working note :-

Carrying and storing cost is calculated as under

10% of Rs. 30 per unit i.e.	= Rs. 3
Add. Rent, insurance, tax etc. per unit	= Re. 1
Total carrying cost per year	= Rs. 4

Problem No.10

The daily demand for an electric component is 25 units. Every time an order is placed, a fixed cost of Rs. 25 is incurred. The daily holding cost per item of inventory is 40 paise. If lead time is 16 days, determine the EOQ and reorder point.

Solution :

1) $$\textbf{EOQ} = \sqrt{\frac{2 \times A \times B}{C \times S}}$$

Where,

EOQ = Economic order quantity

A = Annual requirement i.e. consumption

B = Buying cost per unit.

S = Inventory carrying cost per year per unit.

$$= \sqrt{\frac{2 \times 9125 \text{units} \times \text{Rs.} 25}{0.40 \times 365}}$$

$$= \sqrt{\frac{4,56,250}{146}}$$

= 56 units.

Working notes :-

Annual consumption - 25 units **x** 365 day = 9125 units.

Storing cost per unit per year = 0.40 **x** 365 days = Rs. 146.

2) Re-order point :

Re-order point : i.e. Re-order level

$$\textbf{Reorder Level} = \text{Maximum Consumption} \times \text{Maximum Lead time}$$

$$= 25 \text{ units } \textbf{x } 16$$

= 400 units.

Note : The daily demand i.e. 25 units are considered as maximum consumption per day.

Problem No.11

From the details given below, calculate,

(i) Re-order level   (iii) Minimum level

(ii) Maximum level   (iv) Danger level.

(v) Average stock level and   vi) Re-order Quantity.

Cost of placing a purchase order is Rs. 20

Purchase price per unit inclusive of transportation cost is Rs. 50.

Number of units purchased during the year is 5000.

Annual cost of storage per unit is Rs. 5.

Details of lead time : Average 10 days, Maximum 15 days, Minimum 6 days, For emergency purchases 4 days.

Rate of consumption : Average 15 units per day

Maximum 20 units per day.

Solution :

1) $$\text{Economic order quantity Or Reorder quantity} = \sqrt{\frac{2 \times A \times B}{S}}$$

Where, A = Annual consumption,

B = Buying cost per order,

S = Storing cost per unit per year.

$$= \sqrt{\frac{2 \times 5000 \text{ units} \times Rs.20}{5}}$$

$$= \sqrt{40,000}$$

= 200 units.

2) **Reorder Level** = Maximum Consumption × Maximum Reorder period

= 20 units **×** 15 days

= 300 units.

3) **Maximum Stock Level** = $\text{Re order Level} + \text{Re order quantity} \left(\text{Minimum consumption} \times \text{Minimum reorder periold} \right)$

Note : Minimum consumption is calculated as under.

$$\text{Average Consumption} = \frac{\text{Manimum Consumption} + \text{Maximum consumption}}{2}$$

$$15 \text{ units} = \frac{\text{Minimum consumption} + 20 \text{units}}{2}$$

30 units = Minimum consumption + 20 units

30 units - 20 units = Minimum consumption

10 units = Minimum consumption

i.e. Minimum consumption = **10 units.**

4) Maximum Stock Level $= 300\text{units} + 200\text{units} - (10\text{units} \times 6 \text{ days})$

$$= 500 \text{ units - 60 units}$$
$$= \textbf{440 units.}$$

5) Minimum Stock Level $= \text{Re order Level} - \left(\begin{array}{cc} \text{Average} & \times & \text{Average} \\ \text{Consumption} & \text{reorder period} \end{array} \right)$

$$= 300 \text{ units - } (15 \text{ units} \times 10 \text{ days})$$
$$= 300 \text{ units - 150 units}$$
$$= \textbf{150 units.}$$

6) Average Stock Level $= \dfrac{\text{Maximum Consumption} + \text{Minimum consumption}}{2}$

$$= \frac{440 \text{ units} + 150 \text{ units}}{2}$$

$$= \frac{590}{2}$$

$$= \textbf{295 units.}$$

7) Danger Level $= \begin{array}{cc} \text{Average} & \times & \text{Re order Period in} \\ \text{Consumption} & & \text{emergency Conditions} \end{array}$

$$= 15 \text{ units} \times 4 \text{ days}$$
$$= \textbf{60 units.}$$

Problem No.12

In manufacturing its products, a company uses three raw materials A, B and C as follows.

Raw materials	Usage per unit	Re-order quantity	Price kg (Rs.)	Delivery in weeks.	Order level	Minimum level
A	10	10,000	10	1 to 2	8,000	-
B	4	5,000	30	3 to 5	4750	-
C	6	10,000	15	2 to 4	-	2000

Weekly production varies from 175 to 225 units, averaging 200. What would you expect the quantities of the following to be?

   (i) Minimum stock of A   (ii) Maximum stock of B

   (iii) Average stock of A and   (iv) Re-order level of C.

Solution :

(a) **Minimum Stock of A** $= \text{Re order Level} - \left(\begin{array}{cc} \text{Normal} & \times \text{ Normal Reorder} \\ \text{usage} & \text{period} \end{array} \right)$

$$= 8000 \text{ kgs - (2000 kgs. } \times 1.5 \text{ week)}$$
$$= 8000 \text{ kgs - 3000 kgs} = \textbf{5000 kgs.}$$

Note : -
1) Normal Usage or production $= 200 \text{ units} \times 10 = 2000 \text{ units.}$

2) Normal delivery period $= \dfrac{1+2}{2} = 1.5 \text{ week.}$

b) **Maximum Stock of B** $= \begin{array}{cc} \text{Re order} + \text{Re order} \\ \text{Level} \quad\quad \text{quantity} \end{array} \left(\begin{array}{cc} \text{Minimum} \times & \text{Minimum} \\ \text{usage} & \text{reorder periold} \end{array} \right)$

$$= 4750 \text{ kgs + 5000 kgs - (700 kgs } \times 3 \text{ weeks)}$$
$$= 9750 \text{ kgs - 2100 kgs} = \textbf{7650 kgs.}$$

Note :- Minimum production per week $= 175 \text{ units} \times 4 \text{ kgs.} = 700 \text{ kgs.}$

c) **Average stock of A** $= \text{Minimum level} + 1/2 \text{ Re-order quantity}$

$$= 4000 \text{ kgs.} + \frac{1}{2} \times 10000 \text{ kgs.}$$
$$= 4000 \text{ kgs.} + 5000 \text{ kgs.}$$
$$= \textbf{9000 kgs.}$$

Note : Maximum stock of A is not given, hence above formula for calculation of average stock is used.

Alternatively, average stock of A can be calculated as under.

$\begin{array}{c} \text{Maximum} \\ \text{Stock Of A} \end{array} = \begin{array}{cc} \text{Re order} + \text{Re order} \\ \text{Level} \quad\quad \text{quantity} \end{array} \left(\begin{array}{cc} \text{Minimum} \times & \text{Minimum} \\ \text{consumption} & \text{reorder periold} \end{array} \right)$

$$= 8000 \text{ kgs + 10000 - (175 kgs } \times 10 \times 1 \text{ kg)}$$
$$= 18000 \text{kgs - 1750 kgs}$$
$$= 16250 \text{ kgs.}$$

Now,

$$\text{Average stock level} = \frac{\text{Minimum Stock + Maximum Stock}}{2}$$

$$= \frac{5000 \text{kgs} + 16250 \text{kgs}}{2}$$

$$= \textbf{10650 kgs.}$$

(d) **Reorder Level of 'C'** $=$ Maximum consumption x Maximum reorder period

$\qquad$ $= 1350$ kgs x 4 weeks $= 5400$ kgs.

$\qquad$ $= $ **5400 kgs**

Note : Maximum consumption $= 225$ units x 6 kgs $= 1350$ kgs.

Problem No.13

Bajaj Electrical Ltd Badalapur provides the following cost data in relation to a component.

Maximum stock level $\qquad$ 8,400 units

Budgeted consumption per month :

(i) Maximum : 1500 units

(ii) Minimum : 800 units

$\quad$ Estimated delivery period :

(i) Maximum 4 months

(ii) Minimum 2 months.

You are required to calculate

(i) Re-order level and (ii) Re-order quantity.

Solution :

a) **Re-order Level** $=$ Maximum Consumption $\times$ Maximum delivery period

$\qquad$ $= 1500$ units x 4 months

$\qquad$ $= $ **6000 units**

b) Re-order quantity

In order to calculate re-order quantity we have to have the formula of maximum stock level and by substituting the figures we will get reorder quantity.

c) **Maximum Stock Level** $=$ Re order Level $+$ Re order quantity $\left(\dfrac{\text{Minimum}}{\text{consumption}} \times \dfrac{\text{Minimum}}{\text{Delivery period}} \right)$

Assuming Re-order quantity as 'x'. the value can be substituted as :

8400 units= 6000 units + 'x' - (800 units x 2 months)

8400 units= 6000 + 'x' - 1600

$\qquad$ x $= 8400 + 1600 - 6000$

$\qquad$ x $= 10000$ units - 6000 units

$\qquad$ $= $ **4000 units.**

Problem No.14

The following information is available in respect of a material used by XYZ Ltd Mumbai.

Ordering quantity	900 units
Normal Consumption	25 units per week
Maximum consumption	35 units per week
Minimum consumption	15 units per week

Delivery period :

Maximum	30 weeks
Normal	25 weeks
Minimum	20 weeks

Calculate ordering level, minimum level and maximum level.

Solution

a) **Reorder Level** = Maximum Consumption × Maximum delivery period

= 35 units x 30 weeks.

= 1050 units.

b) **Minimum Stock Level** = Re order Level − (Average Consumption × Averagel delivery periold)

= 1050 units - 25 units x 25 weeks

= 1050 units - 625 units

= 425 units.

c) **Maximum Stock Level** = Re order Level + Re order quantity (Minimum consumption × Minimum Delivery periold)

= 1050 units + 900 units - (15 units x 20 weeks)

= 1050 units + 900 units - 300 units

= 1950 units – 300 units

= 1650 units.

Problem No.15

From the following particulars of Product M. Calculate
1) Re-order level 2) Maximum level 3) Minimum level

Usage per week :

Maximum	1600 units
Normal	1200 units
Minimum	800 units

Delivery period :

Maximum   4 weeks
Minimum   2 weeks
Normal   3 weeks
Re-order quantity 800 units.

Solution :

a) Re-order level : Maximum Usage x Maximum Delivery Period

           = 1,600 x 4
           = 6,400 units.

b) Maximum level :

Re-order level - (Minimum Usage x Minimum Delivery Period) + Re-order Quantity

           = 6,400 - (800 x 2) + 800
           = 7,200 - 1,600
           = 5,600 units.

c) Minimum level :

Re-order level - (Normal Usage x Normal Delivery Period)

           = 6,400 - (1,200 x 3)
           = 6,400 - 3,600
           = 2,800 units.

Problem No.16

Two Components A & B are used in Mahindra Industries as follows:

Normal Usage   150 Units per week each
Minimum Usage   75 Units per week each
Maximum Usage   225 Units per week each
Re-order Quantity   A - 900 units
                          B - 1500 units
Re-order Period   A - 4 to 6 weeks
                          B - 2 to 4 weeks

Calculate for each component :

1) Re-order level
2) Minimum level
3) Maximum level
4) Average stock level

Solution :

Particulars	A	B
a) Re-order Level Maximum Usage x Maxi Re-order Period	225 x 6 1,350 units	225 x 4 900 units
b) Minimum Level Average Usage x Average Level time	1,350-(150x5) 1,350 - 750 600 units	900-(150x3) 900 - 450 450 units
c) Maximum Level ROL + ROQ - (Mini Consumption x Mini Delivery Period) d) Average Stock Level	1,350-(75x4) + 900 1,950 units	900-(75x2) +1,500 2,250 units
$\dfrac{\text{Mini.level + Maxi level}}{2}$	$\dfrac{600 + 1,950}{2}$ = 1275 units **OR**	$\dfrac{450 + 2,250}{2}$ = 1350 units **OR**
	$\text{Mini.level} + \dfrac{1}{2} \text{ ROQ}$	
	$600 + \dfrac{900}{2}$ 1050 units	$450 + \dfrac{1,500}{2}$ 1200 units

Problem No.17

P.Ltd uses two types of materials A & B for production of 'X', the final product. The relevant monthly data for the components are as given below :

Particulars	A	B
Normal Usage (in units)	200	150
Minimum Usage (in units)	100	100
Normal Usage (in units)	300	250
Re-order Quantity (in units)	750	900
Re-order Period (in Months)	2 to 3	3 to 4

Calculate for each component :
a) Re-order Level
b) Minimum Level
c) Maximum Level
d) Average Stock Level

Solution :

Stock Levels

Particulars		A Units B Units
1) Re-order Level	300 x 3 = 900	250 x 4 = 1000
2) Minimum Level	900 - (200 x 2.5) = 400	1000 - (150 x 3.5) = 475
3) Maximum Level	900 - (100 x 2) + 750 = 1450	1000 - (100 x 3) + 900 = 1600
4) Avg.Stock Level	$\dfrac{400 + 1,450}{2}$ = 925 **OR** $400 + \dfrac{750}{2}$ = 775	$\dfrac{400 + 1,600}{2}$ = 1038 **OR** $475 + \dfrac{900}{2}$ = 925

Problem No.18

The following information is available in respect of a material used by XYZ Ltd.

Ordering Quantity (EOQ)	- 900 units
Normal consumption	- 25 units per week
Maximum consumption	- 35 units per week
Minimum consumption	- 15 units per week
Delivery Period -	
Minimum	- 20 weeks
Normal	- 25 weeks
Maximum	- 30 weeks

Calculate :

i) Maximum stock level   ii) Minimum stock level

iii) Re-order stock level

Solution :

a) Re-order level : Maximum Usage x Maximum Delivery Period

$$= 35 \times 30$$
$$= 1050 \text{ units.}$$

b) Maximum level :

Re-order level - (Minimum Usage x Minimum Delivery Period) + Re-order Quantity

$$= 1050 - (15 \times 20) + 900$$
$$= 1050 - (300) + 900$$
$$= 1650 \text{ units.}$$

c) Minimum level :

Re-order level - (Normal Usage x Normal Delivery Period)

$\qquad$ = 1050 - (25 x 25)

$\qquad$ = 1050 - 625

$\qquad$ = 425 units.

Problem No.19

From the following information calculate the Maximum Stock Level, Minimum Stock Level, Re-order Level and Average Stock Level.

Normal consumption	- 300 units per day
Maximum consumption	- 420 units per day
Minimum consumption	- 240 units per day
Re-order quantity	- 3600 units per day
Re-order period	- 10 to 15 days
Normal re-order period	- 12 days

Solution :

a) Re-order level : Maximum Usage x Maximum Delivery Period

$\qquad$ = 420 x 15

$\qquad$ = 6300 units.

b) Maximum level :

Re-order level - (Minimum Usage x Minimum Delivery Period) + Re-order Quantity

$\qquad$ = 6300 - (240 x 10) + 3600

$\qquad$ = 6300 - 2400 + 3600

$\qquad$ = 7500 units.

c) Minimum level :

Re-order level - (Normal Usage x Normal Delivery Period)

$\qquad$ = 6300 - (300 x 12)

$\qquad$ = 6300 - 3600

$\qquad$ = 2700 units.

d) Average Stock level :

$$= \frac{\text{Mini.level} + \text{Maxi level}}{2}$$

$$= \frac{7500 + 2700}{2}$$

= 5100 units

OR

$$= \text{Min.level} + \frac{1}{2} \text{ EOQ}$$

$$= 2700 + \frac{1}{2}(3600)$$
$$= 4500 \text{ units}$$

Problem No.20

Calculate the minimum stock level, maximum stock level and re-order level from the following information :

Normal consumption	- 120 units per day
Maximum consumption	- 150 units per day
Minimum consumption	- 100 units per day
Re-order period	- 10-15 days
Re-order quantity	- 1500 units
Normal re-order period	- 12 days

Solution :

1) Re-order level : Maximum Usage x Maximum Delivery Period

$$= 150 \times 15$$
$$= 2250 \text{ units.}$$

2) Maximum level :

Re-order level - (Minimum Usage x Minimum Delivery Period) + Re-order Quantity

$$= 2250 - (100 \times 10) + 1500$$
$$= 2250 - 1000 + 1500$$
$$= 2750 \text{ units.}$$

3) Minimum level :

Re-order level - (Normal Usage x Normal Delivery Period)

$$= 2250 - (120 \times 12)$$
$$= 2250 - 1440$$
$$= 810 \text{ units.}$$

Problem No.21

Calculate the minimum stock level, maximum stock level and re-order level from the following information :

Normal consumption	- 300 units per week
Maximum consumption	- 400 units per week
Minimum consumption	- 250 units per week
Re-order period	- 4 to 6 weeks
Re-order quantity	- 1500 units

Solution :

1) Re-order level : Maximum Usage x Maximum Delivery Period

$$= 400 \times 6$$
$$= 2400 \text{ units.}$$

2) Maximum level :

Re-order level - (Minimum Usage x Minimum Delivery Period) + Re-order Quantity

$$= 2400 - (250 \times 4) + 1500$$
$$= 2400 - 1000 + 1500$$
$$= 2900 \text{ units.}$$

3) Minimum level :

Re-order level - (Normal Usage x Normal Delivery Period)

$$= 2400 - (300 \times 5)$$
$$= 2400 - 1500$$
$$= 900 \text{ units}$$

Problem No.22

Calculate :

    1) Re-order Level   2) Minimum Level

    3) Maximum Level   4) Average Level from the following
       information

Lead Times :

Average 10 days

Maximum 15 days

Minimum 6 days

Rate of Consumption :

Average - 15 units per day

Maximum - 20 units per day

Minimum - 10 units per day

Solution :

1) Re-order level : Maximum Usage x Maximum Delivery Period

$$= 20 \times 15$$
$$= 300 \text{ units.}$$

2) Minimum level :

Re-order level - (Normal Usage x Normal Delivery period)

$$= 300 - (15 \times 10)$$
$$= 150 \text{ units.}$$

3) Maximum level :

Re-order level - (Minimum Usage x Minimum Delivery Period) + Re-order Quantity

$$= 300 - (10 \times 6) + EOQ$$
$$= 240 + \text{Re-order Quantity}$$

4) Average Stock level :

$$= \frac{\text{Mini.level} + \text{Maxi level}}{2}$$

$$= \frac{150 + (240 + \text{EOQ})}{2}$$

Note : In this problem Re-order Quantity is not given, hence Maximum Level and Average Level can't be calculated.

Problem No.23

Ganesh Enterprises manufactures a special product CAG.

The following particulars are collected for the year 2009 :

1) Monthly demand for product - 1000 units

2) Cost of placing an order - Rs.100/-

3) Annual carrying cost per unit - Rs.15/-

4) Normal usage 50 units per week

5) Minimum usage 25 units per week

6) Maximum usage 75 units per week

7) Re-order period 4 to 6 weeks.

Compute from the above -

1) Re-order quantity   2) Re-order level

3) Minimum level   4) Maximum level

5) Average stock

Solution :

1)Re-order Quantity : $\sqrt{\dfrac{2.A.O}{C}}$

where A = annual consumption, O = ordering cost per order,

C = carrying cost per unit per year

$$\text{EOQ} = \sqrt{\frac{2 \times 12{,}000 \times 100}{15}}$$

= 400 units

2)Re-order Level : Maximum Lead time x Maximum usage

= 6 x 75

= 450 units

3)Minimum Level : Re-order level - (Normal usage - Normal lead time)

= 450 - (50 x 5)

= 450 - 250

= 200 units

4)Maximum Level : ROL + ROQ - (Minimum usage x Minimum lead time)

= 450 + 400 - (25 x 4)

= 850 - 100
= 750 units

5) Average Stock Level : $\dfrac{\text{Mini.level} + \text{Maxi level}}{2}$

$$= \dfrac{200 + 750}{2}$$

$$= \dfrac{950}{2}$$

= 475 units

OR

$$= \text{Min.level} + \dfrac{1}{2}\,\text{EOQ}$$

$$= 2700 + \dfrac{1}{2}\,(400)$$

= 200 + 200

= 400 units.

Problem No.24

You have been asked to calculate the following levels for part no.486 from the information given there under :

    1) Re-order Level   2) Minimum Level   3) Maximum Level
    4) Danger Level   5) Average Level

The ordering quantity is to be calculated from the following data-

1) The total cost of purchasing relating to the order Rs.20/-.
2) No.of units to be purchased during the year Rs.5000.
3) Purchase price per unit including transportation costs Rs.50/-
4) Annual cost of storage of one unit Rs.5.

Lead Times :

Average 10 days
Maximum 15 days
Minimum 6 days

Rate of Consumption :

Average - 15 units per day
Maximum - 20 units per day

Solution :

        1) Calculation of Safety Stock = (Maximum usage x Maximum lead time) -
                                        (Normal usage x Normal lead time)

$$= (20 \text{ units} \times 15 \text{ days}) - (15 \text{ units} \times 10 \text{ units})$$
$$= 300 \text{ units} - 150 \text{ units}$$
$$= 150 \text{ units.}$$

2) Calculation of EOQ $= \sqrt{\dfrac{2.A.O}{C}}$

where,

A = Annual consumption

O = Ordering cost per order

C = Carrying cost per unit per annum.

$$\text{EOQ} = \sqrt{\dfrac{2 \times 5,000 \times 20}{5}}$$

$$= \sqrt{\dfrac{2,00,000}{5}}$$

$$= 200 \text{ units}$$

3) Re-order Level : Safety stock + (Normal usage × Normal lead time)
$$= 150 \text{ units} + (15 \times 10)$$
$$= 150 + 150 \text{ units}$$
$$= 300 \text{ units}$$

3) Maximum Level : Safety stock + EOQ
$$= 150 + 200$$
$$= 350 \text{ units}$$

4) Minimum Level : It is equal to safety stock.
$$= 150 \text{ units}$$

5) Danger Level : Normal Usage × Lead time for emergency purchases
$$= 15 \text{ units} \times 4 \text{ days}$$
$$= 60 \text{ units}$$

6) Average Stock Level : $\dfrac{\text{Safety stock} + \text{Maximum level}}{2}$

$$= \dfrac{150 \text{ units} + 350 \text{ units}}{2}$$

$$= 250 \text{ units}$$

Special Problems on EOQ (Economic Order Quantity)

Economic Order Quantity =

$$\sqrt{\frac{2 \times \text{Annual Usage} \times \text{Buying Cost Per Order}}{\text{Carrying Cost}}}$$

Problem No.1.

a) From the following particulars of Product X.

Calculate : 1) Re-order level   2) Maximum leve   3) Minimum level.

Usage per week :

Maximum	1600 units
Normal	1200 units
Minimum	800 units

Delivery Period :

Maximum	4 weeks
Normal	2 weeks
Minimum	3 weeks

Re-order quantity 800 units.

b) Calculate economic order quantity from the following :

1. Quantity 60,000 units
2. Ordering cost Rs.1200/- per order
3. Carrying cost 20%
4. Price per unit Rs.2000/-.

Solution :

1) $$\frac{\textbf{Economic order quantity}}{\textbf{Or Reorder quantity}} = \sqrt{\frac{2 \times A \times B}{S}}$$

$$= \sqrt{\frac{2 \times 60,000 \times 1,200}{2000 \times \frac{20}{100}}}$$

$$= \sqrt{1,20,000 \times 3}$$

$$= 600 \text{ units}$$

Problem No.2.

From the following particulars calculate the Economic Order Quantity (EOQ)

(1) Annual Requirement = 1600 units

(2) Cost of placing and receiving one purchase order = Rs.50

(3) Cost of Material per unit Rs.40

(4) Annual Carrying Cost of Inventory = 10% of Inventory value

Calculate : 1) Re-order level   2) Maximum level

Solution :

1) $$\text{Economic order quantity Or Reorder quantity} = \sqrt{\dfrac{2 \times A \times B}{S}}$$

$$= \sqrt{\dfrac{2 \times 1{,}600 \times 50}{40 \times \dfrac{10}{100}}}$$

$$= \sqrt{\dfrac{3{,}200 \times 50}{4}}$$

$$= \sqrt{800 \times 50}$$

$$= \sqrt{40{,}000}$$

$$= 200 \text{ units}$$

Problem No.3.

A factory required 20,000 kgs. of a certain material for the year. Cost of carrying one Kg. of material is calculated to be Rs.20 per annum and it is estimated that expenses of placing an order and receiving would amount to Rs.500.

Calculate : Economic Order Quantity

Solution :

1) $$\text{Economic order quantity Or Reorder quantity} = \sqrt{\dfrac{2 \times A \times B}{S}}$$

$$= \sqrt{\dfrac{2 \times 20{,}000 \times 500}{20}}$$

$$= \sqrt{10{,}00{,}000}$$

$$= 1000 \text{ units}$$

Problem No.4.

A manufacturer buys certain equipments from outside suppliers at Rs.30 per unit. Total annual needs are 1600 units. The following further data are available.

Annual return on investment - 10%, Rent, insurance, tax per year Re.1, Cost of placing an order - Rs.50.

Calculate : Economic Order Quantity

Solution :

1) $\begin{array}{c}\textbf{Economic order quantity}\\\textbf{Or Reorder quantity}\end{array} = \sqrt{\dfrac{2 \times A \times B}{S}}$

$$= \sqrt{\dfrac{2 \times 1,600 \times 50}{1}}$$

$$= \sqrt{3,200 \times 50}$$

$$= \sqrt{1,60,000}$$

$$= 400 \text{ units.}$$

Note : The figures of rate per unit, annual return on investment are not to be taken into account for calculation of EOQ.

Problem No.5.

Calculate Economic Order Quantity from the following information. Also state the number of order to be placed in a year.

Consumption of Material per annuam 10,000 kg. order placing cost per order Rs.50, storage costs 8% on average inventory, cost per kg. of raw materials Rs.2/-.

Solution :

1) $\begin{array}{c}\textbf{Economic order quantity}\\\textbf{Or Reorder quantity}\end{array} = \sqrt{\dfrac{2 \times A \times B}{S}}$

$$= \sqrt{\dfrac{2 \times 10,000 \times 50}{2 \times \dfrac{8}{100}}}$$

$$= \sqrt{\dfrac{20,000 \times 50}{0.16}}$$

$$= 2500 \text{ units.}$$

Problem No.6.

Determine the EOQ from the following particulars :

Annual consumption is 675 units.

Cost of Material is Rs.30 per unit
Cost of placing an order Rs.18
Annual carrying cost of one unit 10% of inventory value.

Solution :

1) $\begin{array}{c}\textbf{Economic order quantity}\\ \textbf{Or Reorder quantity}\end{array} = \sqrt{\dfrac{2\times A\times B}{S}}$

$$= \sqrt{\dfrac{2 \times 675 \times 18}{30 \ \times \dfrac{10}{100}}}$$

$$= \sqrt{8,100}$$

$$= 90 \text{ units.}$$

Problem No.7.

Find out Economic Order Quantity from the following Annual Consumption of 2000 units :

Inventory Carrying Cost - 15 %
Cost per order - Rs.15
Cost per unit - Rs.1.00

Solution :

1) $\begin{array}{c}\textbf{Economic order quantity}\\ \textbf{Or Reorder quantity}\end{array} = \sqrt{\dfrac{2\times A\times B}{S}}$

$$= \sqrt{\dfrac{2 \times 2,000 \times 15}{1 \ \times \dfrac{15}{100}}}$$

$$= \sqrt{\dfrac{60,000}{0.15}}$$

$$= \sqrt{4,00,000}$$

$$= 632 \text{ units.}$$

Problem No.8.

Find out Economic Order Quantity from the following information:

Annual Usage   : 6000 units

Cost of material per unit   : Rs.20
Cost of placing and receiving one order : Rs.60
Annual carrying cost of one unit   : 10% of inventory value

Solution :

1) $$\text{Economic order quantity Or Reorder quantity} = \sqrt{\frac{2 \times A \times B}{S}}$$

$$= \sqrt{\frac{2 \times 6{,}000 \times 60}{20 \times \frac{10}{100}}}$$

$$= \sqrt{\frac{12{,}000 \times 60}{2}}$$

$$= \sqrt{12{,}000 \times 30}$$

$$= \sqrt{3{,}60{,}000}$$

$$= 600 \text{ units}$$

Problem No.9.

M/s Raskar Brothers, Pune supplies you the following information-
Annual consumption - 15000 kg.
Cost of placing an order - Rs.48
Cost of Raw materials Rs.2 per kg
Storage Cost is 8% of Average Inventory
You are required to asceratain Economic Order Quantity.

Solution :

1) $$\text{Economic order quantity Or Reorder quantity} = \sqrt{\frac{2 \times A \times B}{S}}$$

$$= \sqrt{\frac{2 \times 15{,}000 \times 48}{2 \times \frac{8}{100}}}$$

$$= \sqrt{\frac{14{,}40{,}000}{0.16}}$$

$$= \sqrt{90{,}00{,}000}$$

$$= 3000 \text{ units.}$$

Problem No.10.

Sachin motors purchase 9000 motor spare parts for its annual requirements, ordering one month usage at a time. Each spare part cost Rs.20/-. The ordering cost per order is Rs.15/- and the carrying charges are 15% of the average inventory per year. You have been asked to suggest a more economical purchasing policy for the company. What advice would you offer and how much would it save the company per year?

Solution :

Present Policy :

1) No. of orders :
$$= \frac{\text{Annual Requirement}}{\text{Order size}}$$
$$= \frac{9000}{750}$$
$$= 12$$

Order size per month
$$= \frac{9000}{12 \text{ months}}$$
$$= 750$$

No. of orders $= 12$

2) Order Cost : $= 12 \times 15 = 180$............(1)

3) Carrying Cost :
$$= \frac{\text{Order sixe}}{2} \times \text{cost price} \times \text{carrying cost in \%}$$

$$= \frac{750}{2} \times 15\% \text{ o fRs.20/-}$$
$$= 375 \times 3 = 1125$$.............(2)

Total Cost
$$= (1) + (2)$$
$$= 180 + 1125$$
$$= 1305$$

Proposed Policy

To purchase in Economic Order Quantity -

1) $\begin{matrix}\textbf{Economic order quantity}\\ \textbf{Or Reorder quantity}\end{matrix} = \sqrt{\dfrac{2 \times A \times B}{S}}$

$$= \sqrt{\frac{2 \times 9{,}000 \times 15}{15\% \text{ of } 20}}$$
$$= 300 \text{ units.}$$

Now the revised total cost will be -

1) No.of orders $= \dfrac{9000}{300}$

$= 30$

2) Ordering cost $= 30 \times 15 = 450.........(4)$

3) Carrying cost $= \dfrac{300}{2} \times 15\%$ o fRs.20/-

$= 150 \times 3 = 450.............(5)$

Total Cost $= (4) + (5)$ i.e. $= 450 + 450$

$= 900/-.$

Thus, purchases in Economic Order Quantity will result into the yearly saying of Rs.405 (i.e.Rs.1305-Rs.900)

Problem No.11.

Xerox Ltd. has been buying a given item in lots of 2400 units in a 12 months supply. The cost per unit is Rs.12. Ordering cost is Rs.8 per order and carrying cost is 25%. You are required to calculate Economic Order Quantity.

A = Annual consumption - 2400 units

B = Ordering Cost = Rs.8 per order

Cs = Carrying Cost = 25% i.e.12 x 25% = Rs.3

(P.U. April, 2006)

Solution :

1) **Economic order quantity Or Reorder quantity** $= \sqrt{\dfrac{2 \times A \times B}{S}}$

$= \sqrt{\dfrac{2 \times 2400 \times 8}{3}}$

$= \sqrt{12,800}$

$= 113.13$ i.e.113 units

Problem No.12.

TATA Electricals Ltd. Pimpri provides the following cost data in relation to a component :

Maximum stock level : 8,400 units

Budgeted consumption per month :

i) Maximum : 1500 units

ii) Minimum : 800 units

Estimated delivery period :
i) Maximum : 4 months
ii) Minimum : 2 months

Reorder Stock level = 6000 units
Calculage Reorder Quantity.

(P.U. April, 2007)

Solution :

1) Reorder Quantity =

Maximum Stock Level - Reordering Level - (Minimum Consumption x Minimum Reorder Period or Delivery Period)

Given,

Maximum Stock Level	= 8400 units/month
Reorder Stock Level	= 6000 units/ month
Minimum Consumption	= 800 units/month
Minimum Delivery Period	= 2 months
Reorder Quantiy	= 8400 - 6000 + (800 x 2)
	= 8400 - 6000 + 1600
	= 2400 + 1600
	= 4000 units.

Problem No.13.

You are supplied with the following information from the books of a concern :

Particulars	Material-x	Material-y
	Rs.	Rs.
Opening stock	7,000	10,000
Purchases	1,15,000	1,68,000
Closing stock	5,000	12,000

Calculate the material turnover ratio of the above materials and state which of the two materials is more fast moving.

(P. U. April, 2007)

Solution :

1) Calculation of Cost of Materials consumed

= Opening Stock + Purchases - Closing Stock

Material X = 7000 + 115000 - 5000 = Rs.1,17,000

Material Y = 10000 + 168000 - 12000 = Rs.1,66,000

2) Calculation of Cost of Average Stock (3 Marks)

$$= \text{Average Stock} = \frac{\text{Opening Stock} + \text{Closing Stock}}{2}$$

$$\text{Material X} = \frac{7000 + 5000}{2}$$
$$= \text{Rs.}6000$$
$$\text{Material Y} = \frac{10000 + 12000}{2}$$
$$= \text{Rs.}11000$$

3) Calculation of Inventory Turnover Ratio =
$$\frac{\text{Cost of Material Consumed}}{\text{Cost of Average Stock}}$$
$$\text{Material X} = \frac{1,17,000}{6,000}$$
$$= 19.5 \text{ times}$$
$$\text{Material Y} = \frac{1,66,000}{11,000}$$
$$= 15.09 \text{ times}$$

Comment - Material X is Fast Moving material.

3:7 EXERCISES

1) **Indicate whether each of the following statements are true or false.**

(a) Purchase requisition is sent by purchase department.
(b) All raw materials are assumed as direct materials.
(c) Tender form is issued by the purchasing department.
(d) Purchase order is prepared by departments which require materials.
(e) Original copy of purchase order is retained by purchasing department.
(f) Purchase control is exercised by the storekeeper.
(g) Goods received note is prepared by the goods receiving clerk.
(h) Purchase order is a written contract between purchaser and seller.
(i) A bill of materials is prepared by a production department.

Answers :- a - false, b - true, c - true, d - false, e - false, f - false, g - true, h - true., i- true

2) **Fill in the blanks.**

(a) Purchase requisition note is sent to............
(b) Goods received note is prepared by...........
(c) Material control starts with control over.........
(d) Oil and grease is treated as..........
(e) Purchase budget is prepared by..........

(f) When all purchases are made by one or single purchase department it is called as..........

(g) Debit note is prepared by..........

(h) Wage Sheet is prepared by the .... department.

Answers : a - Purchase department, b - goods receiving department, c - Purchases, d - Indirect material, e - purchase department, f - centralised purchases, g - purchase department., h- payroll

3) Short answers questions :

(1) Give the essentials of material control.

(2) Explain the need of material control.

(3) Give the classification of materials.

(4) What is purchase order? Draw a specimen of purchase order.

(5) What is material inspection report?

(6) What is goods received note?

(7) What are various types of purchases?

(8) What is purchase requisition? Give the specimen.

(9) Give the list of functions of purchase department.

(10) What are the objects of purchase department?

4) Give the specimens of the following.

(1) Purchase requisition, (2) Quotation,

(3) Purchase order, (4) Material received note,

(5) Inspection report, (6) Debit note,

(7) Invoice.

Essay type questions

1) What is the prime object of material control. state the essentials of material control.

2) State the functions of purchase department in a factory.

3) Explain in detail the purchase procedure.

4) What are the objectives of scientific purchasing. State the functions of purchase department.

5) What is centralised and decentralised purchasing? State the advantages and disadvantages of both.

6) What are the items which are included in purchase cost of materials?

7) Describe briefly the purchase documents which are used in an organisation while purchasing of materials.

Exercises on stock levels and EOQ.

(a) Fill in the blanks.

(1) Store ledger is maintained by the...........
(2) The level between maximum level and minimum level is called..........
(3) The level of materials which must be maintained in hand at all times is called...........
(4) When stock exceeds maximum stock level it is called........
(5) Maximum consumption x Maximum lead time........
(6) The point where carrying costs and ordering costs are equal, is called..........
(7) The quantity of material to be ordered at one time is known as..........

Answers. 1 - Cost accounting department, 2 - Re-order level, 3 - Minimum level, 4 - Overstocking, 5 - Re-order level, 6 & 7 - Economic order quantity.

(b) Short answer type question.

1) What are the different levels of material control?
2) What is re-order level?
3) What is economic order quantity?
4) What is ordering cost?
5) What are included under carrying cost?
6) What is maximum stock level?
7) What is danger level?
8) What is minimum stock level?

Practical problems.

1) **Calculate the maximum level, Minimum level and Reorder level from the following data.**
   Re-order quantity = 3000 units
   Re-order period = 8 to 12 weeks
   Maximum consumption = 800 units per week.
   Minimum consumption = 500 units per week.
   Normal consumption = 400 units per week.

Ans : Maximum level 3800 units, Minimum level 800 units, Ordering level 4800 units.

2) **From the following particulars of product 'K', calculate**
   (1) Re-order level, (2) Maximum level, (3) Minimum level.
   Usage per week.
   Maximum   1600 units
   Normal   1200 units
   Minimum   800 units
   Delivery period

Maximum	4 weeks
Normal	3 weeks
Minimum	2 weeks
Re-order quantity	800 units.

Ans : Re-order level 6400 units, Maximum level 5600 units, Minimum level 2800 units.

3) **P. Limited uses two types of materials x & y for production Z, the final product. The relevant monthly data for the components are given below.**

	x	y
Normal usage (in units)	200	150
Minimum usage (in units)	100	100
Maximum usage (in units)	300	250
Re-order quantity (in units)	750	900
Re-order period (in months)	2 to 3	3 to 4

Calculate for each component

(1) Reorder level, (2) Minimum level, (3) Maximum level, (4) Average stock level.

Answers :	x (units)	y (units)
Reorder level	900	1000
Minimum level	400	475
Maximum level	1450	1600
Average stock level	925	1037.5

4) **Find out minimum level, maximum level and Re-order level from the following particulars**

(a) Maximum consumption = 175 units per day

(b) Minimum consumption = 100 units per day.

(c) Normal consumption = 125 units per day

(d) Re-order quantity = 1500 units

(e) Maximum period for receiving goods = 15 days

(f) Minimum period for receiving goods = 7 days

(g) Normal period for receiving goods = 10 days.

Answers : Re-order level 2625 units, Minimum level 1375 units, Maximum level 3425 units.

5) **From the following particulars, calculate**

(1) Re-order level, (2) Minimum stock level, (3) Maximum level.

Normal usage	- 100 units per day
Minimum usage	- 60 units per day
Maximum usage	- 130 units per day
Economic order quantity	- 5000 units

Re-order period   - 25 to 30 days.

Answers : Re-order level 3900 units, Minimum level 1150 units, Maximum level 7400 units.

6) A company uses 10000 units per year of an item costing Rs. 5 each. The cost of processing a purchase order is Rs. 100 and the stock holding cost amounts to 20% per year of the money value of inventory. Calculate economic order quantity.

Answer : EOQ = 4470 units

7) **Find out EOQ from the following information.**

Annual demand	: 20000 units.
cost per article	: Re. 1
Inventory carrying cost	: 15%
Cost per order	: 15

Answer : EOQ 2000 units

8) **From the following information calculate, (a) Economic order quantity, (b) No of orders to be placed in a quarter of one year.**

(i) Quarterly consumption of material : 2000kgs.
(ii) Cost of placing one order   Rs. 50
(iii) Cost per unit   Rs. 40
(iv) Storage and carrying cost   8% on average inventory.

Answer : (a) 500 units,   (b) 4 orders.

9) **Calculate EOQ from the following.**

(a) Consumption during the year = 600 units
(b) Ordering cost Rs. 12 per order
(c) Carrying cost 20%
(d) Price per unit Rs. 20

Answer : 60 units.

10) **M/s Sandhu Brothers, Dhulia supplies you the following information.**

Annual consumption	: 15000 units
Cost of placing an order	: Rs. 48
Cost of raw materials	: Rs. 2 per kg.

Storage cost is 8% of average inventory.
Calculate EOQ.

Answer : EOQ = 3000 units

11) Calculate Economic order quantity and No. of order to be placed in a year.

1) Quantity 60,000 units.
2) Ordering cost Rs. 1200 per order.
3) Carrying cost 20%
4) Price per unit Rs. 2000.

Answers : EOQ 600 units, No of orders to be placed 100.

12) M/s Tube Limited are the manufacturers of picture tubes for T.V. The following are the details of their operation during 2009.

Average monthly market demand	2000 tubes
Ordering cost	Rs. 100 per order.
Inventory carrying cost	20% per annum.
Cost of tube	Rs. 500 per tube.
Compute Economic order quantity.	

Answers : EOQ = 63 tubes (Approx)

CHAPTER 4

MATERIAL ACCOUNTING

4:1 STORE LOCATION AND LAYOUT

Storekeeping is the function of receiving materials, storing them and issuing these to departments or workshops. As a substantial amount of company's working capital is invested in stores, storekeeping acquires special importance, so location and layout of stores also requires a special attention.

4:1:1 Location of Stores :

Location of stores has a direct impact on the cost of production. So the location of stores should be carefully planned. It should be located in such a way that it will reduce cost in terms of money, labour and time. It should be convenient to all departments. As far as possible, it should be near to receiving department or production department. At the same time, it should be nearer to rail or road transport. This will save the cost of production in terms of money, labour and time. Further, it is very important that bulky and heavy stores should be stored nearest to department requiring them to minimise the labour and transportation charges. Planned location of stores also reduces the material handling charges.

4:1:2 Layout of Stores :

The layout of stores department needs careful consideration. It depends upon the factors like type of industry, nature of materials, size of factory and policy of management. The building of the stores should be properly constructed. It should avoid loss due to damage, pilferage, leakage, evaporation etc.

The stores should be divided into different sections. Each section should have sufficient racks and each rack should be further divided into small spaces which are generally known as 'Bins'. A bin means a box or cupboard or even a small room where materials are stored. Heavy and bulky material is stored in a room, which is also known as a Bin. All bins are serially numbered and have attached bin-cards. On each bin-card entries regarding receipt and issue of materials are recorded. If some materials are costly, it must be kept under lock and key under the possession of a storekeeper. Special attention must be paid to storage of materials which are liable to leakage or evaporation, or deterioration due to atmospheric conditions. In short, the layout of the store should be designed in such a way that, material is well stored and supplied to departments with minimum handling cost.

4:2 TYPES OF STORES ORGANISATION

There are three main types of stores
1) Centralised Stores
2) Decentralised Stores
3) Central Stores with Sub-stores

1) Centralised Stores

The usual practice in most of the concerns is to have a central store. In centralised stores, all materials are stored or kept in one centralised store room and the materials are received and issued from the same room or store. Sometimes, materials are stored in different rooms but they are under the control of one storekeeper. This is also called as centralised purchasing.

Advantages of Centralised Stores.
(1) Better control can be exercised over the stores, because all materials are stored in one department.
(2) Specialised and expert staff can be concentrated in one department.

(3) Clerical costs are reduced because of centralisation of stores records.

(4) Better layout of stores is possible.

(5) Stocks may be checked with greater care and less botheration.

(6) Investment in stocks is minimised.

(7) Bulk buying is facilitated as purchase requisitions are made out by the concerns as a unit and not on departmental basis.

(8) Uniformity in issue procedures and recording stores.

(9) Better safety and security of stock.

(10) Wastages, obsolescencs, and pilferages are minimised.

Disadvantages of Centralised Stores.

(1) Transportation costs are increased, particularly when departments requiring materials are located at a considerable distance from central stores. Further, breakdown in transport may stop production in departments.

(2) More working capital may be locked up in storing various items of materials.

(3) Delay and inconvenience may be caused to departments, which are situated at distance from centralised stores, in drawing materials from central stores.

(4) Loss by fire, flood, earth-quake may be more if materials are stored in one place.

(5) Cost of handling may be increased.

2) Decentralised Stores :

In a large factory, where there are many departments, decentralised stores are more convenient. Under this system independent stores are situated in various departments. An independent storekeeper is appointed in each stores for handling the materials. The departments requiring materials can draw it from the respective stores situated in their departments.

Advantages of Decentralised Stores.

(1) The production department gets materials as and when it is required.

(2) Personal contacts with storekeeper may be developed and thereby delay in issue of material is avoided.

(3) De-centralised storekeeping avoids delay in purchasing and thereby production departments get materials in time.

Disadvantages of Decentralised Stores.

(1) More working capital is required.

(2) Management and administrative expenses are increased due to different stores.

3) Centralised stores with sub-stores.

In a large factory various departments are established and they are far away from the central stores. In order to facilitate the production departments, sub-stores are situated near production departments under the control of central stores. For each item of material, a quantity is determined and this is kept in stock in sub-stores at the beginning of any period. At the end of the period the storekeeper of each sub-stores will requisition from central stores the quantity of material consumed to bring the stock upto the pre-determined quantity. In short, this type of stores operates in similar way to petty cash system, so this system of stores is also known as the imprests system of stores control.

This type of stores combines the advantages of centralised and decentralised stores. This system saves the transpiration and handling charges. It facilitates every day management in quick issues and eliminates maintenance and administrative cost. Delay in issue of materials is avoided. Similarly, burden on central stores is also reduced.

4:3 CLASSIFICATION AND CODIFICATION

Systematic classification and codification of various items of stores is essential for good system of storekeeping. Classification and codification are two different terms. Classification relates to the grouping of materials according to their nature in suitable categories. Sometimes, materials are classified on the basis of their usage. For example, copper, iron, aluminium may be classified as metals, items like soap, cotton wastage, lubricating oil etc. may be classified as consumable stores, all forms of tools including jigs and fixtures may be classified as tools etc. Thus, materials may be classified as consumable materials, spare parts, tools, construction materials, metals etc.

After the classification of materials, materials are assigned some codes for their identification. This is known as coding. Very often names and descriptions of materials are long and vague. In order to avoid length and ambiguity in description and names of materials, a symbol may be assigned to each item of material which is known as code. Thus, codification is the procedure of systematic assignment of symbols for each item of store. Such codes may be either numeric, alphabetic or combination of numerical and alphabetical symbols. Such codes are secret and short names of materials. Codification avoids duplication of materials or stores. It helps for easy location of materials in stores. It helps not only for purchases but also for issue of materials.

Basic Principles of Coding.

While assigning codes, the following principles should be kept in mind.
(1) **Brief :** Code should be brief because longer codes take longer time to write and are prone to error.
(2) **Elastic :** The code should be such that more materials can be added easily and logically.
(3) **Exclusive :** Each code number should relate to only one type of material and there should be no duplication.
(4) **Certain :** The code must identify the material without any ambiguity.
(5) **Mnemonic :** As far as possible, codes should be easier to remember, such as, HCW for Hard Copper Wire.

Procedure for Classification and Codification.

First of all, materials are grouped under various categories such as metals, lubricants, fuel, steel items, spare parts etc. It may be classified further into sub-groups. For example metal may be sub-grouped as ferrous materials and non-ferrous materials. These may further be categorised as indigenous and imported.

Methods of Codification :

There are three methods of Codification.

(1) Alphabetical, (2) Numerical, (3) Alpha-numerical.

(1) Alphabetical :

In this method, alphabets or letters or words are given to each material. As the Alphabets represent the first sound of description of material, it becomes easy to remember codes. This system is also known as Mnemonic. For example.

Brass Screws	- B.S.
Stainless steel Wire	- S.S.W.
Cast Iron Sheet	- C.I.S.
Mild Copper Bar	- M.C.B.

2) Numerical and Decimal :

Under this method, Number is alloted to each item of material. Whole number may indicate the main group and decimals may indicate sub-groups of material like primary, secondary or other group. For example, in a foundry the following codes may be used.

Steel	- 21
Copper	- 31
Aluminium	- 41

Further sub-groups or physical characteristics can be indicated in the code of decimals. This is shown below for copper of which numerical code as shown above is 31.

Copper Bars	31.1
Copper Tubes	31.2
Copper Sheets	31.3
Copper Wire	31.4

This numerical method allows a wide range and is therefore most suited where the number of items is very large.

3) Alpha-numerical or Alphabetic cum Numerical Method.

This method is the combination of alphabetical and numerical method. In this method, numbers are also used along with alphabet. For example :

BS24 for Brass Strips of 1/4" thickness.

MCB16 for Mild Copper Bar of 6" length.

Advantages of Classification and Codification.

(1) The biggest advantage of codification is the distinctive code given to each item of stores and the avoidance of duplication due to multiple names, which results in reduction of number of item of stores carried.

(2) Classification and Codification both help in material control.

(3) Clerical effort is reduced as length in description is minimised.

(4) Secrecy of materials used in production is maintained.

(5) A coding system helps in the maintenance of mechanised accounting.

(6) Ambiguity in description is avoided as a particular code can refer to only one type of item.

(7) It facilitates the identification of various items of stores resulting into prompt issue of stores.

Duties of a Storekeeper.

The incharge of stores department is called store-keeper or store-controller or store superintendent. He is a prime or main officer in the stores. The storekeeper should have technical knowledge and wide experience in stores routine and ability of organising the operations of the stores.

He should be honest and efficient person. The staff working under the storekeeper is controlled by the storekeeper. He is responsible for the store control. He is responsible for the receipt, storage and issue of materials. He knows very well the materials stored in the stores. His duties and responsibilities regarding the stores are as follows.

1) **Receiving Materials :** The storekeeper has to receive the materials ordered by purchase department. While receiving the goods or materials, he has to ensure that every item of stores received is duly supported by an indent, purchase order, an inspection note and the goods received note.

2) **Recording of Materials :-** The storekeeper is responsible for the proper and systematic maintenance of stores record. Proper maintenance of stores can facilitate easy location of various items of materials.

3) **Storage of Materials :-** He stored the materials in bins or racks with the help of staff of stores. He ensures that all entries of receipt and issue of materials are made on concerned bin-cards.

   He has to store the materials in such a manner that minimum space is occupied and it is protected from all types of losses. The principle of good storekeeping is - **A place for every thing and every thing in its place.**

4) **Issue of Materials :-** Issue of materials is the important function of storekeeper. He should ensure that the materials are issued only to those, who present duly signed store requisition note and the quantities issued are correctly recorded in the bin cards.

5) **Protection of Materials :-** He has to take care of all materials in stores. He should ensure that there should be minimum losses due to evaporation, theft or pilferage and preventing unauthorised persons from entering into stores.

6) **Verification of Materials :-** He should arrange for physical verification of stores periodically and find out whether it is in order. He helps the auditor for verification of materials at the time of physical verification of materials.

7) **Supervision :-** In big industrial concern, a large number of staff is appointed in stores. The staff works under the control of storekeeper, so he has to supervise the duties of different staff members under his charge.

8) **Co-ordination :-** The storekeeper is responsible for co-ordination between materials and production.

9) **Supply of Information :-** The storekeeper has to supply necessary information to the management. He has to locate the slow-moving and non-moving materials and report on obsolete stock to the management.

10) **Maintenance of Levels :-** The storekeeper is responsible for the maintenance of stock levels in the godown. He should ensure that the stock should not exceed the maximum level and should not fall below minimum level at any time.

11) **Investigation :-** In case there is any shortage of materials, its causes should be found out by detailed investigation and prompt remedial action should be taken.

12) **Facility of Material Handling :-** He has to store materials in stores in an orderly and tidy manner so that it can be handled easily. The material handling charges should be as low as possible.

13) **Return of Materials :-** Sometimes, the excess materials are returned by production or other departments to store department. The storekeeper has to record the materials properly and proper accounting record of materials are to be kept.

14) **Request for Purchases :-** When the material reaches to the reorder level, the storekeeper has to inform purchase department for further supplies.

15) **Duties relating to Cost Accounting Departments :-**
   The storekeeper has to furnish the following information to the cost accounting department.
   (1) The department, processes, operations or jobs to be debited for all materials issued by him and to be credited for all materials returned to him.
   (2) A record of scrap received, disposed off and balance of stock of scrap.
   (3) A record of finished product or parts delivered by production departments.
   (4) A record of number of all vouchers relating to goods receipt and inspection note, store requisition, material return notes and stock verification vouchers for shortages and excesses so that, all these vouchers are verified in cost accounting department as to their receipt, posting and reconcilation thereof.

4 : 4 STORES AND MATERIAL RECORDS.

The stores records show the movement of materials i.e the receipt of materials, issues of materials to production department and the balance in stock. Two sets of records are maintained. They are Bin-cards and Stores ledger. Bin-cards are maintained by storekeeper and the store ledger is maintained by cost accounting department.

Bin-card : (Stock card)

Bin means a rack, container or space where goods are kept. Separate bin cards are maintained by the storekeeper for each item of material in store. The bin cards show the details of receipts and issues of materials and the balance of stock at any time. Quantity of stores received is entered in the receipt column and the quantity of stores issued is recorded in the issue column of the bin card and the balance of quantity of stores is taken after every receipt or issue, so that the balance at any time can be seen. This card is of immense help to the storekeeper in controlling the stock position. For each item of stores minimum quantity, maximum quantity and ordering quantity are stated on the card. By seeing the bincard, the storekeeper can send material requisition for the purchase of material in time.

A bin card is also known as bin tag or stock card and is usually attached or placed in shelf, rack or bin where the material has been kept. Bin cards may also be in the form of loose sheet which can be maintained in a ledger kept in the stores. For each entry whether relating to receipts and issues, the balance quantity is calculated and recorded in the balance column. It should agree with the physical balance in bins and store ledger balances.

The specimen of bin card is as follows.

ABC Co Ltd.

Bin No..........................   Maximum level...............

Description..................   Minimum level...............

Code No.....................   Ordering level................

Store ledger folio.........   Ordering quantity............

Date	Receipts		Issues		Balance	Stock Verification	
	Ref. No.	Quantity	Ref. No.	Quantity	Quantity	Date	Initials

Two Bin System : In this system, two bins are maintained for each item of material. One bin constitutes the main or regular bin from which material are issued and other bin contains the minimum stock from which issues are made only when stock in the regular bin is exhausted. At the time of stock verification it is usually sufficient to verify stock in the regular bin as the stock in the minimum stock bin is already known. The idea of two bin is to provide automatic information about reaching minimum stock level so that issue of materials for regular production is stopped. At this stage materials are issued only for urgent requisitions till fresh supplies of materials are received.

Problem -

The following is the history of receipts and issues of material 'Z' in a factory during May 2008.

May 1   Opening stock 400 units
May 4   Received from supplier 800 units (GRN No 51)
May 9   Issued to production department 480 units (SR No 61)
May 11   Issued to production department 320 units (SR No 62)
May 13   Received from supplier 1000 units (GRN No 52)
May 14   Issued to production department 800 units (SR No 63)
May 17   Received from supplier 500 units (GRN No 53)
May 18   Received from supplier 1000 units (GRN No 54)
May 23   Issued to production department 500 units (SR No 64)
May 25   Issued to production department 520 units (SR No 65)
May 29   Issued to production department 680 units (SR No 66)

The minimum stock level of material 'Z' is 400 units, Reorder level is 700 units and reorder quantity is 1000 unit. The code No of material is BJ 180.

Prepare Bin Card No 480 for material 'Z' with all necessary details showing transactions in May 2008.

(GRN denotes Goods received Notes, SR denotes Store Requisition.)

Solution :

BIN CARD

Bin No - 480   Minimum level - 400 units.
Description - 'Z'   Re-order level - 700 units.
Code No - BJ 180   Re-order quantity - 1000 units.
Store Ledger Folio -

Year and Date 2008	Receipts		Issues		balance	Stock verification
	Ref. No.	Quantity	Ref. No.	Quantity	Quantity	
May 1	-	-	-	-	400	
May 4	51	800	-	-	1200	
May 9	-	-	61	480	720	
May 11	-	-	62	320	400	
May 13	52	1000	-	-	1400	
May 14	-	-	63	800	600	
May 17	53	500	-	-	1100	
May 18	54	1000	-	-	2100	
May 23	-	-	64	500	1600	
May 25	-	-	65	520	1080	
May 29	-	-	66	680	400	

Utilities of Bin-Card : (advantages)

Bin card is most important document in storekeeping. Its utilities or advantages are as follows.

1) Bin card is used for entering the receipts, issues and closing balances of each item of stores.
2) It provides an independent check on the store ledger.
3) It helps in requisitioning the material when the reorder level is reached.
4) It helps in the implementation of the perpetual inventory system as the bin card contains the quantitative record of receipts, issues and closing balance of each item of store.
5) It is used for controlling the stock by watching the maximum and minimum level stated on the card.
6) As the economic ordering quantity is stated on the bin card, it enables storekeeper as to how much quantity he has to requisition.

Stores Ledger :

Store ledger is kept in the cost accounting department. It gives the same information regarding stores as in bin card and in addition, it gives the money value of materials. It contains an account for every item of stores and makes a record of the receipts, issues and balances, both in quantity and value. Thus, this ledger provides the information for the pricing of materials issued and money value at any time of each item of stores. The ledger sheets may be in loose leaf form or separate binding. There are mainly three section in this ledger. i.e. receipts, issues and balances, each of these with appropriate sub-divisions showing date, quantity, unit price and total cost. The entries in the receipts and issues columns are made from the same documents which are used for posting in bin card. i.e. Goods Received Note and Stores Requisition note etc.

It is often argued that maintenance of bin card along with store ledger is an unnecessary duplication of work. This is no doubt duplication of work but the necessity for it arises from the fact that store ledger constitutes a check on the quantity shown in the bin card. Moreover bin cards are not accounting records and are kept by storekeeper. For costing purpose maintenance of store ledger is necessary. The record of bin card and store ledger acts as a cross check on each other because the balance of stock disclosed by bin cards should agree with balance shown by store ledger. Thus, accuracy of both records is established. It is, therefore, necessary that both stock records should be kept.

SPECIMEN OF STORE LEDGER
Store Ledger

Description...   Maximum level.................
Code No...   Minimum level.................
Location...   Ordering level..................
Unit...Ordering quantity..............

Receipts				Issues				Balance of Stock		
GRN No	Qty.	Rate	Amount	SR No	Qty.	Rate	Amount	Qty.	Rate	Amount

Distinction between Bin Card and Store Ledger.

Bin Card	Store Ledger
1) Bin card is maintained by storekeeper.	1) Store ledger is maintained by Cost Accounting Department.
2) It records only the quantities of material.	2) It records both quantities as well as money value of materials.
3) Posting in bin card normally takes place just before transaction takes place.	3) Posting in store ledger always takes place after the transaction takes place.
4) It is kept inside the stores.	4) It is kept in the costing department.
5) It can be eliminated for avoiding duplication.	5) It can not be eliminated as this contains the money value of materials.
6) Each transaction is individually posted.	6) Transactions may be summarised and posted periodically.
7) Balance in bin card is compared with physical quantity.	7) Balance in store ledger is compared with Bin card quantity.
8) No need of reconciliation with general ledger as it contains quantities only.	8) Total value of all these cards is to be reconciled with the general ledger.

4:5 ISSUES OF MATERIALS :

Various types of materials are stored in the stores. They are issued by the storekeeper whenever they are demanded by the production and other departments. But the storekeeper should not issue materials unless a properly authorised material requisition is presented to him. For authorising the movement of materials various forms are used. The nature of these forms may be as under.

1) Store Requisition Note or Material Requisition Note.

The storekeeper should always issue the material on proper authority to avoid misappropriation of materials. This authority is usually given by the manager or foreman of production department on a form known as Store Requisition or Material Requisition. Thus, store requisition is a prime document which is used to authorise and record the issue of materials from store. Store requisition serves a dual purpose such as (a) Authorising the storekeeper to issue materials and (b) Providing a written record of usage of materials.

A separate requisition may be prepared for each item of material or a single requisition may be prepared to cover the issuance of number of items. The requisitions received are serially numbered by the storekeeper so that no requisition may be left out in accounting. Besides the serial number written by storekeeper, department placing the requisition may put its own serial number on it. After receiving store requisition, The storekeeper issues the material and entries of such issues are made on bin card in the 'Issue' column of the bin card. Thereafter, it is priced by the cost accounting department according to one of the agreed methods of pricing of issue and posted in the 'Issue' column of the store ledger account by debiting the concerned job, process or overhead control account as per particulars furnished in the store requisition note.

Number of copies of stores requisition to be prepared will depend on the requirement of organisation. But minimum 4 copies are required as follows (a) Store department, (b) Cost Accounting Department, (c) Material Control Department and (d) Office copy retained by the foreman. The Specimen or ruling of store requisition is as follows.

ABC COMPANY LIMITED
Material / Stores requisition Note

Department...   No......................
Job No...   Date...................

To,
    The storekeeper,
    please issue the materials stated herein.

Descri-ption	Code No	Quantity	For Cost office		Bin card No	Store Ledger No.	Remarks
			Rate	Amt.			

Authorised by...   Received by....................
Issued by...   Checked by....................

Bill of Materials

Bill of materials is also known as specification of materials. It is a master requisition which lists all the materials required for the completion of job or order or process. Bill of materials serves the purpose of purchase requisition to purchaser, material requisition to the storekeeper and work order to the production department. It is a complete schedule of materials, parts etc. listed by the production department on a single document required for a particular job or work order. A bill of materials is a special form of store requisition which is generally used by departments having standard material requirements. For instance, in assembly type production there will be no variation from the amount of materials which are used. In such a case, much time would be saved if a bill of materials is used, because only quantity is to be indicated against the code or name of materials required.

If a job is of non-standardised nature, a special bill of materials may be prepared to estimate the materials required by the production department before the job is started. A specimen form of a bill of materials is as follows.

ABC LIMITED

Bill Of Materials

Job No....   No....................
Department...   Date...................

Serial No	Description of materials	Stores code	Quantity Required	For Cost Office		Remarks
				Rate	Amount	

Drawing officer...   Priced by...
Received by...   Store ledger folio...
Storekeeper...

Advantages of Bill of Materials :
(1) It serves the purpose of material requisition for the issue of materials to the storekeeper.
(2) It serves the purpose of purchase requisition upon the purchase officer for the purchase of materials required for a job.
(3) It serves the purpose of work order to the production department.
(4) When pre-printed forms of materials are used in standard type of production, it saves lot of clerical labour and risk of error is also reduced.
(5) Costing of jobs becomes easier and speedier.
(6) Procurement of materials can be planned in advance to avoid production delays.
(7) Control over use of materials in case of non-standard jobs is facilitated if materials are issued according to the bill of materials.

Difference between Material Requisition and Bill of Materials.

Material Requisition / Store Requisition	Bill of Materials
1) It authorise storekeeper to issue materials from stores.	1) It gives a complete list of all materials required for a particular job, order or process.
2) Store or material requisition cannot serve the purpose of bill of materials.	2) Bill of materials can serve the purpose of material requisition.
3) Material requisition may be more helpful in case of standardised products or job.	3) It can be helpful in case of non standardised job.
4) Store requisition is prepared only at the time of getting materials issued from stores.	4) A bill of materials is helpful in sending competitive quotations.

Material Return Note :-

Sometimes, materials may be issued in excess of the requirements of a particular job or work order to facilitate convenient handling. The excess material may be returned by production or other departments to stores department or it may be transferred to other job. When material is returned to stores, the concerning department prepares material returned note and sends it along with the materials. Material returned note is also called Store Debit Note or Shop Credit Note.

Material Return Note is usually prepared in triplicate by store clerk. One copy is sent to the department returning materials, second copy is sent to the cost office for appropriate entries and third copy is retained by the store department for entry in bin-card. The form of material return is also similar to the store requisition note. The quantity returned is to be entered in the 'Receipt' column of bin card preferably with red ink so as to be distinct from receipt of new material. The money value may also be entered in red ink in the store ledger. Then the information regarding the material returned may be obtained easily for the purpose of managerial information. The ruling of material return note is given below.

```
┌─────────────────────────────────────────────────────────────────────┐
│                      ABC COMPANY LIMITED                              │
│                      Material Return Note                             │
│                                                                       │
│  Credit...                                    No.....................│
│  Job No...                                    Date.................   │
│  Department...                                                        │
├──────────┬──────────────┬────────────┬───────────────────────────────┤
│ Quantity │ Description  │  Code No   │         Cost Office           │
│          │              │            ├──────────────┬────────────────┤
│          │              │            │  Rate        │  Amount        │
│          │              │            │  (Rs)        │  (Rs.)         │
├──────────┼──────────────┼────────────┼──────────────┼────────────────┤
│          │              │            │              │                │
│          │              │            │              │                │
├──────────┴──────────────┴────────────┴──────────────┴────────────────┤
│  Bin No...                              Received by......             │
│  Store ledger Folio...                  Priced by.........            │
│  Authorised by...                                                     │
└─────────────────────────────────────────────────────────────────────┘
```

Material Transfer Note :

Sometimes, the excess material from one job is transferred to another job. Such transfer should be avoided as far as possible. The main objection is that, record for the transfer may not be made and actual material cost for job may be inaccurate. An exception to the return of surplus materials to the stores is that, returning of materials to the stores may be costly due to the distance or excessive amount of handling charges, material may be transferred to another job which is near the transferring job. This saves the transportation cost.

The transfer of materials from one job to another should be strictly prohibited unless the procedure is adequately recorded on material transfer note. This should indicate all the necessary data for debiting and crediting the concerned job or processes affected.

Material transfer note is prepared in the department where the material is in excess and one copy of the note is sent to the cost office for making necessary records. The job receiving the material is debited and the job transferring the material is credited. No entry is required in bin card and store ledger. The ruling of this note is given below.

```
┌─────────────────────────────────────────────────────────────────────┐
│                      ABC COMPANY LIMITED                              │
│                      Material Transfer Note                           │
│                                                                       │
│  From                                                                 │
│  Job No...                                    No.....................│
│  Department / shop                            Date...................│
│                                                                       │
│  To                                                                   │
│                                                                       │
└─────────────────────────────────────────────────────────────────────┘
```

Job No... Department / shop					
Description	Code No	Quantity	For Cost Office		Remarks
			Rate (Rs)	Amount (Rs.)	
Approved by... Debited Job No...		Received by...		Priced by... Credited Job No...	

4:6 PRICING METHODS OF ISSUE OF MATERIALS.

After posting of the store requisition in the issue column of bin-card, One copy is sent to costing department for necessary posting in the store ledger, pricing of issue and accounting thereof. But when the materials are issued from stores to production department, a difficulty arises regarding the price at which materials issued are to be charged. This is because the same type of material may have been purchased in different lots at different time at several different prices. This means that actual cost can take on several different values and some methods of pricing of issues of materials must be selected. The price of material changes according to market conditions. Now the question is whether the pricing of material should be original purchase price or the current market price on the date of issue or some other price that should be used for this purpose. The pricing of issues affect directly the profit or loss of the industry. Hence, the selection of appropriate and suitable method becomes somewhat difficult. The various methods are based on different assumptions. Such methods are classified as those based on actual cost price, average price and notional price.

Methods of Pricing

a) Based on Actual Cost   b) Average Cost   c) Notional Cost

1) First in First out
2) Last in First out
3) Highest in First out
4) Next in First out
5) Base Stock price.

1) Simple Average price
2) Periodic simple average price
3) Moving simple average price
4) Weighted average price
5) Periodic weighted average price.
6) Moving weighted average price

1) Standard price

2) Inflated price

3) Replacement or market price

4) Re-issue price.

Note :- The syllabus is restricted to First-in First out, Last-in First out, Simple Average and Weighted Average methods. Hence other methods are not discussed here.

4:6:1 First - In First Out Method :- (FIFO)

This method is commonly recognised as FIFO. It is based on the assumption that materials which are purchased first are issued first. The price of first lot or batch purchased is charged for all the issues until the stock of that lot is exhausted. After the first lot is fully issued, the price of next lot received becomes the issue price. Upon this lot also fully issued, the price of still next lot is used for pricing and so on. In other words the issues are priced in the chronological order of receipts. In this case issues to production and other departments are valued at historical price and stock is valued at the latest price paid.

Advantages :-

(1) The main advantages of FIFO is that it is simple to understand and easy to operate.

(2) The value of closing stock represents the current market price.

(3) It is a logical method as it takes into consideration the normal procedure of utilising first those materials which are received first.

(4) This method is useful when prices are falling.

(5) This method is useful in case of slow moving materials, bulk items and also when transactions are not too many and prices of materials are fairly steady.

(6) As the materials are charged at actual cost, no adjustment for profit or loss is necessary.

Disadvantages :-

(1) When the prices of materials fluctuate considerably, it involves number of calculations which may increase the possibility of errors.

(2) Useful comparison of material cost of one job to another is not possible, if the prices fluctuate too often.

(3) The issue prices do not reflect the current market price. Hence, profit calculated on the issues of this method may not disclose real position.

(4) Sometimes, more than one price has to be adopted for pricing a single issue of materials.

(5) This method involves more clerical work, when the defective or excess materials are returned by production department.

4:6:2 Last-In First Out Method :

This method is exactly opposite to the earlier method. It is based on the assumption that the last material purchased are the first materials issued. Then the price of last batch purchased is used first for all issues until stock of that batch is exhausted. Hence, issues are valued at current prices and stock is valued at historical prices. This method is sometimes known as replacement cost method because materials are issued at the current cost to the job or work order. This method is suitable in times of rising prices because materials will be issued from the latest consignment at a price which is closely related to the current price level. This method was first introduced in U.S.A. during the second world war in order to get the advantage of rising prices.

Advantages :
   (1) This method is simple to operate and is useful when transaction are not too many and prices fairly steady.
   (2) Materials are charged to production at the latest prices paid. In times of rising prices, quotation of prices for company's product will be safe and profitable.
   (3) It obviates the necessity of ascertaining the replacement price of materials.
   (4) This method like FIFO does not result in any unrealised profit or loss.
   (5) Issues are valued at current prices and hence charge to production is more appropriate.

Disadvantages :-
   (1) Like FIFO, this method may lead to clerical errors as every time an issue is made, the store ledger clerk will have to go through the record to ascertain the price to be charged.
   (2) This method is not realistic as it does not conform to the physical flow of materials.
   (3) This method is cumbersome when prices are subject to frequent fluctuations.
   (4) The closing stock is valued at the old prices and does not represent the current economic value.
   (5) If the latest receipt rate is not finalised, the work of pricing of issues will be held up.
   (6) Like the FIFO system, sometimes more than one price has to be adopted for pricing a single issue of materials.

4:6:3 Simple Average Method :-

A price which is calculated by dividing the total of the prices of the materials in the stock from which the material to be priced out could be drawn by number of prices used in that total.

Under this method issues of materials are priced at the average price of materials on hand. Average cost price is obtained by dividing the total price by the number of prices i.e.

$$= \frac{\text{Total of Different Prices per unit}}{\text{Number of Prices}} = \text{Rate of Issue.}$$

In this method, issues are not charged at actual cost, hence there may be profit or loss. This method is most useful when materials are purchased at uniform quantities and prices do not fluctuate.

Advantages :-
  (1) It is simple and easy to operate.
  (2) Cost distortion is not much because of adopting an average price.
  (3) It does not involve much calculations.

Disadvantages :-
  (1) A serious drawback is that, even a solitary small purchase at a very high or low price distorts the issue price.
  (2) It does not take into consideration the quantity of materials purchased at different prices.
  (3) Materials are not charged out at actual cost. This may give rise to profit or loss.
  (4) When prices rise sharply, the closing stock may show a minus balance.

4:6:4 Weighted Average Method :

  This method gives due weight to the quantities held at each price when calculating the average price. The weighted average price is calculated by dividing the total cost of material in stock from which the material to be priced could have been drawn by the total quantity of material in that stock. The simple formula is that weighted average price at any time is the balance value figure divided by the balance units figure.

  In short the weighted average price takes into account the price and quantity of the material in stores. In the period of heavy fluctuations in the price of materials, the average cost method gives better results because it tends to smooth out fluctuation in prices by taking the average prices of various lots in stores.

Advantages -
  (1) No unrealised profit or loss arises by the use of this method.
  (2) It is easy to calculate.
  (3) This method maintains the issue prices near to the market prices as possible.
  (4) Value of closing stock can be accepted for the purpose of Balance Sheet under this method.
  (5) This method is suitable where there are wide fluctuations in purchase prices and it evens out prices over the whole period of accounting because of considering the quantities also.

Disadvantages :
  (1) This method requires lot of calculations, if purchases are made frequently.
  (2) Issue prices may not be at the current market prices.
  (3) To avoid errors, the average price must be calculated to sufficient number of decimal points. This makes the operation of this method somewhat tedious.
  (4) Inventory on hand does not represent current economic value.
  (5) As the issues are not valued at actual cost, profits or loss may arise.

4:6:5 Stock Valuation :

Receipts Valuation :

Generally the materials are purchased from the regular suppliers against approved quotations. However sometimes the materials may be purchased in bulk at an auction or a sale or sometimes free gifts as sample may be received. When goods are received they have to be issued to production even before the invoice of material is received. In order to determine the purchase price the purchase order is referred to however the price of material needs adjustments for the discount allowed, transport charges, cost of containers, sales tax, duty,etc. On the basis of earlier purchases the total cost and rate per unit is determined and entered in the stores Ledger. When the invoice is received the difference between the actual amount and the amount already entered in stores register needs adjustments.

Discount :

Discount may be of the following type :

a) Trade Discount : This document is given by the supplier to the purchaser. The purchaser has to break the bulk or sell in small quantities or repack the goods hence the supplier is relieved of the burden of these costs.

b) Quantity Discount : The supplier makes some savings because of orders. These benefits are passed on by the supplier to the purchaser in the form of quantity discounts.

c) Cast Discount : This is allowed by a supplier to encourage prompt payment. If payment is made within 15 days the purchaser is given a cash discount. Generally speaking cash discount is excluded from cost accounts but if cash discount is always earned for prompt payment then it may be considered in determining the final rate for material.

Transport and Storage Cost :

If the price charged by a supplier does not include transport and storage cost and if the purchaser is required to bear these costs then they are to be added to the purchase price. However, sometimes it is difficult to analyse and calculate these costs. In that case, they are treated as factory overheads and absorbed accordingly.

Cost of Containers :

With regard to containers the supplier may or may not make a separate charge for these. However, if there is a charge on the containers the treatment may vary according to,

a) Non-returnable containers

b) Returnable containers credited at reduced value on return

c) Returnable containers credited at full value on return

Issue Valuation :

Pricing of Material Issues : The price of which the material is issued is important from the point of view of cost accounting. The issues are made out of various purchases at different prices. Therefore, the question arises as to how to price the issues. There are several methods used for pricing the issues the selection of the proper method depends upon.

1) The type of business - job or process
2) Market trends and range of price fluctuations
3) Length of inventory turnover period, E.O.Q.
4) Clerical cost involved in maintain records
5) The need for maintaining uniformity in the cost of the product within an industry,

4:6:6 Use of Computer in Stores Accounting :

Computer system is widely spread and accepted by people. New generation has great affection about advance technology and time saving transferent systems.

Computer Data Base Management system i.e.DBMS is now a days a key tool for MIS and Management decision making process.

Every industry and business is now function with less labour efforts and less cost if computer is used effectively.

Store keeping is not a manual task now. Starting from a small medical store to any MNC with CNC, HNC, VMC, now uses the software for store keeping and accounting.

* Computer can work from material inward upto material dispatch.

* Computer can identify the bin for material.

* Computer can note and update the quantity of each quality and specification of material.

* If material requisition is received through system, it automatically calculate the rate, amount and also warns about the stock level.

* System once instructed properly and connected in network generates P.O.and send it to the vendor on its own when the material is at reorder level.

* Nearly all softwares of MIS and ERP has these features of storekeeping and store accounting.

* It is seen in the malls now a days that the barcode system is used to identify the material and manage the inventory.

* Now a days CNC and VMC machines if connected to the system passes the MRN directly without human intervention.

* It is a need of time to have computer based store keeping and accounting as if you are a vendor of a big company they want your store and godown details, to note the process and other details for production transferency.

* New techniques of store accounting i.e.JIT, just in time as well as carring cost' or supply chain management system,etc.needs a strong backup of computer stored data base for further analysis and decision about the material.

* All kinds of analysis and all forms of data presentation is possible on computer which is very useful to know the store situation at a glance.

* Decision making about production and cost calculation has made very easy if computer is used in store accounting system.

4:7 PROBLEMS ON PRICING OF ISSUES

Problem - 1

The following transactions took place in respect of material 'X' during the month of January 2014.

Date	Particulars	Quantity kgs.	Rate per unit (Rs.)
January 2	Received	2000	10
January 6	Received	300	12
January 9	Issued	1200	-
January 10	Received	200	14
January 11	Issued	1000	-
January 22	Received	300	15
January 31	Issued	200	-

You are required to prepare store ledger account under FIFO method.

Closing Stock on 31-1-2014	Qty kgs.	Rate Rs.	Amt. Rs.
	100	14	1400
	300	15	4500
	400		5900

Solution : (FIFO Method)

In the books of...

Store ledger account of material x for the month ended 31st Jan. 2014.

Year & Date 2014 January	Parti-culars	Receipts				Issues				Balance		
		GRN	Qty. kgs	Rate Rs.	Amt Rs.	M.R.	Qty. kgs.	Rate Rs.	Amt Rs.	Qty kgs	Rate Rs.	Amt Rs.
2nd	Purchases	-	2,000	10	20,000	-	-	-	-	2,000	10	20,000
6th	Purchases	-	300	12	3,600	-	-	-	-	2,000	10	20,000
										300	12	3,600
9th	Issues	-	-	-	-	-	1,200	10	12,000	800	10	8,000
										300	12	3,600
10th	Purchases	-	200	14	2,800	-	-	-	-	800	10	8,000
										300	12	3,600
										200	14	2,800
11th	Issues	-	-	-	-	-	800	10	8,000	100	12	1,200
							200	12	2,400	200	14	2,800
22nd	Purchases	-	300	15	4,500	-	-	-	-	100	12	1,200
										200	14	2,800
										300	15	4,500
31st	Issues	-	-	-	-	-	100	12	1,200	100	14	1,400
							100	14	1,400	300	15	4,500

Problem - 2

Prepare store ledger as per First In First Out method of pricing of issue of materials.

		Units	Rate(Rs.)
April 1, 2014	Opening balance	1,000	5
April 3, 2014	purchased	5,000	6
April 4, 2014	Issued	3,000	-
April 6, 2014	Issued	2,000	-
April 8, 2014	Purchased	3,000	5
April 9, 2014	Issued	2,000	-

The weekly physical stock taking on 7 th April 2014 showed a shortage of 100 units.

Closing Stock on   Qty   Rate   Amt.
                   kgs. Rs.   Rs.
                   1900 5   9500

Note : Shortage of 100 units is to be entered in the issue column only and is to be valued at Rs. 6 per unit as per FIFO method.

Problem - 3

The stock in hand of a materials as on 1st March, 2014 was 500 units at Rs. 10 per unit. From the following transactions of purchases and issues of Sunshine Co. Ltd. Prepare ledger account under First In First out method.

Purchases

6 th March	100 units at Rs. 11
20th March	700 units at Rs. 12
27th March	400 units at Rs. 13
13th April	1000 units at Rs. 14
20th April	500 units at Rs. 15
17th May	400 units at Rs. 16

Issues

9th March	500 units
22nd March	500 units
30th March	500 units
15th April	500 units
22th April	500 units
11th May	500 units
30th May	Missing units 20

On 1st April, 2014, there was a discrepancy of 50 units.

Solution : (FIFO Method)

Store Ledger Account
For the period 1st April to 9th April, 2014

Year & Date 2009 January	Particulars	Receipts GRN No.	Units	Rate Rs.	Amt Rs.	Issues M.R.	Units	Rate Rs.	Amt Rs.	Balance Units	Rate Rs.	Amt Rs.
1st	Opening balance	-	1,000	5	5,000	-	-	-	-	1,000	5	5,000
3rd	Purchases	-	5000	6	30,000	-	-	-	-	1,000 5,000	5 6	5,000 30,000
4th	Issues	-	-	-	-	-	1,000 2,000	5 6	5,000 12,000	3,000	6	18,000
6th	Issued	-	-	-	-	-	2,000	6	12,000	3,000 1,000	6 6	18,000 6,000
7th	Shortage						100	6	600	1,000 900	6 6	6,000 5,400
8th	Purchases	-	3000	5	15,000	-	-	-	-	900 3,000	6 5	5,400 15,000
9th	Issues	-	-	-	-	-	900 1100	6 5	5,400 5,500	1,900	5	9,500

Closing Stock on	Qty units	Rate Rs.	Amt. Rs.
	130	15	1,950
	400	16	6,400

Problem - 4

The receipts and issues from materials in a factory in January 2014 are as under.

January

1	Opening balance	300 kgs. at Rs. 12 per kg.
4	Issued	1300 kgs.
5	Purchases	800 kgs. at Rs. 12.50 per kg.
9	Issued	600 kgs.
10	Purchases	400 kgs. at Rs. 12.50 per kg.
11	Issued	600 kgs.
12	Retuned from workshop issued on 3rd January	40 kgs.
13	Issued	900 kgs.
16	Purchases	1000 kgs. at Rs. 13 per kg.
18	Issued	800 kgs.
20	Returned from workshop issued on 9th January	120 kgs.
22	Issued	600 kgs.
27	Purchases	800 kgs. at Rs. 12 per kg.
29	Issued	400 kgs.

Pricing of issue is to be done on FIFO. A shortage of 20kgs. was noticed on 16th January. Prepare store ledger account for the month of January 2014 in respect of materials.

Closing Stock on	Qty kgs.	Rate Rs.	Amt. Rs.
	20	13	260
	120	12	1440
	800	12	9660
	940		11300

Note :

(1) **Return from workshop :** It should be entered in receipt colum and is valued at the rate at which it was originally issued.

(2) **Shortage :** The shortage in stock is to be entered in issue column and is valued at the rate as per method adopted treating as one of the issues i.e. FIFO in this case.

Solution : (FIFO Method)　　　　**Store ledger Account for January 2014.**

Year & Date 2014 January	Receipts Particulars	Receipts				Issues				Balance		
		GRN	Qty. kgs.	Rate Rs.	Amt Rs.	M.R.	Qty. kgs.	Rate Rs.	Amt Rs.	Qty kgs	Rate Rs.	Amt Rs.
Jan 1	Opening stock									3000	12.00	36,000
Jan 4	Issues						1300	12	15600	1700	12.00	20,400
Jan 5	Purchases		800	12.50	10,000					1700	12.00	20,400
										800	12.50	10,000
Jan 9	Issued						600	12	7200	1100	12.00	13,200
										800	12.50	10,000
Jan 10	Purchased		400	12.50	5000					1100	12.00	13,200
										800	12.50	10,000
										400	12.50	5,000
Jan 11	Issued						600	12	7200	500	12.00	6,000
										800	12.50	10,000
										400	12.50	5,000
										500	12.00	6,000
Jan 12	Returned from workshop		40	12	480					800	12.50	10,000
										400	12.50	5,000
										40	12.00	480
Jan 13	Issued						500	12.00	6000	400	12.50	5,000
							400	12.50	5000	400	12.50	5,000
										40	12.00	480

Date	Particulars	Receipts Qty	Rate	Amount	Issues Qty	Rate	Amount	Balance Qty	Rate	Amount
Jan 16	Purchases	100	13	13,000				400	12.50	5,000
								400	12.50	5,000
								40	12.00	480
								1000	13.00	13000
Jan 16	Shortage				20	12.50	250	380	12.50	4750
								400	12.50	5,000
								40	12.00	480
								1000	13.00	13000
Jan 18	Issued				780	12.50	9750	20	12.00	240
					20	12.00	240	1000	13.00	13,000
Jan 20	Returned from workshop	120	12.00	1440				20	12.00	240
								1000	13.00	13,000
								120	12.00	1,440
Jan 22	Issued				20	12	240	420	13.00	5,460
					580	13	7540	120	12.00	1,440
Jan 27	Purchases	800	12.00	9600				420	13.00	5,460
								120	12.00	1,440
								800	12.00	9,600
Jan 29	Issued				400	13	5200	20	13.00	260
								120	12.00	1,440
								800	12.00	9,600

Problem - 5

The following particulars have been extracted in respect of material 'Z', prepare Store Ledger Account pricing the material issue on the basis of Last In First Out method.

Receipts

1-3-2014	Opening stock	200 units at Rs. 3.50
3-3-2014	Purchased	300 units at Rs. 4.00
13-3-2014	Purchased	900 units at Rs. 4.30
23-3-2014	Purchased	600 units at Rs. 3.80

Issues

5-3-2014	Issued	400 units
15-3-2014	Issued	600 units
25-3-2014	Issued	600 units
29-3-2014	Issued	200 units

Closing Stock on	Qty units	Rate Rs.	Amt. Rs.
	200	4.30	860

Solution : (LIFO Method)

Store Ledger Account

Year & Date 2014 March	Particulars	GRN	Receipts			M.R.	Issues			Balance		
			Qty. units	Rate Rs.	Amt Rs.		Qty. units	Rate Rs.	Amt Rs.	Qty units	Rate Rs.	Amt Rs.
1	Opening Stock									200	3.50	700
3	Purchased		300	4.00	1200					200 / 300	3.50 / 4.00	700 / 1,200
5	Issued						300 / 100	4.00 / 3.50	1,200 / 350	100	3.50	350
13	Purchased		900	4.30	3870					100 / 900	3.50 / 4.30	350 / 3,870
15	Issued						600	4.30	2,580	100 / 300	3.50 / 4.30	350 / 1,290
23	Purchased		600	3.80	2280					100 / 300 / 600	3.50 / 4.30 / 3.80	350 / 1,290 / 2,280
25	Issued						600	3.80	2,280	100 / 300	3.50 / 4.30	350 / 1,290
29	Issued						100 / 100	3.50 / 4.30	350 / 430	200	4.30	860

Problem - 6

The following transaction relate to purchase and issue of material, RM-51 in Bajaj Ltd, Pune during June 2014. Prepare store ledger account under LIFO method of charging materials.

June 2014

1st	Opening balance	500 units at Rs. 25
8th	Issues	250 units
13th	Received from vendor	200 units at Rs. 24
14th	Returned of surplus from a work order	15 units at Rs. 24
16th	Issued	180 units
20th	Received from vendor	240 units at Rs. 23
24th	Issued	304 units
25th	Received from vendor	320 units ar Rs. 23.50
26th	Issued	112 units
27th	Excess found in stock 12 units due to wrong weighing during the month.	
29th	Received from vendor	100 units at Rs. 24.

A stock verifier noted that on 15th he had found a shortage of 5 units and on 28th a damage of 8 units.

Closing Stock on	Qty	Rate	Amt.
	Units	Rs.	Rs.
	216	25	5,400
	212	23.50	4,982
	100	24	2,400
TOTAL	**528**		**12,782**

Solution : (LIFO method)

In the books of bajaj limited Store Ledger Account of RM. 51 For the month of April 2014.

Year & Date 2014 June	Parti-culars	Receipts				Issues					Balance		
		GRN	Qty. units.	Rate Rs.	Amt Rs.	M.R.	Qty. units.	Rate Rs.	Amt Rs.		Qty units	Rate Rs.	Amt Rs.
June 1st	Opening Stock										500	25	12500
8th	Issues						250	25	6250		250	25	6250
13th	Purchased		200	24	4800						250	25	6250
											200	24	4800
14th	Return of Surplus		15	24	360						250	25	6250
											200	24	4800
											15	24	360
15th	Shortage						5	24	120		250	25	6250
											200	24	4800
											10	24	240
16th	Issues						180	24	4320		250	25	6250
											30	24	720
20th	Purchases		240	23	5520		-	-	-		250	25	6250
											30	24	720
											240	23	5520

Date	Particulars	Receipts Qty	Receipts Rate	Receipts Amount	Issues Qty	Issues Rate	Issues Amount	Balance Qty	Balance Rate	Balance Amount
24th	Issues				240 / 30 / 34	23 / 24 / 25	5520 / 720 / 850	– / – / 216	– / – / 25	– / – / 5400
25th	Purchases	320	23.50	7520				216 / 320	25 / 23.50	5400 / 7520
26th	Issues				112	23.50	2632	216 / 208	25 / 23.50	5400 / 4888
27th	Excess in stock	12	23.50	282				216 / 208 / 12	25 / 23.50 / 23.50	5400 / 4888 / 282
28th	Damages				8	23.50	188	216 / 208 / 4	25 / 23.50 / 23.50	5400 / 4888 / 94
29th	Purchases	100	24	2400				216 / 208 / 4 / 100	25 / 23.50 / 23.50 / 24	5400 / 4888 / 94 / 2400

Problem - 7

The following is the receipts and issues of coal in a factory during March 2014.

1	Opening stock 200 tons at Rs. 460 tons.
4	Issued 140 tons
6	Purchased 350 tons at Rs. 450 per ton.
8	Condemned due to deterioration in quantity and transferred to scrap 30 tons.
9	Issued 80 tons
14	Issued 210 tons
17	Purchased 200 tons at Rs. 480 per ton.
20	Issued 120 tons
25	Purchased 180 tons at Rs. 470 per ton
28	Issued 280 tons
31	Excess found in stock 43 tons due to wrong weighting during the month.

The maximum level fixed is 400 tons the minimum 75 tons and re-order level is 100 tons. Show the store ledger account under LIFO system

Closing Stock on	Qty (tons)	Rate (Rs.)	Amt. (Rs.)
	60	460	27,600
	10	450	4,500
	43	470	20,210
Total	**113 tons**		**52,310**

Note :- Excess found in stock on 31st March is valued at Rs. 470 which is the latest purchase price.

Solution : (LIFO Method)

Store Ledge Account

Maximum level 400 tons
Minimum level 75 tons
Re-order level 100 tons

Year & Date 2014 March	Particulars	Receipt				M.R.	Issues			Balance		
		GRN	Qty. tons	Rate Rs.	Amt Rs.		Qty. tons	Rate Rs.	Amt Rs.	Qty. tons	Rate Rs.	Amt Rs.
March 1	Opening Stock									200	460	92,000
4	Issues						140	460	64,400	60	460	27,600
6	Purchases		350	450	1,57,000					60	460	27,600
										350	450	1,57,500
8	Detoriorati on of coal						30	450	13,500	60	460	27,600
										320	450	1,44,000
9	Issues						80	450	36,000	60	460	27,600
										240	450	1,08,000
14	Issues						210	450	94,500	60	460	27,600
										30	450	13,500
17	Purchases		200	480	96,000					60	460	27,600
										30	450	13,500
										200	480	96,000

Date	Particulars	Receipts Qty	Rate	Amount	Issues Qty	Rate	Amount	Balance Qty	Rate	Amount
March 20th	Issues				120	480	57,600	60	460	27,600
								30	450	13,500
								80	480	38,400
25th	Purchases	180	470	84,600				60	460	27,600
								30	450	13,500
								80	480	38,400
								180	470	84,600
28th	Issues				180	470	84,600	60	460	27,600
					80	480	38,400			
					20	450	9,000			
31th	Excess stock	43	470	20,210				60	460	27,600
								10	450	4,500
								43	470	20,210

Problem - 8

The receipts side of the store ledger account shows the following particulars.

2014 Jan 1   Opening balance   500 units at Rs. 4
2014 Jan 5   Received from vendor   200 units at Rs. 4.25
2014 Jan 12   Received from vendor   150 units at Rs. 4.10
2014 Jan 20   Received from vendor   300 units at Rs. 4.50
2014 Jan 25   Received from vendor   400 units at Rs. 4

Issues of materials were as follows.

Jan 4 - 200 units, Jan 10 - 400 units, Jan 15 - 100 units, Jan 19 - 100 units, Jan 28 - 200 units and Jan 30 - 250 units.

Issues are to be priced on the principle of Last In First Out. Write out store ledger account in respect of materials for the month of January.

Closing Stock on	Qty (Units)	Rate Rs.	Amt. Rs.
	50	4	200
	250	4.50	1125
Total	**300**		**1325**

Solution : (LIFO Method)

Store Ledger Account

Year & Date 2014 Jan.	Particulars	Receipts				Issues				Balance		
		GRN	Qty. units	Rate Rs.	Amt Rs.	M.R.	Qty. units	Rate Rs.	Amt Rs.	Qty units	Rate Rs.	Amt Rs.
Jan. 1	Opening Stock									500	4	2000
Jan. 4	Issues						200	4	800	300	4	1200
Jan. 5	Purchases		200	4.25	850					300 200	4 4.25	1200 850
Jan. 10	Issues						200 200	4.25 4	850 800	- 100	- 4	- 400
Jan. 12	Purchases		150	4.10	615					100 150	4 4.10	400 615
Jan. 15	Issues						100	4.10	410	100 50	4 4.10	400 205
Jan. 19	Issues						50 50	4.10 4	205 200	- 50	- 4	- 200

Problem - 9

The following transactions took place in respect of 'Y' materials.

	Receipts Quantity	Rate Rs.	Issue Quantity
2-9-2014	200	2.00	-
10-9-2014	300	2.40	-
15-9-2014	-	-	250
18-9-2014	250	2.60	-
20-9-2014	-	-	200

Record the above transactions in store ledger pricing the issues at :

(a) Simple Average Method, (b) Weighted Average Method,

Solution

(a) Simple Average Method

Store Ledger Account

Date and Year	Particulars	Receipts			Issues			Balance	
		Qty	Rate Per unit Rs.	Amt. Rs.	Qty	Rate Per unit Rs.	Amt. Rs	Qty	Amt. Rs.
2014 2-9	Purchases	200	2	400	-	-	-	200	400
10-9	Purchases	300	2.40	720	-	-	-	500	1120
15-9	Issues				250	2.20	550	250	570
18-9	Purchases	250	2.60	650	-	-	-	500	1220
20-9	Issues				200	2.50	500	300	720

1) Calculation of Simple Average Rate. (Issue price)

$$15\text{-}9\text{-}2009 = \frac{2 + 2.40}{2} = \text{Rs. } 2.20$$

$$20\text{-}9\text{-}2009 = \frac{2.40 + 2.60}{2} = \text{Rs. } 2.50$$

(b) Weighted Average Rate

Store Ledger Account

Date and Year	Particulars	Receipts			Issues			Balance	
		Qty	Rate per unit Rs.	Amt Rs.	Qty	Rate per unit Rs.	Amt. Rs.	Qty	Amt. Rs.
2-9	Purchases	200	2.00	400	-	-	-	200	400
10-9	Purchases	300	2.40	720	-	-	-	500	1120
15-9	Issues	-	-	-	250	2.24	560	250	560
18-9	Purchases	250	2.60	650	-	-	-	500	1210
20-9	Issues	-	-	-	200	2.42	484	300	726

Calculation of Weighted Average Rate. (Issue price)

$$15\text{-}9\text{-}2014 = \frac{400+720}{200+300} \text{ or } \frac{1120}{500} = \text{Rs. } 2.24$$

$$20\text{-}9\text{-}2014 = \frac{560+650}{250+250} \text{ or } \frac{1210}{500} = \text{Rs. } 2.42$$

Problem - 10

The following materials have been extracted in respect of material. Prepare the store ledger account showing the receipt and issues, pricing the materials issued on the basis of simple average and weighted average.

2014	Particulars	Quantity Kgs.	Rate per kg. Rs.
Feb. 2	Received	2000	10
Feb. 6	Received	300	12
Feb. 9	Issued	1200	-
Feb. 10	Receipt	200	14
Feb. 18	Issued	1000	-
Feb. 22	Received	300	11
Feb. 28	Issued	200	-

Solution :

(a) Simple Average Method

Store Ledger Account

Date and Year	Particulars	Receipts			Issues			Balance	
		Qty kgs	Rate Rs.	Amt Rs.	Qty kgs	Rate Rs.	Amt. kgs	Qty	Amt. Rs.
Feb.2	Purchases	2000	10	20,000	-	-	-	2000	20,000
Feb.6	Purchases	300	12	3600	-	-	-	2300	23600
Feb.9	Issues	-	-	-	1200	11	13200	1100	10400
Feb.10	Purchases	200	14	2800	-	-	-	1300	13200
Feb.18	Issues	-	-	-	1000	12	12000	300	1200
Feb.22	Purchases	300	11	3300	-	-	-	600	4500
Feb.28	Issues	-	-	-	200	12.33	2466	400	2034

Calculation of Simple Average Rate. (Issue price)

$$9\text{-}2\text{-}2014 \ = \ \frac{10+12}{2} \ \ \ \ = \text{Rs. } 11$$

$$18\text{-}2\text{-}2014 = \ \frac{10+12+14}{3} \ = \text{Rs. } 12$$

$$28\text{-}2\text{-}2014 = \ \frac{12+14+11}{3} \ = \text{Rs. } 12.33$$

(b) Weighted Average Rate.

Store Ledger Account

Date and Year	Particulars	Receipts			Issues			Balance	
		Qty kgs	Rate Rs.	Amt Rs.	Qty kgs	Rate Rs.	Amt.	Qty kgs	Amt. Rs.
Feb. 2	Purchases	2000	10	20,000	-	-	-	2000	20,000
Feb. 6	Purchases	300	12	3600	-	-	-	2300	23600
Feb. 9	Issues	-	-	-	1200	11	13200	1100	11288
Feb. 10	Purchases	200	14	2800	-	-	-	1300	14088
Feb. 18	Issues	-	-	-	1000	10.84	10840	300	3248
Feb. 22	Purchases	300	11	3300	-	-	-	600	6548
Feb. 28	Issues	-	-	-	200	10.91	2182	400	4366

Calculation of Weighted teer ed Average Rate. (Issue price)

$$9\text{-}2\text{-}2014 \quad = \frac{Rs.\, 23600}{2300} \quad = Rs.\, 10.26$$

$$18\text{-}2\text{-}2014 = \frac{Rs.\, 14088}{1300} \quad = Rs.\, 10.84$$

$$28\text{-}2\text{-}2014 = \frac{Rs.\, 6548}{600} \quad = Rs.\, 10.91$$

Problem - 11

The following transactions occur in the purchase and issue of a material in thed year 2014.

Jan. 2	Purchased	4000units at Rs. 4.00 per unit
Jan. 6	Purchased	500units at Rs. 5.00 per unit
Feb. 5	Issued	2000units
Feb. 10	Purchased	6000units at Rs. 6 per unit
Feb. 12	Issued	4000 units
March 2	Issued	1000 units
March 5	Issued	2000 units
March 15	Purchased	4500units at Rs. 5.50 per unit
March 20	Issued	3000 units

From the above, prepare store ledger account using the following methods.

(a) Simple average price

(b) Weighted average price

Solution :

(a) Simple Average Price

Store Ledger Account

date Year	Particulars	Receipts			Issues			Balance	
		Qty units	Rate Rs.	Amt Rs.	Qty units	Rate Rs.	Amt.	Qty units	Amt. Rs.
Jan. 2	Purchases	4000	4.00	16000	-	-	-	4000	16,000
Jan. 20	Purchases	500	5.00	2500	-	-	-	4500	18500
Feb. 5	Issues	-	-	-	2000	4.50	9000	2500	9500
Feb. 10	Purchases	6000	6.00	36000	-	-	-	8500	45500
Feb. 12	Issues	-	-	-	4000	5.00	20000	4500	25500
Mar 2	Issued	-	-	-	1000	6.00	6000	3500	19500
Mar 5	Issued	-	-	-	2000	6.00	12000	1500	7500
Mar 15	Purchases	4500	5.50	24750	-	-	-	6000	32250
Mar 20	Issued	-	-	-	3000	5.75	17250	3000	15000

Calculation of simple average price. (Issue price)

On Feb 5 $= \dfrac{Rs.\,4 + Rs.\,5}{2}$ = Rs. 4.50

On Feb. 12 $= \dfrac{Rs.\,4 + Rs.\,5 + Rs.\,6}{3}$ = Rs. 5.00

On Mar. 20 $= \dfrac{Rs.\,6 + Rs.\,5.50}{2}$ = Rs. 5.75

(b) Weighted Average Price

Store Ledger Account

date Year	Particulars	Qty units	Rate Rs.	Amt Rs.	Qty units	Rate Rs.	Amt.	Qty units	Amt. Rs.
		Receipts			Issues			Balance	
Jan. 2	Purchases	4000	4.00	16000	-	-	-	4000	16,000
Jan. 20	Purchases	500	5.00	2500	-	-	-	4500	18500
Feb. 5	Issues	-	-	-	2000	4.111	8222	2500	10278
Feb. 10	Purchases	6000	6.00	36000	-	-	-	8500	46278
Feb. 12	Issues	-	-	-	4000	5.445	21780	4500	24498
Mar 2	Issues	-	-	-	1000	5.445	5445	3500	19053
Mar 5	Issues	-	-	-	2000	5.445	10890	1500	8163
Mar 15	Purchases	4500	5.50	24750	-	-	-	6000	32913
Mar 20	Issues	-	-	-	3000	5.486	16457	3000	16456

Calculation of Weighted average price (Issue price)
On Feb 5   = Rs 18500 ÷ 4500   = Rs. 4.111
On Feb 12 = Rs. 46278 ÷ 8500 = Rs. 5.445
On Mar 20 = Rs. 32913 ÷ 6000 = Rs. 5.486

Problem - 12

From the following information prepare store ledger under (i) Simple Average method and (ii) Weighted Average method for the month of March 2014.

March 2014

1   Opening stock 200 pieces at Rs. 2 each
    Purchases
5   100 pieces at Rs. 2.20 each
10   150 pieces at Rs. 2.40 each
20   180 pieces at Rs. 2.60 each.

Issues

6 150 pieces

11 100 pieces

31 200 pieces

On 13th March 2014 the stock verifier reported that there was a shortage of 10 pieces.

Solution :

(i) Simple Average Method

Store Ledger Account

date	Particulars	Receipts			Issues			Balance	
Year		Qty pieces	Rate Rs.	Amt Rs.	Qty pieces	Rate Rs.	Amt.	Qty pieces	Amt. Rs.
Mar. 1	Opening stock	-	-	-	-	-	-	200	400
5	Purchases	100	2.20	220	-	-	-	300	620
6	Issues	-	-	-	150	2.10	315	150	305
10	Purchases	150	2.40	360	-	-	-	300	665
11	Issues	-	-	-	100	2.30	230	200	435
13	Shortage	-	-	-	10	2.30	23	190	412
20	Purchases	180	2.60	468	-	-	-	370	880
31	Issued	-	-	-	200	2.40	480	170	410

Calculation of simple average rate (Issue price)

On 6th March 2014 $= \dfrac{Rs.2 + Rs.2.20}{2} = Rs.\ 2.10$

On 11th & 13th March 2014 $= \dfrac{Rs.2 + Rs.2.20 + Rs.2.40}{3} = Rs.\ 2.30$

On 31st March $= \dfrac{Rs.2.20 + Rs.2.40 + Rs.2.60}{3} = Rs.\ 2.40$

(ii) Weighted Average Method

Stock Ledger Account

date Year	Particulars	Receipts Qty pieces	Rate Rs.	Amt Rs.	Issues Qty pieces	Rate Rs.	Amt. Rs.	Balance Qty pieces	Amt. Rs.
Mar. 1	Opening stock	-	-	-	-	-	-	200	400
5	Purchases	100	2.20	220	-	-	-	300	620
6	Issues	-	-	-	150	2.067	310	150	310
10	Purchases	150	2.40	360	-	-	-	300	670
11	Issues	-	-	-	100	2.233	223.30	200	446.70
13	Shortage	-	-	-	10	2.233	22.33	190	424.37
20	Purchases	180	2.60	468	-	-	-	370	892.37
31	Issued	-	-	-	200	2.411	482.20	170	410.17

Calculation of Weighted Average Rate (Issue price)
On 6th March 2014 = Rs 620 ÷ 300 = Rs. 2.607
On 11th and 13th March 2014 = Rs. 670 ÷ 300 = Rs. 2.233
On 31st March 2014 = Rs. 892.37 ÷ 370 = Rs. 2.411

Problem - 13

The following transactions occur in the purchase and issue of a material :

Jan. 2   Purchased 4000 units @ Rs. 4.00 per unit
Jan. 20   Puchased 500 units @ Rs. 5.00 per unit
Feb. 5   Issued 2,000 units
Feb. 10   Purchased 6,000 units @ Rs. 6.00 per unit
Feb. 12   Issued 4000 units
March 2   Issued 1000 units
March 5   Issued 2000 units
March 15 Purchased 4500 units @ Rs. 5.50 per unit
March 20 Issued 3000 units.

From the above, prepare the Store Ledger Account by adopting LIFO method of charging material issued.

Solution :

LIFO Method

Year & Date	Particulars	Receipts Qty Rs.	Rate Rs.	Amt. kgs.	Issues Qty Rs.	Rate Rs.	Amt kgs	Balance Qty Rs.	Rate	Amount Rs.
Jan 2	Purchases	4000	4.00	16000	-	-	-	4000	4.00	16000
Jan 20	Purchases	500	5.00	2500	-	-	-	4000 500	4.00 5.00	16000 2500
Feb 5	Issues	-	-	-	500 1500	5.00 4.00	2500 6000	2500	4.00	10000
Feb 10	Purchases	6000	6.00	36000	-	-	-	2500 6000	4.00 6.00	10000 36000
Feb 12	Issues	-	-	-	4000	6.00	24000	2500 2000	4.00 6.00	10000 12000
Mar 2	Issues	-	-	-	1000	6.00	6000	2500 1000	4.00 6.00	10000 6000
Mar 5	Issues	-	-	-	1000 1000	6.00 4.00	6000 4000	1500	4.00	6000
Mar 15	Purchases	4500	5.50	24750				1500 4500	4.00 5.50	6000 24750
Mar 20	Issues				3000	5.50	16500	1500 1500	4.00 5.50	6000 8250

Problem - 14

From the following particulars write up the priced Stores Ledger under Last-in-first-out. **[10]**

Date	Particulars
Dec. 1	Stock in hand 500 units at Rs. 20
Dec. 2	Issued 200 units
Dec. 3	Purchased 150 units at Rs. 22
Dec. 4	Issued 100 units
Dec. 5	Purchased 200 units at Rs. 25
Dec. 6	Issued 300 units
Dec. 7	Purchased 10 units at Rs. 22
Dec. 8	Issued 100 units
Dec. 9	Issued 50 units

On 10th Dec. it was noticed that there is shortage of 10 units.

Solution :

FIFO Method

Year & Date Dec.	Particulars	Receipts Qty. kgs.	Receipts Rate Rs.	Receipts Amt. Rs.	Issues Qty. kgs.	Issues Rate Rs.	Issues Amt. Rs.	Balance Qty kgs	Balance Rate Rs.	Balance Amount Rs.
1	To bal b/d	-	-	-	-	-	-	500	20	10000
2	Issues	-	-	-	200	20	4000	300	20	6000
3	Receipts	150	22	3300	-	-	-	300 150	20 22	9300
4	Issues	-	-	-	100	22	2200	300 50	20 22	7100
5	Receipts	200	25	5000	-	-	-	300 50 200	20 22 25	12100
6	Issues	-	-	-	200 50 50	25 22 20	7100	250	20	5000
7	Receipts	10	22	220	-	-	-	250 10	20 22	5220
8	Issues	-	-	-	10 90	22 20	2020	160	20	3200
9	Issues	-	-	-	50	20	1000	110	20	2200
10	Shortage	-	-	-	10	20	200	100	20	2000

4.8 EXERCISES

1) Indicate whether each of the following statements are true or false

a) Store ledger is maintained by the storekeeper.
b) Bin card is the part of accounting.
c) Bill of material is a cash memo sent by a supplier along with the goods.
d) Material requisition is prepared by storekeeper.
e) Purchase requisition is sent by the purchase department
f) Goods received note is prepared by the goods receiving clerk.
g) Purchase control is exercised by the storekeeper.

Answers : True - (f), False - (a), (b), (c), (d), (e), (g)

2) Fill in the blanks

(a) Store ledger is maintained in the....
(b) Bin card is a record of ... only.
(c) Bin card is maintained by....
(d) Goods received note is prepared by... .
(e) Identification of material is made by... .
(f) The incharge of store department is called as... .
(g) Store ledger records both... and... of materials.
(h) A document which gives a complete list of all materials required for a particular job or order is called....

Answers. (a) Cost Accounting Department, (b) Quantities, (c) The Storekeeper, (d) Receiving Department, (e) Codes, (f) Storekeeper, (g) Quantities, Money Value, (h) Bill of Materials

3) Short answer type questions.

(1) What are various types of stores?
(2) What is goods received note?
(3) What is the difference between classification and codification?
(4) What do you mean by the impress system of store control?
(5) What is Bin-card?
(6) What do you mean by double bin system?
(7) State the difference between bin card and store ledger.
(8) State the difference between store requisition and bill of material.
(9) Explain any five functions of the storekeeper.
(10) What are the basic principles of coding?
(11) Write Short Note : a) Centralised store with sub-stores
                        b) Stores Location
                        c) Weighted Average Price Method

4) Long Answer type questions.

(1) Explain the importance of good stockkeeping in an organisation. What are duties of a store keeper?

(2) What is bin-card? Give a specimen form of it and discuss its utility.

(3) Distinguish between,
   (i) Bill of material and Store requisition.
   (ii) Material requisition note and material transfer note.
   (iii) Bill of material and purchase requisition.

(4) What are centralised and decentralised storage? State its advantages and disadvantages.

(5) What are (a) Bin card, (b) Store ledger? State what purposes do they serve and bring out the dinstinction between the two.

(6) Give the specimens of the following documents.
   (a) Bin cards, (b) Store ledger, (c) Store requisition, (d) Bill of materials, (e) Material return note, (f) Material transfer note.

5) Indicate which of the following statements are true or false.

1) In LIFO Method of pricing materials issues, closing stock is valued at the oldest prices in stock.

2) During the period of rising material prices FIFO Method results in profit inflation.

3) Simple average method should be used when there are wide fluctuations in prices.

4) Weighted average method is considered better than simple average method.

Answers : True :- 1, 2, 4,   False - 3

6) Fill in the blanks

1) In... method and... method materials are charged to production department at actual cost.

2) Under LIFO method, profit will be... when prices are rising.

3) Materials should be issued by storekeeper against...

4) FIFO method of valuing material issues is suitable in times of...

5) LIFO method is suitable in time of...

6) Average price method of valuing materials issues is suitable when...

7) A bill of material serves the purpose of...

8) Last in first out method is suitable in times of ....

Answers : 1 - FIFO, LIFO, 2 - lower, 3 - Material Requisition, 4 - Falling prices, 5 - Rising prices, 6 - Prices fluctuate considerably, 7 - Material Requisition., 8-Rising Prices

7) Short Answer Type Questions

1) Give the Three names of valuing material issues.

2) What is material requisition? Give its specimen?

3) What is LIFO?

4) What is FIFO?

Practical Problems

1) The following transactions occur in the purchase and issue of a material.

Jan 2 Purchased 400 units at Rs4=00 per unit.

Jan 20 Purchased 500 units at Rs 5=00 per unit

Feb 5 Issued 2000 units.

Feb 10 Purchased 6000 units at Rs 6=00 per unit

Feb 12 Issued 4000 units.

March 2 Issued 1000 units

March 5 Issued 2000 units.

March 15 Purchased 4500 units at Rs 5.50 per unit.

March 20 Issued 3000 units.

From the above, prepare a store ledger account by adopting FIFO and LIFO method.

Ans : (a) Value of closing stock 3000 units, at Rs 5.50 =Rs16500

(b) Value of closing stock. 1500 units at Rs 5.50 per unit and

1500 units at Rs 4.00 per unit

2) Bharat Manufacturing Company uses copper, is which purchased from the market as and when necessary. The following purchases and issues were made during the month of Jan.2014

Jan 1   Opening balance 300kg at Rs 25 per kg.

Jan 3   Purchased 500kg at Rs 26.60 per kg

(Purchase order No 101)

Jan 4   Issued 220 kg (Material requisition No 201)

Jan 10   Issued 440 kg (Material requisition No 202)

Jan 20   Purchased 490kg at 23 per kg

(Purchase order No 102)

Jan 25   Issued 300 kg (Material requisition No 203)

Jan 26   Surplus 20 kg returned to store out of quantity issued on Jan 4 (Material requisition Note No 20)

Prepare store ledger account for the above transaction according to LIFO method of pricing issues

Ans : Value of closing stock   140 units at Rs 25=Rs 3500

20 units at Rs 26.60= Rs 532   190 units at Rs 23 = Rs 4370

3) **The following are the receipts and issues of material in Bharati Ltd during the month of March 2014.**

1   Opening stock 2000 units at Rs 46 per unit
4   Issued 1400 units
6   Purchased 3500 units at Rs 45 per unit
8   Condemned due to deterioration in quantity and hence transferred to scrap 300 units.
9   Issued 800 units
14   Issued 1400 units
17   Purchased 2000 units at Rs 48 per unit
20   Issued 1200 units
25   Purchased 1800 units at Rs. 47 per unit.
28   Issued 2800 units
31   Excess found in stock 430 units due to wrong weighing during the month.
Show the store ledger account under last in first out method.

Ans. Closing stock, 600 units at Rs 46 = Rs 27600, 100 units at Rs 45 = Rs 4500, 430 units at Rs 47 = Rs 20210.

4) **Prepare store ledger account on the basis of FIFO method of pricing the issue of stores using the following information.**

Date	particulars	Quantity units	Rate per unit
1st	Material on hand	300	9.70
3rd	Purchases	250	9.80
11th	Issues	390	-
14th	Shortage	10	-
15th	Purchases	300	10.05
18th	Purchases	150	9.60
20th	Issues	210	-
24th	Purchases	110	9.90
25th	Issues	300	-
28th	Purchases	150	10.30
29th	Issues	210	-

Ans. 140 units at Rs 10.30 = Rs 1442

5) **The following transactions took place in respect of a material for the month of March 2014**

Date of March 2014	Receipts		Issues
	Quantity units	Rate Rs	Quantity units
2	200	2	-
10	300	2.40	-
15	-	-	250
18	250	2.60	-
20	-	-	200
24	200	2.50	-
30	-	-	300

   Record the above transactions in store ledger Account on the basis of
   (a) Simple average method and (b)   Weighted average Method

Ans.(a) Closing Stock 200 units Rs 470.
      (b) Closing Stock 200 units Rs 490.40

(6) **From the following information relating to material, Prepare Store Ledger Account for the month of Dec 2014 on the basis of**

(i) Simple average method and (ii) Weighted average method
   1st   Purchases 100 units at Rs10 per unit
   2nd   Purchases 200 units at Rs10.20 per unit
   5th   Issues 250 units.
   7th   Purchases 300 units at Rs 10.50 per unit.
   10th Purchases 200 units at Rs 10.80 per unit.
   13th Issues 200 units
   18th Issues 200 units
   20th Purchases 100 units at Rs 11per unit
   28th Issues 150 units

Ans : (i) 100 units Rs 1060 (ii) 100 units 1074.55

INVENTORY CONTROL

INTRODUCTION

Materials constitute a very important proportion of total cost of finished product in most of the manufacturing industries. Hence, proper recording and control over the material costs is essential. In respect of materials, it is necessary to have control because the price paid should be the minimum possible, wastage during the process of manufacture should be the minimum possible, wastage and losses while the materials are in store should be avoided as far as possible.

Meaning:

Materials control may be defined as,the regulation of the procedures for requisitioning, buying.receiving, storing, handling and usage of materials.

The-main requirements of a system of material control are:

(1) Proper system of stock control.
(2) Centralisation of purchases.
(3) Use of standard form.
(4) Use of material purchase budget and material requirement budget.
(5) Planning and fixation of definite responsibility for each function of material control.
(6) Co-ordination between departments responsible for requisitioning, purchasing, receiving, inspecting, storing and utilising the materials.
(7) Efficient storage of all materials under proper safeguard.

5.1 PERIODIC INVENTORY CONTROL

5.1.1 Meaning :

Under this system, the entire stock is verified at periodic intervals, usually once a year at the close of the annual accounting period, so as to value the closing stocks for preparation of final accounts. If it is chosen to verify the stocks at two or more periodic intervals, the verification is arranged during the slack season. For periodic verification, the factory work is stopped for the required number of days and the verification has got to be done hurriedly. The closure of the works even for a day is quite a costly affair and so this system is not favoured by the big business houses.. Secondly, the risk of loss or theft of stores is not minimised due to long interval between the two checking periods.

5.1.2 Procedure of Periodical Verification :

It is normally the practice to close the stores for some days while carrying out the stock verification. Before starting the process of stock verification the following procedure should be adopted:

(1) The store-keeper must ensure that the bin-card postings are all complete and upto date.
(2) To see that the bin-cards are kept alongside the corresponding items.
(3) On the dates fixed for verification of the stock, verification personnel should verify the stock of each item.
(4) Post the same in the bin-card and prepare the relevant stock verification sheets.
(5) The stock verification sheets, as and when completed, are sent to the stores accounting section who carry out the necessary adjustments in the stores ledger.
(6) In each bin a tag is kept on which the stock verification personnel record the following data, (a) the description of the item,,(h), location code, (c) the quantity of stock.
(7) These tags are forwarded to the stores accounting section who compare them first with the bin-card to arrive at the surplus or deficit and then with the stores ledger to make the necessary adjustments therein.

5.1.3 Advantages :

(1) To facilitate valuation of stores for exhibition in the final accounts.
(2) Periodic verification is, however, good for the item which do not find place in the perpetual (continuous) inventory records e.g., work-in-progress, components and consumable stores at site, capital assets, loose tools and spare parts lying in the departments or workshops, measuring devices and tools in the custody of inspection staff etc.
(3) The correctness of the description in the bin-card can be checked up.
(4) Irregularities in Store keeping are automatically checked.
(5) Mix-up of more than one item in one bin or keeping the same stock in two places, are also brought out.

5.1.4 Disadvantages :

(1) If stock is verified at frequent intervals of less than a year it becomes expensive.
(2) The need for stoppage of activities even for small period for the purpose of stock verification makes the method costly.
(3) No regular or special staff is employed for stock-taking, inexperienced persons are appointed at short notice. The result of this is that the stock-taking becomes inaccurate.
(4) Periodic stock verification can have more mistakes.

5.2 CONTINUOUS STOCK TAKING :

5.2.1 Nature :

The other name for continuous stock-taking is "Perpetual Inventory Control", In this system the stocks are checked throughout the year in a systematic manner. The verification plan and programme are so chalked out and the work of counting, weighing, measuring and listing of items is so well distributed that, the entire stock is checked in routine way, without duplication throughout the year. The notice regarding the particular stock to be checked is given to the storekeeper only on the day of checking of that stock, and not earlier. The factory work goes on normally during the checking period. As the checking is a continuous process, the bulky items of minor value are checked only once in a year, while items of importance and high value are checked even twice or thrice a year.

5.2.2. Procedure for continuous stock taking :

(1) The stock verification staff plans the programme of stock-taking in a systematic manner with proper distribution of work among themselves.
(2) Different sections of the stores are taken up for verification turn by turn.
(3) Notice of the particular stock to be verified each day is given to the Store-keeper only on the date of actual verification.
(4) Consignments of stores which are received in the godown and which have not been inspected and recorded should not be mixed up with the stock at the time of stock verification.
(5) The physical stock of an item in the godown is counted and recorded.

5.2.3 Methods of recording the results of stock verification :

(I) Inventory Tags :
The tag consists of two parts viz.
(a) The Upper Part : This is attached to the particular stores bin at the location to indicate that the item has been verified.
(b) The Lower Part : This part is torn off and kept together. (a)Advantages of Inventory Tags Method:

(1) Most suitable method for any industry.

(2) Useful for verification of the slow-moving items.

(3) The Columns Provided at the bottom of the tag record information Verification of Receipts and issues between the actual date and last date of verification.

(4) Useful as verification is done without shutting down the factory.

(5) Useful for preparing final accounts; because closing balance of stock is necessary to be recorded in final accounts.

(6) Useful in case of stock-verification if done after the closing date. A proforma for Inventory Tag is given below in Fig. 8.2.3 (1).

INVENTORY TAG		
Store Code :	No.	
(Bin - card / Ledger Folio No.)	Unit Code No.:	
Nomenclature :	Stock Verifier :	
Quantity :	Date :	
Store Code :	No.	
Nomenclature :	Unit :	
Quantity :	Stock Verifier :	
Godown No.:	Date :	
Date	Issue after Verification	Receipts after Verification

Fig Inventory Tag

(II) Record in Bin Cards:

The result of stock verification may be entered in the bin-cards. The balance found on physical verification is entered in red ink. The physically counted figure; may be recorded on the bin-card even if it differs from the bin-card balance. The date of stock verification is also recorded on the bin-card, so that the check of the records will indicate whether any item has been left unverified.

(III) Stock Verification Sheets:

These sheets are maintained date-wise. This helps us to give the list of the items verified date-wise. The quantity actually found at the time of stock verification is recorded on the stock sheet. The bin-card balances are also recorded. Finally, these sheets are sent to the stores ledger clerk who enters the balance as recorded in the stores ledger. This will help for verification of any difference between actual quantity and quantity as per bin card.

5.2.4 Advantages of Continuous Stock-Taking :

1) Final Accounts can be prepared quickly.
2) The system generally has a sobering influence on the stores staff.
3) Closure of normal functioning is not necessary.
4) Stock discrepancies are likely to be brought to the surface and corrected much earlier than under the annual stock-taking system.
5) The movement of stores items can be watched more closely by the stores auditor so that, chances of obsolescence are reduced.
6) It avoids labourious and costly work of stock taking at the end of the year.
7) Moral check exists upon the employees concerned with stock records.
8) Discrepancies are detected in time so that necessary action can be taken to avoid repetition of mistakes in future.

5.3 RECONCILIATION OF PHYSICAL STOCK-BIN CARD AND STORES LEDGER.

5.3.1 Necessity :

If stock is verified physically and if there is any difference in physical stock recorded on bin-card or stores ledger, then in such cirumstances there is need to reconcile physical stock with bin-card and stores ledger. e.g. if on the date of verification of some spcified items, physical balance is, 100 kg and corresponding bin-card and ledger balances are 125 kg and 120 kg respectively. In this case the correct balance is always the physical balance.

If bin-card and ledger balances disagree with physical balance, then these balances should be adjusted to the physical balance.

Sometimes, bin-card and stores ledger balances differ from one another. In such circumstances there is a need to reconcile these two balances and come down to the agreed book figure. Secondly, if there is difference between physical balance and bin-card balance, then it is transferred to the surplus or deficiency in stock account.

The bin-card and ledger balances are independently reconciled when physical stock taking is going on.

RECORD OF STOCK-TAKING

Serial No.....

Date of Verification	Nomenclature of Stores	Stores Code No.	Location	Frequency of Verification	Date Verified Last	Unit	Stores Balance			Surplus	Deficit	Adjustment
							Physical	Bin Bard	Stores Ledger			

FIG. 5.2.3 (2) FORM OF STOCK VERIFICATION SHEET :

5.3.2 Causes For The Differences in Balances of Bin-card and Stores Ledger :

1) Wrong positing in wrong sheet of store ledger and wrong bin-card.
2) Posting of issue documents in receipts column or vice-versa.
3) Sometimes, some materials are received or issued for approval and recorded temporarily in the cards only. Such types of transactions are not recorded in the store ledger.
4) Totalling mistake is committed while working out the balances.
5) Sometimes, posting is not done in the bin card or in the stores ledger.

Hence, there is need to reconcile the difference regularly and to keep all the postings updated.

5.4 ABC ANALYSIS :

5.4.1. Meaning :

It is a system of inventory control. To exercise proper control on stores, it is essential that the store items should be classified according to values so that the most valuable items may be paid greater and due attention regarding their safety and care, as compared to others. The stores are divided into three categories, Viz. A, B and C.

5.4.2 Nature :

An analysis of the material costs will show that a smaller percentage of items of materials in the stores may contribute to a large percentage of the value of items may represent a smaller percentage of the value of consumption and on the other hand a large percentage of items consumed. Between these two extremes will fall those items, the percentage number of which is more or less equal to their value of consumption. Item falling in the first category are treated as "A' items, of the second category as "B' items and items of the third category are taken as "C' items. Such an analysis of material is known as ABC analysis.

5.4.3 Categories :

1) "A' category of items consists of only a small number i.e. 5% to 10% of the total items but they are quite valuable, the values being 70% to 75% in the total cost of inventory.
2) "B' category of items are relatively less important. They may be 15% to 25% of the total items of material handled by stores and have 15% to 25% of the total value of inventory.
3) "C' category of items consists of a large number i.e. 70% to 75% of the total items but carrying little value ranging from 5% to 10% of the total value of inventory.

PROFORMA OF A BIN CARD

BIN CARD

Description of Material :
Maximum level :
Minimum level :
Re-order level :

Bin No.
Code No. of Material :
Stores Code No.
Unit :
Location of Material :

Date	Receipts		Issues		Balance	Stock Verification	
	GRN No.	Quantiy	Reqn. No.	Quantity	Quantity	Date	Initials

Fig. 3

5.4.4 Control Over ABC Items :

In the ABC system, greatest care and control is to be exercised on the items of "A' list as any loss or breakage or waste of any items of this list may prove to be very costly.

In the case of "B' category of items as the sum involved is moderate, proper care need be exercised.

In the case of "C' category of items there is no need of exercising constant control.

5.4.5 The Report of The Indian Productivity Team on "Stores and Inventory Control in U.S.A. Japan and West Germany" :

Example of ABC Analysis :

Group	Percentage of item	Percentage of costs
A	8%	75%
B	25%	20%
C	67%	5%

For example, a stores has 1000 items of consumption and monthly consumption of Rs. 5,00,000. In this example according to the above report, 80 items will have a consumption of Rs. 3,75,000,250 items will account for Rs. 1,00,000 and 670 items consume material worth Rs. 25,000 only.

5.4.6 Importance :

1) The greatest degree of control would be exercised over the items of group "A'.
2) Little control would be exercised over the items of group "C'.
3) Purchase, stores and issues are to be strictly applied in case of the item of A group.
4) The time, efforts and costs can be saved on the "C' group items by not having an elaborate control.
5) To provide maximum overall protection against stock outs for a given investment in safety stocks.

5.4.7 Advantages :

1) Storage cost is reduced.
2) It ensures that, without involving any danger of interruption of materials or stores, minimum investment will be made on the inventories of the stocks of the materials.
3) Investment in inventory is reduced to the minimum possible level.
4) Large part of the work connected with purchases can be systematized on a routine basis to be handled by sub-ordinate staff.
5) Management time is saved.
6) A strict control is exercised on the items having high percentage in the material costs.

PROFORMA OF A STORES LEDGER

STORES LEDGER

Description of Material :
Maximum level :
Minimum level :
Re-order level :
*Normal lead time :

Bin No.
Code No. of Material :
Stores Code No.
Unit :
Location of Material :

Date	Receipts					Issues					Balance			Remarks
	GR. No.	Quantiy	Rate Rs.	Amount Rs.	Reqn. No	Quantity	Rate Rs.	Amount Rs.		Quantity	Rate Rs.	Amount Rs.		

Fig. 4

Normal lead time means the time taken to receive the materials in stores from the time of placing the order.

5.4.8 Practical Problems :

Problem - 1

From the following information calculate the Average Value per item of stores:
1) If a stores has 5,000 items of consumption and a monthly consumption of Rs. 5,00,000.
2) If a stores has 7,000 items of consumption and a yearly consumption of Rs. 12,00,000.

Class	Percentage of total Number of items	Percentage of the total Value
A	6%	70%
B	30%	20%
C	64%	10%
	100%	100%

Solution :

1)

Class	Number of items	Percentage of the total No. of items	Value Rs.	Percentage of the total value	Average value per item Rs.
A	300	6	3,50,000	70	1,16,667
B	1500	30	1,00,000	20	66.67
C	3,200	64	50,000	10	15.63
Total	5,000	100	5,00,000	100	

Working Notes :

1) Calculation of No. of items :

	Categories		
	A	B	C
Percentage of each category of item x Total No. of items i.e.	6% of 5,000 300	30% of 5,000 1,500	64% of 5,000 3,200

2) Calculation of Total Value per items :

	Categories		
	A	B	C
Percentage of each category of item x Total i.e.	70% of Rs. 5,00,000 Rs. 3,50,000	20% of Rs. 5,00,000 Rs. 1,00,000,	10% of Rs. 5,00,000 Rs. 50,000

3) Calculation of Average Value per item :

	Categories		
	A	B	C
Total value per item	3,50,000	1,00,000	50,000
No. of items	300	1,500	3,200
i.e.	1166.67	66.67	15.63

Solution (ii) :

Class	Number of items	Percentage of the total No. of items	Value Rs.	Percentage of the total value	Average value per item Rs.
A	420	6	8,40,000	70	2,000
B	2,100	30	2,40,000	20	114.28
C	4,480	64	1,20,000	10	26.78
Total	**7,000**	**100**	**12,00,000**	**100**	-

Working Notes :

1) Calculation of No. of items :

	Categories		
	A	B	C
Percentage of each category of item x Total No. of items i.e.	6% of 7,000 420	30% of 7,000 2,100	64% of 7,000 4,480

2) Calculation of Total Value per items :

	Categories		
	A	B	C
Percentage of each category of item x Total No. of items i.e.	70% of Rs.12,00,000 Rs. 8,40,000	20% of Rs. 12,00,000 Rs. 2,40,000	10% of Rs. 12,00,000 Rs.1,20,000

3) Calculation of Average Value per item :

	Categories		
	A	B	C
Total value per item	Rs. 8,40,000	Rs. 2,40,000	Rs. 1,20,000
No. of items	420	2,100	4,480
i.e.	Rs. 2,000	Rs. 114.28	Rs. 26.78

Problem - 2

From the following information calculate Average Value of Consumption per item, if a stores has 4,000 items of consumption and a monthly consumption of Rs. 8,00,000.

Class	Percentage of the total No. of items	Percentage of the total value
A	10	70
B	20	20
C	70	10
	100%	**100%**

Solution :

Class	Number of items	Percentage of the total No. of items	Value Rs.	Percentage of the total value	Average value per item Rs.
A	400	10	5,60,000	70	1,400
B	800	20	1,60,000	20	200
C	2,800	70	80,000	10	28.57
Total	**4,000**	**100**	**8,00,000**	**100%**	-

Working Notes :

I) Calculation of No. of items :

	Categories		
	A	B	C
Percentage of each Category of items x Total No. of item i.e.	10% of 4,000 400	20% of 4,000 800	70% of 4,000 2,800

2) Calculation of Total Value per item :

	Categories		
	A	B	C
Percentage of each category of item x Total No. of items i.e.	70% of Rs. 8,00,000 Rs. 5,60,000	20% of Rs. 8,00,000 Rs. 1,60,000	10% of Rs. 8,00,000 Rs. 80,000

Problem - 3 :

From the following information determine category of items and total value per item if a store has 5,000 items and if the total monthly consumption is Rs. 5 lakhs.

% of item	% if cost
8%	75%
25%	20%
67%	5%

Solution :

Class	Number of items	Percentage of the total No. of items	Total Value of consumption	Percentage of the total value	Average value per item Rs.
A	400	8	3,75,000	75	937.5
B	1,250	25	1,00,000	20	80
C	3,350	67	25,000	5	7.47
	5,000	**100**	**5,00,000**	**100**	-

Working Notes :

1) Calculation of No. of items :

	Categories		
	A	B	C
Percentage of each Category of items x Total No. of item i.e.	8% of 5,000 400	25% of 5,000 1,250	67% of 5,000 3,350

2) Calculation of Total Value per item :

	Categories		
	A	B	C
Percentage of the total value x Total value i.e.	70% of Rs. 5,00,000 3,75,000	20% of Rs. 5,00,000 1,00,000	5% of Rs. 5,00,000 25,000

3) Calculation of Average Value per item :

	Categories		
	A	B	C
Total value per item	3,75,000	1,00,000	25,000
No. of items	400	1,250	3,350
i.e.	937.50	80	7.47

Conclusion : Average value per item is more in category A and average value per item is less in "C' category.

Problem - 4

From the following information calculate Total Value per item and percentage of the Total Value, if a stores has 10,000 items of consumption.

Class	Percentage of the total No. of items	Percentage of the total value
A	10%	Rs. 2,000
B	25%	Rs.100
C	65%	Rs.10

Solution :

Class	Number of items	Percentage of the total No. of items	Value Rs.	Percentage of the total value	Average value per item Rs.
A	1,000	10	20,00,000	86.40	2,000
B	2,500	25	2,50,000	10.80	100
C	6,500	65	65,000	2.80	10
	10,000	**100**	**23,15,000**	**100**	

Working Notes :

1) **Calculation of No. of items :**

Categories

	A	B	C
Percentage of the total No. of items x Total No. of items i.e.	10% of 10,000 1,000	25% of 10,000 2500	65% of 10,000 6,500

2) **Calculation of Total Value per item :**

Categories

	A	B	C
No. of items x Average value per item i.e.	1,000 x Rs. 2,000 20,00,000	2,500 x Rs. 100 2,50,000	6,500 x Rs. 10 65,000

3) Calculation of percentage of the Total Value :

	Categories		
	A	B	C
$\dfrac{\text{Total value per item}}{\text{Total Value}}$ x 100	$\dfrac{20,00,000}{23,15,000}$ x 100	$\dfrac{2,50,000}{23,15,000}$ x 100	$\dfrac{2,65,000}{23,15,000}$ x100
i.e.	86.40	10.80	2.80

Problem - 5

From the following information calculate Total Value per item and percentage of the Total Value, if a stores has 1,00,000 items of consumption.

Class	Percentage of the total No. of items	Percentage of the total value
A	10%	Rs. 2,000
B	25%	Rs.100
C	65%	Rs.10

Solution :

Class	Number of items	Percentage of the total No. of items	Value Rs.	% of the total value	Average value per item Rs.
A	10,000	10	2,00,00,000	86.40	2,000
B	25,000	25	25,00,000	10.80	100
C	65,000	65	6,50,000	2.80	10
	1,00,000	**100**	**2,31,50,000**	**100**	

Working Notes :

1) No.of items   **A**   **B**   **C**
   % x total items   10,000   25,000   65,000

2) Total value of each
   class (No.of items x   2,00,00,000   25,00,000   65,000
   Value per item

3) % of Total Value
   Total value of each class   86.40%   10.80%   2.80%
   x 100 Total value

5.5. INVENTORY RATIOS

There are various methods of judgement of efficiency of material management. Ratio analysis is one of the effective methods of inventory control. Following are some of the ratios:

1. Inventory Turnover Ratio :

This ratio is a relationship between cost of materials consumed and average inventory held during the period. It is calculated by applying the following formula;

$$= \frac{\text{Cost of Material Consumed}}{\text{Cost of Averages Stock held during the period}}$$

$$\text{Cost of Average Stock} = \frac{\text{Cost of Opening Stock} + \text{Cost of Closing Stock}}{2}$$

Higher ratio indicates fast moving stock. Low ratio indicates locking up of working capital.

The ratio can be calculated in days as follows :

$$\frac{\text{Days during the period}}{\text{Inventory Turnover Ratio}}$$

This ratio shows the period for which inventory is held. The period should be as minimum as possible. Shorter the period, better is the management.

In order to find out investment in stock, the following ratios can be calculated :

$$\frac{\text{Total Inventory}}{\text{Cost of Production}} \quad \text{and} \quad \frac{\text{Cost of Sales}}{\text{Average Finished Goods Inventory}}$$

2. Input Output Ratio :

This ratio is a relationship between finished goods and material consumed. It is calculated as follows :

$$= \frac{\text{Value of Output}}{\text{Value of Input of Materials}}$$

The ratio can be calculated by applying the following formula.

$$:= \frac{\text{Standard Cost of Actual Quantity}}{\text{Standard Cost of a Standard Quantity}}$$

This ratio facilitates to know the performance of the firm. It also helps to know whether the use of material is favourable or unfavourable.

3. Ratio of slow moving items to Total Inventory :

This ratio is calculated to find out the proportion of slow moving items to total inventory. It is given by the following formula:

$$= \frac{\text{Slow moving Stores}}{\text{Total Inventory}}$$

This ratio helps to identify the slow moving items. Higher ratio indicates that there are many slow moving items and therefore capital is locked up. Management should take immediate steps to set right this situation.

Practical Problems - Problem : 1

Calculate inventory turnover ratio.

	Material X Rs.	Material Y Rs.
Opening Stock	25,000	87,500
Closing Stock	15,000	62,500
Purchases	1,90,000	1,25,000

Determine fast moving material.

Solution :

1. Material Consumed :

	X	Y
Opening Stock	25,000	87,500
+ Purchases	1,90,000	1,25,000
	2,15,000	2,12,500
- Closing Stock	15,000	62,500
	2,00,000	1,50,000

2. Average Inventory $= \dfrac{25,000+15,000}{2} \quad \dfrac{87,500+62,500}{2}$

$= \qquad 20,000 \qquad 75,000$

3. Material Turnover

Ratio $= \dfrac{2,00,000}{2,000} \qquad \dfrac{1,50,000}{7,500}$

$\dfrac{\text{Cost of Materials}}{\text{Average Inventory}} = \qquad 10 \text{ times} \qquad 2 \text{ times}$

4. Material Turnover

$$\text{in days} = \frac{365}{10} \qquad \frac{365}{2}$$

$$\frac{\text{Days during the period}}{\text{Inventory Turnover}} = \qquad 36.5 \text{ days} \qquad 182.5 \text{ days}$$

$$\text{(i.e. 37 days)} \quad \text{(i.e. 183 days)}$$

Material X is fast moving as compared to material Y as it takes only 37 days to consume the average stock. In case of Y it takes 183 days to consume the average stock. By considering low turnover ratio of Y, its stock level should be refixed and change the Purchasing Policy.

Problem - 2

Inventory records of Sunlight Ltd. shows the following information :

Material	Opening Stock	Purchaes	Closing Stock
A	700 kg	11.500 kg	200 kg
B	200 litres	11.00 litres	1200 litres
C	100 kg.	1800 kg.	1200 kg.

The inventory is valued @ Rupee 1 per kg or litre.

Calculate material turnover ratio for each of the material.

Solution :

Material Consumed	=	Opening Stock + Purchases – Closing Stock.
Material A	=	700 + 11,500 - 200 = 12,000 kg.
Material B	=	200 + 11,000 - 1,200 = 10,000 litres.
Material C	=	1,000 + 1,800 - 1,200 = 1,600 kg.

$$\text{Average Inventory} = \frac{\text{Opening Stock} + \text{Closing Stock}}{2}$$

$$\text{Material A} = \frac{700 + 200}{2} = \frac{900}{2}$$
$$= 450 \text{ kgs. of Rs. } 450$$

$$\text{Material B} = \frac{200 + 1,200}{2} = \frac{1,400}{2}$$
$$= 700 \text{ kgs of Rs. } 700$$

$$\text{Material C} \quad = \frac{1,000+1,200}{2} = \frac{2,200}{2}$$
$$= 1,100 \text{ kgs of Rs. } 1,100$$

Material Turnover

$$\text{Ratio} \quad = \frac{\text{Cost of Materials consumed}}{\text{Average Inventory}}$$

$$\text{Material A} \quad = \frac{12,000}{450} = 26.67 \text{ times}$$

$$\text{Material B} \quad = \frac{10,000}{700} = 14.29 \text{ times}$$

$$\text{Material C} \quad = \frac{1,600}{1,100} = 1.46 \text{ times}$$

Material Turnover

$$\text{(in days)} \quad = \frac{\text{Days of the period}}{\text{Inventory Turnover}}$$

$$\text{Material A} \quad = \frac{365}{26.67} = 14 \text{ days}$$

$$\text{Material B} \quad = \frac{365}{14.29} = 26 \text{ days}$$

$$\text{Material C} \quad = \frac{365}{1.46} = 250 \text{ days}$$

Material "C" is slow moving and it takes 250 days to consume the average stock.

Problem - 3

The following information is available from the books of Ramesh Enterprises for the year 2014.

Particulars	Material A	Material B
1. Opening Stock	2,000	3,000
2. Purchases	20,000	7,000
3. Closing Stock	3,000	3,500

Calculate the material turnover ratio and determine which material is fast moving.

Solution :

	Material A Rs.	Material B
Opening Stock	2,000	3,000
Add : Purchases	26,000	7,000
	28,000	10,000
Less : Closing Stock	3,000	3,500
Material consumed	25,000	6,500

$$\text{Average Inventory} = \frac{\text{Opening Stock + Closing Stock}}{2}$$

For Material A $= \dfrac{2,000 + 3,000}{2} = 2,500$

Material B $= \dfrac{3,000 + 3,500}{2} = 3,250$

$$\text{Material Turnover Ratio} = \frac{\text{Materials Consumed}}{\text{Average Inventory}}$$

For Material A $= \dfrac{25.000}{2,500} = 10 \text{ times}$

Material B $= \dfrac{6.500}{3,200} = 2 \text{ times}$

As Material Turnover Ratio of Material "A' is high Material "A' is fast moving material.

Problem - 4

The following information is available from the books of Akash Enterprises for the year 2014.

Particulars	Material A	Material B
1. Opening Stock	1,400	2,000
2. Purchases	23,000	3,600
3. Closing Stock	1,000	2,400

Calculate the material turnover ratio of the above types of materials and determine which of the material is fast moving.

Solution :

	Material A Rs.	Material B Rs.
Opening Stock	1,400	2,000
Add : Purchases	23,000	3,600
	24,400	5,600
Less : Closing Stock	1,000	2,400
Cost of Material consumed	23,400	3,200

Average Inventory $= \dfrac{\text{Opening Stock + Closing Stock}}{2}$

For Material A $= \dfrac{1,400 + 1,000}{2} = 1,200$

For Material B $= \dfrac{2,000 + 2,400}{2} = 2,200$

Material Turnover Ratio $= \dfrac{\text{Materials Consumed}}{\text{Average Inventory}}$

For Material A $= \dfrac{23,400}{1,200} = 19.5$ times

For Material B $= \dfrac{3,200}{2,200} = 1.45$ times

As Material Turnover Ratio of Material "A' is high, Material "A' is fast moving material.

Problem - 5

From the following for the year ending 31st March, 2014.

Compute :

a) Cost of Materials Consumed

b) Average Inventory

c) Inventory Turnover Ratio

	Material A Rs.	Material B Rs.
Opening Stock	40,000	36,000
Purchases during the year	2,08,000	1,08,000
Closing stock	24,000	48,000

Solution :

1. Materials Consumed = Opening Stock + Purchases – Closing Stock

   Material A   = 40,000 + 2,08,000 - 24,000

                     = Rs. 2,24,000

   Material B   = 36,000 + 1,08,000 - 48,000

                     = Rs. 96,000

2. Average Inventory $= \dfrac{\text{Opening Stock + Closing Stock}}{2}$

   Material A $= \dfrac{40,000 + 24,000}{2} = \text{Rs.}32,000$

   Material B $= \dfrac{36,000 + 48,000}{2}$

                   = Rs. 42,000

3. Inventory Turnover

   Ratio $= \dfrac{\text{Materials Consumed During the year}}{\text{Average Inventory}}$

   Material A $= \dfrac{2,24,400}{32,000} = 7 \text{ times p.a.}$

   Material B $= \dfrac{96,000}{48,000} = 2.3 \text{ times p.a.}$

   Inventory Turnover in

   Number of days $= \dfrac{365}{\text{Inventory Turnover Ratio}}$

   Material A $= \dfrac{365}{7} = 52 \text{ days}$

   Material B $= \dfrac{365}{2.3} = 159 \text{ days}$

Problem - 6

Calculate the material Turnover Ratio for the year 2014 from the following information and determine which of the two materials is fast moving.

	Material A Rs.	Material B Rs.
Material in hand 1.1.2014	60,000	80,000
Material in hand 31.12.2014	20,000	60,000
Purchases during the year	2,00,000	1,20,000

Solution :

Cost of Material Consumed	Material A	Material B
Opening Stock	60,000	80,000
Add : Purchases	2,00,000	1,20,000
	2,60,000	2,00,000
Less : Closing stock	20,000	60,000
	2,40,000	1,40,000
Average Stock		
Opening Stock	60,000	80,000
Closing Stock	20,000	60,000
	80,000	1,40,000

Average Stock $\quad \dfrac{80,000}{2} \qquad \dfrac{1,40,000}{2}$

$\qquad\qquad\qquad = 40,000 \qquad = 70,000$

$$\text{Material Turnover Ratio} = \frac{\text{Cost of Material Consumed}}{\text{Cost of Average Stock}}$$

$$\text{Material Turnover} = \frac{2,40,000}{40,000}$$

Ratio of A $\qquad = 6$ times p.a.

$$\text{Turnover Ratio of B} = \frac{1,40,000}{70,000}$$

Material Turnover in

days $\qquad = \dfrac{\text{Days during the year}}{\text{Material Turnover Ratio}}$

Material Turnover of A

$$\text{in days} \quad = \frac{365}{6} = 60.83 \text{ days (i.e. 61 days)}$$

Material Turnover of B

$$\text{in days} \quad = \frac{365}{2} = 182.5 \text{ days (i.e. 183 days)}$$

A turnover ratio of 60.83 days shows that the average stock of material A is held for 60.83 days whereas the average stock of material B is held for 182.5 days which means that material A is fast moving whereas material B is slow moving.

Problem - 7

Calculate Material Turnover Ratio for the year 2013-14 from the following information and determine which of the two materials is most fast moving.

	Material A Rs.	Material B Rs.
Material in hand :		
On 1.4.2113	50,000	1,75,000
On 31.3.2014	30,000	1,25,000
Material purchased during the year	3,80,000	2,50,000

Solution :

	Material A Rs.	Material B Rs.
1. Cost of Material Consumed :		
Opening Stock	50,000	1,75,000
Add : Purchases	3,80,000	2,50,000
	4,30,000	4,25,000
Less : Closing Stock	30,000	1,25,000
Cost of Material Consumed :	4,00,000	3,00,000
2. Average Stock :		
Opening Stock	50,000	1,75,000
Closing Stock	30,000	1,25,000
	80,000	3,00,000
Average Stock	$\dfrac{80,000}{2}$	$\dfrac{3,00,000}{2}$

3. Material Turnover Ratio $= \dfrac{\text{Cost of Material Consumed}}{\text{Cost of Average Stock}}$

   a) Material Turnover Ratio of Material A $= \dfrac{4,00,000}{40,000} = 10$

   b) Material Turnover Ratio of Material B $= \dfrac{3,00,000}{1,50,000} = 2$

4. Material Turnover in days $= \dfrac{\text{Days during the year}}{\text{Material Turnover Ratio}}$

Material Turnover of A Material in

days $= \dfrac{365}{10} = 36.5 \text{ days}$

Material Turnover of B Material in

days $= \dfrac{365}{2} = 182.5 \text{ days}$

     A turnover ratio of 36.5 days shows that the an average stock is being held for 36.5 days. On the other hand a turnover of 182.5 days shows that an average stock is being held for 182.5 days. Therefore, material B is very slow moving while material A is fast moving.

Problem - 8

     Calculate the material Turnover Ratio for the year 2013-14 from the following information and determine which of the two materials is slow moving.

	Material No.1 Rs.	Material No. 2 Rs.
Material in hand :0000		
On 1-4-2013	10,000	15,000
On 31-3-2014	25,000	5,000
Material purchased during the year	1,00,000	75,000

Solution :

	Material No. 1	Material No. 2
	Rs.	Rs.
1. Cost of Material Consumed :		
Opening Stock	10,000	15,000
Add : Purchases	+ 1,00,000	75,000
	1,10,000	90,000
Less : Closing Stock	25,000	5,000
Cost of Material Consumed :	85,000	85,000
2. Average Stock :		
Opening Stock	10,000	15,000
Closing Stock	+ 25,000	5,000
	35,000	20,000

$$\text{Average Stock} \qquad \frac{35000}{2} \qquad \frac{20,000}{2}$$

$$= 17,500 \qquad = 10,000$$

3. Material Turnover Ratio $= \dfrac{\text{Cost of Material Consumed}}{\text{Cost of Average Stock}}$

a) Material Turnover Ratio of Material No. 1 :

$$\frac{85,000}{17,500} = 4.85$$

b) Material Turnover Ratio of Material No. 2 :

$$\frac{85,000}{10,000} = 8.5$$

4. Material Turnover in days $= \dfrac{\text{Days during the year}}{\text{Material Turnover Ratio}}$

a) Material Turnover of Material No. 1 in days :

$$\frac{365}{4.85} = 75.25 \text{ (i.e. 75 days)}$$

b) Material Turnover of Material No. 2 in days :

$$\frac{365}{8.5} = 42.94 \text{ (i.e. 43 days)}$$

Conclusion : Material No. 1 is slow moving.

Problem - 9

Calculate material turnover ratio for the year 2014 from the following details.

Particulars	Material X Rs.	Material Y Rs.
Opening Stock	25,000	87,500
Closing Stock	15,000	62,500
Purchases	1,90,000	1,25,000

Solution :

	Material X Rs.	Material Y Rs.
Opening Stock	25,000	87,500
Add : Purchases	1,90,000	1,25,000
	2,15,000	2,12,500
Less : Closing Stock	15,000	62, 500
Material Consumed	2,00,000	1,50,000

$$\text{Average Inventory} = \frac{\text{Opening Stock} + \text{Closing Stock}}{2}$$

$$\text{Material X} = \frac{25,000+15,000}{2} = 20,000$$

$$\text{Material Y} = \frac{87,500+62,500}{2} = 75,000$$

Material Turnover

$$\text{Ratio} = \frac{\text{Material Consumed}}{\text{Average Inventory}}$$

$$\text{Material X} = \frac{2,00,000}{20,000} = 10$$

$$\text{Material Y} = \frac{1,50,000}{75,000} = 2$$

Problem - 10

Calculate the Material Turnover Ratio for the year 2013-14 from the following information and determine which of the two materials should be immediately disposed off.

	Material X Rs.	Material Y Rs.
Material in hand :		
On 1-4-2013	25,000	20,000
On 31-3-2014	75,000	90,000
Material purchased during the year	50,000	90,000

(P.U.)

Solution :

	Material X Rs.	Material Y Rs.
1. Cost of Material Consumed :		
Opening Stock	25,000	20,000
Add : Purchases	+ 50,000	90,000
	75,000	1,10,000
Less : Closing Stock	75,000	90,000
Material Consumed :	Nil	20,000
2. Average Stock :		
Opening Stock :	25,000	20,000
Closing Stock	+ 75,000	90,000
	1,00,000	1,10,000
Average Stock	$\dfrac{1,00,000}{2}$	$\dfrac{1,10,000}{2}$
	= 50,000	= 55,000

3. Material Turnover Ratio = $\dfrac{\text{Cost of Material Consumed}}{\text{Cost of Average Stock}}$

a) Material Turnover Ratio of Material X :

$$\frac{0}{50,000} = 0 \text{ times p.a.}$$

b) Material Turnover Ratio of Material Y :

$$\frac{20,000}{55,000} = 0.36 \text{ time p.a.}$$

Conclusion : Material X should be immediately disposed off.

Problem - 11

From the following data for the year ended 31st December, 2013.

Calculate the Inventory turnover ratio of two items and determine which of the two materials is fast moving.

	Material X Rs.	Material Y Rs.
Opening Stock 1-1-2013	40,000	60,000
Purchases during the year	2,08,000	2,00,000
Closing Stock 31-12-2013	24,000	20,000

Solution :

1. Calculation of cost of material consumed :

$$= \text{Opening Stock} + \text{Purchases} - \text{Closing Stock.}$$

Material X $= 40,000 + 2,08,000 - 24,000 = \text{Rs. } 2,24,000$

Material Y $= 60,000 + 2,00,000 - 20,000 = \text{Rs. } 2,40,000$

2. Calculation of Average Inventory :

$$= \frac{\text{Opening Inventory} + \text{Closing Inventory}}{2}$$

Material X $= \dfrac{40,000 + 24,000}{2} = \text{Rs. } 32,000$

Material Y $= \dfrac{60,000 + 20,000}{2} = \text{Rs. } 40,000$

3. Calculation of Inventory Turnover Ratio :

$$= \frac{\text{Cost of Material Consumed}}{\text{Average Inventory}}$$

Material X $= \dfrac{2,24,000}{32,000} = 7 \text{ times p.a.}$

$= \dfrac{2,40,000}{40,000} = 6 \text{ times p.a.}$

Problem - 12

The following information is available from the books of Prakash Co.Ltd. for the year 2013-14.

Particulars	Material A Rs.	Material B Rs.
Opening Stock	1,400	2,000
Purchases	23,000	3,600
Closing Stock	1,000	2,400

Calculate the material turnover ratio of the above types of materials and determine which of the materials is fast moving.

Solution :

Calculation of cost of materials consumed.

Particulars	Material A Rs.	Material B Rs.
1. Opening Stock	1,400	2,000
Add : Purchases	+ 23,000	3,600
	24,400	5,600
Less : Closing Stock	1,000	2,400
Material Consumed :	23,400	3,200

Formula : Opening Stock + Purchases - Closing Stock

$$\text{Material Turnover Ratio} = \frac{\text{Cost of Material Consumed}}{\text{Cost of Average Stock}}$$

$$\text{Cost of Average Stock} = \frac{\text{Cost of Opening Stock} + \text{Cost of Closing Stock}}{2}$$

$$\text{Material A} = \frac{1400 + 1000}{2}$$

$$= 1200$$

$$\text{Material B} = \frac{2000 + 2400}{2}$$

$$= 2200$$

Material Turnover Ratio :

$$\text{Material A} = \frac{23,400}{1,200}$$

$$= 19.5$$

$$\text{Material B} = \frac{3,200}{2,200}$$

$$= 1.45$$

Material A is fast moving material as the ratio is high.

Problem - 13

From the following information relating to two materials A and B for the year 2013-14, determine which of the two materials is to be disposed off immediately.

Particulars	Material A Rs.	Material B Rs.
Materials in hand on 1/4/2013	25,000	20,000
Material purchased during the year	50,000	40,000
Material in hand on 31/3/2014	75,000	20,000

(P.U.May 1997, Oct 2004)

Solution :

Calculation of cost of materials consumed.

Formula : Opening Stock + Purchases - Closing Stock

Particulars	Material A Rs.	Material B Rs.
1. Opening Stock	25,000	20,000
Add : Purchases	+ 50,000	40,000
	75,000	60,000
Less : Closing Stock	-75,000	-20,000
Material Consumed :	NIL	40,000

Formula : Opening Stock + Purchases - Closing Stock

$$\text{Material Turnover Ratio} = \frac{\text{Cost of Material Consumed}}{\text{Cost of Average Stock}}$$

$$\frac{\text{Cost of}}{\text{Average Stock}} = \frac{\text{Cost of Opening Stock} + \text{Cost of Closing Stock}}{2}$$

$$\text{Material A} = \frac{25{,}000 + 75{,}000}{2}$$

$$= 50{,}000$$

$$\text{Material B} = \frac{20{,}000 + 20{,}000}{2}$$

$$= 20000$$

Material Turnover Ratio :

$$\text{Material A} = \frac{0}{500}$$

$$= 0$$

$$\text{Material B} = \frac{40{,}000}{20{,}000}$$

$$= 2$$

Material A should be immediately disposed off as it has zero turnover ratio.

Objective Type

A. State whether the following statements are True of False.

1) Continuous stock taking is an inseparable feature of perpetual invertory system.
2) Low value and high volume of items fall in "C" category under ABC Analysis.
3) ABC Analysis for material control is based on general principle of pareto Distribution.
4) Perpetual inventory system and continuous stock taking are synonymous.
5) ABC Analysis is based on the principle of 'Management by exception.'
6) Inventory Sheet is prepared by the storekeeper.
7) Under periodic inventory control system the entire stock is verified at periodic intervals.
8) ABC Analysis is a system of inventory control.
9) More control would be exercised over the items of group 'C'
10) Ratio Analysis is one of the effective methods of inventory control.
11) Under the ABC analysis of material contorl 'A' stands for highest number of items.

Answer : 1) True 2) True 3) True 4) False 5) True 6) False 7) True 8) True 9) Fasle 10) True, 11) False

B. Fill in the blanks.

1) In continuous stock taking, the stocks are checked ...... the year.
2) Under periodic inventory system the entire stock is verified at .... intervals.
3) The result of stock verification is entered on ...... cards.
4) The bin card and ledger balances are ...... reconciled.
5) "A' Catagory of item consists of only a .... numbers.

Answer : 1) throughout 2) Periodic 3) bin 4) independently 5) small

C) Essay Type

1) Explain in brief the meaning of periodic Inventory control. State the procedure of periodical verification of stocks.
2) Enumerate the advantages and disadvantages of Periodic Inventory control.
3) What are the advantages of continuous Stock Taking over the "Annual Stock taking?
4) What is meant by continuous stock taking? State the procedure of continuous stock taking.
5) What are "Invertory Tags" and "Stock verification sheet?" Give proforma of each of them.
6) Explain the significance of ABC Analysis.
7) What is Inventory Ratio. State the different catagories of Inventory ratios.
8) Give the meaning of the terms "Invertory Ratio". Explain the advantages of Inventory ratio. How it is useful to management?

D) Write Short Notes on :

1) Periodic Inventory Control
2) Continuous Stock taking
3) Inventory Tags
4) Bin cards
5) ABC Analysis
6) Inventory Ratios.
7) Periodic Inventory System
8) Inventory Ratios

LABOUR COST, REMUNERATION AND INCENTIVES

6.1 Records and Methods - Time Keeping and Time booking

6.2 Methods of Remuneration.

6.2.1 Time Rate System

6.2.2 Piece Rate System

6.2.3 Taylor's Differential Piece Rate System

6.3. Incentive plans

6.3.1 Halsey Premium plan

6.3.2 Rowan Premium plan

6.3.3 Group Bonus Schemes :

6.1 TIME KEEPING AND TIME BOOKING

INTRODUCTION - Labour being an important element of cost requires a careful thought. Under any system of costing there must be an adequate provision for proper control over expenditure on labour. Accurate and systematic record of time keeping and time booking facilitates effective managerial control over labour cost. Thus, control over labour cost is very much essential, which can be effected by the co-ordinated efforts of the personnel department, cost-accounting department and time - keeping department.

Meaning.

Time keeping - It is an accurate record of each worker's exact time of arrival and departure from the factory during regular working hours and overtime during irregular working periods and of reporting the time of each worker for every departmental operation and production order. Thus, time-keeping is the detailed recording of attendance of the employees. In a large organisation a separate time keeping department looks after the time keeping function whereas a small organisation time keeping section functions under the personnel department. Accurate system of time keeping is very essential in every organization.

i) to have a correct record of workers - attendance to meet statutory requirements.
ii) to maintain discipline and regularity in attendance.
iii) to prepare the payroll when the workers are remunerated on time rate basis.
iv) to distinguish between normal time and overtime, regular and latecomers.
v) to use it for research and other statistical purposes.
vi) for overhead recovery rates, if based on labour hours.

The time keeping department functions under a head time keeper assisted by a number of time keepers and time clerks. The time keeper records the time of arrival and departure of the workers at and from the factory. This recording of time is normally done twice during the day but where the workers are allowed to leave the factory premises during the lunch break, it is done at four times during the day.

Time - Booking - It is the process of recording the time spent by the worker on each job or operation if he is a direct worker, or against each standing order number, if he is engaged on direct work. Thus, time booking is the recording of work-time of the workers spent by them during their period of attendance in the factory. It is the recording of work-time for purposes of cost analysis and apportionment of labour costs between various jobs. Accurate record of the time spent by the worker for individual cost centres is very essential in every organisation.

i) to ensure that the time paid for is properly utilized.
ii) to ascertain exact labour cost for each individual job and the cost of work done.
iii) to provide a basis for apportionment of overheads.
iv) to ascertain and control idle time and work evasion.
v) for evaluation of labour performance.

Difference between Time keeping and Time booking.

Time - Keeping	Time - Booking
1) It is the recording of attendance time of the workers.	1) It is the recording of time spent by the worker on different jobs during his period of attendance.
2) It is the recording of time for the purpose of attendance and wage calculations.	2) It is the recording of time for the purpose of cost analysis and apportionment of labour.
3) It helps to maintain discipline in attendance.	3) It helps to minimise idle time.
4) Attendance time can be recorded through register disc or token system or time recording clocks.	4) Work-time can be recorded through daily time sheet, weekly time sheet, job card or labour cost card.
5) An efficient system of time keeping should be smooth and quick.	5) An efficient system of time booking should provide proper instructions for filling the work-time.

Methods of Time-keeping.

The methods of recording the time of the workers vary considerably according to the prosperity and outlook of the company. Old fashioned methods like attendance registers and metal tokens, etc. still function satisfactorily in small concerns. However, modern Time Recorders represent an advanced technology in this field and prove economical only large concerns.

The methods of time-keeping can be broadly classified into two categories. a) Manual methods, and b) Mechanical methods.

Manual Methods. There are mainly two manual methods. These are :

a) Attendance Register or Muster Roll. This is the oldest method of time keeping and is still used in small establishments. Under this method, a register is maintained which provides for sufficient number of columns for each worker's attendance. This register may be kept either in the time office near the factory gate or with the foreman in the department. Alternatively, workers may be asked to sign the register noting down their "in' and "out' time.

This method is quite cheap and simple to operate. But it can be used only in small factories.

b) Token or Disc Method. Under this system each worker is allotted a number of his identification. Metal tokens bearing these numbers are hung on a board, serially arranged, at the entrance of the factory. As and when a worker arrives, he picks up his token or disc and drops it into the box provided for this purpose. Instead of dropping the tokens into the box, workers may be asked to hang their tokens on another board, called attendance board.

After the expiry of the time, the first box is removed and replaced by another for latecomers. Alternatively, workers coming late may be required to report at the time office so that the exact time of their arrival can be noted.

After the factory gates are closed, the time clerk marks the attendance in register on the basis of tokens in the boxes. The absentees are indicated by the missing tokens in the box.

This method is an improvement on the attendance register method and can be used in small and medium size concerns. But this method has certain defects.

a) It is difficult to check one worker dropping more than one token into the box, one for himself and the other for his friend.

b) The accuracy of the record depends entirely on the integrity of the time keeper. Frauds can be committed by inclusion of dummy workers in the payroll.

c) In case of disputes, doubts etc. this method does not offer any proof of accuracy.

Mechanical Methods. These methods have been devised to overcome the shortcomings of the manual methods.

a) Time Recording Clocks : The use of time recording clocks has now become almost universal except in small businesses. Under this method, time cards, also known as clock cards, are used. These cards, are of uniform size and made of stiff paper. Each worker is allotted a card which bears his identification number. A specimen of time card is given below

ABX Co. Ltd.						
Time Card						
Worker's Name				Department		
Worker's No				Week ending		
Day	Morning		Afternoon		Total Hours	
	In	Out	In	Out	In	Out
Monday						
Tuesday						
Wednesday						
Thursday						
Friday						
Saturday						
Time keeper					Total	

These cards are kept in racks near the clock at the entrance gate. There are usually two racks known as "In' and "Out' racks. The "In' rack contains the cards of all workers who are inside the factory, and the "Out' rack, which is on the other side of the clock, holds the cards of the workers who are not in the factory. When a worker enters the gate, he picks up his card from the "out' rack, inserts it into the clock and the time is stamped at the relevant space. He takes his card out and keeps it in the "in' rack. This process is reversed when he goes out of the factory. i.e., he stamps the departure time and places back his card in the "out' rack.

Some clocks print particulars of late arrival and overtime in red ink. The change of stamping colours is automatically made at the predetermined time.

A time-keeper will be in charge of the clock to ensure that workers do not stamp the cards of their absent friends.

This method has the following advantages.

1) The clocks produce a definite, unchallengeable record.
2) It reduces the chances of false and fraudulent entries.
3) It makes easier the work of calculation of wages and preparation of payroll.

b) **Dial Time Recorders :** This is a variation of Time Recording clocks. It consists of a mechanism with dial having about 150 holes around the circumference. When a worker enters the factory, he presses the dial arm into a hole which denotes his particular number and the time is recorded automatically on an attendance sheet placed inside the clock. This attendance sheet forms a part of the payroll and there is no need of copying out the record. But this method has the following defects.

a) The time of worker's arrival and departure are widely separated on the paper, making the calculation of worker's total time cumbersome.

b) The capacity to this machine is quite limited as the number of holes is only about 150.

Time Booking : In addition to the recording of the attendance of a worker, it is also necessary to record the time spent by him on each job or operation, if he is a direct worker. Time booking is a process of recording the time spent by a worker on different jobs carried out by him during his period of stay in the factory. Objects of time booking are.

a) To ascertain the cost of work done.

b) To ensure that the time for which worker has been paid is properly utilised.

c) To ascertain the idle time so as to control it.

d) To provide a basis for the apportionment of overheads.

There are various methods of time booking and various types of forms are used for this purpose. Four types of cards are commonly in use.

a) **Combined time and job card :** This card records the attendance time and the time spent on different jobs on the same form. It consists of two sections - one for recording attendance and the other for recording the work time, i.e., time spent on different jobs. This combined time and job card can be more conveniently used when the recording of time is done by time clocks. One advantage of this method is that reconciliation of attendance time and work time is simplified as any difference between the two can be easily brought to light. A specimen of this card is given below.

ABX Co. Ltd.

Time -cum-job card

Worker's Name .....   Department ....
Worker's No .....   Week ending ....

Day	Job No.	Clock time		Job time		Ordinary time	Over time	Job time	Idle time
		In	Out	From	To				
Monday									
Tuesday									
Wednesday									

Thursday Friday Saturday								
				Total				

Hourly rate of pay ....
Total Wages ......   Signed ....

b) Job Card : This card is prepared for each job. When a worker takes up a job, a job card bearing its job number is given to him. Times of starting and finishing the job are recorded in this card.

ABX Co. Ltd.			
Job card			
Job No. ...... Name of Worker ..... No. of Worker		Department .... Date 20	
Description of job	Quantity		
	Produced	Accepted	Rejected.
Time start ...... Time finish ..... Hours taken ...... Hourly rate of pay .... Total cost		Worker's Sign .... Foremen's Sign	

When the job is completed or suspended for any reason, the worker is given another card bearing the next job number.

c) Labour Cost Card. This is a type of circulating job card. It is meant to record the time taken on the job by all the workers employed on it. Instead of allotting one card to each worker, the same card is passed round and the time taken by each worker on that job is recorded on it. Thus, this card gives the total labour cost of a job.

d) Piece-Work Card. Where workers are paid on piece rate system, piece-work card is used. Such a card is maintained for each job separately.

* New methods of Time Keeping & Time Booking -

* Biometric attendence - Employee attendence is taken on biometric machine through thumb punching, eye scarning,etc. biometric way of attendence is most popular and used in govt.offices in India.

* **Card punching -** Alongwith biometric card attendence is also used for security purpose.

* **System log in -** System oriented working conditions are now inevitable part of commerce industry computers & other devices are connected to each other through network and employees should log in on system through his/her password and Id.

* **Online time sheet -** This method is mainly used in all BPO and IT oriented service sector, daily reporting is mandatory for employees. Time sheet is to be submitted and mailed by employees daily before logging off the system.

* **Softwares like SAP, ERP -** Softweres i.e.MIS system of company has inbuilt facility of time keeping & time booking nearby 80% of companies in India use softweres for MIS and record keeping. These system has their own method of time keeping & time booking.

* **GPS Icards -** In countries like USA, UK employees are given GPS Icards to note their time in campus and off campus.

Wages Abstract
(Wages Analysis Sheet)

Wages abstract is ""a document which is a classified record of time and / or wages compiled from labour time records" I.C.M.A. This is a summary of wages paid during a period on different Jobs. It is prepared after analysing the Time and Job Cards. It is prepared in the following form.

ABX' Co. Ltd. Wages Abstract								
Dept							Week ending	
	Job No.							Total
Worker No.	301 Rs.	302 Rs.	303 Rs.	304 Rs.	305 Rs.	306 Rs.	307. Rs.	Wages Rs..
11			150		30			180
12	40	15						55
13				65		30		95
14			40				85	125

	Job No.							Total
15		36			24			60
16	54						15	69
17						170		170
18		34						34
19				45				45
20			25				20	45
Total	94	85	215	110	54	200	120	878

PAYROLL

A payroll (or wage sheet) is a list of all employees showing major details relating to their pay, particularly gross wages, deductions and net wages payable for a particular period. Preparation of a payroll falls into two parts :

(a) Computation of employees' gross wages

(b) Computation of employees' net wages.

The wages payable to an employee vary according to the basis on which he is paid. The main bases are :

(a) **Time basis.** Where the employee is paid a fixed daily or monthly rate irrespective of the amount of work he does.

(b) **Piece basis.** Where the employee is paid a fixed rate per unit or piece produced irrespective of the time taken.

(c) **Bonus Plan.** Where the employee is paid on time basis or piece basis and receives in addition a bonus relating to the amount of work he produces.

In large concerns a separate department known as Payroll Department is set up for the computation and disbursement of wages. A proforma wages sheet is given on page 281 :

Payment of Wages

On completion, the wage sheets are sent to the cash office for the payment of wages. Generally, payment is made in the department in which workers are working, in the presence of a responsible official. Payment for an absent worker is not made to any other person unless a duly authorised letter from the absent worker is produced.

Frauds in the Payment of Wages. The preparation of wage sheet and the payment of wages provide ample scope for frauds. The common types of frauds are :

(a) The inclusion of dummy or fictitious workers in the payroll.

(b) Marking an absent worker as present.

(c) Inclusion of fictitious overtime.

(d) Showing higher rate of wages in the payroll.

(e) Omission to record deduction from wages.

(f) Manipulating in the computation of wages.

(g) Ignoring to mark late arrivals or early departures.

Prevention of Frauds. The following steps may be taken to prevent frauds :

1. Every employee should be issued an identity card. This card should be produced at the time of payment of wages.

2. Attendance should be recorded by time recording clock. The work of punching time card should be properly supervised by the time keeper so that no worker punches the card of his absent friend.

3. No payment for overtime should be made unless it is properly sanctioned.

4. A comparison should be made between the attendance and time booked to Jobs.

5. The cashier should not have any hand in the preparation of wage sheet.

6. The payroll should bear the signature of each clerk concerned with its preparation.

7. The exact amount of total wages payable should be drawn from the bank and exact cash payable to each worker should be put into individual envelopes or pay packets.

8. The distribution of wages should be in the presence of some responsible officer and foreman who can identify the worker.

9. A proper account should be maintained in respect of unclaimed wages and entered in "undistributed wages book."

6.2 METHODS OF REMUNERATION

Introduction

Remuneration is the price or compensation paid for labour and services offered by the workers. The term remuneration includes wages, salaries, fees, allowances etc. Wages are paid for the physical work while salary is paid to the staff and executives for the services rendered by them. Fees are paid to the consultants, auditors, professional practitioners etc. Allowances are paid for house rent, leave travel assistances etc. Remuneration of labour is the most complicated problem in the developing countries like India, because there connot be a single method of wage payment which is acceptable to the employers as well as to the workers. Wages is the only means of income to the workers. Hence, they try to get maximum from the employers. On the other hand the employers try to keep down the labour cost as low as possible. The result of these two situations taken together is that labour management relations are strained. The methods of payment of wages should be such that labour cost per unit is reduced and at the same time workers are paid sufficiently for their work.

Essential Features (Characteristics) of a Good Wage System :

The choice of a paritcular method depends upon general consideration such as the nature of the industry, prevailing economic conditions, availability of the required type of labour and the standard of education and skill attained by workers. Howerver, a good wage system should have the following features.

PAYROLL / WAGES SHEET

Department....

For the month of......

No.	Worker's Name	Rate Rs.	Hours Worked		Earnings				Gross Wages	Deductions					Net Amt payable	Signature of Workers
			Regular	Over time	Regular	over time	Bonus	D.A.	Allowances		P.F	E.S.I.	Fines	I.Tax	Total		

1. **Simplicity :** It should be simple and capable of being understood by the workers, so that workers can make their own calculations. Also it should be easy to operate with minimum scripty work.

2. **Suitability :** It should be suitable to industry. For example, time wage system is suitable of work where quality is important.

3. **Fair and Just :** It should be just and fair to both the worker and employer. It should be based upon scientific time and motion study to ensure a standard output to the employer and a fair amount of wages to the workers.

4. **Guarantee of minimum wages :** It should guarantee a minimum living wage to ensure a satisfactory standard of living.

5. **Linking with efficiency :** There should be direct relation between reward and efforts and skill and responsibility. More the efforts and skill, higher should be the wages.

6. **Incentives offered :** The incentives offered to workers should be such that the workers are encouraged to work more and more to get more wages.

7. **Standard of performance :** Any system of wages should set attainable objectives. This means the standard of performance fixed should be within the abilities of an average worker.

8. **Resembleness in particular locality :** The system should keep in view the wage rate in the same area or industry. The method selected by an organisation should be as far as possible in line with that of its competitors. It should not in anyway be entirely different from that of industry or locality.

9. **Minimum cost :** The cost in terms of money, clerical labour and time should be minimum in deciding any wage system.

10. **Flexibility :** It should be flexible and capable of being adapted to changed circumstances.

11. **Quality should not be affected :** The wage system should be such as "Better wages for better quality." Otherwise in order to earn more and more wages, the workers, may produce inferior quality goods.

12. **Worker's morale :** The system should be such which should boost the morale of the workers and should minimise labour turnover, absenteeism and late attendance.

13. **Equal wages for equal work :** The system should be such that the workers with equal efficiency get equal wages, otherwise there will be dissatisfaction among the workers.

14. **Permanent wage system :** It should not be changed frequently, otherwise the workers will not trust the system.

15. **Changes in prices should be considered :** There should be an escalation clause providing for an automatic rise in wages as cost of living index number increases.

16. **Within the framework of various laws :** It should be in conformity of various labour laws and regulations both local and national. It should not violate any local or national trade unions agreements.

Methods of Remuneration :

Basically, there are only two methods of remuneration of labour :

1. **Time - rate system and**
2. **Piece - rate system.**

Under time - rate system. payment is made to the workers on the basis of time spent by him in the factory irrespective of the amount of work done. **Under piece - rate system,** payment is made to the workers on the basis of work done by him in the factory irrespective of the time taken by him.

From the combination of the above two systems, various other premium bonus plans have also been prepared and are vogue in different industries. All these various wage systems can be shown in the following chart.

Methods

1) Time wages	2) Piece - work wages	3) Incentive wage plans
1. Flat Time - Rate	1. Straight Piece - Rate	1. Halsey premium plan
2. High Day Rate	2. Taylor's Differential Piecc - Rate.	2. Rowan premium plan
3. Measured Day Rate	3. Merrick's Multiple Piece Rate	3. Halsey - Weir System
4. Graduated Time - Rate	4. Group Piece - Rate	4. Barth Premium Plan
5. Differential Time Rate		5. Gantt Task and Bonus Plan
		6. Emerson's Efficiency Bonus system
		7. Bedaux Points Premium system
		8. Priestman's Production Bonus Plan
		9. Towne Plan
		10. Profit sharing and Co-partnership

6.2.1 Time - Rate System

In this method, the worker is paid on the basis of time attended by him irrespective of the work done by him. The time unit may be per month, per week, per day or per hour. Extra payment for overtime work will also be paid under this system.

This method is suitable in the following cases.

i) Where quality of goods produced is of utmost importance e.g. artistic goods.
ii) Where accuracy of the output is very important e.g. in watch-making, tool making etc.
iii) Where the speed of production is beyond of the control or energy of the workers e.g. when production is automatic or depends on heat treatment or a chemical reaction.
iv) Where the work is incapable of exact measurement.
v) Where strict supervision is possible.
vi) Where production passes through different operations and disturbances cannot be avoided.
vii) Where work demands high degree of skill.

Advantages

1) **Easy understanding -** This method is simple to understand and calculate. The amount of wages to be paid can be calculated without any tedious mathematical calculations.

2) **Guarantees minimm wage -** Hourly, daily, weekly or monthly rates are fixed and workers are assured of certain amount of wages to be received after a definite period. This creates sense of security among them.

3) **Quality output -** The wages of the workers are fixed hence the worker is not hasty. The worker uses best of his talents to make a quality of production. Thus, quality is not sacrified for quantity.

4) **Trade unions favour -** Labour unions favour this method because no distinction is made between efficient and inefficient workers.

5) **Most economical -** As remuneration is not based on work done, the workers avoid over speeding and thus cause less damage to equipment. Detailed records of work done is not required. All this results in the economy in the cost of administering the system.

Disadvantages -

1) **No inducement -** Efficient and inefficient workers are treated alike and thus there is no inducement for hard work.

2) **Labour cost per unit increases -** As reward is not directly linked up with work performed, inefficiency may creep in. Amount of work done shall reduce and labour cost per unit of product shall increase.

3) **Loitering by workers -** Workers are paid on the basis of time spent in the factory

premises, it may encourage loitering by workers within the premises of the factory to waste their time in unproductive activites.

4) **Requires more supervision and control -** Workers develop tendency to work slow or idle away the time. This necessitates more supervision and control.

5) **Production suffers -** The workers become lazy and dull and try to avoid work. In this way the production suffers.

System of time - wage - There are various systems of Time wage. They may be summarised as follows.

1) **Flat time - rate** (or time-rate at ordinary level) - When concerns pay at a flat rate on the basis of the time they are employed, it is known as flat time rate of wages. The normal duration is fixed in advance. The flat rate may be per hour, day week or month. The flat rate is usually fixed keeping in view the rate prevailing in similar trades in the same locality for the same grade and skill.

Formulae :
   Earnings = Hours worked x rate per hour.

2) **High day rate (or time rate at high wage level) -** Under this method, the rate of wages is fixed by hour or day but the amount specified is relatively higher. The purpose behind this method is to attract efficient workers who can easily be motivated to achieve pre-determined standards of efficiency and output. The salient features (advantages) of this system are :

Advantages
   1) It provides incentive to best workers which is not available in the ordinary time rate system.
   2) It is simple and cheap as ordinary time rate system.
   3) It attracts the best and talented workers.
   4) It increases labour productivity.
   5) It results in reduced labour cost per unit.
   6) It demands less supervision.

Disadvantages.
   1) It cannot be adopted in the case of concerns where output cannot be measured.
   2) It becomes useless if output levels are not properly fixed.
   3) It does not benefit the less efficient workers and
   4) The purpose of the method may be defeated if local employers also raise their rates to attract better workers.

3) **Measured day-rate -** The workers employed under this method are given specified work and the level of wages is fixed in accordance with the levels of performance specified by the employer.

4) **Graduated time-rate** - Under this method the cost of living index factor is taken into consideration. The rate of wages are linked up with the cost of living index.

Though, this method is favourable both to the employers and employees, the determination of a wage index is difficult.

5) **Differential time rate** - Under this method different rates of wages are fixed for different workers in the same group according to the differences in their personal abilities and skill. Higher rates are given to efficient workers in their merits and there is a positive incentive for improvement of performance by the workers.

6.2.2 Piece-rate System

Under this system a worker is paid a fixed amount per unit produced irrespective of the time taken. A rate per unit of output is fixed and wages are calculated as follows.

Formula :

Earnings = No. of units produced × Rate per unit.

Under this method the rates are fixed by systematic work study, time and motion study, and job evaluation. This method of remuneration is more suitable in following cases.

1) Where quantity of work is main factor and quality is not important e.g. mining. quarries etc.
2) Where work can be measured in convenient units.
3) Where job rate can be easily fixed.
4) Where there is continuous work etc.

This method is also known as "Payment by Results.' Because in this method wages are paid to the workers on the basis of work done by him and not on basis of time taken by him.

Advantages :

1) **Simple** - It is simple to operate and is also understood easily by the worker.
2) **Strong incentive** - It provides a strong incentive because remuneration is in direct ratio to the worker's effort.
3) **Cost fixed in advance** - Labour cost per unit of product or for particular job can be fixed in advance.
4) **Saving in cost of supervision** - Not much supervision is needed as the workers themselves take care of the time and output.
5) **Inefficient worker is easily located** - Inefficient workers can be easily located and it is possible to adopt suitable measures to improve their performance or replace them by efficient men.
6) **Exact labour cost determination is possible** - The employer is able to know his exact labour cost per unit which will help him in making quotations confidently.
7) **Reduction in idle time** - Idle time is not paid for as in time wage system. Thus, idle time will be reduced to minimum.

Disadvantages -

1) **Quality suffers** - Increase in production is likely to affect the quality of work. Where quality is more important the employer has to spend more on supervision, inspection and quality control.

2) **Careless handling** - Owing to careless handling, material wastage may increase and tools, machines etc. may not receive proper care, as they are in hurry to produce maximum possible limits of product in order to earn more wages. This also leads to heavy wear and tear of machinery.

3) **Fixing proper piece rate is difficult** - Fixation of a suitable piece rate is a real problem. Too low piece rate is disadvantageous to the workers and too high piece rate is disadvantagous to the management.

4) **Feeling of insecurity** - Workers have the fear of losing wages if they are not able to work due to some reason.

5) **Useless for trainees** - For trainees this system is not very good as they may not be able to earn anything.

6) **Labour-union disputes** - Disputes between labour union-management generally arise about piece-rates. This system does not provide guarantee of minimum payment of wages of the worker. Hence, trade unions generally oppose this mode of payment.

7) **Rigidity** - Piece-work rates may be fixed too high and once they have been fixed, it is difficult to alter.

8) **Adverse effect on health of worker :** In order to get more and more wages, workers may work for long hours beyond their capacity. Thus, they may spoil their health.

9) **Interruption in constant flow of production** - Workers may work at a furious speed for a few days to earn good wages and then absenting themselves for a few days, upsetting the uniform flow of production.

Methods of Piece-work wages.

6.2.2. 1 Straight Piece-Rate

Under this method, workers are paid wages at a fixed amount per unit of product manufactured, irrespective of the time taken to produce it.

Formula -

i) **Where rate per unit is known -**

Total earnings = No. of units x Rate per unit.

ii) **Where standard hour rate is known.**

Total earnings = Standard hours of work produced x rate per standard hour.

Units produced may be jobs, operations or another convenient units in terms of which product is expressed. A rate of payment fixed for the unit produced is known as the piece-rate.

The advantages and disadvantages of piece-rate system which are mentioned above are generally - associated with straight piece -rate system. So students are requested to mention the above advantages and disadvantages to the straight piece-rate system if asked.

Difference between Time-Rate and Piece-Rate.

Time Rate	Piece-Rate
1) Worker is paid on the basis of time spent in the factory.	1) Worker is paid on the basis of work done in the factory.
2) Work done is not considered.	2) Time spent is not considered.
3) Extra payment for over-time work is generally paid to the workers.	3) No question of overtime wages arises under this method.
4) This method is useful where quality of work is most important.	4) This method is useful where quantity of work is most important.
5) Trade unions favour this method because no distinction is made between efficient and inefficient workers.	5) Trade unions generally oppose this method because here, dinstinction is made between efficient and inefficient workers.
6) Tools and equipment are carefully handled by workers because there is no hurry to complete the work.	6) To get more and more wages workers are in hurry to complete a work. It may result in damage to tools and equipments.
7) Minimum day wages are guaranteed.	7) Day wages are not guaranteed.
8) No incentives are given under this method.	8) Incentives are given to efficient workers under this method.
9) Certainty of income.	9) Uncertainty of income.
10) Strict supervision and control is necessary under this method.	10) There is no need of strict supervision and control.
11) Idle time may increase in this method.	11) Idle time cannot arise under this method, because all workers are in hurry to complete their work.
12) Exact labour cost cannot be determined, so difficulty in sending tenders quotations may arise.	12) Determination of exact labour cost is possible. So preparation of tenders and quotations becomes quite easy.

6.2.2.2. Piece work with guaranteed time rate.

In the straight piece-rate system no minimum wages is guranteed to a worker who is paid according to output. But in this case, minimum wages based on time rate for 8 hours is guaranteed. When the piece rate earnings are less than time rate earnings, he will be paid at piece rate earnings. In short, worker will be paid Time-Rate earnings or piece rate earnings whichever is higher.

This is to safeguard worker's earnings when there are delays, shortages, tool breakages etc. which make it impossible for workers to earn more.

Labour cost per unit decreases with increase in production until piece-rate earnings exceed the guarantee, thereafter the labour cost per piece remains constant.

This system has the same advantages as straight piece-rate system. In addition, the worker is not unduly penalised when his piece-work earnings are low through circumstances beyond his control. Disadvantages of this method are also similarly to straight piece-rate system except the cause of insecurity of the worker is avoided.

6.2.2.3 Differential Piece-Rate

Under straight piece rate method a flat rate per unit is paid for the entire output produced. Naturally, the incentive for higher production declines. The differential piece rate system seeks to overcome this disadvantage by paying at different rates for different levels of efficiency reflected in the output. Consequently, an efficient worker is induced to increase his level of efficiency. This method has the following three variants.

6.2.3. Taylor's Differential Piece-rate - This scheme was introduced in the U.S.A. by Dr. F.W. Taylor who is the father of scientific management. Under this method, no minimum time rate is guranteed. Standard time for a job is fixed by time and motion study. The scheme provides two different piece-rates.

Formulae - Low piece-rate i.e. 80% of normal piece-rate when below standard.

High piece - rate i.e. 120% of normal piece-rate when at or above standard. This system has the following features.

Features -
1) Day wages are not guaranteed.
2) It provides two piece rate for output below standard and high piece-rate for output above standard.
3) Scheme is suitable in mass production industries.
4) If a worker produces more than standard output within time he will be given higher piece-rate. And if worker is below the standard, he shall be given lower rate of wages.
5) It provides strong incentive to the efficient worker.

Advantages -
1) It stimulates workers to achieve high rate of production.
2) It is simple and easily understandable.
3) It attracts only the efficient workers.
4) Due to increased production, incidence of fixed overheads per unit is reduced.

Disadvantages -
1) It penalises inefficient workers.
2) It affects the quality of work.

3) It does not guarantee minimum wages.
4) It creates disparity among workers and may weaken their unity.
5) It is not good for the human being or the quality of his work.

    Lower rate is criticised by labour as primitive and unfair and possibly this is the reason for Taylor's system which could not become popular.

Example -

    From the following information calculate wages earned by Mr.A & B under the Taylor's system -

Stanard time allowed	- 10 units per hour
Normal wage rate	- Rs.2 per unit

Differential wage rate to be applied -

    80% of piece rate when output below standard 120% of piece rate when output at or above standard. The production on a day of 8 hour - A 70 units & B 90 units.

Solution :

    Wages : No of unit produced **x** low or high piece rate.
    Standard output for a day = 10 **x** 8 = 80 units
    Wages Rate - Rs.2 per unit.

Wages -

    Mr.A = 70 **x** 2 **x** 80% = Rs.112
    Mr.B = 90 **x** 2 **x** 120% = Rs.216

Practical Problems -

Problem - 1

    On the basis of the following information, calculate the earnings of Anita and Sunita on the straight piece-rate basis and Taylor's Differential piece-rate system.

Standard production	8 units per hour
Normal time rate	Rs. 0.40 per hour.
Differential to be applied.	
80% of piece-rate below standard.	
120% of piece rate at or above standard.	

In a 9 hour day, Anita produces 54 units and Sunita produces 75 units.

Solution -

Standard production	8 units per hour.
Normal time rate	Re. 0.40 per hour.
Hence, for 8 units	Re. 0.40
For 1 unit	Re. 0.40 ÷ 8 = Rs. 0.05
∴ Piece rate	Re. 0.05 (i.e. 5 paise)

Straight piece rate -

Anita 54 units @ Rs. 0.05 = Rs. 2.70

Sunita 75 units @ Rs. 0.05 = Rs. 3.75

Differential piece rate -

Low piece rate 80% of the piece rate $\dfrac{0.05 \times 80}{100}$ = Re. 0.04

High piece-rate 120% of piece-rate $\dfrac{0.05 \times 120}{100}$ = Rs. 0.06

Standard output in a day of 9 hours at 8 units per hour is 72 units (9 x 8) Anita produces 54 units and Sunita produces 75 units. Accordingly Anita is below the standard while Sunita is above the standard. So Anita is paid at the lower piece-rate and Sunita at the higher piece-rate.

Anita 54 units @ Re. 0.04 = Rs. 2.16

Sunita 75 units @ Re. 0.06 = Rs. 4.50

Problem - 2

Standard time allowed = 20 units per hour

Normal rate per hour   = Rs. 2

Differential rate -

80% of piece rate when below standard

120% of piece-rate when at or above standard.

On a particular day of 8 hours.

"A' produces 140 units.

"B' produces 160 units.

"C' produces 180 units.

Calculate the wages of A, B and C.

Solution :

$\dfrac{2}{20}$ x 100 = 10 Paise per unit

Standard output in a day of 8 hours at 20 units per hour is 160 units (20 x 8)

'A' produces 140 units i. e. below the standard. So he is paid at low - piece rate i. e. 8 paise per unit (80% of 10 paise)

'B' produces 160 units which is exactly at standard so he is paid at high piece rate i. e. at 12 paise per unit (120% of 10 paise)

'C' produces 180 units which is above standard so he is paid at high piece - rate i. e.

at 12 paise per unit. (120% of 10 paise)

$\therefore$ 'A' world be paid 140 x Rs. 0.08 = Rs. 11.20

'B' world be paid 160 x Rs. 0.12 = Rs. 19.20

'C' world be paid 180 x Rs. 0.12 = Rs. 21.60

6.3 INCENTIVE PLANS

In between the two basic methods of remuneration described above, there are many bonus and premium plans, which are also known as incentive plans. The basic objectives of these various plans are :

1. To induce the workers to increase the production and productivity
2. To provide them additional wages for their skill and efforts
3. To raise the morale of the labour high
4. To reduce the cost of production
5. To retain the services of good workers
6. To induce the workers to serve the organisation with loyalty and sincerity and
7. To establish better labour-management relations.

General features :

1. They are a combination of time and piece rate systems.
2. Benefit is shared by both employer and the employee.
3. They relate payment to output directly or indirectly.
4. They regulate speed in such a way that workers neither tend to slow down or not accelerate their speed.
5. Wages cost per unit reduces as efficiency increases.
6. Employee's remuneration per hour increases with production but not in that proportion.
7. Time rate is guaranteed in some cases.

Essential features / Principles / Factors of sound wage incentive plans :

Before introducing an incentive plan, it is necessary to take the following factors into consideration :

1. It should be simple and easily understandable.
2. It should be fair to both the parties.
3. It should motivate workers to produce more.
4. The nature of work should permit its production.
5. Standards should be fixed by time and motion study.
6. It should guarantee time wages.
7. Standards once fixed should not be altered.
8. Workers should be taught the best method of doing a job.
9. The cost of operating the scheme should be the minimum.
10. Work should be of a repetitive nature.

11. There should be continuous flow of work.
12. It should not be opposed by trade unions.
13. Supervision should be satisfactory.
14. There should be no rate-cutting.
15. Once introduced, the scheme should be permanent.
16. It should be made applicable to indirect workers also.
17. It should aid the introduction of budgetary control and standard costing.
18. The working conditions should be uniform and the factors affecting output should be non-existent.
19. It should be flexible, so as to incorporate minor changes in the method of calculation, without disturbing the basic system of wage-payment.

Precautions : The following precautions should be taken while introducing a satisfactory incentive plans :
1. The system should be introduced first in a particular department or in a particular job. While selecting particular department or job it should be seen that there are cordial labour-management relations.
2. A proper methods study should be made in order to determine improved method of production, routing etc.
3. The scheme should be discussed with the worker's representatives.
4. Suitable instructions regarding the method of calculation of bonus and the payment of wages should be given to time office, wage office and other related department.
5. Suitable forms should be designed for booking of time, recording performance and the payment of bonus and other incentives.

Incentive plan : There are various incentive wage plans :
1. Halsey premium plan
2. Rowan premium plan
3. Halsey-weir system
4. Barth premium plan
5. Gantt task and Bonus plan
6. Emerson's efficiency bonus plan
7. Bedaux or points system.
8. Priestman's production bonus plan
9. Towne plan
10. Profit sharing and co-partnership

According to syllabus only three plans are required to be studied. They are :
1. Halsey premium plan.
2. Rowan premium plan.
3. Piece work plan
So we will see now these plans one by one :

6.3.1. Halsey-Premium-Plan :

1. Halsey premium plan : This plan was introduced by F.A Halsey, a mechanical engineer in America in 1891. Under this plan standard time is fixed for doing a job by time rate. If a worker completes the job within less than the standard time he gets a bonus of 50% of the time saved, besides his time wages for the time taken. If he cannot reach the standard, he is paid his time wages. Thus, this system guarantees time wages and does not penalise an inefficient worker. Since under this plan the benefit of time saved is shared by both the employer and the employee, it is also known as the split bonus plan or the 50 : 50 plan.

Formula :

Total earnings = Time taken x rate per hour
+ 50% (Standard time - Time taken) x Rate per hour

$$\text{OR } E = (T \times R) + \left(\frac{S-T}{2} \times R \right)$$

Where E = Total earnings
T = Time taken (i.e hours worked)
R = Rate per hour
S = Standard time (i.e time allowed)

$$\left(\text{Bonus} = \frac{S-T}{2} \times R \right)$$

Advantages :

1. It is simple to operate.
2. It is capable of being understood by workers.
3. It guarantees time wages.
4. The benefit of time saved is shared equally by both.
5. Efficient workers are induced to earn more.
6. Fixed overhead cost per unit is reduced with increase in production.
7. Since the employer also gets a share of the benefit of time saved, he is induced to provide the best equipments and methods.

Disadvantages :

1. The incentive is not strong enough to induce efficient workers to work hard.
2. Workers do not like the employer also getting a share of the benefit of time saved.
3. The workers may be encouraged to rush through work and neglect the quality of production in order to earn extra bonus.
4. If a rate is not properly fixed there is the possibility of bonus amounting to a large figure.

6.3.2 Rowan Premium Plan : This plan was introduced in Glassgow in 1891 by James Rowan.

This plan is similar to Halsey plan except for the calculation of bonus. Under this plan, bonus is that proportion of actual wages which time saved bears to the standard time. Time rate wages are guaranteed. Bonus is calculated as following.

$$\text{Bonus} = \frac{\text{Time saved}}{\text{Standard time}} \text{Time taken} \times \text{Rate per hour}$$

$$= \frac{S-T}{S} \times T \times R$$

Total earnings will be calculated as follows :

Total earning= (Time taken x Rate Per hour) + Bonus

$$= T \times R + \frac{S-T}{S} \times T \times R$$

where T = Time taken (Actual time)
  S = Standard time (Time allowed)
  R = Rate per hour

Advantages :
1. It guarantees wages according to time basis.
2. Upto 50% of the time saved, it provides a higher bonus than under Halsey plan.
3. It offers protection to the employer when - standard has not been properly fixed.
4. It is good for beginners and learners.
5. Quality of work is not neglected as this system does not induce worker to rush through work because bonus increases at a decreasing rate with higher level of efficiency.
6. Sharing of the benefit will encourage the employer to provide the best equipment and methods.

Disadvantages :
1. It is a complicated and is not easily understandable by the workers.
2. Where time saved is more than 50% of the standard time, the total earnings start decreasing.
3. Wage rate per hour can never be doubled as in Halsey plan.
4. It pays the same amount of bonus to beginners and efficient workers.
5. It provides too easy excuses for loose rate - fixing.

Comparison of Halsey and Rowan Plan :
Rowan system gives more bonus than Halsey Plan until the job is performed in half the standard time. For job performing exactly in half the standard time, bonus is the same in both the systems. But when job is performed in less than half the standard time the Rowan - system gives less bonus than the Halsey Premium plan.

Pratical Problems -

Problem - 1

Compute the earnings of a worker under :

a) Time rate method

b) Halsey plan

c) Rowan plan

Information given : Wage rate - Rs. 2 per hour

Dearness allowance - Re. 1 per hour

Standard hours - 80

Actual hours - 50

Solution :

a) Time rate system :

Wages = Hours worked x Rate per hour + D.A.

= 50 x 2 + 50

= 100 + 50

= Rs. 150

b) Halsey plan :

$$\text{Earnings} = (T \times R) + \left(\frac{S\text{-}T}{S} \times R \right) + DA$$

$$= (50 \times 2) + \left(\frac{80 - 50}{2} \times 2 \right) + 50$$

$$= 100 + 30 + 50$$

$$= Rs. 180$$

c) Rowan plan :

$$\text{Earnigs} = T \times R + \frac{S - T}{S} \times T \times R + D.A.$$

$$= 50 \times 2 + \frac{80 - 50}{80} \times 50 \times 2 + 50$$

$$= 100 + \frac{30}{80} \times 100 + 50$$

$$= 100 + 37.50 + 50$$

$$= Rs. 187.50$$

Problem -2

A worker takes 9 hours to complete a job on daily wages and 6 hours on a scheme of payment by results. His day rate is 75 paise per hour. The material cost of the product is Rs. 4 and overheads are recovered @ 150% of the total direct wages. Calculate the factory cost of the product under (a) Piece-work plan (b) Rowan plan (c) Halsey plan

Solution :

Wages under three plans :

a) Piece work plan :

Statement showing factory cost under three plans.

	Piece-work Rs.	Halsey Rs.	Rowan Rs.
Materials	4.00	4.00	4.00
Direct labour (wages)	4.50	5.62	6
Overtheads (150% of direct wages)	6.75	8.43	9
Factory cost Rs.	15.25	18.05	19.00

Problem - 3

From the following information calculate the earnings per employee under each of the following methods of wage payment :
i) Halsey Premium Plan
ii) Rowan Premium Plan

Employee :	A	B	C
Time allowed - hrs. per 100 units	30	36	40
Wages per unit Rs.	1.20	2.00	2.50
Hourly rate Rs.	5.00	6.00	7.00
Actual time taken hrs.	48	40	38
Actual units produced	220	150	150

Solution : Working :

	A	B	C
Time allowed-hours	66	54	60
Actual time taken	48	40	38
Time saved-hours	18	14	22
50% of time saved	9	7	11
Bonus 50%			
of time saved at hourly rate	Rs. 45	42	77
(under Halsey Plan)	(9 x 5)	(7 x 6)	(11 x 7)
Bonus under Rowan Plan	Rs. 65.45	62.23	97.54
by applying formulae			

$$= \frac{S-T}{S} \times T \times R$$

Statement showing total earnings of the three employees under different two plans :

Employee	Halsey plan			Rowan plan		
	Wages Rs.	Bonus Rs.	Total Rs.	Wages Rs.	Bonus Rs.	Total
A	240	45	285	240	65.45	305.45
B	240	42	282	240	62.23	302.23
C	266	77	343	266	97.54	363.54

(Note : Wages under both plans calculated as follows)

A - 48 x Rs. 5

B - 40 x Rs. 6

C - 38 x Rs. 7

Problem - 4

In a factory, guaranteed wages are paid @ Rs. 2 per hour and the payment is made on a weekly basis for a week of 48 hours. By time and motion study, it is estimated that manufacture of a product requires 25 minutes. To this, personal time and contingency allowance of 20% is to be added. During one week Nilmoni Das produced 110 articles. Calculate his wages under.

   i) Time - rate

   ii) Piece rate with a guaranteed weekly wage

   iii) Rowan premium plan

   iv) Halsey Premium plan

Solution :

   i) Time - rate

     Earnings = Hours worked x Rate per hour

           = 48 x 2

           = Rs. 96

   ii) Piece-rate :

Standard time : Time taken per unit	= 25 minutes
Add allowance 20%	= 5 minutes
Standard time	= 30 minutes

     $\therefore$ Piece rate will be Rs. $\dfrac{2 \times 30}{60}$ = Re. 1

Earnings = No. of units produced × piece rate

= 110 × 1

= Rs. 110

Alternatively, standard hours of work produced 110 units × $\frac{1}{2}$ hr. = 55 hours @ Rs. 2 per hour = Rs. 110

As piece rate earnings is greater than guaranteed weekly wages, he will get Rs. 110 for the week.

iii) Halsey plan :

$$\text{Total earnings} = T \times R + \frac{S-T}{2} \times R$$

$$= 48 \times 2 + \frac{55-48}{2} \times 2$$

$$= 96\frac{7}{2} \times 2$$

$$= 96 + 7$$

$$= Rs.\ 103$$

iv) Rowan plan :

$$\text{Total earnings} = T \times R + \frac{S-T}{S} \times T \times R$$

$$= 48 \times 2 + \frac{55-48}{55} \times 48 \times 2$$

$$= 96 + \frac{7}{55} \times 96$$

$$= 96 + \frac{672}{55}$$

$$= 96 + 12.22$$

$$= Rs.\ 108.22$$

Problem - 5

In order to finish a task, standard time of 15 hours was determined by time and motion study. Ram took 16 hours to finish the job while Shyam took 12 hours. Time rate is Rs. 3 per hour. Calculate the earnings of the workers if 50 : 50 Halsey premium plan is in operation.

Solution :

$$\text{Earnings} = T \times R + \frac{S-T}{2} \times R$$

Ram could not finish his work within the standard time. So he will not be paid any bonus, His earnings will be :

Hours worked × Rate per hour

= 16 × 3

= Rs. 48

Shyam's earnings will be as follows by applying the formula.

$$\text{Earnings} = 12 \times 3 + \frac{15-12}{2} \times 3$$

$$= 36 + \frac{3}{2} \times 3$$

$$= 36 + \frac{9}{2}$$

$$= 36 + 4.50$$

$$= \text{Rs. } 40.50$$

Problem - 6

From the following particulars work out the earning of the week of a worker under -

(a) Straight piece rate

(b) Differential piece rate

(c) Halsey premium plan

(d) Rowan premium plan

    No. of workers hours per week - 48 hrs.

Wages per hour	- Rs. 3.75
Normal time per piece	- 20 minutes
Normal output per week	- 120 pieces
Actual output for the week	- 150 pieces
Differential piece rate	- 80% of piece rate when output is below standard and 120% when above standard.

    (P.U)

Solution :

(a) Straight piece-rate system :

Earnings = No. of units produced × Rate per unit

= 150 × 1.50

= Rs. 225

(Note : weekly wages = 48 x Rs. 3.75 = Rs. 180

$$\text{Rate per unit} = \frac{180}{120} = \text{Rs. 1.50})$$

(b) Differential piece-rate system :

Output is above standard so high piece-rate is paid as follows:

$$\text{High piece-rate} = 1.50 \times \frac{120}{100} = \text{Rs. 1.80}$$

∴ Earnings will be 150 x Rs. 1.80 = 270

(C) Halsey premium plan :

Time allowed (Standard time) 150 x 20 minutes =	50 hours
Hours worked	48 hours
Time saved	2 hours

$$\text{Earnings} = T \times R + \frac{S-T}{2} \times R$$

$$= 48 \times 3.75 + \frac{50-48}{2} \times 3.75$$

$$= 180 + \frac{2}{2} \times 3.75$$

$$= 180 + \frac{7.50}{2}$$

$$= 180 + 3.75$$

$$= \text{Rs. } 183.75$$

Alternatively,

Time allowed for 120 pieces   - 48 hours

∴ Time allowed for 150 pieces   - 60 hours

$$\left(\frac{150}{120} \times 48 \right)$$

Time saved   = 60 - 48

              = 12 hrs.

$$\text{Earnings} = T \times R + \frac{S-T}{2} \times R$$

$$= 48 \times 3.75 + \frac{12}{2} \times 3.75$$

$$= 180 + 22.50$$
$$= Rs.\ 202.50$$

(d) Rowan premium plan :

Earnings $= T \times R + \dfrac{S-T}{S} \times T \times R$

$\qquad = 48 \times 3.75 + x\ \dfrac{60-48}{60} \times 48 \times 3.75$

$\qquad = 180 + \dfrac{12}{60} \times 180$

$\qquad = 180 + 36$

$\qquad = Rs.\ 216$

Problem - 7

From the following information calculate the earnings of two workers, Shiva and Hari under,

(i) Halsey plan (40% of workers)

(ii) Rowan plan

Hourly rate of wages (guaranteed) - Rs. 0.75

Standard time for producing one dozen articles is - 3 hours

Actual time taken for producing 20 dozen articles is as under.

Shiva - 48 hours

Hari - 54 hours

Solution :

Standard time for 20 dozen 60 hrs. (20 x 3)

Under Halsey Plan generally 50% of the time saved is given as a bonus. But here it is specifically mentioned that 40% of workers, hence in the formula instead of 50% we have to take 40%.

Halsey plan :

Formula :

Earnings $= T \times R + 40\% (S-T) \times R$

Shiva's earnings :

$\qquad = 48 \times Re.\ 0.75 + 40\% (60 - 48) \times Re.\ 0.75$

$\qquad = 36 + 40\% (12) \times 0.75$

$\qquad = 36 + 40\% (9)$

$\qquad = 36 + 3.60$

$\qquad = Rs.\ 39.60$

Hari's earnings :

$$= 54 \times 0.75 + 40\% (60 - 54) \times 0.75$$
$$= 40.50 + 40\% (4.50)$$
$$= 40.50 + 1.80$$
$$= Rs. 42.30$$

Rowan plan :

$$\text{Earnings} = T \times R + \frac{S - T}{S} \times T \times R$$

Shiva's earnings :

$$= 48 \times 0.75 + \frac{60 - 48}{60} \times 48 \times 0.75$$

$$= 36 + \frac{12}{60} \times 36$$

$$= 36 + 7.20$$

$$= 43.20$$

Hari's earnings :

$$= 54 \times 0.75 + \frac{60 - 54}{60} \times 54 \times 0.75$$

$$= Rs. 40.50 + \frac{6}{60} \times 40.50$$

$$= Rs. 40.50 + 4.05$$

$$= Rs. 44.55$$

Problem - 8

The following are the particulars as regards a worker who worked on Job No. 666 and 999.

Job No.	Time allowed	Time taken
666	26 hours	20 hours
999	30 hours	20 hours

His normal and basic rate of wages was Rs. 8 per day of 8 hours and his dearness allowance was Rs. 12 per week of 48 hours.

Calculate the amount payable to him on,

1. Time basis
2. Halsey premium plan (bonus at 50% of time saved)
3. Rowan premium plan

Solution :

Basic rate per hour Rs. 1

D.A per hour Re. 0.25 $\left(\dfrac{12}{48}\right)$

1. Time basis : Earnings = Hours worked **x** Rate per hour

	Job. No. 666	Job. No. 999
Basic wage @ Re. 1 per hour	20	20
D.A @ Rs. 0.25 per hour	5	5
Rs.	25	25

2. Halsey plan : Job. No. 666 :

$$\text{Earnings} = T \times R + \dfrac{S-T}{2} \times R + D.A$$

$$= 20 \times 1 + \dfrac{26-20}{2} \times 1 + 5$$

$$= 20 + \dfrac{6}{2} \times 1 + 5$$

$$= 20 + 3 + 5 = 28$$

Job No. 999 :

$$\text{Earnings} = 20 \times 1 + \left(\dfrac{30-20}{2} \times 1\right) + 5$$

$$= 20 + \left(\dfrac{10}{2}\right) + 5$$

$$= 20 + 5 + 5$$

$$= Rs. \ 30$$

3. Rowan Plan :

$$\text{Earnings} = T \times R + \left(\dfrac{S-T}{S} \times T \times R\right) + D.A.$$

Job No. 666 :

$$= 20 \times 1 + \left(\dfrac{26-20}{26} \times 20 \times 1\right) + Rs. \ 5$$

$$= 20 + \left(\dfrac{6}{26} \times 20\right) + 5$$

$$= 20 + \frac{120}{26} + 5$$

$$= 20 + 4.62 + 5$$

$$= Rs. \ 29.62$$

Job No. 999 :

$$= 20 \times 1 + \left(\frac{30-20}{30} \times 20 \times 1 \right) + 5$$

$$= 20 + \left(\frac{10}{30} \times 20 \right) + 5$$

$$= 20 + \frac{200}{30} + 5$$

$$= 20 + 6.67 + 5$$

$$= Rs. \ 31.67$$

Problem - 9

A worker takes 9 hours to complete a Job on daily wages and 6 hours on a scheme of payment by results. His day rate is Rs. 30 per hour, the material cost of the product is Rs. 40 and the overheads are recovered at 150% of the total direct wages.

Calculate the factory cost of the product under :
1. Piece Work Plan.
2. Rowan Plan.
3. Halsey Plan.

Solution :

1. Wages under Piece Work Plan :

$$6 \ hours \times Rs. \ 30$$
$$= \ Rs. \ 180$$

2. Wages under Rowan Plan :

$$\text{Wages} \ = \ T \times R + \frac{S-T}{S} \ T \times R$$

where T = Actual time   = 6 hours
S   = Standard time   = 9 hours and
R   = Rate per hour   = Rs. 30

$$= \ 6 \times 30 + \frac{3}{9} \times 6 \times 30$$

$$= \ 180 + 60$$

$$= \ Rs. \ 240$$

3. Wages under Halsey Plan :

$$\text{Time} \times \text{Rate} + \frac{50}{100} \times \text{Time Saved} \times \text{Rate}$$

$$= 6 \times 30 + \frac{50}{100} \, 3 \times 30$$

$$= 180 + 45$$

$$= \text{Rs. } 225$$

Statement of Factory Cost

Particulars	When wages are paid according to piece Work Plan Rs.	When wages are paid according to Rowan Plan Rs.	When wages are paid according to Halsey Plan Rs.
Material	40	40	40
Wages	180	240	225
Prime Cost	**220**	**280**	**265**
Factory Overheads 150% of Wages	270	360	337.5
Factory Cost	**490**	**640**	**602.5**

Problem - 10

Calculate the total earnings and effective rate of earnings per hour of the two operators. Gopal and Hassan. under :

1. Halsey plan
2. Rowan Plan

The standard time fixed for producting 100 articles is 50 hours
The rate of wages is Rs. 15 per hour.

The actual time taken for producting 100 articles is as under :

Gopal 42 hours.
Hassan 38 hours.

Solution :

Calculation of Earnings

	Earnings of	
	Gopal Rs.	Hassan Rs.

1. Halsey Plan :
@ Rs. 15 per hour
a) or 42 hours (42 x 15)   630
b) for 38 hours (38 x 15)   570
  Bonus - 50% of time saved i.e.
      50 - 42 = 8 and 50 - 38 = 12

  $\dfrac{8}{2}$ x 45 and $\dfrac{12}{2}$ x 15   <u>60</u>   <u>90</u>

  Hence, Total Earnings   <u>690</u>   <u>660</u>

2. Rowan Plan :
  Wages for the hours worked as above   630   570

  $Bonus = \dfrac{Time\ saved}{Time\ allowed}$ x Time Taken x Rate

a) $\dfrac{8}{50}$ x 42 x 15 =   <u>100.80</u>

b) $\dfrac{12}{50}$ x 38 x 15 =   <u>136.80</u>

                                  <u>730.80</u>   <u>706.80</u>

Problem - 11

Calculate the total monthly remuneration of three workers A, B, C from the following data :

a) Standard production per month per worker : 1,000 units.
b) Actual production during the month
   A - 850 units, B - 750 units, C - 950 units.
c) Piece work rate is 10 Rs. per unit of production.
d) Additional production bonus is Rs. 100 for each percentage of actual production exceeding 80% of standard production.
e) Dearness allowance - fixed @ Rs. 500 p.m.

Solution :

Statement of Monthly Wages

	A	B	C
No. of Units produced	850	750	950
% to standard production of 1,000 units	85%	75%	95%
	Rs.	Rs.	Rs.
Wages @ Rs. 10 per unit			
Bonus @ Rs. 100 for each	8,500	7,500	9,500
Percentage of efficiency in excess of 80%	500		1,500
Dearness allowance	500	500	500
Total monthly wages	**9,500**	**8,000**	**11,500**

Problem - 12

Standard time is 30 minutes per unit and Hourly Rate is Rs. 25 per hr. Bonus is paid at 30% of time saved. In a week of 48 hrs. a worker produced 120 units of which 5 units were found defective.

Calculate cost per good unit produced.

Solution :

Standard Time   :   1 unit = 30 minutes

120 unit = 3600 minutes

i.e. 60 hours

Actual Time   :   48 hours

Time saved   :   12 hours

Earning $= \text{Time} \times \text{Rate} + \dfrac{30}{100} \times \text{Time Saved} \times \text{Rate}$

$= 48 \times 25 + \dfrac{30}{100} \times 12 \times 25$

$= 1200 + 90$

$= \textbf{Rs. 1,290}$

Cost per Good Unit $= \text{Rs. } \dfrac{1,290}{115}$

$= \text{Rs. } 11.22 \text{ per unit.}$

Problem - 13

Calculate the earnings of a worker from the following information :

1. Time Rate Method.
2. Piece Rate Method.
3. Halsey Plan.
4. Rowan Plan.

Information given :

    Standard Time : 30 hours
    Time taken   : 20 hours

Hourly rate of wages is Rs. 50 per hour plus a dearness allowance @ Rs. 5 per hour worked.

Solution :

1. Earnings under Time Rate Method :

	Rs.
Wages for 20 hours (time taken) @ Rs. 50 per hour.	1,000
Dearness allowance for 20 hours @ Rs. 5 per hour	100
	1,100

2. Earnings under Piece Rate Method :   Rs.

	Rs.
Wages for 300 hours (i.e. time allowed) @ Rs. 50 per hour	1,500
Dearness allowance for 20 hours (i.e. actual hours worked) @ Rs. 5 per hour	100
	1,600

3. Earnings under Halsey Plan :   Rs.

	Rs.
Wages for 20 hours (i.e. actual hours worked) @ Rs. 50 per hour	1,000
Bonus for the half of the time saved (i.e. $\dfrac{S-T}{2} \times R = \dfrac{30-20}{2} \times$ Re. 50)	250
Dearness allowance for 20 hours @ Rs. 5.00 per hour	100
	1,350

4. Earnings under Rowan Plan :

	Rs.
Wages for 20 hours @ Rs. 50 per hour	1,000

Bonus $\dfrac{S-T}{S} \times T \times R$

where S = Standard Time; T = Actual Time and R = Rate per hour

i.e. $\dfrac{30-20}{30}$ x 20 x Rs. 50   333.33

Dearness allowance for 20 hours Rs. 5 per hour   100.00
                                                  ―――――
                                                  1.433.33

Problem - 14

Compute the earnings of a worker under :
1. Time Rate Method.
2. Piece Rate Method.
3. Halsey Method.
4. Rowan Plan.

Information given :

Wages Rate - Rs. 20/- per hour.
Dearness Allowance - Re. 10/- per hour.
Standard Hours - 80
Actual Hours - 50

Solution :

Calculation of Earning

1. According to Time Rate Method :

	Rs.
Basic wages @ Rs. 20 per hour for 50 hours	1,000
Dearness Allowance @ Rs. 10 per hour for 50 hours	500
Total Earnings	1,500

2. Piece Rate Method :

	Rs.
Wages @ Rs. 20 per hour for time allowed i.e. 80 hours	1600
D.A. @ Rs. 10 per hour for 50 hours	500
Total Earnings	2,100

3. Halsey Plan :

	Rs.
Basic Wages @ Rs. 20 per hour for 50 hours	1,000
D.A. @ Rs. 10 per hour for 50 hrs.	500

$$\text{Bonus} = \frac{50}{100} \text{ Time saved} \times \text{Rate} = \frac{50}{100} \times 30 \times 20 \qquad 300$$

Total Earnings $\qquad\qquad\qquad\qquad\qquad\qquad\qquad\qquad$ 1,800

4. Rowan Plan :

	Rs.
Basic Wages @ Rs. 20 per hour for 50 hours	1,000
D.A. @ Rs. 10 per hour for 50 hrs.	500

$$\text{Bonus} = \frac{\text{Time saved}}{\text{Standard Time}} \times \text{Time} \times \text{Rate}$$

$$= \frac{30}{80} \times 50 \times 20 \qquad\qquad\qquad\qquad 375$$

Total Earnings $\qquad\qquad\qquad\qquad\qquad\qquad\qquad\qquad$ 1,875

Problem - 15

Standard time set for Job X and Job Y is 40 hrs and 200 hrs. respectively. Mahesh is engaged on Job X and Mr. A is paid under Halsey plan Mr. B. is paid under Rowan Plan.

	Mr. A	Mr. B
Time rate per hour	Rs. 40	Rs. 25
Actual time taken	24 hrs.	120 hrs.

Calculate earnings and effective rate of earning of both.

(P.U.)

Solution :

	Mr.A	Mr.B
Standard Time	40 hrs.	200 hrs.
Time taken	24hrs.	120 hrs.
Time saved	16 hrs.	80 hrs.
Time Rate	Rs. 40	Rs. 25

Earnings of Mr. A under Halsey Plan :

Normal Earnigs	=	Time taken × Time rate
	=	24 hrs × Rs. 40/-
	=	Rs. 960

$$\text{Bonus} \quad = \quad \frac{1}{2} \text{ (time saved} \times \text{time rate)}$$

$$\qquad\qquad = \quad \frac{1}{2} \text{ (hrs 16} \times \text{Rs. 40/-)}$$

$$\qquad\qquad = \quad \text{Rs. 320}$$

Total wages	=	**Rs. 1,280**
Effective rate of		

$$\text{Earnings} = \frac{\text{Total Wages}}{\text{Hours worked}}$$

$$= \frac{\text{Rs. 1280}}{24 \text{ hours}}$$

= **Rs. 53.33** per hour.

Earnings of Mr. B under Rowan Plan :

Normal Earning	=	Time taken x Time rate
	=	120 hours x Rs. 25
	=	**Rs. 3,000**

$$\text{Bonus} = \frac{\text{Time saved}}{\text{Standard Time}} \times \text{Normal earning}$$

$$= \frac{80 \text{ hours}}{200 \text{ hours}} \times \text{Rs. 3,000}$$

	=	**Rs. 1,200**
Total wages	=	Normal Earnings + Bonus
	=	Rs. 3,000 + Rs. 1,200
	=	**Rs. 4,200**
Effective Rate of		

$$\text{Earning} = \frac{\text{Total Wages}}{\text{Time taken}}$$

$$= \frac{\text{Rs. 4,200}}{120 \text{ hours}}$$

= Rs. 35 per hour

Problem - 16

On the basis of the following information, calculate earning of Mr.Ram and Mr.Shyam on the Straight Piece Rate & Taylor's Differential piece rate.

Standard production per hour = 8 units

Normal time rate = Rs.0.40 per hour

Differential to be applied -

80% of piece rate for below std.production and 120% of piece rate for above std production.

In a 9 hours day, Ram produced 50 units and Shyam produced 80 units.

Solution :

        Rate per hour = Rs.0.40

        Std.production per hour = 8 units

        Total std production for 9 hours = 8 x 9 = 72 units

$$\text{Piece Rate} = \frac{\text{Hrly Rate}}{\text{Hrly production}} = \frac{0.40}{8 \text{ units}}$$

        = Rs.0.05

        i) Straight piece rate = Actual production x piece rate

Mr.Ram	= 50 x 0.05
	= Rs.2.50
Mr.Shyam	= 80 x 0.05
	= Rs.4.00

ii) Differential piece rate = Actual production x 80% OR 120% of piece rate.

        Mr.Ram produced 50 units i.e.below std.production

        wages = 50 x 0.05 x 80%

        = Rs.2.00

        Mr.Shyam produced 80 units i.e.above std.production

        wages = 80 x 0.05 x 120%

        = Rs.4.80

Problem - 17

        From the following particulars calculate the amount of wages & Bonus earned by worker under Halsey plan.

        Job start on Monday 1st Jan at 8 a.m. and completed on Saturday 6th Jan at 1p.m.

        Wages rate Re.1 per hour

        Standard time allowed per unit = 6 minutes

        Bonus 50% of time save & No.of units produced 600.

        The worker works 9 hours a day & no overtime is allowed.

Solution :

        Std.time for 600 units = 600 units x 6 minutes = 3600 minutes = i.e.60 hrs

Actual time = Monday to friday i.e.5 days = 5 days x 9hr = 45

+ Saturday hours = $\dfrac{5}{50 \text{ hrs}}$

Time saved = 10 hrs (60-50)

Halsey Plan :

Total wages = Time wages + Bonus

        = Actual hrs x hrly rate + 1/2 time saved x hrly rate

        = 50 x 1 + 1/2 x 10 x 1

        = 50 + 5

        = Rs.55

Problem - 18

Following are the particulars relating to three worker X,Y & Z.

Normal time rate   = Rs.0.80 per hour

Normal piece rate   = Rs.0.60 per piece

Std output per hour = 4 units

In a 40 hours week, the production of the worker is as follows -

x - 100 units

y - 160 units

z - 240 units

Calculate the earnings of the worker under -

i) Taylors differential piece rate system.

ii) Merrick's multiple piece rate system

iii) Gantt's Task and Bonus system.

Solution :

Std.production = 40 hrs x 4 units = 160 units.

1) Taylor's Differential piece rate system -

Wages = Actual production x 80% OR 120% of piece rate

Mr.X - produced 100 units i.e.below std.

Therefore 80% of the piece rate

wages = 100 x 0.60 x 80%

    = Rs.48

Mr.Y - produced 160 units i.e.at std.

Therefore 120% of the piece rate

wages = 160 x 0.60 x 120%

    = Rs.115.20

Mr.Z - produced 240 units i.e.above std.

Therefore 120% of the piece rate

wages = 240 x 0.60 x 120%

    = Rs.172.80

2) Merrick's multiple piece rate system

Wages = Actual production x Applicable piece rate

Different piece rates

upto 83% of std output

= Normal piece rate

83% to 100 % of std.output = 110% of Normal piece rate above 100% of std.output = 120% of normal piece rate.

percentages of output $= \dfrac{\text{Actual production}}{\text{Std.production}} = $ x 100

$X = \dfrac{100}{160}$ = x 100 = 62.5% i.e. below 83% of std.output

$X = \dfrac{100}{160}$ =x 100 = 100% i.e. between 83% to 100% of std.output

$X = \dfrac{240}{160}$ = x 100 = 150% i.e. above 100% of std.output

wages according to merrick's system -

X = 100 x 0.60 = Rs.60

Y = 160 x 0.60 x 110% = Rs.105.60

Z = 240 x 0.60 x 120% = Rs.172.80

3) Gantt's Task Bonus System

a) If output below std. = Time wages

b) It output at std. = Time wages + 20%

c) If output above std. = High piece rate

Mr.X - produced 100 unit i.e.below std. Therefore time wages

= Actual hours x Rate per hr

= 40 x 80

= Rs.32

Mr.Y - produced 160 unit i.e.at std. Therefore time wages + 20%

= Actual hours x Rate per hr

= 40 x 80 + (40 x 80) x 20%

= 32 + 6.40

= Rs.38.40

Mr.Z - produced 240 unit i.e.above std. Therefore high piece rate i.e. 120% of piece rate

Wages = Actual production x piece rate x 120%

= 240 x 0.60 x 120%

= Rs.172.80

Problem - 19

Following are the particulars related to the workers Ram, Shyam & Govind.

Time Rate per hr. = Rs.2

Std.Output per hour = 2 units

Low piece Rate per unit = Rs.0.75

High piece rate per unit = Rs.1.10

In a 40 hours week the production were -

Ram - 60 units

Shyam - 80 units

Govind - 100 units

Calculate the earning under -

i) Taylors differential piece rate system.

Solution :

   Std.production = 40 x 2 units = 80 units.

1) Taylor's Differential piece rate system -

   Wages = Actual production x High/Low piece rate

Mr.Ram - 60 x 0.75 (Low Rate) = Rs.45

Mr.Shyam - 80 x 0.1.10 (High Rate) = Rs.88

Mr.Govind - 100 x 1.10 (High Rate) = Rs.110

6.3.3 Group Bonus Schemes :

The premium plans discussed so far viz. Halsey Plan, Rowan Plan etc. are applicable to individal direct workers. However, in certain industries, there are particular type of jobs which require combined work of a a group of workers together. Individual work can not be separaterd. The Work is so inter related that completion of the job requires joint efforts of all the wrokers in the group. A worker's work depends on the work done by one or two of his fellow workers & therefore, it is not possible to measure separately, the output of each worker. In such a case as the individual work can not be separated, the incentive scheme to be applied should be applicable to all the persons together of that group or team. The number of persons performing the job jointly is considered as one group or team & the time spent by each of them on that specific job is paid on time basis. Then the number of units produced or output produced by that group is counted & if the actual output is more thatn the standard output then bonus is given to them as an incentive. The bouns is distributed to all the workers in that group in any of the following ways :

1) If all the workers in the group are at the equal efficiency, grade & skill then, bonus is distributed equally to them.

2) If all the workers in the group are of unequal efficiency & grade, then their time rate will be different & bouns in such case is distributed to all the workers in the ratio of time rate.

3) If all the workers in the group have unequal efficiency & at the same time, they spent different number of hours on the job then the bonus is distributed to all the worker in the ratio of their time earnings.

4) Sometimes the bonus is given to all the workers in the group on percentage basis. The precentage of each worker is calculated by considering his efficiency & the rate of pay.

5) If the group consists of skilled & unskilled workers then, the unskilled workers get bonus at their time rates & remaining bouns is disttribued to skilled workers on some basis.

The main object of introducing group bonus schemes is to create team spirit in the group. All the workers working in the group, who are working together should have the same interest in completing the work early, to achieve efficiency. When group incentive schemes are introduced, efficient workers will work more to get the advatage of group bonus & with them even the indefficent workers will have to work speedily with the result that all the workers in the group will work more. As all the workers themselves are made more interested in the work, to get group bonus, the supervision costs are less. The efficient workers of the group themselves will work as the su[pervisors to extract more work from the inefficient workers. As efficient workers are working hard, even inefficient workers in the group will get no chance to waste their time or to remain absent. Because of this production will increase.

Advantages of Group Bonus Schemes :

1) It encourages cooperation & team spirti among the workers, which will improve the labour relations.

2) As efficient & inefficient, all the workers are working hard, it results in more production.

3) In order to get the benefit of group bonus, each & every worker in the group will have to remain present because their work is interrelated. This reduces labour absenteeism.

4) As all the workers in the group are interested in the work & try to produce more, supervision costs are reduced.

5) Inefficient workers will also have to work hard as they are pulled up by the efficient workers.

6) Clerical work is reduced as the records are to be kept for the entire group & individual record is not necessary. This simplifies costing work.

Disadavatagees of Group Bonus Schemes :

1) The amount paid as bonus to each worker is very small.

2) If the bonus is distributed equally to all the workers in the group, inefficient workers will get the same amount of bonus as that of efficient workers. & in such a case efficient workers remain unsatisfied.

3) Disctribution of bonus on some suitable basis to all the workers in the group is the real problem of this method.

4) Proper care is to be taken while selecting the group. The group as far as possibkle should be homogeneous. If the workers in the group show high degree oef differences in their efficiency, seniority & speed of work then naturally both efficient & inefficient workers will remain unhappy.

5) Efficient workers suffer because of inefficiency of other workers.

6) It there is rivalry among the different workers in the group, the very purpose of this system is lost.

Suitability of Group Bonus Schemes :

Group Bonus Scheme can be advantageously used in the following cases :

1) Where output of the individual workers can not be nmeasured but output of the entire group can be measured.

2) Where the work is inter-connected & the output depends on the fforts of all the persons in the group.

3) Where management wants to create team spirit amongst the workers & thereby keep labour relations satisfactory.

4) In can be used in line production or conveyer belt system of production.

5) This system is suitble in ship building industry, iron & steel industry, Heavy engineering industry & industries having mass production.

Different types of Group Bonus Systems :

The main Group Bonus Schemes are as follows :

1) Budgeted expense bonus

2) Cost effiecency bonus

3) Priestman system

4) Towne gain sharing scheme

5) Waste reduction bonus

1) Budgeted Expense Method : In this system, the budgeted or standard expense of a certain job is calculated & actual expenses of the job are compared with it. If there are savings that is if actual expenses are less than the budgeted expenses, then workers are given bouns equal to some percentage which is predetermined. e.g. If the budgeted expenses of a job is Rs. 400. A, B & C together have completed the job in 350Rs. As per the group bonus scheme, they are entitiled to 10% bonus each, for the savings in the expenses, then their bonus is calculated as follows :

Saving in Expenses = Budegeted experises - Actual expenses

= 400 - 350

= 50 Rs.

Out of 50Rs. A, B & C will get 10% each i.e.Rs. 5 each as bonus.

This scheme can be applied to direct workers as well as to indirect workers & to the office staff.

2) Cost Efficiency Bonus : As the name suggest, in this system bonus is given for efficiency in reducing cost. The cost reduciton may be for total cost or some particulatr cost such as reduction of labour cost or reduction of overhead et. In this method, Standard cost is predetermined. Actual cost is sompared with the standard cost & if there is savings in cost then out of this saving a partcular amount is given to workers as bonus :

Problem - 20

In a factory bonus is payable for reduction in cost of labour & overheads on the following basis :

Upto 10% Savings - bonus is 5% of earnings

Upto 20% Savings - bonus is 15% of earnings

Upto 50% Savings - bonus is 30% of earnings

Upto 80% Savings - bonus is 50 % of earnings.

Upto 80% Savings - bonus is 60% of earnings.

Wage rate per hour of 4 workers A, B,C & D is Rs. 2/- , Rs. 2.50 Rs. 1.50 & Rs. 2/- respectively. The overheads are 200% of the labour cost. The standard cost per unit is Rs. 18 If time taken by A, B, C & D to finish 10 units is 25, 16, 30 & 10 hours respectively. Calculate the amount of bonus they would get.

Solution :

Statement of Calculation of Bonus

	A	B	C	D
Time Taken	25	16	30	10
Wage Rate per hour	x 2	x 2.5	x 1.5	x 2
Labour cost/ wages	50	40	45	20
overheads (200% of wages)	100	80	90	40
Total cost (Labour + Overheads)	150	120	135	60
Standard cost	180	180	180	180
Savings in cost	30	60	45	120
Percentage in reduction of cost	16.67%	33.33%	25%	66.67%
Percentage of Bonus	15%	30%	30%	50%
Amount of bonus in Rs.	**7.50**	**12.00**	**13.50**	**10.00**

3) Priestman's Bonus System : In this system, time rate is guaranteed. The standard output is fixed & if actual output is more than standard output, then all workers in the group get bonus equal to percentage increase output over the standard output. If in a particular month production is not more than the standard output, then bonus is not given.

Problem - 21

There are 200 workers in a factory & the standard output is 4000 tones. In a month, actual output is 5000 tones. Calculate percentage increase in the time rate if they receive bonus equal to 75% of the increase in actual output over the standard output.

Solution :

    Standard Output   4000 tones

    Actual output   5000 tones

    Increase in output   1000 tones.

$$\text{\% increase in actual output over the standard output is} = \frac{1000}{4000} = \text{x } 100 = 25\%$$

Now 75% of 25% is given as bonus

        100 : 75

        25 : ?

$$\frac{25}{100} \times \frac{75}{1} = 18.75\%$$

Group bonus is 18.75% of their wages.

4) Towne Gain Sharing Plan : This group bonus system was introduced by H. R. Towne in U.S.A. in 1886. In this system time wages are guaranteed & bonus is paid for reduciton of labour cost. Standard labour cost is calculated & actual labour cost is compared with it. If actual labour cost is less than the standard labour cost then there is saving in the labour cost. Half of this saving of labour cost is given to all workers in the proportion of the wages earned by the workers. The supervisor also receives a part of this bouns.

5) Waste Reduction Bonus System : In this system bouns is paid to workers if the waste in material is minimum. This system of giving bouns is applied where material cost is very high. Some specific percent of reduction in material cost is distributed to workers as bonus on some suitable basis.

Problem - 22 :

    A manufacturing concern has intoduced a bonus system on a slabe rate based on cost of reduction towards labour and overheads, the slab rates being.

Up to	10% saving	5% of the earning
"	20% saving	15% of the earning
"	40% saving	30% of the earning
"	70% saving	40% of the earning
Above	70% saving	50% of the earning

    wage rates per hour for three workers X, Y and Z are Rs. 0.50. Rs. 0.60 and Rs. 0.55 respectively. The overhead recovery rate is 500% on productive wages. The standard cost towards wages and overhead per unit is determined at Rs. 1.20 per unit.

    If the time taken by X, Y and Z ro finish 100 units is 26 hours, 30 hours and 20 hours respectively, what is the amount of bonus earned by the three workers?

Solution :

	Worker X	Worker Y	Worker Z
Time taken	26 hours	30 hours	20 hours
Rate of wages per hour	Rs. 0.50	Rs. 0.60	Rs. 0.55
Wages earned	Rs. 13.00	Rs. 18.00	Rs. 11.00
Overheads (500% of wages)	65.00	90.00	55.00
Total (wages and overheads)	78.00	108.00	66.00
Standard wages and overheads	120.00	120.00	120.00
Saving in wages and overheads	42.00	12.00	54.00
% of reduction on standard	35%	10%	45%
Bonus entitlement slab	up to 40%	up to 10%	up to 70%
% of bonus earnings	30%	5%	40%
Amount of bonus	Rs. 3.90	Rs. 0.90	Rs. 4.40

Problem - 23 :

Calculate the material turnover ratio for the year 2010 from the following infromation and determine which of the two materials is most fast moving :

Particulars	Material x Rs.	Material y Rs.
Material in hand on 1-1-2010	1,00,000	3,50,000
Material in hand on 31-12-2010	60,000	2,50,000
Material purchased during the year	7,60,000	5,00,000

320 / Cost and works Accounting Paper - I

B. Calculate the total earning of the workers under Halsey and Rowan Palns :

     Standard Time - 20 hours

     Hourly Rate - Rs. 4

     Time Taken - 12 hours.

(P. U. April, 2014)

Solution :

1.Computation of Material Consumed :

	X	Y
Opening Stock	1,00,000	3,50,000
+ Purchases	7,60,000	5,00,000
	8,60,000	8,50,000
- Closing Stock	60,000	2,50,000
	8,00,000	6,00,000

Computation of Average Stock :

	X	Y
	$\dfrac{1,00,000 + 60,000}{2}$	$\dfrac{3,50,000 + 2,50,000}{2}$
	$\dfrac{1,60,000}{2}$	$\dfrac{6,00,000}{2}$
	= 80,000	= 3,00,000

Computation of Material Turnover Rotio :

$\dfrac{\text{Cost of Material Consumed}}{\text{Cost of Average Stock}}$	$\dfrac{8,00,000}{80,000}$	$\dfrac{6,00,000}{3,00,000}$
	= 10 times	= 2 times

Conputation of Turnove in days :

$\dfrac{\text{Days during the year}}{\text{Material Turnover Ratio}}$	$\dfrac{365}{10}$	$\dfrac{365}{2}$
	36.5 days	182.5 days

Comment : Material X is fast moving than Y.

(B)

     Time Allowed - 20 hours

     Time Taken - 12 hours

     Time saved - 8 hours

Halsey Plan :

Wages for time taken : 12 hours @ Rs.4 per hour   = Rs.48.00

Bonus = 50% of 8 x Rs.4   = Rs.16.00

                                           Rs.64.00

Rowan Plan :

Wages for time taken : 12 hours @ Rs.4 per hour   = Rs.48.00

Bonus = $\dfrac{\text{Time Taken}}{\text{Time Allowed}}$ x Time Saved x Hrly Rate

$\dfrac{12}{20}$ x 8 x 4   = Rs.19.20

                                           = Rs.67.20

Problem - 24 :

Calculate the earnings of A and B under Taylor's Differential Piece Rate System, from the following information :

    Standard production: 21 units per hour

    Factory day   : 8 hours

    Normal time rate   : Rs. 8.40 per hour

    Differential to be applied : 80% of piece rate below standard, 120% of piece rate at or above standard

    Mr. A produces 150 units a day.

    Mr. B produces 180 units a day.

(P. U. Oct, 2012)

Solution :

Calculation of Wage Rate

Normal Time Rate   - Rs.2.40 per hour

Standard Production per hour - 21 units

Straight piece rate = Rs.8.40 / 21 units = Rs.0.40 per unit

Taylor's Differential Piece Rates -

i) Below standard (80% of piece work rate of Rs.0.40) = Rs.0.32 per unit

ii) At or above standard (120% of piece work rate) = Rs.0.48 per unit

Calculation of Wages -

1) Straight piece rate system :

Worker A - 150 units x Re.0.40 = Rs.60

Worker B - 180 units x Re.0.40 = Rs.72

2) Taylor's Differential piece rate system :

Worker A - 150 units x Rs.0.32 = Rs.48

Worker B - 180 units x Rs.0.48 = Rs.86.40

Problem - 25 :

From the following, calculate earnings of a worker under :

(i) Halsey plan and

(ii) Rown plan

Time allowed - 48 hours
Time taken   - 40 hours
Rate per hour - Rs. 10.

(P. U. Oct. 2012)

Solution :

1) Earnings under Halsey Plan

      Time Allowed - 48 hours

      Time Taken - 40 hours

      Time Saved - 8 times

      Rate per hour - Rs.10

$$\text{Total earnings} = \text{TT x HR} + \frac{50}{100}(\text{TA - TT}) \text{ x HR}$$

$$= 40 \text{ x Rs.}10 + \frac{50}{100}(48\text{-}40) \text{ x Rs.}10$$

$$= \text{Rs.}400 + \text{Rs.}40 \text{ (2 Marks)}$$

$$= \text{Rs.}440 \text{ (1 Mark)}$$

2) Earning under Rowan Plan

      Time Allowed - 48 hours

      Time Taken - 40 hours

      Time Saved - 8 hours

      Rate per hour - Rs.10

$$\text{Total earnings} = \text{TT x HR} + \frac{\text{TS}}{\text{TA}} \text{x TT x HR}$$

$$= 40 \text{ x } 10 + \frac{8}{48} \text{ x } 40 \text{ x Rs.}10$$

$$= \text{Rs.}400 + \text{Rs.}66.67 \text{ (2 Marks)}$$

$$= \text{Rs. }466.67 \text{ (1 Mark)}$$

EXERCISES :

Objective Type

A. State whether the following statements are True or False:

1) Time keeping helps in ascertainment of wages of employees.
2) Time booking is required for piece workers.
3) Time keeping is the recording of Job time of the workers.
4) The objective of time booking is to ascertain the Labour cost of work done.
5) The job of preparation of the wage sheet is the work assigned to the pay-roll department.

6) Time rate system of wage payment is more suitable where the quantity of work is of highest importance.
7) Where the job is of a repetitive nature, piece rate system of wage payment is more suitable.
8) Piece-rate system of wage payment does not ensure minimum wages of warkers.
9) Time card is normally used for accounting of labour cost.
10) Time keeping is essential for ensuring discipline in attendance.
11) A Taylor's differential piece rate system does not guarantee a minimum time wages.
12) Under Rowan Preminm plan labour cost per unit decreases with corresponding increase in efficiency.
13) Bin Card shows the time devoted by a worker on a specific job.
14) When time-Cum-Job card is maintained there is no need of keeping a separate time card.
15) Time keeping facilitates the preparation of payroll.
16) Time booking is not necessary, when time keeping is accomplished.
17) Halsey plan guarantees a minimum hourly rate.
18) Time wage System is generally forwarded by the Trade Unions.
19) Labour cost can be redued by employing worker at low rates.
20) Incentive plans benefit both the employers and employees.
21) Time rate system of wage payment is more suitable where the quantity of work is of highest importance.
22) Workers are guaranteed minimum time wage under Taylor's differential piece rate system.

Answer : (1) True (2) False (3) False (4) True (5) True (6) False (7) True (8) True (9) True (10) True (11) True (12) True (13) False (14) True (15) True (16) False (17) True (18) True (19) False (20) True (21) False (22) False

B. Fill in the blanks :

1) The process of recording the attendane of workers is known as ......
2) The process of recording the time spent on jobs is known as .....
3) A record in time keeping is known as ......
4) A record is time booking is known as .....
5) The attendance records form the basis of preparing the .....
6) In small establishment, the attendance record is known as ...
7) Time not spent on production is known as ......
8) Remuneration is the ..... paid for labour and services offered by the workers.
9) Under ...... rate system a worker is paid on the basis of time attended by him.
10) Under ..... system a worker is paid a fixed amount per unit product.
11) Maintaining .... is the most simple and economical method of time keeping.

Answer : (1) Time keeping (2) Time booking (3) Time card (4) Job card (5) Payroll (6) muster roll (7) elapsed time (8) Price (9) Time rate (10) Piece rate (11) Attendence Register

C. Theory Questions

1. What are the essentials of a good wage plan?
2. Enumerate general principles to be considered in designing a system of remuneration of workers. What are the factors which govern the determination of wages level in an organisation?
3. What are the salient features to be considered before formulating a system of remunerating labour?
4. What are piece-rates? What advantages are attributed to their use? What principles should govern the determination and revision of piece-rates?
5. Discuss the advantages and disadvantages of piece-work system of payment of wages. Distinguish between Time Rate Wages and Piece Rate Wages.
6. Compare and contrast the Halsey scheme and Rowan Premium systems of payment bringing out differences in formula, purpose and effect and advantages and disadvantages.
7. a) Define piece rate.
   b) Tabulate the advantages and disadvantages of piece rates.
8. a) Define time rates.
   b) Tabulate the advantages and disadvantages of time rates.
9. Distinguish between a 'straight piece-rate' and a "differential piece-rate?" What are the benefits of differential piece-rate?
10. Explain the factors which affect wages.
11. State the characteristics of a wage plan which promotes efficiency.
12. What do you think to be an ideal plan for remunerating workers?
13. What do you understand by payment by results? Explain three different types of payment by results commonly in use.
14. a) Explain main features of time-rate method.
    b) Examine its suitability as a method of labour remuneration.
15. Evaluate time-rate method as a system of remuneration to workers.
16. Explain the main features of Flat Time-Rate method of wage payment. In what cases, this method of remuneration is suitable?
17. Enumerate the merits and demerits of Flat Time-Rate method of remuneration.
18. What are the advantages and shortcomings of Time-Rate method of remuneration?
19. What do you understand by "High Wage' system of remuneration? Examine its suitability as a method of remuneration.
20. Explain the meaning of piece-rate method of remuneration of labour. What are its merits and demerits?

21. Write short notes on:
    a) Straight piece-rate method.
    b) Piece rates with graduated time rates.
22. Explain, in brief, Differential Piece-Rate Method of remuneration and the schemes based on the principles of differential piece-rate.
23. Explain the following:
    a) Halsey plan.
    b) Rowan Plan.
24. a) Time-keeping
    b) Rowan Premium Plan

Practical Problems

1. A factory works 9 hours per day and has a 5-day week. A worker requires 9 hours for completion of a job on daily wages. However, under incentive schemes, he completes the same job in 6 hours. A worker is entitled to day rate of Rs. 7 per hour.

You are asked to calculate his wages to be charged to the job under the following plans :

a) Piece-work plan.
b) Halsey premium plan.
c) Rowan plan.

Ans. : (a) Rs. 63; (b) Rs. 52.50; (c) Rs. 56

2. An employee working under a bonus scheme saves 4 hours in a job for which the standard time is 32 hours.

Calculate the rate per hour worked and wages payable for the time taken under the following alternative Scheme (award rate is Re. 1 per hour) :

a) Employee receives an increase in the hourly rate based on percentage.
b) A bonus of 10% on award rate is payable when standard time (namely, 100% efficiency) is achieved plus a further bonus of 1% award rate for each 1 percent in excess of 100% efficiency.

Ans.: (a) wages, Rs. 31.50; (b) Rate per hour, Rs. 1.24

3. You are required to calculate the wages payable to Bhanudas and Nilkanth under straight piece-rate and Taylor's Differential Piece-Rate system with the help of following details :

a) Standard output 8 units per hour.
b) Normal Time-Rate Rs. 4 per hour.
c) Differential to be applied are :

80% of piece-rate below standard.

120% of piece-rate at or above standard

d) In a 9-hour day, Bhanudas produced 56 units whereas Nilkanth produced 80 units.

Ans. : Under straight Piece-Rate wages : Bhanudas Rs. 28, Nilkanth Rs. 40, Under Taylor's Differential Piece rate wages : Bhanudas Rs. 22.40, Nilkanth Rs. 48

4. From the following data calculate total monthly remuneration of three workers X, Y and Z:

a) Standard production per month per worker is 1,000 units.

b) Actual production during the month :
   X : 800 units, Y : 700 units, Z : 900 units.

c) Piece work rate per unit of actual production : 15 paise.

d) Dearness wages : Rs. 40 per month (fixed).

e) House rent allowance : Rs. 20 per month.

f) Additional production bonus at the rate of Rs. 5 for each percentage of actual production exceeding 75 per cent actual production over standard.

5. The standard time for a job is 60 hours. The hourly rate of guaranteed wages is Re. 0.75. Because of saving in time, a worker gets an hourly wage of Re. 0.90 under Rowan Premium Bonus System.

For the same saving in time, calculate the hourly rate of wages a worker B will get under Halsey Weir Preminum Plan assuming 40% bonus for time saved.

Ans. : Hourly rate of wages under Halsey-Weir plan : Re. 0.825

6. In a factory two workmen A and B Produce the same product using the same material. They are paid bonus according to Rowan System. The time allotted to the product is 40 hours. A takes 25 hours and B takes 30 hours to finish the product. The factory cost of the product A is Rs. 193.75 and for B Rs. 205. The factory overhead rate is one rupee per man hour.

Find the normal rate of wages and the cost of materials used for the product.

Ans. : Normal Rate of wages Rs. 2 per hour. Cost of Material for each product Rs. 100

7. a) Explain in brief, Rowan Premium Plan.

b) Production sections of a factory working on the Job-Order system pay their worker under the Rowan Premium Bonus Scheme. Workers also get a Dearness allowance of Rs. 12 per week of 48 hours.

A worker's basic wage is Rs. 2 per day of 8 hours and his time sheet for a week is summarised below :

Job No	Time allowed	Time take
1844	25 Hrs.	20 Hrs.
1926	30 Her.	20 Hrs.
Idle time (waiting)		8 Hrs.
		48 Hrs.

Calculate the gross wages he has earned for the week and indicate the accounts to which the wage amount will be debited.

8. **Given the following details you are required to calculate the labour cost chargeable to Job No. 531 in respect of a worker who is paid wages according to -**

a) the Rowan Scheme

b) the Halsey Premium Plan.

Time allowed : 22 hours. Time actually taken : 18 Hours. Rate of pay : Re. 1 per hour

Ans. : Wages under Rowan Scheme Rs. 21.27 : Wages under Halsey Plan Rs. 20

9. An operator engaged in machining certain components receives an ordinary rate of Rs. 1.60 per day of 8 hours. The standard output for machining the component has been fixed at 80 pieces per hour (time as fixed for premium bonus). On a certain day the output of the worker on this machine is 800 pieces. Find the labour cost per 100 piece and the wages that would have been earned by the workman under the following :

a) If a bonus of Re. 0.23 is paid per 100 of the extra output.

b) If paid on straight piece-work basis at the standard rate.

c) If Halsey premium bonus system is being adopted (50-50)

10) **Wage negotiations are going on with the recognised Labour Union and the Management wants you as the Cost Accountant of the Company to formulate an incentive scheme with a view to increase productivity.**

The case of three typical workers. Achyuta, Ananta and Govinda who produce respectively 180, 120 and 100 units of the Company's product in a normal day of 8 hours is taken up for study.

Assuming that day wages would be guaranteed at 75 paise per hour and the piece rate would be based on a standard hourly output of 10 units, calculate the earnings of the three workers and the labour cost per 100 pieces under :

a) Day wages,   b) Piece rate.

c) Halsey scheme and   d) The Rowan scheme.

Also calculate under the above schemes the average cost of labour for the company to produce 100 pieces.

(Ans.

Scheme	Earnings of workers			Labour Cost per 100 Pieces			Average Cost of Labour (100 pieces) Rs.		
	Achyuta Rs.	Ananta Rs.	Govinda Rs.	Achyuta Rs.			Ananta Rs.	Govinda Rs.	
a) Daily Wages	6	6	6	3.33			5	6	4.50
b) Piece Rate	13.50	9	7.50	7.50			7.50	7.50	7.50
c) Halsey Plan	9.75	7.50	6.75	5.42			6.25	6.75	6
d) Rowan	9.33	8	7.20	5.18			6.67	7.20	6.13

11. An operator engaged in machining certain components receives an ordinary rate of Rs. 1.60 per day of 8 hours. The standard output for machining components has been fixed at 80 pieces per hour (time as fixed for preminum bonus). On a certain day the output of the worker on this machine is 800 pieces.

   Find the labour cost per 100 pieces and the wages that would have been earned by the workman under the following:
   a) If a bonus of Rs. 0.23 is paid per 100 of the extra output.
   b) If paid for on a straight piece-work basis at the standard rate.
   c) If Halsey premium bonus system is adopted.

Ans. : (a) Rs. 1.97; (b) Rs. 2.00; (c) Rs. 1.80

CHAPTER 7

OTHER ASPECTS OF LABOUR

7.1 Labour Turnover
7:1.1   Meaning
7.1.2   Definition
7.1.3   Rate of Labour Turnover
7.1.4   Causes of Labour Turnover
7.1.5   Measures to Reduce Labour Turnover
7.1.6   Cost of Labour Turnover
7.1.7   Measurement of Labour Turnover

7. 2 Job Analysis and Job Evalution Key
7.2.1   Why Job Study?
7.2.2   Terminology - Job Analysis, Job Description, Job Specification, Job Evaluation etc.

7. 3 Merit Rating
7.3.1   Meaning
7.3.2   Purpose of Merit Rating
7.3.3   Methods of Merit Rating

7.1 LABOUR TURNOVER

7.1.1 Meaning

In every industrial enterprise there is a continuous flow of workers, as some workers leave their jobs for some reason or the other and some new workers are replaced to take their position. Thus, there is not only a movement of labour out of industrial concerns but also a corresponding number of new persons joining them. This continuous process of change in the composition of labour represents an important chareteristic of labour in India. This change in the composition of labour force during a specified period measured against a suitable index is termed as labour turnover. Thus, it is the shifting or movement of a workforce into and out of an industrial enterprise.

330 / Cost and works Accounting Paper - I

7.1.2. Definition of Labour Turnover:

According to Dr. R.C. Saxena, " Labour turnover is the rate of change in the working staff of a concern during a definite period. It is a measure of the extent to which old workers leave and new workers enter the service of a concern in a given period."

7.1.3. Rate of Labour Turnover :

The rate of labour turnover in a business concern depends upon several factors such as nature of the industry, its size, location and composition of labour force. In any organisation some rate of labour turnover will always occur due to personal factors where the employers can practically do nothing to avoid the situation. As such normal labour turnover does not create any severe problem. High rate of labour turnover will not only mean a higher cost of recruitment and training but would also adversely affect the working efficiency of the concern. It causes permanent ill effect on the labour morale and hampers the building up of healthy employer-employee relationship. It is an important indication of high labour cost. Hence, it has to be kept at the minimum. Low rate of labour turnover is an indication of well managed organisation.

7.1.4. Causes of Labour Turnover :

For an effective control over labour turnover every concern should analyse the number of persons leaving the concern during a particular period under the following causes which normally contribute to labour turnover.

(A) Personal Causes : -
 (i) lack of interest in the work.
 (ii) attraction of high salaries and wages outside.
 (iii) family responsibilities.
 (iv) ill-health, sickness, incapability due to old age.
 (v) death and retirement.
 (vi) marriages, in case of women workers.

These are the various causes where the workers leave their jobs purely on personal grounds. In all such cases the concern can practically do nothing to improve the situation.

(B) Avoidable Causes :
 (i) lower rates of pay and allowances.
 (ii) long and odd hours of work.
 (iii) lack of job satisfaction.
 (iv) dissatisfaction with working conditions.
 (v) unhappy relations with other co-workers and with supervisors.
 (vi) disputes between rival trade-unions.
 (vii) bad recruitment policy.
 (viii) lack of adequate recreational facilities.
 (ix) inadequate medical, housing, transport and other necessary facilities.

(x) unfair methods of promotion.

These are the various causes which need proper attention of the management to prevent the same so that the turnover may be kept low.

(C) Unavoidable Causes :
  (i) retrenchment due to seasonal trade.
 (ii) discharge due to long absenteeism.
(iii) national and emergency services during periods of war.
(iv) expansion and development programmes.
 (v) rationalisation of industries such as automation and computerisation.

These are the various causes where the workers may be unsuitable for the jobs or may be discharged for indiscipline. It is obligatory on the part of the organisation to take such decisions under the exceptional circumstances.

7.1.5. Measures to Reduce Labour Turnover:

The causes mentioned above responsible for high labour turnover, resulting a heavy drain on a concern, should be studied very carefully and scientifically and an attempt should be made to reduce the causes as far as possible by adopting the following measures.
  (i) introducing scientific methods of recruitment and job placements.
 (ii) conducting employee orientation and induction training programmes.
(iii) provision for attractive pension and gratuity schemes.
(iv) improvement in the working conditions.
 (v) providing opportunities for advancement.
(vi) fair wages and wage incentives.
(vii) promotion by merit and promotion from within.
(viii) introducing effective methods of labour participation in management.
(ix) maintenance of job interest and job satisfaction.
 (x) conducting employee welfare benefit programmes.

7.1.6. Cost of Labour Turnover:

Increased rate of labour turnover is mainly responsible for loss of output, heavy training cost, under utilization and mishandling of equipments, high cost of selection, increased overtime, low team-spirit which ultimately results into a loss to the organisation. When such losses are measured in terms of monetary value they are termed as cost of labour turnover which may be classified into the following.

(A) Preventive costs :

It refers to all those items of expenses which are incurred to keep the workers satisfied and discourage them against leaving employment. Generally, it includes the cost of personnel administration, cost of medical services, cost of welfare activities and schemes, cost of other incentive schemes like pension, provident fund, bonus, high wages plans etc.

(B) Replacement costs :

It referes to all those items of expenses which are incurred for recruitment and training of new employees and the resulting losses wastage and decrease in productivity due to inexperience and inefficiency of new employees. Generally, it includes the cost arising due to inefficiency of new workers like cost of tools and machine breakage, cost of defective work, cost of accidents, loss of output due to delay in getting new workers, cost of selection and placement, cost of training programme etc.

Labour turnover costs are usually treated as factory overheads. The preventive costs should be distributed among different departments on the basis of workers in each department. The replacement costs should be distributed among the departments affected by the labour turnover on the basis of number of workers replaced.

The management should try to control the labour costs by preparing various important labour reports. The personnel department prepares periodically a labour turnover report with a view to minimise labour turnover costs by taking appropriate measures. This report includes the comparative positions of labour turnover relating to current period and previous period. It also contains the causes of labour turnover classifying avoidable and unavoidable causes. Usually, the report includes the specific analysis of turnover into various sub-classification such as men and women, old and new employees, skilled and unskilled workers, time and piece workers etc. This type of systematic analysis helps the management to take corrective action in time which minimises the labour turnover.

7.1.7. Measurement of Labour Turnover:

Three different methods are used for measuring the labour turnover viz., separation method, replacement method and flux method. The selection of a particular method depends upon the emphasis given on either labour separations or labour replacements or on the average of the number of separations and the number of replacements. But once a specific method is selected it must be used.

The following are some important methods followed for measurement of labour turnover :

1. Separation Method:

Under this method, labour turnover is considered as a relationship between the total number of separations for a given period and the average number of workers on the pay roll during the corresponding period.

$$\text{Labour Turnover Rate} = \frac{\text{Number of Separations in a period}}{\text{Average No. of Workers during the same period}} \times 100$$

2. Basis of Avoidable Separation Method :

It is argued that in any organisation a certain amount of labour turnover is inevitable. The percentage of separation can be high due to unavoidable causes such as sickness, old age, death, family conditions, seasonal and cyclical fluctuations in business. Therefore, separation should be segregated as "avoidable" and "unavoidable". Labour turnover should be measured as relationship between "avoidable separation" and average working force during the related period. The only limitation of this method is that it is rather difficult to accurately classify separation between "avoidable" and "unavoidable".

$$\text{Labour Turnover Rate} = \frac{\text{Avoidable Separations in a period}}{\substack{\text{Average Workers Force} \\ \text{during the Period}}} \times 100$$

3. Basis of Accession :

There are some experts who hold the view that the logical way to measure labour turnover is to calculate it as relationship between accessions and average working force during the period.

$$\text{Labour Turnover Rate} = \frac{\text{Accessions}}{\text{Average Workers Force}} \times 100$$

4. Replacement Method or Net Labour Turnover Method :

In this method, labour turnover is measured as relationship between the actual replacement of labour during the period and the average number of workers in the period. It does not take into consideration the separations.

$$\text{Labour Turnover Rate} = \frac{\substack{\text{Number of Workers Replaced} \\ \text{in a period}}}{\substack{\text{Average No. of Workers} \\ \text{in a Period}}} \times 100$$

5. Flux Method :

This method takes into account both separations and replacements for calculation of labour turnover.

$$\text{Labour Turnover Rate} = \frac{\substack{\text{No.of} \qquad \text{No.of} \\ \text{Seperations} + \text{Replacements}}}{\substack{\text{Average No. of Workers} \\ \text{during the period}}} \times 100$$

6. Equivalent Annual Rate of Labour Turnover :

In case it is desired to relate the labour turnover rate for a month or fraction of a month to annual rate of turnover, this may be done by finding out. "Equivalent Annual Rate" with the help of the following formula.

$$\text{Equivalent Annual Rate} = \frac{\text{Turn over Rate} \times 365 \,(\text{or } 366 \text{ in a leap year})}{\text{No. of days in the Relevant Period}}$$

Practical Problems

Problem - 1

From the following data of Abhay Co. Ltd. calculate Labour Turnover Rate under Separation Method, Replacement Method and Flux Method :

Labour force at the Beginning	2,900
Labour force at the end	3,100
Separations	320
Total Number of work force recruited (inclusive of 200 for expansion)	500

Solution :

$$\text{Average No. of workers during the period} = \frac{2,900 + 3100}{2}$$
$$= 3,000$$

Labour Turnover Rate :

1. Separation Method :

$$\text{L. T. R.} = \frac{320}{3,000} \times 100$$
$$= 10.67\%$$

2. Replacement Method :

$$\text{L. T. R.} = \frac{300}{3,000} \times 100$$
$$= 10\%$$

3. Flux Method :

$$\text{L. T. R.} = \frac{(320 + 300)}{3,000} \times 100$$
$$= 20.67\%$$

Problem - 2

Following information is available from the records of the personnel office for a particular period :

Working force at the beginning	4,900
Working force at the end	5,100
No. of workers left during the period	650

(of those 350 workers left on account of avoidable causes)

Calculate labour Turnover Rate on the basis of avoidable separation.

Solution :

$$\text{Average No. of Work Force during the period} = \frac{4,900 + 5,100}{2}$$

$$= 5,000$$

$$\text{Labour Turnover Rate} = \frac{\text{Avoidable Separation in the period}}{\text{Average Working Force during the period}} \times 100$$

$$= 7\%$$

Problem - 3 :

In XYZ Co. Ltd., there were 1,900 workers at the beginning of the period and 2,200 at the end of the period. 100 workers left the company. Calculate labour Turnover Rate on the basis of accession.

Solution :

$$\text{Average Working Force} = \frac{1,900 + 2,200}{2}$$

$$= 2,050$$

The accessions during the period will be :

$$= [(2,200 + 100) - 1,900]$$
$$= 400.$$

$$\text{Labour Turnover Rate} = \frac{\text{Accessions}}{\text{Average Working Force}} \times 100$$

$$= 19.51\% .$$

Problem - 4

Following are the details of the workers in the factory for the Month of April 2014 given by the personnel department.

No. of workers on 1.4.2014	5000
No. of worker on 30.4.2014	3000
No. of workers discharged	160

No. of workers left the job   80

No. of workers newly appointed against the vacancies   120

Calculate labour turnover rate and equivalent rate under three methods.

Solution :

$$\text{Average No. of Workers} = \frac{\text{Workers at the beginning} + \text{Workers at the end}}{2}$$

$$= \frac{5,000 + 3,000}{2}$$

$$= 4,000$$

1. Separation Method :

$$\text{Labour turnover} = \frac{\text{No. of Workers leaving}}{\text{Average No. of Workers}} \times 100$$

$$= \frac{240}{4,000} \times 100$$

$$= 6\%$$

Equivalent

$$\text{Annual turnover} = \frac{\text{Labour Turnover Rate}}{\text{No. of days of the month}} \times 365$$

$$= \frac{6}{30} \times 365$$

$$= 73\%$$

2. Flux Method :

$$\text{Labour turnover} = \frac{\text{No. Of Workers left} + \text{No. Of Workers replaced}}{\text{Average No. of Workers}} \times 100$$

$$= \frac{240 + 120}{4,000} \times 100$$

$$= 9\%$$

Equivalent

$$\text{Annual turnover} = \frac{9}{30} \times 365$$

$$= 109 - 5\%$$

3. Net Labour Turnover Method :

$$\text{Labour turnover} = \frac{\text{No. of Workers replaced}}{\text{Average No. of workers}} \times 100$$

$$= \frac{120}{4,000} \times 100$$

$$= 3\%$$

Equivalent

$$\text{Annual turnover} = \frac{3}{30} \times 365$$

$$= 36.5\%$$

Problem - 5 :

The following details are obtained from the records of department of a factory relating to the year 2014 :

Total strength of workers on 31.12.2013	1900
Total strength of workers on 31.12.2014	2100
No. of employees expired during 2015	5
Cases of statutory retirement during 2015	30
Cases of dismissal and termination during 2015	25
Workers resigned their jobs during 2015	40

During the year, the factory recruited totally 300 workers, out of which 220 were for the new project launched in April, 2015.

Calculate labour turnover rates under three methods.

Solution :

$$\text{Average No. of workers} = \frac{\text{workers at the beginning} + \text{Workers at the end}}{2}$$

$$= \frac{1,900 + 2,100}{2}$$

$$= 2,000$$

1. Separation Method :

$$\text{Labour Turnover} = \frac{\text{No. of workers leaving}}{\text{Average No. of workers}} \times 100$$

$$= \frac{100}{2,000} \times 100$$

$$= 5\%$$

$$\text{Equivalent Annual Turnover} = \frac{\text{Labour Turnover Rate}}{\text{No. of days of the year}}$$

$$= \frac{0.5}{365} \times 365$$

$$= 5\%$$

2. Flux Method :

$$\text{Labour Turnover} = \frac{\text{No. of workers left} + \text{No. of workers replaced}}{\text{Average No. of Workers}} \times 100$$

$$= \frac{100 + 80}{2,000} \times 100$$

$$= 9\%$$

3. Net Labour Turnover Method :

$$\text{Labour Turnover} = \frac{\text{No. of workers replaced}}{\text{Average No. of Workers}} \times 100$$

$$= \frac{80}{2,000} \times 100$$

$$= 4\%$$

Problem - 6 :

The personnel department of Duplex Co. Ltd. has the following information relating to its workforce during the month of January 2014.

Number of workers on 1.1.2014   900
Number of workers on 31.1.2014   1,100

During the month 15 persons quit and 25 persons are discharged. 150 workers were engaged out of them 20 persons were appointed in the vacancy caused. Calculate labour turnover rate during the period under different methods.

Solution : Calculation of average number of workers on the payroll in the month of January, 2014.

= Number of workers on 1.1.2014 + Number of workers on 31.1.2014

$$= \frac{900 + 1100}{2}$$

$$= \frac{2000}{2}$$

$$= 1000$$

Calculation of Labour Turnover Rate –

1. Separation Method :

$$\text{Labour Turnover rate} = \frac{\text{Number of workers replaced in a period}}{\text{Average number of workers on the payroll in the period}} \times 100$$

$$= \frac{40}{1000} \times 100$$

$$= 4\%$$

2. Replacement method :

$$\text{Labour turnover rate} = \frac{\text{Number of Workers replaced in a period}}{\text{Average number of workers on the payroll in the period}} \times 100$$

$$= \frac{20}{1000} \times 100$$

$$= 2\%$$

3. Flux method :

$$\text{Labour turnover rate} = \frac{\text{Number of workers left in a period} + \text{Number of workers replaced in a period}}{\text{Average number of workers on the payroll in the period}} \times 100$$

$$= \frac{40 + 20}{1000} \times 100$$

$$= \frac{60}{1000} \times 100$$

$$= 6\%$$

Problem - 7

From the following data given by personnel department of Duckback Co. Ltd. calculate the monthly and annual labour turnover rate by applying different methods.

Number of workers on payroll -
    (i) at the beginning of the month   :   853
    (ii) at the end ot the month   :   1,147

During the month 10 workers left. 40 workers were discharged and ISO workers were newly recruited. Of these 25 workers were recruited in the vacancies of those leaving, while the rest were for an expansion scheme.

Solution : Calculation of average number of workers on the payroll in the month.

$$= \frac{\text{Number of workers at the beginning of the month + Number of workers at the end of the month}}{2}$$

$$= \frac{853 + 1147}{2}$$

$$= \frac{2000}{2}$$

$$= 1000$$

Calculation of Labour Turnover Rate –

1. **Separation method :**
   Labour turnover rate –

$$= \frac{\text{Number of workers left in a period}}{\text{Average number of workers on the payroll in the period}} \times 100$$

$$= \frac{50}{1000} \times 100$$

$$= 5\%$$

Monthly labour turnover rate = 5%

Annual labour turnover rate $= \frac{5 \times 365}{30} = 60.83\%$

2. **Replacement method :**
   Labour turnover rate –

$$= \frac{\text{Number of workers replaced in a period}}{\text{Average number of workers on the payroll in the period}} \times 100$$

$$= \frac{25}{1000} \times 100$$

Monthly Labour Turnover Rate = 2.5 %

$$\text{Annual Labour Turnover Rate} = \frac{2.5 \times 365}{30} = 30.42\%$$

3. **Flux method :**

Labour Turnover Rate –

$$= \frac{\begin{array}{c}\text{Number of workers left in a period} + \\ \text{Number of workers replaced in a period}\end{array}}{\begin{array}{c}\text{Average number of workers} \\ \text{on the payroll in the period}\end{array}} \times 100$$

$$= \frac{50 + 25}{1000} \times 100$$

$$= \frac{75}{1000} \times 100$$

$$= 7.5\%$$

Monthly Labour Turnover Rate = 7.5%

$$\text{Annual Labour Turnover Rate} = \frac{7.5 \times 365}{30} = 91.25\%$$

Problem - 8

During February 2014 the following information was obtained from the personnel department of Moderate Co. Ltd. Labour force at the beginning of the month - 1,767 and 2,233 at the end of the month. During the month 60 persons were discharged and 20 left the company. During the month 200 workers were engaged out of which only 40 workers were appointed against the vacancy caused by the number of workers separated and the remaining on account of an extension programme of the company. Calculate labour turnover rate and equivalent annual rate under (i) separation method, (ii) replacement method and (iii) flux method.

Solution : Calculation of average number of workers on the payroll in the month of February, 2014.

$$= \frac{\text{Number of workers on 1.2.2014} + \text{Number of workers on 29.2.2014}}{2}$$

$$= \frac{1767 + 2233}{2}$$

$$= \frac{4000}{2}$$

$$= 2000$$

Calculation of Labour Turnover Rate

1. Separation Method :
Labour Turnover Rate -

$$= \frac{\text{Number of workers left in a period}}{\begin{array}{c}\text{Average number of workers}\\ \text{on the payroll in the period}\end{array}} \times 100$$

$$= \frac{80}{2000} \times 100$$

$$= 4\%$$

Monthly Labour Turnover Rate $= 4\%$

Annual labour Turnover Rate $= \frac{366 \times 4}{29} = 50.48\%$

2. Replacement Method :
Labour Turnover Rate -

$$= \frac{\text{Number of workers replaced in a period}}{\begin{array}{c}\text{Average number of workers}\\ \text{on the payroll in the period}\end{array}} \times 100$$

$$= \frac{40}{2000} \times 100$$

$$= 2\%$$

Monthly Labour Turnover Rate $= 2\%$

Annual Labour Turnover Rate $= \frac{366 \times 2}{29} = 25.24\%$

3. Flux Method :
Labour Turnover Rate -

$$= \frac{\begin{array}{c}\text{Number of workers left in a period +}\\ \text{Number of workers replaced in a period}\end{array}}{\begin{array}{c}\text{Average number of workers}\\ \text{on the payroll in the period}\end{array}} \times 100$$

$$= \frac{80 + 40}{2000} \times 100$$

$$= \frac{120}{2000} \times 100$$

$$= 6\%$$

Monthly Labour Turnover Rate $= 6\%$

Annual Labour Turnover Rate $= \dfrac{365 \times 6}{29} = 75.72\%$

7.2 JOB ANALYSIS AND JOB EVALUATION

Thorough knowledge about jobs has come to be accepted as a basic prerequisite for intelligent attack upon many personnel problems. No employment office can hope to make a proper selection of workers for a job without the precise knowledge of the duties, responsibilities, conditions of work and qualifications required for success in it. Before psychological tests are devised or other procedures set up for selection purpose, it is absolutely necessary to know in detail the nature of the job in question. According to Thorndike, in a programme of personnel selection, the first step logically and to a certain extent chronologically is an analysis of jobs to determine the activities carried out in the job and the circumstances under which it is performed.

Some of the questions which need to be answered before any programme of test-construction or personnel selection is launched upon are: What does the worker do? What are the conditions of work, indoor or outdoor? Does it require dealing with people or only mechanical handling? What sorts of skills are required in the job? What are the physical, social and intellectual demands of the job? The rich background of knowledge and information only can become the solid foundation-stone for selection of the right man for the right job.

7.2.1 Why Job Study

There are several reasons for making a job study and as these reasons influence the method of study, it is important that they be fully understood. They are:

1. The study of job ingredients is a 'must' to select the best individual for a particular job. Scientific recruitment necessitates the knowledge of the requirements of the job and the opportunities it affords for advancement, so that each applicant's interests, abilities and aspirations may be checked against those inherent in the job.
2. Job study is essential to develop information to be used in building organization charts and for use in organization studies.
3. Knowledge of job ingredients is essential for developing operating manuals.
4. The primary purpose of job study is to determine the 'one best way' of doing a job and establishing the standard method and time (Motion and Time study).
5. It is also required to determine the job values in order to establish wage rates (Job Evaluation).
6. Job ingredients help in the determination of hazards existing in job situations (Health and Accident Investigations).
7. Job study facilitates the task of merit rating.

8. No adequate training programmes can be devised without the knowledge of operating techniques.

9. For the development of more effeetive work-methods, analysis of current methods forms a good guide.

10. Labour legislations, labour agreements, labour negotiations and establishment of rational pay-schedules can be meaningful only if the jobs are understood thoroughly.

11. Lastly, exact knowledge of the working conditions and the working requirements is essential to (i) develop job values as part of a sound salary-administration programme, (ii) settle disputes about the duties and to serve as a basis for the assignment of new duties, (iii) establish a standard for comparison with salaries paid by other companies on the basis of job specifications, and (iv) help stimulate interest in the job and duties.

7.2.2 Terminology

It is important that the meaning behind the true terms used in job study and job analysis be understood. Unless there is a meeting of minds on some common ground of understanding, confusion will result. For this reason, the definitions and explanations of the more common terms are presented. They are used as the springboard from which the plunge into the technique is made.

I. Job

A *Job* is a collection of task, duties and responsibilities which as a whole is regarded as the regular assingnment to individual employees. A 'Job' may include many positions, for 'position' is a job or series of tasks performed by a single individual employee. Thus, an employee has his *position,* but many positions may be so much alike as to constitute a single job. Hence, *Otis* and *Leukart* defined a job as "a group of positions involving substantially the same duties, skills, knowledge and responsibilities." The job is impersonal; the position is personal. Each job or sub-division of a job must have an unambiguous name or title, based upon standardized Trades Specifications. This will avoid confusion. Without this, it is possible that a mechanical draftsman may be supplied with a task of a machine designer or fitter, or an assembler may be sent where a semiskilled machinist is required, and so on. After preparing the 'job' definition, the next step is to analyse the job.

II. Job Analysis

Meaning : In order to evaluate the jobs in terms of their requirements, it is necessary to describe the job in detail. And rating of jobs requires that a careful study should be made of the activities of an employee on a particular job. It is possible only with the help of job analyst, who watches the job while it is performed, often talk to the operator and supervisors and then write up a report of their observation or what is technically called Job Analysis Report. Job Analysis is, indeed the procedure by which the facts with respect to each job are secured, organized and combined. It is also known as Job Study suggesting the cure with which job contents, processes, responsibilities and personnel requirements are considered. According to Harry L. Wylie, "Job analysis deals with the anatomy of the job.... This is the complete study of the job (or position) embodying every known and determinable factor including the duties and responsibilities invovled in its performance; the conditions under which performance is carried on; the nature of the task; the qualifications required in the worker; and the conditions of employment, such as pay, hours, opportunities and privileges."

Difference between Job and Worker Analysis. Job analysis is something different from 'Worker analysis'. Job analysis is in fact a procedure designed to discover the facts about jobs, including each job's requirements in terms of personal qualities for a satisfactory job-holder. Worker analysis, on the other hand, focusses attention on appraisal of the characteristics of employees, using physical examinations, tests, interviews and other procedures for this purpose.

Four-point Job Analysis Formula. A four-point job analysis formula to be used in making an accurate and useful job study is included in the Guide for Analysing Jobs published by War Man-power Commissioin, U.S.A. The points included in the formula are: (1) What the worker does? (2) How he does it? (3) Why he does it? (4) The skill involved in doing.

The Guide points out that, the analyst must establish the complete scope of the job and consider all the physical and mental activities involved in determining what the worker does. In determining how the worker does it, the analyst studies the physical methods used by the worker to accomplish his tasks, including the use of machinery, tools and his own movements, as well as the necessary 'know-how', of normal operations. The 'why' of the job is the overall purpose for which the job is done and includes why each task is essential to the overall result. The skill factors which comprise the fourth point in the formula are necessary to discriminate betwen jobs and to establish the degree of difficulty of any job. The definition given by the National Personnel Association helps a clearer understanding of job analysis. It states: "Job Analysis is a process which results in establishing the component elements of a job and ascertaining the human qualifications necessary for its useful performance."

Thus, basically, there are three parts of the job analysis: (1) the job must be completely and accurately identified; (ii) the task of the job must be precisely described: (iii) the requirements that the job makes upon the worker for successful performance must be indicated as accurately as possible. This means that every job analysis has two aspects: (i) job aspect— description of features of the work, and (ii) man aspect – consisting of the detailed description of the necessary physical, mental and personal characteristics of the worker. But it should be borne in mind that, job analysis involves the study of the duties on the job and obtaining facts about the qualifications required for the job itself, rather than about individual worker who happens to be working on that job at the time the analysis is made. In job analysis, one will observe the worker, but one is seeking observation about the job rather than the worker who is presently employed on it.

Methods of Job Analysis. Three most current methods of obtaining information for analysis are: (i) Sending out questionnaires to job-holders for their answers, (ii) conducting interview with the job-holders and supervisors, (iii) observing job-holders in action. Study of previous works in the field and pertaining documentary material often serves as a starting point for the job analysis. Actual performance of the job for securing valid and first hand information, though considered as the best method of job analysis, is usually discarded because of the time and cost involved in it. Experiments in India too have proved that analysis and description on the basis of actual observation of workers is the most reliable of all methods in analysing the worker's characteristics—physical, mental and personal.

Critical Appraisal. Job analysis, as mostly in use in the industries, suffers from a number of serious defects. Generally, job analysis is confined to the job aspect, describing duties and working conditions only. Description of personal requirements is often limited to the facts like age, sex, health and so on. Analysis of mental capacities and personality traits essential for success are conspicuous by their absence only. If at all an attempt to describe personal qualities is made, it is generrly abstract, vague and in qualitative terms only. No definition of the terms used is given and the qualities are not rated quantitatively with the result that, many job analysis schedule can be attached to a number of job titles.

It is here that the psychologist can help to improve upon the general practice of job analysis. Psychologists stress that the extent to which specific abilities are involved in different jobs often differentiate one job from another. The difference between two jobs may not be found in the content but in the pattern of abilities called forth. Thus, much more detailed study of the personal requirements than generally in practice is very much needed. The emphasis in the psychological study of occupation is not only upon the wider scope of the study but also upon the specific, concrete and quantitative description on the activities and requirements of the job.

Secondly, psychology with its modern techniques of rating scale, specialized methods of analysing skills, patterned interviewing, more scientific observation of behaviour and psychological testing contributes considerably in making job analysis more precise, exact, scientific and hence useful.

III Job Description

In the words of Bethel, Atwater, Smith and Stockman, "The Job Description is a 'boiled down' statement of the job analysis and serves to identify the job for consideration by other job analysts." In other words, it is an abstract of information gained from the job analysis report. It describes the work performed, the responsibilities involved, the skill or training required, the conditions under which the job is done and the type of the personnel required for the job.

IV. Job Specification

Job Specification is a product of job analysis and description. This term has been popularised by the United States Employment Service, which uses it to refer to a summary of the personnel requirements for a job. 'Job Specification' specifics the type of employee required and further assists in the selection of appropriate personnel by outlining the particular working conditions which will be encountered on the job. In short, 'Job specification' is the name given to the part of the job study involving the detailed statement of particulars required of an employee which are based on opinion supported by fact and which are necessary for ideal performance on a specific job.

V. Job Standardization

This involves the establishment of uniform mechanical facilities and methods and combines the specifications of human standards with the specifications of physical standards, so that efficiency can be maintained in keeping with the human element. Job standardization includes the establishment of specifications for tools, equipment, working conditions and methods. These specifications are arrived at by scientific analysis. Standards of performance cannot be maintained unless conditions of work, systems and personnel are standardized.

VI. Job Classification

This branch of job study deals with the comparative study of jobs. Classification embodies the comparison of individual jobs and the determination of identical duties and qualifications for the purpose of grouping similar jobs into classes so that identical and consistent titles may be assigned.

VII Job Grading

It is the process by which the relative levels of various jobs are determined. Usually, the grading of jobs does not include the assignment of rupee values to the jobs in the various classifications, but is limited to the establishment of the relative place of each job in the organization. Jobs may be classified into several groups, such as clerical, stenographic, accounting, skilled, unskilled, etc. They may further be classified within the group according to similarity of duty and specifications. Difference within these classes, as expressed by difference in duties and responsibilities accompanied by comparatively similar specifications or differences in specifications accompanied by similarity of duties, can be designated by the job grades, e.g., Junior Stenographer, Senior Stenographer, Secretary, or Stenographer 3rd class, Stenographer 2nd class and Stenographer 1st class; or Stenographer A grade, Stenographer B Grade and -Stenographer C Grade.

VII. Job Evaluation

This is the study of the job's worth in relation to other jobs in the organization. It involves the conversion of numerical value into rupee values, or it may involve the direct assignment of rupee value to jobs depending upon the method used. Job evaluation is the process of comparing jobs with other jobs in terms of the demands the jobs make on the worker. 'Job evaluation' as a personnel term has both a specific and a generic meaning. Specifically, it means job rating or the grading of occupations in terms of duties; generally, it means the entire field of wage and salary administration along modern lines.'According to Kimball and Kimball Jr., "Job Evaluation represents an effort to determine the relative value of every job in a plant and to determine what the fair basic wage for such a job should be." The same idea is conveyed by Alford and Beatty in their pioneer work, Industrial Management, who write as below: "Job evaluation is the application of the job analysis technique to the qualitative measurement of relative job worth, for the purpose of establishing consistent wage rate differentials by objective means. It measures the difference between jobs, based on the job requirements and establishes the differential numerically (job rating) so that it can be converted to wage rate after the wage level is determined (job evaluation)." In the words of Dale Yoder, "Job Evaluation is a practice, which seeks to provide a degree of objectivity in measuring the comparative value of jobs within an organization and among similar organizations. It is essentially a job rating process, not unlike the rating of employees."

Purposes of Evaluation

The primary objective of job evaluation is to establish the relative requirements of the job for the purpose of properly rewarding workers for the work performed. Its other objectives are:

1. **Eliminating inequalities.** It is a common experience of all concerned that the biggest single factor contributing to job dissatisfaction is inequality of base rate for comparable work. The actual rate paid on comparable jobs will vary between incumbents according to length of service and merit rating of the incumbents. Inasmuch as job evaluation establishes the relative values, inequalities of rate can be eliminated if the findings of the study are tested and applied.

2. **Solving wage controversies.** Job evaluation provides a relatively objective basis for resolving wage controversies involving comparative rates.

3. **Eliminating personal prejudices.** Job evaluation also helps in the elimination of personal prejudices in establishing rates by putting the rate structure on an objective basis. Personal prejudices in rate setting usually take the form of favouritism in respect of certain employees. In job evaluation the job is rated, and not the employee. The employee's rating is done by the process of merit rating, which balances the job and the employee.

4. **Facility of comparison and survey.** The job description on which job evaluation is based provides the information needed for community wage surveys and comparisons.

5. **Establishing a definite plan for salary administration.** When rates are established for the various jobs, they are guides whereby management can evaluate the incumbent

in terms of the job. Further, the job description may provide information needed in establishing lines of promotion.

6. **Proper emphasis on job factors.** These factors are determined during job analysis. When they are applied to the job, job values are established; when these same factors are applied to the incumbent, they will constitute the job's specifications.

7. **Standardization.** Job evaluation enables a company with plants in other areas to maintain a high degree of standardization even though the wage levels may be different.

8. **Simplification of rate structure.** If there are fewer job classes as a result of determining the similarity of jobs, minor variations in specifications are provided for by establishing job grades in the same occupational class, if minimum and maximum rate ranges are established within each job class. If salaries are periodically reviewed by management, then the rate structure will be simpler and salary administration will be made easier.

Principles of Job Evaluation

According to A.K. Kress, there are eight principles of Job Evaluation:

1. **Rate the job and not the man.** The requirements of the job are usually definite and fixed. The man on the job may have plus qualifications or may not quite measure up to the job requirements. A job rating plan should not be concluded with any plan to grade employees. The man on the job may be paid more or less than the job itself is worth, in relation to other jobs. Each element should, therefore, be rated on the basis of what the job itself requires.

2. **The elements selected for rating purposes should be easily explainable** in terms that will avoid any overlapping which might lead to rating the same qualifications under several headings. The elements should be as few in number as will cover the necessary requisite for every job.

3. **Success with job rating** is absolutely dependent on a uniformity of understanding with regard to the definitions of the elements and on consistency in the selection of the degrees of those elements.

4. **Any job rating plan must be sold** to foreman and employees.. Success in selling it will depend on a clear-cut explanation and illustration of the plan.

5. **Foremen should participate** in the rating of jobs in their own departments.

6. **The greatest degree of co-operation from employees,** in job rating will be achieved where they themselves have no opportunity to discuss the rating.

7. **In talking to foremen and employees,** avoid discussion of money values. Talk point values and degrees of each element. Discussion, of money values will lead to juggling.

8. **Too many occupational wages (or rate ranges for given labour grades) should not be established.** It would be unwise to adopt an occupational wage for each total of point values.

The principles of job evaluation can be applied to all kinds of employees' operative as well as executives. They can be applied to businesses of all sizes.

The principal objective of job evaluation is to divide up any given pay roll so that all jobs are paid according to their relative difficulties. For example, the job of machinist and that of an electrician may appear to be quite different but if they are of the same relative difficulty requiring similar skill, effort and intelligence, both would be paid at the same rate. Job evaluation is advantageous in a number of ways; and with the job evaluation plan in operation, inconsistency in rates is minimized and the entire wages structure becomes unified. According to Knowles and Thomson evaluation is useful in eliminating many of the evils to which nearly all systems of wage and salary payments are subjected to. These are:

1. Payment of high wages and salaries to persons who hold jobs and positions not requiring great amount of skills, effort and responsibilities;
2. Paying beginners less money than they are entitled to receive in terms of what is required of them;
3. Giving raises to persons whose performances do not justify them;
4. Deciding rates of pay and increase in pay on the basis of seniority rather than ability;
5. Payment of widely varied wages and salaries of the same or closely related jobs and positions; and
6. The payment of unequal wages and salaries because of race, sex, religion and political differences.

Methods of Job Evaluation

There are three methods of job evaluation and they are as follows:

I. The Ranking or Grading Method

Under this method of job evaluation, the job descriptions are arranged in rank according to the value of the work as judged by the analysis. The Ranking or Grading method consists of three stages, viz., 1. Making a thorough job analysis, 2. Expressing the findings of this analysis in a job description, and 3. Ranking each job by arranging them in ascending order, starting with the one with the minimum requirements and ending up with the one with the maximum requirements. In ranking the jobs attention is sometimes given to a number of factors such as the following: 1. Volume of work, 2. Difficulty of work, 3. Monotony of work, 4. Responsibility involved, 5. Supervision required, 6. Knowledge and experience required, and 7. Working conditions.

Each of these factors are considered generally rather than specifically, and the various factors are not weighted or given a point value when ranking the jobs. Sometimes, the jobs are ranked first by departments. A comparison of departmental rankings is advisable so as to even up discrepancies in work of a similar character.

The advantages of Ranking System are: (1) It is very simple, and (2) It requires less time than the other system. Its disadvantages are: (1) It does not tell how much one job differs from another, merely that it is higher or lower; (2) Unless the same detail is followed as in the other systems, the analysis cannot possibly be so familiar with the jobs as they should and hence the ranking is likely to be inaccurate; (3) In the absence of details analysis compromise plays an undue part, and wages for the job are likely to influence the ranking.

Ranking method is best suited to small organizations in which a committee can be expected to know all jobs.

II. The Factor Comparison or Weight-in-Money Method

It is also known as the Benge Plan. Eugene originated it in 1928. This method consists of analysing jobs on the basis of the following five factors:

1. **Mental requirements.** This factor is gauged on the basis of concentration of attention (tension), intensity and frequency of thought necessary.

2. **Skill requirements.** The measurement of this job characteristic or requirement is broken down into three considerations: (i) the length of training required for an average employee to reach acceptable proficiency; (ii) the variety and complexity of the operations or activities of the job; (iii) the dexterity and manual skill necessary to perform job satisfactorily.

3. **Physical requirements.** This factor gauges fatigue, the laboriousness of the job and its posture requirements.

4. **Responsibility.** It is judged by the possible and probable product-damage value, the job is responsible for the equipment damage possible or probable, the tool and fixture damage and the responsibility for safety of other employees.

5. **Working conditions.** Requirements of the job are gauged on the basis of work location. (Is it inside, outside etc.? Is the work in a damp, wet or very wet location? What are the conditions of working temperature, noise involved, eye-strain, physical contact with oil, accident hazard, and health due to dust or fumes?)'

The jobs are ranked according to each of the above factors, one factor being taken at a time, each job compared with the other with respect to its worth on this factor alone. The weighing of the relative value of this factor in each job is done by applying money values to the ranking. After all the jobs have been rated on each factor, a wage rate for job is determined by obtaining the sum of the money weighings determined for each of the five job factors. These wage rates then become the basis for determining the wage scale.

Among the advantages of the factor-comparison method is the fact that unlike jobs can be evaluated. The system may be applied to combinations of clerical, manual, and supervisory positions. On the other hand, factor-comparison systems are complicated, and installation is expensive. They may not be readily explainable to employees. They cannot be developed by an inexpert, but require leadership by a component and experienced practitioner.

III. Point Systems

The most important characteristic of most point systems is their use of a Manual. The Manual outlines elements of factors upon which each job is to be rated and provides scale and yardsticks by which each degree of each factor is to be valued. It describes several job elements and prescribes the weighing to be applied to each element. It includes a scale for each element by means of which varying degrees are to be appraised. These degrees determine the number of points to be credited to the job. The total of such points establishes the point value of the job.

The four job factors common to practically all point methods of job rating are skill, effort, responsibility and job conditions. These may be, and usually are, further sub-divided. The following table shows the factors with the point values assigned to the various degrees:

Points Assigned to Characteristics and Degrees

Characteristics	First degree	Second degree	Third degree	Fourth degree	Fifth degree
Skill					
1. Education	14	28	42	58	70
2. Experience	22	44	66	88	110
3. Initiative and ingenuity	14	28	42	56	70
Effort					
4. Physical demand	10	20	30	40	50
5. Mental or visual demand	5	10	15	20	25
Responsibility					
6. Equipment or process	5	10	15	20	25
7. Material or product	5	10	15	20	25
8. Safety of others	5	10	15	20	25
9. Work of others	5	—	15	—	25
Job Conditions					
10. Working conditions	10	20	30	40	50
11. Unavoidable hazards	5	10	15	20	25
Total Points					500

Most of these methods are expensive to administrate and are not designed for small businesses. But every business can attempt to arrive at equitable job rating by classifying the job requirements and determining the degree of which these requirements are needed. A comparison of the jobs may be undertaken, for instance, on the basis of the following check list:

Factors In Job Rating

Factors	Comparative Law	Requirement of Medium	Grade High
I. Skill			
1. Education	—	—	—
2. Experience	—	—	—
3. Initiative and Ingenuity	—	—	—
II. Effort			
4. Physical Exertion	—	—	—
5. Mental Strain	—	—	—
6. Decision-making	—	—	—
7. Training others	—	—	—
8. Reporting	—	—	—
9. Recording	—	—	—
III. Responsibility			
10. For Work of others	—	—	—
11. For Process	—	—	—
12. For Equipment	—	—	—
13. For Safety	—	—	—
14. For Material or Product	—	—	—
IV. Job Conditions			
15. Speed and Pressure	—	—	—
16. Hazardous Activity	—	—	—
17. Unpleasant place or Period of work			

On the basis of analysis of such factors, one may rank or grade the jobs. When the magnitude of an operation justifies the paper work, this examination of job requirements may be used to make written job specifications, *i.e., a.* list of all functions required of employee who fills each job. There may also be a rating sheet for each job, listing the degree of skill, responsibility and effort, and the job conditions that are required, so that the enterprise may at all times have evidence that, its policy in setting comparative wage rates is equitable.

Scope of Job Evaluation

Evaluation of clerical, technical, professional and supervisory jobs is handled more or less on the principles that are used in evaluating manual of factory jobs. The chief differences that are found to exist revolve round a different approach to the collection of information about the job and a different method of classification and control. Production of factory employees are usually studied from within; other employees usually assist in their own job rating either by filling out questionnaires or by answering questions about the job. Items of 'responsibility' and 'confidential information' must often be added to the clerical rating, while factors such as 'physical effort' and 'hazards of the job' lose their significance. Regardless of the job or position that is evaluated, the prime requirement is to identify those characteristics that are essential to success on the job. For example, the outstanding requirements of a radio announcer is that he has a pleasing voice and be able to read the script that is prepared for him. Some people with an eighth grade education can meet this requirement, and others with a doctorate in English could not. Most office positions are evaluated in terms of the following requirements: (1) education in years of schooling; (2) accuracy; (3) memory: (4) supervision required: (5) special skills such as typing, shorthand, etc.; and ((b) relations with others, especially the public. While considering supervisory position, another set of requirements are evaluated. These usually include: (1) technical knowledge; (2) experience; (3) exercise of judgment; (4) planning; (5) conditions of work; (6) number of employees; (7) responsibility for equipment and product, and other factors that the particular company may deem important. The higher up the ladder of supervision, the more difficult it becomes to evaluate supervisory or executive positions. One large company in evaluating its executives considers the executives' responsibility for: (1) planning: (2) policy formulation: (3) methods; (4) administration: (5) personnel relations: ((i) executive contracts; (7) original thinking; (8) analysis; and (9) influence upon profits.

Limitations and Criticism of Job Evaluations

Job rating research experiments have been repeatedly shown that the factors generally included in job evaluation are not independent. More often than not, they overlap, consequently. the weights applied in many systems are subject to serious questions. At the same time, and perhaps for this reason, the reliability of job ratings is often questionable. (Reliability here means the consistency with which the same jobs are given similar ranks and ratings).

Some of the most telling criticisms of current job evaluation practice have been made by Viteles, whose major points may be summarized as follows:

1. Job evaluation gives a false sense of accuracy and there is great deal of chaos yet to be eliminated by careful research.
2. Too many rating factors are used. These should never be more than 5 or 10.
3. Definitions of factors and degrees are not so accurately made as they could be in terms of action patterns and objective situations.
4. Too wide a range of factors is assumed and too many degrees are defined.

5. Too great, a controversy is raised over method and not enough attention paid to results.
6. 'Mental-set' of raters is allowed to influence results.
7. Since workers who feel that they are paid on the basis of merit will tend to be happier and more productive than those who have reason to question the wage scale. More job evaluation is needed but it should be better job evaluation and might be made better if commonsense and a due regard for the scientific method were followed.

7.3 MERIT RATING

7.3.1 What is Merit Rating?

Merit Rating is the name applied to the system of evaluating and recording the abilities and personal characteristics of an employee. It is the evaluation or appraisal of the relative worth to the company of a man's services or his job. According to Edwin B. Flippo, merit rating is "a systematic, periodic and, so far as humanly possible, an impartial rating of an employee's excellence in matters pertaining to his present job and to his potentialities for a better job."[1] It is, in fact, the formal process of evaluating some or all of the individuals who make up the work team. The credit for the origin of this system goes to Robert Owen, the Scottish mill-owner who in the early 19th century kept 'character books' for his employees and displayed a colour block indicative of merit on each worker's bench. It is called by various names. For example, in certain government concerns of U.S.A., it is known as 'Efficiency Rating' whereas in American private industry, it is often described as 'Employee Rating', 'Service Rating', 'Performance Rating' or 'Experience Rating'.

Difference between Job and Merit Rating

The principal object of both job rating and personnel rating is to systematically determine the wage rates to be paid to a worker on the job, but the former rates the job and establishes the limits of compensation for it, while the latter rates the man and determines what his compensation will be within the limits. Job evaluation relates to the relative value of jobs. Merit or personnel rating on the other hand, has to do with the relative value of the men as related to particular jobs. The former has to do with the base rates of pay; the latter with the efficiency of the worker performing the job.

7.3.2 Purpose of Merit Rating

Merit rating is an important tool of business administration. It has a wide range of uses. Several worthwhile purposes are served by merit rating, such as:

1. **It unifies the rating procedure.** The system of performance appraisal unfies the rating procedure so that, all the employees are rated on the same qualities by the same method of measurement.

2. **It is more equitable and just.** Although workers and their unions are often opposed to personnel rating and they advocate the payment of the same wage rate to all the

workers on the same job, yet, in order to reward those who produce more and better work, merit rating, is essential. It serves as a basis for granting salary increases and promotion that are based on merit awards.

3. **It serves to stimulate and guide employee's development.** Merit rating can be used for measuring an employee's improvement in concrete, common terms. Conversely, it also measures an employee's deterioration in respect to application and efficiency. Thus, employer rating may be used to help employees gauge their own value and accomplishments. The attention of the raters can be drawn to the personal deficiencies described by the raters and suggestions can be given to them as to how they may improve and reduce such shortcomings. If used properly, such periodic appraisal will establish an atmosphere in which criticism can be taken without resentment and can be used constructively in self-improvement.

4. **Balance the employee's qualifications.** It is a means of determining whether an employee's qualifications are in balance (and have remained in balance) with the job's requirements.

5. **Appraisal of training needs.** Rating may be used to disclose the need for training programmes, where certain types of educational deficiencies are found to characterize a large number of employees.

6. **Weeds out the inefficient employees.** It weeds out inefficient employees and those whose views are not in harmony with the company's objectives or its philosophy of management. Through the objective analysis of merit ratings, it is possible to observe the chronically dissatisfied employees who are out of tune with the objectives of a company. For these cases severance may be the kindest and best solution.

7. **An aid to management.** Some find a rating plan helpful in reducing grievances, especially when ability is considered a part of seniority. The practice of personal rating is a defined aid to management in promoting fairness and a better understanding in regard to many of the decisions affecting employees. Ratings may provide a check at the end of probationary period for new employees.

8. **Other uses.** Merit ratings may be used to provide leaders with a more effective too for rating their personnel; one which requires careful analysis on their part and gives them a better knowledge and understanding of their men. Last but not the least, it may provide better employer-employee relations through mutual confidence, which comes as a result of frank discussions between leader and followers regarding ratings.

According to Roland Benjamin, the principal uses of personnel ratings are to determine who shall receive merit increases, to counsel employees, to determine training needs, to determine promotability, and to identify those who should be transferred. Many concerns use ratings in lay-off and recall, demotion, disciplinary actions, and to evaluate probationary employees, validate tests, and improve placement.

In some business concerns, personnel ratings are avoided as a matter of policy. Employers, employees or both may object to such ratings on the ground that, they are unreliable or that an informal appraisal can provide all the information that is necessary. Formal ratings may be regarded as superfluous especially in small organizations where employees are well-known to their own and other supervisors. In larger organizations, however, policy may favour systematic personnel ratings to provide evaluation of some or all employees.

7.3.3 Methods of Merit Rating

There are several methods of merit rating; but the more popular are as follows: I. Ranking. II. Man-to-man comparison, III. Grading, IV. Graphic scales, V. Check lists, VI. Forced-choice description, VII. Selection of critical incidents, and VIII. Descriptive evaluation. Now let us discuss the rationale of each system of performance appraisal.

I. Ranking

It is the oldest and the simplest method of performance appraisal. Here, the appraiser considers the man and his performance as an entity. No attempt is made to fractionize the rater of his performance; the rater simply compares the whole man with the whole men.

It is the simplest method of separating the most efficient man from the least efficient. But the greatest objection to this system is that, in practice it is very difficult to compare a single individual with the entire mass of human beings possessing varying traits. Well, to solve this problem the *compared-comparison technique* may be employed. According to this technique each man can be compared with every other man, one at a time. For instance, suppose there are five employees. Employee A's performance is compared to B's and a decision is made concerning whose is the better performer. Then A is compared to C, D and E in order. Next, B must be compared with all others individually. He has already been compared with A and there remains only C, D and E. Similar process of comparison can be applied in respect of other personnel. Thus, the use of the paired-comparison technique with these employees would mean a total of decisions, only two people being involved in each decision. The number of decisions can be determined by the following formula:

$$\text{Number of comparisons} = \frac{N(N-1)}{n}$$

Here N represents the number of personnel to be compared. The results of these comparisons can be tabulated, and a rank can be created from the number of times each person is considered to be superior.

II. Man-to-Man Comparison

This system was used by the army during the First World War. Hence, certain factors are selected for the purpose of analysis (such as initiative, leadership, dependability, etc.) and a scale is designed for each factory by the rater. Moreover, a scale of men is also created for each selected factor. Then each man to be rated is compared with the men in the scale and certain scores for each factor are awarded to him. Thus, under this system, instead of comparing whole man to whole men, personnel are compared to *key men,* one factor at a time. This system of appraisal is utilized today in job evaluation and is known as the 'Factor-comparison method'.

Although this system is useful for job evaluation, it is of limited use for personnel appraisal, because the devising of scales is a complicated task.

III. Grading

Under this system certain categories of worth (eg, excellent, very good, good, poor, very poor *or* outstanding, satisfactory, unsatisfactory, etc.) are established and they are carefully defined. The actual performance of the employee is then compared with these grade definitions and the person is allocated to the grade which best describes his performance.

IV. Graphic Scales

It is similar to the man-to-man approach but for the difference that here the degrees on the factor scales are represented by *definition* rather than by key men. The selection of the factors to be measured is a crucial part of the graphic scales method. These factors can be divided into two parts—(i) employee characteristics, and (ii) employee contributions. The term 'characteristic' denotes the quantity of the person, such as initiative, enthusiasm, dependability, loyalty etc. On the other hand, 'contribution' is something the employee produces, such as quality of work, quatity, responsibilities assumed and specific goals accomplished. In appraising employee characteristics, the theory is that, if the employee possesses certain characteristics, he will produce the desired contribution. Some of the more commonly utilized factors are as below: 1. Quantity of work, 2. Quality of work, 3. Dependability of an employee, 4. Regularity of attendance 5. Safety record, 6. Attitudes towards associates and superiors, 7. Ability to learn, 8. Initiative, 9. Ability to instruct others, and 10. Supervisory talent etc., etc.

As in school report card, these and similar characteristics of a work may be scored in the form of grades, such as excellent, good, poor, unsatisfactory. Rating of performance for purpose of selecting those who are to be promoted, trained for promotion, warned or dismissed should be based on objective measurement whereby not only the past and present performance of the same employee is compared, but also the record of several employees. Personnel should be informed about its ratings and it should understand the rating system that is used as a basis for wage increment and promotion. Those who perform below standards should be notified, and suggestions should be made for improvement of their work. If they cannot improve their performance, they may be assigned to less exacting duties that fit better to their capabilities, or they may be dismissed.

The objection to factor scale lies in the arbitrariness that accompanies their design. What factors are to be used? How many? Are they to be equally weighted? How many degrees per factor? What kind of factor and degree definitions? But on the whole it may be said that it is possible to design a fairly reliable system that will produce consistent results.

V. Check Lists

Here the rater does not evaluate the performance of the employee, but simply *reports* about it, and the final rating is done by the personnel department. Under this system, a series of questions is presented concerning the subject 'employee and his behaviour'. The rater then, checks to indicate if the answer to a question about the employee is positive or negative. The value of each question may also be weighted. An example of such question is given below:

	Yes	No
1. Is the employee really interested in the job?	( )	( )
2. Is his attendance satisfactory?	( )	( )
3. Does he make sure that his equipment is maintained in good condition?	( )	( )
4. Does he possess a good working knowledge of the job?	( )	( )
5. Is he respected by his men?	( )	( )
6. Does he keep his temper?	( )	( )
7. Does he follow orders?	( )	( )
8. Does he usually complete what he begins?	( )	( )
9. Does he evade responsibility?	( )	( )

This system is subject to bias or prejudice of rater. Further, it is difficult to assemble, analyse and weigh a number of statements about employee; characteristics and contributions. But at the same time, it is very simple, because in the check-list approach the rater has simply to report the factors and not compare the various points.

VI. Forced-Choice-Description

One of the fundamental objectives of the method is to reduce or eliminate the possibilities of rater bias by forcing him to choose between descriptive statements of seemingly equal worth. For example, the rater might be asked to state which of the following statements is more descriptive of the employee in question:

(i) Gives good, clear instructions to his subordinates, (ii) Can be depended upon to complete any job assigned. Both these statements are descriptions by desirable traits. The rater here cannot place his bias into operation because he is forced to choose one statement even though he feels that *both* apply in the case of a particular employee. Thus, elimination of the bias or prejudice is the greatest *advantage* of this method. There are certain *disadvantages* also, *e.g.,* (i) it is difficult, if not impossible, to keep the key secret; (ii) the system is not very satisfactory if it is to be utilized for employee development; (iii) the rate often objects to being found to make decisions which he feels cannot or should not be made. On account of these disadvantages, this system is not very popular.

VII. Selection of Critical Incidents

Here there are certain key acts of behaviour that make the difference between success and failure of a job. According to this system, the rater selects certain kinds of events which occur in the performance of the rater's job. An example of such events is given as follows: (i) Became upset or angry over work; (ii) Refused to co-operate with a fellow worker; (iii) Suggested an improvement in the work method; (iv) Refused a change to take further training; (v) Tried to get a fellow worker to accept a management decision.

These critical events are discovered by a thorough study of the personnel on-work. Then the collected incidents are ranked in order of frequency and importance. They may also be weighted, thereby providing the basis for a rating score.

VIII. Description of Evaluation

Here the employees are rated on the basis of written descriptions of the performance of each employee. The descriptions should be as factual and concrete as possible. Such a programme of merit rating requires great amount of time and skill on the part of the supervisor.

Other Principles Relating to Merit Rating

Ratings should be made by the employee's immediate supervisor—the only one who really knows the employee—and the result produced by his efforts. Further, the skill and enthusiasm of the rater is the key to a good performance appraisal system. He must be thoroughly indoctrinated in the importance and value of systematic rating. The initial training of the rater must, of course, incorporate complete explanations of the nature of the training system. Factors and factor scales, if any, must be thoroughly defined, analysed and discussed in conference sessions. The rater must thoroughly understand the tool that he is to use. As regards the frequency of rating, it may be observed that the employees be rated semi-annually (though sometimes annually or quarterly) and all personnel be rated at the same time in a given department or plant. The time intervals between rating must not be too short; else ratings will suffer from hasty appraisal owing to the annoyance and irksomeness of the task. These ratings should also be frequently checked by the supervisors, so as to check the thoroughness of the job rather than to find fault with individual rating. A final check should be made in the department of personnel management using past ratings as a guide in order to question any unusual changes in ratings that occur.

EXERCISES :

Objective Type

A. State whether the following statements are True of False:

1) A certain amount of Labour turnover is bound to take place in every organisation.
2) Labour turnover can be controlled by providing conducive working environments.
3) High rate of labour turnover decreases labour cost.

4) High Labour turnover indicates stability of work-force.
5) At the top level management the labour turnover rate should be very low.
6) The total number of separations in the organisation is the important factor while measuring labour turnover by replacement method.
7) Job analysis deals with the anatomy of the Job.
8) Job analysis has both aspects i.e. Job aspect and man aspect.
9) Job evaluation is the application of the job analysis techniques.
10) Merit rating is a system of recording and evaluating the abilities and personal characteristics of an employee.
11) Job evaluation is the comparative appraisal of worker on different jobs.
12) Job evaluation is a systematc evaluation of the personality and performance of each employee by his supervisor.

Ans : 1) True 2) True 3) False 4) False 5) True 6) False 7) True 8) True 9) True
10) True 11) False 12) False

B. Fill in the blanks.

1) Labour turnover rate is the .... in the working staff.
2) Death and retirement is a ...... cause of a worker.
3) Low rate of Labour turnover indicates ..... of work-force
4) Job analysis facilitates the task of .....
5) Job analysis is necessary for ...... good and efficient workers.
6) Job evaluation is necessary for establishing ..... rates.
7) ...... is the oldest and simplest method of performance appraisal.
8) Job evaluation relates to the ...... value of Jobs.

Ans : 1) rate of change 2) Personal 3) Stability 4) Merit Rating 5) Selecting 6) Wage
7) Ranking 8) Relative

C. Essay Type

1) Define the term "Labour Turnover'. What are the causes responsible for labour turnover?
2) What are the costs of Labour turnover? How they are treated in cost accounts?
3) "The cost of Labour turnover is always reflected in Product cost" Discuss.
4) What is Labour "Turnover'? What are the effects of Labour turnover?
5) What are the reasons why Labour turnover should be kept within limits?
6) What is labour turnover? How will you meansure it? What are its causes and effects on labour costs?
7) How is labour turnover measured? Why is high Labour turnover a mater of serious concern to management?
8) What do you mean by costs of Labour Turnover? Give some examples of "preventive costs."?

9) What are the different methods of measuring labour turnover?
10) What do you understand by "Job Analysis'? What is its singificance in personnel administration?
11) Discuss the purposes and methods of Job Analysis.
12) What do you understand by job evaluation? What are the principles of job evaluation?
13) Briefly summarise the merits of Job evaluation.
14) Define the term "merit ratings'. Is it different from job evaluation?
15) What are the different methods of merit rating? Briefly explain each.

D) Write short notes.

a) Job Analysis
b) Job Evaluation
c) Merit Rating
d) Effects of Labour Turnover
e) Causes of Labour Turnover
f) Measurement of Labour Turnover
g) Reduction of Labour Turnover.

Practical Exercise

1) During June, 2014 the following information was obtained from the personnel department of Bombay Co.Labour force at the beginning of the month 800 and 1,200 at the end of the month. During the month 20 persons quit while 40 persons are discharged. 150 workers were engaged out of which only 30 persons were appointed in the vacancy created by the number of workers separated and the rest on account of an expansion programme.

   Calculate the monthly labour turnover rate and equivalent annual rate under the following : (i) Separation method, (ii) Replacement method and (iii) Flux method.

2) From the following data given by the personnel department of Poona Co., Pune, calculate the labour turnover rate by applying -
   (a) Separation method (b) Replacement method (c) Flux method. Number of workers on the payroll: At the beginning of the month -- 913 at the end of the month - 1087

During the month 10 workers left, 40 persons were discharged and 150 workers were recruited. Of these 25 workers are recruited in the vacancies of those leaving, while the rest were engaged for an expansion scheme.

DIRECT COST

8.1 Direct Costs
8.2 Features of Direct Cost
8.3 Direct Cost Vs Direct Materials
8.4 Direct Cost vs Indirect Expenses
8.5 Accounting of Direct Cost in Cost Accounts
8.6 Control of Direct Cost

8.1 DIRECT COST

INTRODUCTION

Direct Cost otherwise known as chargeable expenses, as the name itself indicates, are those expenses, other than direct material cost & direct labour cost which are directly incurred on a specific cost unit. They form part of prime cost because they are incurred directly on a specific cost unit. The ICMA terminology defines direct cost as "expenses which can be identified with and allocated to cost centre or cost units". However, in some cases, the direct cost cannot be very easily identified with the cost unit but it can be identified with cost centre. In such cases these expenses are direct cost of the cost centre and it becomes indirect cost of all jobs manufactured in the department. A factory with large number of departments will have a greater proportion of direct cost.

8.2 Features of Direct Cost

1. Direct costs are solely incurred on a particular cost centre. The benefit of incurring direct expenses is available only for a particular cost unit or cost centre but not for others.
2. Direct cost may sometimes include material, labour or indirect expense, e.g. cost of a special mould.

3. Direct cost vary in direct proportion with production volume.
4. The proportion of direct cost to total cost of production is very less.
5. They can be controlled easily when compared to indirect expenses.
6. The direct cost can be identified with the total cost of production.

The following are some of the examples of direct expenses :

1. Carriage inward and import duty paid on materials purchased.
2. Excise duty and octroi paid on materials specifically purchased for specific job.
3. Primary packing materials.
4. Cost of patents and royalty paid.
5. Travelling expenses incurred in securing an order to supervise a work being carried out at the premises of customer.
6. Architect's or surveyor's fee.
7. Sub-contract cost.
8. Cost of spare parts.
9. Cost of special drawing, design, pattern or mould.
10. Cost of special tools or equipments hired.
11. Maintenance charges of such tools or equipments.

8.3 Direct Cost vs Direct Materials

Though direct material cost and direct cost form part of prime cost, yet there is a difference between the two. Direct materials can be conveniently identified with the finished product. Whereas direct costs are incurred for providing services for center the production and can not be identified with the finished product. For example, when power is used substantially to produce goods, say to the extent of 75 per cent of the total cost of production it is to be treated as direct cost, because power us inevitable to production process,.

8.4 Direct Cost vs Indirect Expenses

Direct Cost differ from indirect expenses in following respects :

(a) Direct cost is part of prime cost whereas indirect expenses is part of overheads.
(b) Direct cost vary in direct proportion of output, whereas indirect expenses do not.
(c) The benefit of incurring direct cost with the completion of a job, whereas the benefit of incurring indirect expenses extends to other jobs also.
(d) The direct cost can be identified with the total cost of production, whereas it is not possibe in case of indirect expenses.
(e) Direct cost can be allocated whereas indirect expenses are to be apportioned.
(f) Direct cost can be easily controlled when compared to indirect expenses.

8.5 Accounting of Direct Cost in Cost Accounts

The following entry is passed when direct costs are incurred.

    Direct cost a/c   Dr.

        To cost ledger control a/c

When charged to respective jobs, the following entry is passed

    Individual job a/c   Dr.

     (In the work-in-progress ledger)

        To direct expenses a/c

8.6 Control of Direct Cost

Though direct cost constitute only a small proportion to the total cost of production it should not be allowed to go unchecked. Care must be taken to see that these expenses do not exceed the predetermind amount. Standard cost can be fixed for direct cost and the actuals can be compared with standard cost to know variances. In case of adverse variance, it should be analysed and reported for taking remedial measures.

EXERCISES :

1. Define direct cost.
2. State any four features of direct cost.
3. Give four examples of direct cost.
4. Distinguish between direct material and direct cost.
5. Distinguish between direct cost and indirect expenses.
6. How is direct cost accounted in cost account?
7. How is direct cost controlled?

APPENDIX

KEY TERMS

Chapter 1 to 2 – Indroduction and Elements of Cost

1) **Cost :** Cost is the total of all expenses incurred, whether paid or due, in the manufacture and sale of product or whose incurred in giving service.

2) **Costing :** The technique and process of ascertaining cost is called costing.

3) **Cost Accounting :** Cost Accounting is the branch of general accounting and covers the application of accounting principles relating to recording. classifying and analysing of cost within the organisation.

4) **Cost Accountancy :** Cost Accountancy is a very wide term. It includes the various aspects such as costing, cost accounting, cost control, cost audit and budgetery control. It is the application of costing and cost accountancy principles, methods and techniques.

5) **Cost Unit :** Cost unit is the quantity of product, service or time in relation to which cost may be ascertained or expressed.

6) **Cost Centre :** "A location or person or item of equipment in or connected with the understanding in relation to which cost may be ascertained and used for the purpose of cost control.

7) **Material :** The cost of commodities purchased by undertaking is called as material. The material may be direct material or indirect material.

8) **Wages or Labour cost :** The cost of remmuneration (wages, salaries, commission, bouns etc.) of the empolyees of an undertaking.

9) **Expenses :** The cost of services provided to an undertaking and the nominal cost of use of owned asset is called expenses.

10) **Indirect Expenses :** The aggregate of indirect material, indirect labour and indirect expenses is called indirect expenses.

11) **Factory Expenses :** The expenses which are incurred in the premises of factory for converting raw materials into finished product is called factory expenses.

12) **Office and Administrative Overheads :** The expenses incurred for the planning, directing and contolling the office activities are called office and administrative expenses.

13) **Selling and Distribution Expenses :** The expenses incurred for sales promotion and distribution of goods are called selling and distribution expenses.

14) **Fixed Cost :** The cost which is not affected as per variation of production is called fixed cost.

15) **Variable Cost :** The cost which varies as the production varies is called variable cost.

16) **Research Cost :** Reserarch cost is the cost of serarching for new and improved products, new application of materials or new or improved methods.

17) **Development Cost :** The cost which is incurred for the development of product or to employ a new or improved methods is called development cost.

18) **Controllable Cost :** The cost which is controlled or regulated by the management is called controllable cost.

19) **Uncontrollable Cost :** The cost which can not be controlled by management is called uncontrollable cost.

20) **Historical Cost :** The actual cost of production, which has already been incurred is called historical cost.

21) **Predetermined Cost :** Predetermined costs are future cost, which are ascertained in advance of production on the basis of specification of all factors affecting cost. It is future cost.

22) **Capital Cost :** The cost incurred for the purchase of fixed.

Chapter 3 : Material Control

1) **Components :** The manufactured or finished Parts enter into the products are called components.

2) **Consumable stores :** consumables stores are the items used in the products but do not become the part of finished product.

3) **Stores :** Stock laying in godown.

4) **Centralised purchasing :** If all purchases are made by a single or one purchase departament it is called centralised purchasing.

5) **Decentralising purchasing :** When purchases are made by various department, according to their needs, it is called decentralised purchasing.

6) **Scientific Purchasing :** The procurement by purchase of proper materials, machinery equipments and supplies of stores used in the manufacture of a product adopted to marketing in the proper quantity and quality at proper time and the lowest price consistent with the quality desired is called scientific purchasing.

7) **Purchase requisition :** A purchase requisition is a form used as formal request by storekeeper to purchase department for the purchase of goods.

8) **Quotation :** Quotation is sent by seller to buyer. It is statment which discloses the description of materials to be purchased.

9) **Debit note :** If the goods are not sent by seller as per specification to the Purchaser, the purchaser prepares a debit note and informs supplier that his account is debited for wrong supplies received.

10) **Reorder level :** It is a level or point, where orders for fresh supplies are to be placed.

11) **Lead time :** It is the time required to replenish the supply i.e. time required from order placed to the time to receive the materials.

12) **Maximum stock level :** The maximum stock level is that quantity above which stock should not normally be allowed to exceed. It is the upper limit of quantity which can be held in stock at any time.

13) **Minimum stock level :** Minimum stock level represents the minimum quantity of materials which must be maintained in hand at all times.

14) **Average stock level :** It is the average of maximum and minimum stock level.

15) **Danger stock level :** Danger stock level indicates the danger and immediate actions for purchasing of material is necessary.

16) **Economic order quantity :** When carrying costs and ordering costs are equal, the cost of materials to be purchased is equal and this point or situation is called economic order quantity.

17) **Ordering Cost :** Ordering cost is the cost of placing an order for the purchase of materials.

18) **Carrying cost :** It is the cost of holding the material in store.

Chapter 4 : Material Accounting

1) **Centralised Store :** If only one store or godown is located in the factory or industry, it is called centralised stores.

2) **Decentralised Store :** If independent stores are located in various department. These are called decentralised stores.

3) **Classification :** Classification mean grouping of materials according to their nature in suitable categories.

4) **Codification :** A particular symbol assigned to a material is called codification.

5) **Bind Card :** Bin means a box or cupboard or even a small room where a material is stored on each bin a separate card is attached for recording receipts and issues, this card is called as Bin Card.

6) **Store ledger :** A ledger which records the quantities and money value of materials, is called store ledger.

7) **Store requisition :** A form or ship on the basis of which store keeper issues material from stores is called store requisition.

8) **Bill of material :** Bill of requisition is a master requisition which lists all the materials required for completion of job or order or process.

9) **FIFO method :** According to this method the material received first, is issued first the the production department. Hence it is called 'First In first Out' method.

10) **LIFO method :** According to this method, the material received last, is issued first, hence it is called 'Last In First Out' method.

Chapter 5 : Inventory Control

1) **Inventory :** Any kind of idle resources which have some economic value.

2) **Inventory control :** It is the process whereby the investment in materials and parts carried in stock is regulated within predetermined limits set in accordance with inventory policy established by the management.

3) **Inventory Turnover Ratio :** It is a ratio which measures the number of times a firm's average inventory is sold during a year.

4) **Periodic Inventory System :** A system of stock taking undertaken at the end of the accounting year.

5) **Perpetual Inventory System :** A system of records maintained by the controlling departments, which reflects physical movements of stock and their current balance.

6) **Bin card :** A bin is a container in which materials are kept.

7) **Stores Ledger :** It records all receipts and issues of material.

8) **Continuous Stock Taking :** It is an integral part of perpetual inventory system which confirms that perpetual inventory system is functioning properly. It varifies the balances shown by bin card and stores ledger by physical counting.

9) **Inventory Tags :** They are used for stock verification. It has two portions i.e. the upper and lower. The upper portion attached to the particular bin indicates that, the item has been verified. The lower portion indicates shortages or surpluses if any, after verification.

10) **Stock Verification Sheets :** These are the sheets which are maintained by the stock verifiers in a chronological order and balances, after verification are enternal therein.

11) **ABC Analysis :** It is a technique of inventory control. According to this analysis materials are analysed as per their economic value so that costly materials are given proper attention.

Chapter 6 : Labour Cost, Remuneration and Incentives

1) **Labour :** These are the expenses incurred for obtaining the services of human being.

2) **Labour cost :** It represents the human contribution to production and is an important element of cost.

3) **Direct Labour :** Direct labour is that which can identified with and allocated to cost centres or cost units.

4) **Indirect labour :** Indirect labour is that which cannot easily identified with a particular cost unit.

5) **Time-keeping :** It is the system in which worker's time of coming in and going out of the factory for the purpose of attendance and wage calculations.

6) **Time Booking :** It is the process of recording the time spent by a worker on different Jobs carried out by him during his period of stay in the factory.

7) **Attendance Register :** It is the register in which worker's attendance is recorded.

8) **Token :** A token is given to each worker bearing the number for his identification.

9) **Job card :** It is a card in which time of starting and time finishing the job of each worker is recorded.

10) **Labour Cost Card :** It is a card which is circulated to all workers in which a worker records his time on a particular Job.

11) **Piece-work Card :** When workers are paid on piece-rate system, piece-work card is used and maintained for each job separately.

12) **Payroll :** It is a list of all employees showing the details of his salary.

13) **Overtime :** Work done beyond the normal working hours is known as overtime.

14) **Casual Worker :** A worker who is appointed temporary on daily basis in order to meet increase in production or to replace the absentee workers.

15) **Out workers :** A worker who works outside the factory premises on behalf of the company is known as out worker.

16) **Idle Time :** It represents the time cost and for which the employer has to pay to the workers - on the basis of time.

17) **Labour Turnover :** It is the tendency of a worker of leaving their Job.

18) **Preventive cost :** It is a cost which is incurred to discourage or prevent the workers from leaving the job.

19) **Replacement cost :** It is a cost which is incurred / after the worker has left his Job. It includes cost of recruitment, selection, training of the workers. etc.

20) **Time rate system :** It is a system of wage payment in which payment is given on the basis of time.

21) **Piece-rate system :** It is a system of wage payment in which payment is made on the basis of fixed amount per unit produced, irrespective of time taken.

22) **Incentive schemes :** It is a system which is a combination of good points of time rate and piece rate system. Under incentive schemes, time rate and piece rate systems are combined in such a way that workers are induced to increase their productivity.

Chapter 7 : Other Aspects of Labour

1) **Labour Turnover :** It refers to the movement in and out of an organisation by the workforce.

2) **Time Study :** It involves determination of standard time for an operation by direct time measurement.

3) **Motion Study :** It is concerned with determination of standardised methods for performing different operations.

4) **Job Analysis :** It involves preparation of description and classification of each Job, with a list of qualification needed by workers to perform the work satisfactorily.

5) **Job Evaluation :** It is a process of analysis and assessment of Jobs to ascertain their comparative labour worth.

6) **Merit Rating :** It is the comparative appraisal of individual merits of an employee. It is the qualitative or quantitative assessment of an employee's performance or his personality made by his supervisor or any other competent person.

FORMULAS AT A GLANCE

Chapter 2 : Elements Of Cost

1) Material Consumed = Opening stock of Raw Materials + purchases + Expenses on purchases – closing stock of Raw Materials – scrap of raw materials.
2) Prime Cost = Material consumed + Direct wages + Direct Expenses.
3) Factory cost = Prime cost + Factory Expenses
4) Cost of Production = Factory Cost + office and Administrative Expenses.
5) Total Cost = Cost of Production + Selling and Distribution Expenses.
6) Sales = Total Cost + Profit.
7) Cost = Sales – Profit or sales + Loss.
8) Profit on cost of Production = $\dfrac{\text{Cost of production x percentage of profit}}{100}$
9) Profit on selling price = $\dfrac{\text{Cost of production x percentage of profit on sales}}{100 - \text{percentage of profit on sales}}$

Chapter 3 : Material Control

Formulas

1) **Reorder Level**

 = Maximum consumption x Maximum reoder period

OR

 = Minimum stock + Consumption during the lead time

OR

 = Minimum stock + (Average usage x Avrage reorder period)

2) **Minimum stock level**

 = Reorder Level – Normal consumption x Normal reorder period

OR

 = Minimum rate of consumption – Average rate of consumption x Leadtime

3) **Maximum stock level**

 = reorder level + reorder quantity – Minimum consumption x Minimum reorder period

OR

 = reoder level – consumption during the time required to get supplies at minimum rate + Economic order size / level

4) **Average stock level**

 = $\dfrac{\text{Maximum Stock level} + \text{Minimum level}}{2}$

OR

 = Minimum Stock Level + ½ Reorder quantity.

5) Danger stock level

= Minimum Consumption x Minimum reorder period

OR

= Average Consumption x Maximum reorder period for emergency purchases.

Chapter 5 : Inventory Control

1) Inventory Turnover Ratio (in number of times) :

$$\text{Inventory Turnover Ratio} = \frac{\text{Cost of Materials Consumed}}{\text{Cost of Avereye Stock}}$$

2) Inventory Turnover Ratio (in number of days) :

$$\text{Inventory Turnover Ratio} = \frac{\text{No of days during the period}}{\text{Inventory Turnover Ratio}}$$

3) Cost of Materials Consumed : Opening stock + Purchases - Closing Stock

4) Cost of Average Stock : $\dfrac{\text{Opening Stock + Closing Stock}}{2}$

Chapter 6 : Labour cost, Remuneration and Incentives

1) Time Rate System :

Earnings = Hours worked x Rate per hour

Earnings = No. of days worked x Rate per day

2) Piece - Rate System :

i) Straight Piece - Rate System (when rate per unit is known)

Earnings = No. of units produced x Rate per unit

When Standard Hour Rate is given

Total Earnings = Standard Hour of work produced x Rate per Standard hour

ii) Taylor's Differential piece rate system :

Low piece rate - when production is **below** standard.

High piece rate - when production is **at or above** standard

Low piece Rate - 80% of Normal Piece Rate.

High Piece Rate - 120% of Normal Piece Rate.

Incentive Plans

1) Halsey Plan :

Total Earnings = Hours worked x Rate Per hour + 50% of Time saved rate per hour

Where Time Saved = Standard Time - Time taken

Symbolically,

$$E = T \times R + \left(\frac{S\text{-}T}{2} \times R \right)$$

When   E = Total Earnings
       T = Time taken (i.e. hours worked)
       R = Rate per hour
       S = Standard time (i.e. time allowed)

2) Rowan Premium Plan :

Total Earnings = Hours worked x Rate per hour + $\dfrac{\text{Time Taken} \times \text{Time Saved}}{\text{Time Allowed}}$ x rate

per hour

OR

Total Earnings = Hours worked x Rate per hours + $\dfrac{\text{Time Allowed} \times \text{Time taken}}{\text{Time Allowed}}$ x

hours worked x Rate per hour
Symbolically,

$$E = T \times R + \frac{S\text{-}T}{S} + T \times R$$

When   T = Time taken (Actual time)
       S = Standard time (time allowed)
       R = Rate per hour

Effective Rate of earnings per hour = $\dfrac{\text{Total Earnings}}{\text{Time Taken}}$

D. A. Amount should be added (if D.A. rate per hour is given) to Earnings for calculating total Earnings.

Chapter 7 - Labour Turnover

1) Separation Method :
Labour Turnover Rate =

$$\frac{\text{No. of workers left in a period}}{\text{Averege No. of workers on the payroll in a period}} \times 100$$

2) Replacement Method :
Labour Turnover Rate =

$$\frac{\text{No. of workers replaced (joined)in a period}}{\text{Averege No. of workers on the payroll in a period}} \times 100$$

3) Flux Method :
Labour Turnover Rate =

$$\frac{\text{No. of workers left in a period +No. of workers replaced in a period}}{\text{Averege No. of workers on the payroll in a period}} \times 100$$

IMPORTANT FORMULAS OF COSTING

---

1. BASICS OF COST ACCOUNTING :
1. Cost = Usage x Price
2. Cost + Profit = Price
3. Cost - Loss = Price

2. ELEMENTS OF COST :
a. Cost of Materials Consumed :
= Opening Stock of Raw Materials (+) Purchases of Raw Materials (+) Expenses for Purchases of Raw Materials (-) Closing Stock of Raw Materials (-) Sale of Scrap of Raw Materials (-) Defective Materials returned to suppliers.

b. Prime Cost :
= Direct Materials + Direct Labour + Direct Expenses

c. Works Cost :
= Prime Cost + Factory Overheads

d. Cost of Production :
= Works Cost + Office Overheads

e. Total Cost :
= Cost of Production + Selling and Distribution Overheads

f. Overheads :
= Indirect Material + Indirect Labour + Indirect Expenses

g. Conversion Cost :
= Direct Labour + Direct Expenses + Overheads

h. Selling Price :
= Total Cost + Profit or - Loss

3. MATERIAL :

a. Re-order Level :

i. Wheldon's Formulae :

= Maximum Rate of Consumption **x** Maximum Re-Order Period

ii. Minimum Level + Consumption during the time required to get fresh delivery of materials.

b. Maximum Stock Level :

= Re-Order Level + Re-Order Quantity - (Minimum rate of Consumption **x** Minimum Re-order Period)

c. Minimum Stock Level :

= Re-Order Level - (Average Rate of Consumption **x** Average Re-Order Period)

d. Average Stock Level :

i. Averaging Formulae :

$$= \frac{\text{Minimum Stock Level} + \text{Maximum Stock Level}}{2}$$

ii. Re-order Quantity Formulae :

$$= \text{Minimum Stock Level} + \frac{1}{2} \text{(Re-Order Quantity)}$$

e. Danger Level :

= Average Rate of Consumption **x** Maximum Re-order period for emergency purchases.

f. Economic Order Quantity :

Simpson's Mathematical Formulae :

$$= \sqrt{\frac{2.A.O}{C}} \quad 2AQ / C$$

Where,

A = Annual Consumption

O = Cost of Placing and Receiving an order

C = Inventory Carrying Cost

g. Number of Orders to be placed in a particular period or Order Schedule :

$$= \frac{A}{EOQ}$$

A = Total Consumption of Material

EOQ = Economic Order Quantity

4. INVENTORY CONTROL :

a. Inventory Turnover Ratio (In number of times)

$$= \frac{\text{Cost of Material Consumed}}{\text{Cost of Avarage Stock}}$$

b. Inventory Turnover Ratio (In number of days)

$$= \frac{\text{Number of Days during the period}}{\text{Inventory Turnover Ratio}}$$

c. Cost of Materials Consumed :

= Opening Stock + Purchases - Closing Stock

d. Cost of Average Stock :

$$= \frac{\text{Opening Stock + Closing Stock}}{2}$$

5. LABOUR COST, REMUNERATION AND INCENTIVES :

a. Time Booking = Attendance Time - Lost Time

b. Idle Time = Attendance Time - Job Time

c. Time Wage System :

i. Earnings = Hours Worked x Rate Per Hour

ii. Earnings = Number of Days Worked x Rate Per Day

d. Piece Rate System :

i. Straight Piece Rate System :

= Number of Units x Rate Per Unit

ii. Taylor's Differential Piece Rate System :

* Low Piece Rate - Below Standard.

80% of Normal Piece Rate

* High Piece Rate - At or Above Standard

120% of Normal Piece Rate

e. Incentive Plans :

i. Hasley's Premium Plan :

Earnings = Hours Worked x Rate Per Hour +50% (Time Allowed - Time Taken) x Rate Per Hour

ii. Rowan Premium Plan :

Earnings = Hours Worked x Rate Per Hour

$$+ \text{Time Taken} \times \frac{\text{Time Saved}}{\text{Time Allowed}} \times \text{Rate Per Hour}$$

Earnings = Hours Worked x Rate Per Hour

$$+ \text{Time Allowed} \times \frac{\text{Time Taken}}{\text{Time Allowed}} \times \text{Hours Worked} \times \text{Rate Per Hour}$$

* Effective Rate of Earnings Per Hour = Total Earnings / Time Taken

* Calculation of Efficiency Percentage :

$$\text{On Time Basis} = \frac{\text{Time Taken}}{\text{Time Allowed}} \times 100$$

$$\text{On Production Basis} = \frac{\text{Actual Production}}{\text{Standard Production}} \times 100$$

6. OTHER ASPECTS OF LABOUR :

i. Measurement of Labour Turnover Rate :

a. Separation Method :

$$\frac{\text{Number of Workers left in a Period}}{\text{Average Number of workers on the pay-roll}} \times 100$$

b. Replacement Method :

$$\frac{\text{Number of Workers replaced in a Period}}{\text{Average Number of workers on the pay-roll in the period}} \times 100$$

c. Flux Method :

Number of workers left in a period.

$$\frac{\text{Number of Workers replaced in a Period}}{\text{Average Number of workers on the pay-roll in the period}} \times 100$$

LIST OF PRACTICALS

LIST OF PRACTICALS FOR COST AND WORKS ACCOUNTING - 1

Topic :	Particulars :	Mode of Practical
1. Cost Units and Cost Centres	Collecting of data on various cost units and cost centres identified / determined by industries. Making illustrative lists and commenting on the same.	Industrial Visit or Guest Lecture
2. Cost Sheets	Specimen of Job/Work Cost Sheet for a Standard / Repetitive Job or Product. Types of Cost Sheet.	Library Assignment by collecting the Cost Sheets of Jobbing concerns.
3. Tender	Speciman of Standard form of Tender.	Collection of Advertise-ment from Newspapers, etc.
4. Purchase Procedure Documentation	Making a complete set of various Speciman documents used in a Particular Company i.e.GRN / MR/ Bill of materials. Transfer note. Return Note.	Group Discussion / Industrial Visit.
5. EOQ and Stock Levels	Survey on whether these techniques are used in practice and how illustrations of ordering costs / carrying costs. Where and how the Stock Level Fixed are referred.	Group Discussion / Industrial Visit.
6. Codification	Information on : a. Methods selected b. Bases used. Example on the methods and in practice with illustrative items.	Class-room Assignment / Industrial Visit
7. Stores Accounting	Speciman on Bin card, stores - ledger card and study of their utilities.	Industrial Visit / Liabrary Assignment.
8. ABC Analysis	Analysing the data with quantity and value according to ABC principles and making report thereon.	Class room Assignment / Industrial Visit
9. Time-keeping	Collecting the Specimen documents to particular industrial unit and study thereof.	Industrial Visit.
10.Labour Turnover	Collection the information about reasons and remedies.	Guest Lecture.

REFERENCES

1) Advanced Cost Accounting – Made Gowda, Himalaya Publication.

2) B.L. Lal and G.L. Sharma – Theory and Techniques of Cost Accounting.
   Himalaya Publishing House, New Delhi.

3) Cost Accounting – Bhatta HSM, Himalaya Publication

4) Cost Accounting – Prabhu Dev, Himalaya Publication

5) Horngrain and Datar – Cost Accounting and Managerial Emphasis.

6) Jain and Narang – Cost Accounting Principles and Practice. Kalyani Publishers

7) M.N.Arora – Cost Accounting Principles and Practice,
   Vikas Publishing House Pvt.Ltd., New Delhi.

8) N.K.Prasad – Principles and Practice of Cost Accounting Book Syndicate Pvt.Ltd.,
   Calcutta.

9) R.K.Motwani – Practical Costing. Pointer Publisher, Jaipur.

10) R.S.N.Pillai and V.Bhagavati – Cost Accounting.

11) Ravi Kishor – Advanced Cost Accounting and Cost Systems Taxman's Allied Service
    Pvt.Ltd., New Delhi.

12) Ravi Kishor – Students Guide to Cost Accounting Taxman's, New Delhi.

13) S.N.Maheshwari and S.N.Mittal – Cost Accounting, Theory and Problems,
    Mahavir Book Depot, New Delhi.

14) S.P. Iyengar – Cost Accounting Principles and Practice,
    Sultan Chand & Sons Accounting Taxman's, New Delhi.

15) V.K.Saxena and Vashista – Cost Audit – Text book.
    Sultan Chand and Sons, New Delhi.